# PRAISE FOR RICK ACKER

"TOP PICK! . . . Acker whips up a winner with appealing characters and a plot wound as tight as a ticking bomb . . . Action in and out of the courtroom tops off this exceptional read."

—RT Book Reviews on *Dead Man's Rule*

"Gripping, edge-of-your-seat fiction. *When the Devil Whistles* is a fast mix of suspense, compelling characters, and legal intrigue as only Acker can write it. I dare you to try to put this book down."

—*New York Times* bestselling author Tosca Lee

"High-stakes intrigue that will keep you flipping pages long into the night."

—Bestselling and award-winning author James Scott Bell on *When the Devil Whistles*

"[A] fast-paced book with subtle references to faith and doing what is right . . . This would be a good addition for those readers who shy away from traditional Christian fiction as too 'preachy.' I liked the book very much."

—Church and Synagogue Library Association on *Dead Man's Rule*

"*Blood Brothers* is a riveting thriller of drugs and business gone bad, a grade-A pick."

—Midwest Book Review

"I love so many things about being a reviewer, but I think my favorite is the nudge to read books I might not normally choose to read. Sometimes I stumble across a new author that I absolutely fall in love with . . . and that has happened with Rick Acker . . . Rick Acker joins the league of Randy Singer, Robert Whitlow, and Craig Parshall with intense and realistic courtroom drama. He's now on my favorites list . . ."

—from *A Peek at My Bookshelf* blog on *Blood Brothers*

# DEATH
## IN THE
# MIND'S
# EYE

# ALSO BY RICK ACKER

*Dead Man's Rule*

*Blood Brothers*

*When the Devil Whistles*

# DEATH
## IN THE
# MIND'S
# EYE

## RICK ACKER

**Waterfall**
PRESS

Text copyright © 2016 Rick Acker

Published by Waterfall Press, Grand Haven, MI

www.brilliancepublishing.com

Amazon, the Amazon logo, and Waterfall Press are trademarks of Amazon.com, Inc., or its affiliates.

ISBN-13: 9781503937680
ISBN-10: 1503937682

Cover design by Cyanotype Book Architects

Printed in the United States of America

*for Anette, of course*

# PROLOGUE

*March*

Death is a woman.

She spoke to Seth Bell from the dark, glittering waters of the San Francisco Bay as the ferry chugged toward Alameda. Her voice was deep, throaty, seductive. She wanted him. If he would only climb over the rail and jump, she would let him inside. She would take him down to her black secret places and hold him forever.

"Shut up!" He pushed himself away from the rail and staggered toward a bench. "Get away from me!"

Other passengers edged away, watching him surreptitiously. *Let them watch.* They were always watching, always plotting.

He pulled a flask of vodka from inside his leather coat and took a swig. The familiar heat in his throat comforted him. He hadn't eaten anything that day, so the alcohol hit his bloodstream a few minutes later, relaxing his tight-strung nerves. The voice of Death faded to an insistent whisper in the back of his mind.

The monthly trust-fund deposit had landed in his account last night, so he had plenty of cash. He'd blown some of it right away on a truly epic bar crawl. He also apparently had bought a new tattoo—a woman's eye on the back of his right hand, crying a single blood-red tear. He thought he recognized the eye but couldn't quite place it.

Some indistinct time later, he woke up on a BART train. He didn't remember getting off of the ferry or onto the train, and he had no idea where he was headed. But that was okay. Most BART lines ran through San Francisco, so he could stay on the train and it would eventually take him back to the city. He hitched himself up on the blue vinyl seat and looked out the window. Late-afternoon sun slanted across the rolling green hills outside, casting sharp shadows that made the darkened hillsides look like cliffs. Shadow Cliffs.

Now he knew where he was going. "You put me on the train, didn't you?"

She agreed, her voice light and musical now. He hadn't heard that voice in a long time, but he remembered it well.

He laughed, harsh and loud.

A homeless guy sleeping in the seat across from him stirred and muttered something. Seth ignored him. "It's been a long time, girl. Okay, Shadow Cliffs it is. I haven't been out there in years."

He spent the rest of the train ride drinking and wandering among old memories. He used to enjoy thinking about Shadow Cliffs and his time there with Maddie. Most of it, anyway. The end had always unnerved him. But reliving the rest of it had been an exciting, illicit pleasure. Maddie had been one of his favorites in the secret library of memories he kept locked away in the dark places of his soul.

He rubbed his hand across his face and a twinge of pain reminded him of his new tattoo. He held his hand up for a better look. The eye stared at him, accusing and seductive at the same time. The red of the tear mingled with fresh little droplets of his own blood, glittering like tiny rubies in the shaky sunlight from the train window. He recognized the eye now. It was Maddie's.

Maybe going out to Shadow Cliffs would bring back some of the old savor. He comforted himself with that thought and with more vodka.

The train reached the end of the line. A maintenance worker rousted Seth from a troubled slumber, and he staggered off the train and out of the station.

He collapsed into a cab and mumbled "Shadow Cliffs" to the driver.

The driver glanced into the backseat uncertainly. "It'll be closed by now."

Seth shoved money at the cabbie. "Just drop me at the gate!"

Fifteen minutes later, the taxi arrived at the deserted park. Seth stumbled out of the cab and down the dark path. He knew where he needed to go, and it was suddenly urgent that he get there.

He staggered along the empty paths, now gray and lonely in the deepening gloom. They were different in his memory—ribbons of fresh gravel bordered by bright green under a dome of clear-blue sky. He hadn't been lonely then either. Maddie had been there, burbling happily about what a blast they would have. He'd smiled, knowing that he would have more of a blast than she would ever realize.

They had left the path and gone up to an isolated hilltop crowned with a thicket of brush and small trees. In the middle of the thicket lay a tiny meadow, filled with wildflowers at that time of year. She had wanted to take pictures of the flowers for a photography contest, and he'd offered to bring a picnic lunch and help carry her equipment. They took pictures all morning, Seth's anticipation rising deliciously the whole time. When lunchtime came, he surprised her by pulling a bottle of wine (stolen from his parents' kitchen) out of the picnic basket. He slipped a roofie into her second glass, and she was out cold fifteen minutes later.

Then the real fun began.

When it ended, he realized she wasn't breathing. Maddie would never wake up again.

He sighed and took another swig from his bottle, trying to conjure up the old happy memories of walking there with Maddie.

"I've missed you," said a voice at his side. Her voice.

He spun, nearly falling. His vision doubled and the world whirled. When his eyes cleared, he saw only darkness.

"Maddie?" he called, staggering in a full circle on the path. "Are you here?"

"Come to me. I want you." Her voice came from the shadows off the path, sweet and flirtatious.

He stumbled after the sound. "Maddie?"

He reached a gate and stopped, uncertain. Thick, tangled weeds and mounds of gravel lay beyond it. It looked abandoned and foreboding.

A ripple of unease swept across him. He had known Shadow Cliffs well as a child, but his memory had faded over the years. His conscious mind did not remember this spot, but he had a vague sense that it was dangerous and that he shouldn't go any farther.

He listened to the darkness. Silence, broken only by the chittering of a bat. Then a soft breeze blew on his face, carrying a snatch of distant laughter. Her laughter.

"Wait! I'm coming!" he called.

He struggled over the gate. It wasn't high, but alcohol and urgency made him clumsy. He fell heavily on the other side. The impact knocked the air out of his lungs and he lay there for a moment, gasping.

The laugh came again, even fainter. He pushed himself to his feet and staggered on.

"Seth," she called, barely audible. He broke into a run. Weeds and uneven ground tripped him. Brambles scratched his hands and face.

Then he stopped suddenly and nearly fell. He stood at the edge of a steep, rocky slope. Black water spread below, glinting in the moonlight. A cold breeze blew over him, chilling his sweaty face.

He stared down. Deep below the surface, Maddie's face stared back, unblinking and luminescent.

"Come here," her voice whispered, but her lips did not move.

The lake was an old gravel pit. The bottom was forty feet down, even right by shore. Seth couldn't swim and the water would be icy at this time of year. But Maddie was calling to him.

He stood on the bluff, looking down and trembling. Bitter black water lay below him, but maybe he could fly.

"Come to me," she said in the voice of many women. The voice of Death.

He went. Without making a conscious decision, he jumped. He flew for two long seconds, sailing several yards from shore. The rational fragment of his mind was still trying to comprehend what he had done when he hit the water.

It was very cold.

# CHAPTER 1

*October*

It had been a bad day. So bad that Dr. Johanna Anderson had eaten her entire emergency stash of Dove Bars. And it was about to get worse.

Jo's day had begun with a fender bender on Van Ness at eight thirty. She finally got into the office at quarter after nine. Five minutes after that, the Mind's Eye operating system crashed while booting up and refused to restart, forcing her to cancel the morning's therapy appointments. That's when she hit the Dove Bars the first time.

At ten thirty, Jo determined that the problem was a software issue and that she couldn't fix it. Mind's Eye was her invention, a sophisticated mix of biosensors and algorithms that gave her an unparalleled ability to understand what her patients were thinking and feeling. On a good day, Mind's Eye enabled her to do something very close to reading her patients' minds. On a bad day, it crashed. Today was a very bad day.

She knew Mind's Eye better than anyone, but she was a neuropsychologist, not a programmer. So she'd had to call her programmer for an emergency service visit, which would not be cheap. He returned the call at three—from Paris. The earliest he could be back in San Francisco was two days from then, and since he'd be coming back especially for Jo, she would have to pay all his travel expenses. She cleaned out the rest of the Dove Bars after she got off the phone with him.

She spent the rest of the day responding to e-mail and handling paperwork. She left the office at six, feeling a little queasy from a nascent chocolate hangover. As she walked to her car, a man got out of an old Toyota Camry parked next to her Audi. He looked like a cross between a bike messenger and a low-rent security guard.

He stepped in front of her. "Dr. Johanna Anderson?"

"Yes."

He handed her a stack of paper, stepped back, and took a picture of her holding it. Then he got back in the Camry and drove off without saying another word.

Jo looked down at what he had handed her. It was a lawsuit. She was being sued for causing the death of one of her patients, Seth Bell.

She stood there, rooted to the floor of the parking garage in shock. She knew Seth was dead, of course. The police report was in her files. A jogger had found his body floating in Shadow Cliffs Lake seven months ago. Toxicology tests showed that he'd been both very drunk and abusing multiple drugs at the time of his demise. The police concluded that suicide was the most likely cause of death. So why would anyone blame her?

Her knees felt weak and she leaned against her car for support. Hands shaking, she flipped through the legal papers. The first few documents were forms filled with boilerplate legalese. Then she came to something titled "Complaint." It laid out the case against her in more-or-less clear English. Seth Bell's parents had sued her on behalf of his estate. She was allegedly responsible for Seth's death for two reasons: she used "dangerous experimental technology"—i.e., Mind's Eye—on Seth, and she "failed to identify the clear red flags warning that Seth would take his own life."

As she read, her shock and fear gave way to anger. This was outrageous! The lawyers who wrote this didn't understand psychology, and they especially didn't understand Mind's Eye. It couldn't kill anyone—it was just a tool that helped her see what her patients were thinking and feeling. Not that the truth mattered to the people suing her. Seth's parents doubtless wanted to blame his death on someone other than their son or themselves, so they hired some ambulance chasers to go after Jo.

Jo's fingers tightened on the sheaf of papers, crumpling them slightly. After a moment, she brought her emotions to heel. Standing in a parking garage being mad wouldn't do any good. She needed to think and act rationally.

She got in her car and headed home, forcing herself to drive carefully and deliberately. Night gathered around her as she drove. The mood of the city shifted subtly as the streets darkened, the professionals went home, and the night people came out. It felt alien and menacing. Or was she just projecting her worries about the Bell lawsuit?

She needed a lawyer, of course. A very good one. By the time she arrived at the Bay Bridge toll plaza, she had decided to set three requirements for her attorney. First, she needed a medical-malpractice specialist. Second, she needed someone who had tried at least ten cases and never lost one. Third, she needed to see him or her in action. She was not about to rely on Yelp reviews or word of mouth.

By eleven that night, she had found six lawyers in the entire Bay Area who met her first two criteria, and only one of those was in a trial now. His name was Mike Webster and he seemed perfect on paper—with one minor problem. He was a plaintiffs' lawyer. He might not want to take a defense case, but that didn't worry her too much. She could be very persuasive when she wanted to be.

# CHAPTER 2

At eight thirty the next morning, Jo slipped into the courtroom and found a seat on one of the benches in the rear of the gallery. Court was not yet back in session, and both the judge's chair and the jury box were empty. Men and women in conservative suits stood or sat around two large tables in front of the railing that separated the gallery from the rest of the courtroom.

Jo scanned the pack of lawyers for Mike Webster. She had assumed that a successful plaintiffs' lawyer would wear a flashy suit and a glittering Rolex, but no one fit that description. They all looked like they had just stepped out of a convention of Republican accountants.

There he was. His face had been hidden as he leaned to talk to a dark-haired woman in the front row, but Jo recognized him from his website picture as soon as he stood. He had the same bright-blue eyes and toothpaste-commercial smile, but in person it was charming and insouciant rather than plastic.

It looked like Webster must not have gotten the dress-code memo after all. He wore a charcoal-gray suit and white shirt, but he had decided to complement them with a bright-pink tie that was as out of place as an electric guitar in a string quartet.

A door at the back of the courtroom opened and a woman in a police uniform—presumably the bailiff—entered. She stepped to the side of the doorway and called out, "All rise. The Superior Court for the County of San Francisco is now back in session, the Honorable Hamilton Williams presiding."

Jo joined the rest of the courtroom in standing as the judge and jurors filed in and took their seats. Over half of the jurors were women, and one of them had a little pink-ribbon pin on her blouse.

Then it hit Jo: October was Breast Cancer Awareness Month. She looked more closely at Webster's tie and saw a matching pink tie tack in the shape of a looped ribbon. The corners of Jo's mouth curled upward. Smart man.

Judge Williams nodded toward an aristocratic-looking gray-haired man sitting in the front row.

The man stood and walked to the witness stand, where he sat without letting his back touch the chair. The judge looked down on him, stretching out his long neck like a turtle. "You realize you're still under oath, Dr. Harrington?"

The witness gave a single sharp nod. "I do."

"All right, then." The judge waved to Webster, who had moved to the lectern. "You may resume your examination, Mr. Webster."

"Thank you, Your Honor. Dr. Harrington, what are the symptoms of a cerebral aneurysm before it bursts?"

A woman with a severe gray bun rose from the table to the left. "Objection, calls for expert testimony."

Judge Williams turned to Webster, who shrugged. "Your Honor, if Ms. Strickner is suggesting that Dr. Harrington does not have the ability to accurately diagnose a cerebral aneurysm, we're willing to so stipulate."

A couple of jurors smiled.

"I'm not suggesting anything of the sort," snapped Strickner. "Dr. Harrington is a fact witness. It's improper to ask him for expert opinions."

The judge stroked his well-trimmed gray beard. "Overruled."

Dr. Harrington gave a tight smile. "I'm sorry. I forgot the question."

"What are the symptoms of a cerebral aneurysm before it bursts?" repeated Webster.

"Usually, there are none."

"But in those cases where there are symptoms, what are they?"

Dr. Harrington shook his head. "The symptoms don't matter. The thing you have to remember is that there's always a more likely explanation than cerebral aneurysm because it's almost always asymptomatic."

"That's not what I asked. What are the symptoms of an unburst cerebral aneurysm?"

"As I said, there aren't usually symptoms."

Webster regarded the witness silently for several seconds. "You know, Doctor, I've asked you that question four times now and I still haven't gotten an answer. Are you afraid to answer it?"

Strickner jumped to her feet again. "Objection! He's just harassing the witness."

The judge nodded. "Ask another question, Counsel."

Webster leaned forward, resting his elbows on the lectern. "Let's try this a little differently. Do you remember that during your deposition I asked you what medical treatises you relied on in your practice?"

"Yes."

"And you gave me a list, right?"

"Yes."

"And isn't it a fact that three of those treatises discuss cerebral aneurysms, and each of those three includes severe headaches and vision problems in the list of symptoms of an unburst aneurysm?"

The witness stretched his thin mouth into an unnatural smile. "I don't know. I haven't memorized them. They're quite large."

"Fair enough." Webster picked up a sheaf of papers. "Would it help if I gave you the relevant sections of each treatise to read?"

"Right now?"

"Right now."

The muscles in Dr. Harrington's neck were taut as piano wires. "That . . . that won't be necessary."

"So you'll agree that severe headaches and double vision are symptoms of an unburst cerebral aneurysm?"

He looked at his lawyer with pleading eyes, but she stayed in her seat. "I suppose so," he said at last.

"Thank you. Isn't it true that when Daniel Lee called your office on the morning of July 23, 2014, he complained of severe headaches and double vision?"

"No."

Webster paused for a moment, as if surprised. "All right. Let's see about that. Your Honor, may I publish Plaintiffs' Exhibit Twenty-Three to the jury?"

Strickner stood. "Your Honor, defendants object to that exhibit. You said you would rule on our objections at trial."

A light of recognition gleamed in the judge's bored eyes. "Oh, yes, yes. That's right. Objection sustained."

"Thank you."

Webster stood frozen for an instant. "Plaintiffs' Twenty-Three is an absolutely critical piece of evidence, Your Honor. Could I be heard at sidebar?"

"Certainly."

Strickner and Webster went up to the bench and held a whispered conversation with the judge. Jo couldn't hear them, of course, but she was an expert at reading body language. Webster was surprised and angry, the muscles of his shoulders tensing and bunching as he leaned forward to make his case. Judge Williams listened politely but looked like he had made up his mind. Strickner . . . Now that was interesting. Strickner was relaxed and a little disengaged—even though she seemed to be in the process of winning a major tactical victory. It was almost as if she had known all along how the judge would rule.

Did the judge and Strickner have some sort of understanding about Exhibit 23? If asked for her professional opinion, Jo would have said yes. No one had asked, of course, but she was half-tempted to speak up somehow.

The sidebar conference broke up and the judge turned to the jury. "Ladies and gentlemen, we're going to break for lunch a little early today. Please be back here by one o'clock."

The courtroom began to empty and Jo considered saying something to Webster as he walked out. She decided against it. She was there to see if he was as good as advertised. This would be an interesting test.

# CHAPTER 3

Mike Webster muttered under his breath as he walked toward the elevator. He should have seen this coming. He really should have.

Julia Strickner was too smart to take this case to trial against him—unless she knew something he didn't. On the face of it, he held all the cards: he had at least six million in provable economic damages, there was clear evidence of malpractice, and he had beaten her firm four times in a row in earlier med-mal cases. Plus, his clients were a pretty, young widow and her children.

So when Strickner refused his offer to settle for three million—refused to even make a counteroffer—he should have known she had an ace in the hole. And once he'd figured that out, it would have been obvious that her ace was the Honorable Hamilton Williams. Judge Williams had always gotten campaign contributions from defense firms, spoken at defense bar dinners, and so on. Now he was rumored to be considering retirement, and a cushy partnership at a big defense firm would add a lot of gold to his golden years.

Had Strickner offered the judge an explicit bribe? She probably hadn't needed to. A subtle hint over dinner at some uptown bar function would have been enough.

And with two words—"Objection sustained"—Judge Williams had turned a case worth millions into a case worth nothing. Exhibit 23 was a voice mail that Daniel Lee had left for Dr. Harrington, complaining of a headache and double vision. Mike had given his paralegal, Val, an impromptu bonus when she discovered that gem buried in the backup tapes of Harrington's answering service. It was great evidence—a dramatic voice from the grave, giving textbook cerebral-aneurysm symptoms. And it was almost the *only* direct evidence that Daniel had told Harrington he had those symptoms. Without that exhibit, Mike's odds were slim.

So now what? Mike could probably get the judge reversed on appeal, but that would take years and would only get him a retrial. And his clients didn't have the resources to wait out an appeal and a new trial. With the family breadwinner dead due to Dr. Harrington's malpractice, the Lees were running out of money. They would probably take whatever lowball offer Strickner made after the trial just so they could pay the mortgage and put food on the table for a few more months.

Mike clenched his jaw. There was a special place in hell for those who trampled on the rights of widows and orphans. Maybe they roasted forever over a fire fueled by the money they paid to bribe judges.

He reached the elevators and found the lunch-rush crowd already waiting. It included half the jurors from his case. Lawyers weren't supposed to talk to jurors outside the courtroom, so he didn't greet them or even acknowledge their presence. But he couldn't help overhearing their conversation. They were discussing where to eat lunch. "Subway?" said one.

"We ate there yesterday," said another. "How about that Cajun place, Brenda's? It's only eleven thirty, so maybe there won't be a wait."

"Oooh, I've heard good things about it," replied a third.

Mike stared at the wall, well-oiled gears whirring in his head. Then he turned and headed for the stairwell, which would be faster than the elevators. He leaped down the stairs two at a time and was walking out the courthouse doors as the elevator pinged behind him.

He speed-walked to Brenda's and arrived at the restaurant while the jurors were still at least two blocks away. He quickly surveyed the interior. No jurors yet, and no one from Team Strickner.

Like many eateries near the courthouse, Brenda's was a tiny place. It had only one table big enough to seat half a dozen, and that table was right next to the restaurant's counter. Perfect. Mike hopped on a counter stool with his back to both the door and the big table. While he waited for the server, he fired off a quick text to Val to let her know she was on her own for lunch.

He ordered chicory coffee with steamed milk and a shrimp po'boy sandwich. His stomach rumbled in anticipation. Good thing the jurors had decided on a decent place for lunch.

The jurors came in, and, as he expected, they were seated behind him. Mike couldn't speak to them, of course, but if they happened to come into the same restaurant where he was having lunch, sit down right behind him, and overhear him having a phone conversation . . . who could blame him for that?

He pulled out his cell phone while the jurors were ordering and dialed his rock-climbing partner and sometime cocounsel, Colin West. Colin wasn't helping him with this case, but they talked about it a fair amount. There would be nothing unusual or suspicious about them chatting about it over lunch. Nothing at all.

Colin picked up on the second ring. "Mike! How's it going?"

"It went great for a while. Harrington had to admit that Daniel Lee had the symptoms of an unburst aneurysm—or, well, he *almost* admitted it."

"What do you mean?"

"I mean I got him to admit the symptoms, but he denied that Daniel mentioned having them."

"Really? Wow."

Mike raised his voice a little, which was perfectly natural in a busy restaurant. "Yeah, a flat-out lie. I know. It's right there in that voice mail

Daniel left for Harrington: 'Doctor, I've got this terrible migraine and double vision. Can you please see me?'"

Mike caught low murmuring from the big table behind him, followed by someone shushing.

"So what did he say when you played it for the jury?" Colin asked.

"Nothing. The judge kept it out. He said the voice mail was hearsay."

Colin snorted. "What? That's nuts!"

"No kidding. Any second-year law student could list three reasons why it isn't hearsay. But the judge had his mind made up. And he didn't give any hint before trial that he wouldn't let the voice mail into evidence. He totally blindsided me just now. And it's interesting that Harrington seemed to know it was coming. Otherwise he would have been crazy to lie like that, knowing I could prove the truth by playing that voice mail."

"You're up against Strickner, right? Think she got to him?"

Mike whistled. "I hear what you're saying, but I don't know that I'd go that far. Yes, Judge Williams is friendly with Strickner's firm, and yes, they've probably offered to triple his salary when he retires, but—"

"It looks bad."

"I know it looks bad, but I'm going to give him the benefit of the doubt. Not that I have much choice right now. I'm stuck with him for the rest of this case. I just hope the judge's career planning doesn't leave the Lees out on the street. Daniel didn't have any insurance and his wife was home with the kids, so their money is running out."

"Sorry to hear it, man. Let me know if there's anything I can do to help."

Mike smiled and mouthed "Thanks" as the waitress brought him his sandwich. "I appreciate that, Colin. Just talking to you has been a big help."

Mike clicked off the phone and smiled. "Justice is served," he whispered to himself. "Good and hard."

# CHAPTER 4

"My, my, my." David Klein dropped the *Estate of Bell v. Anderson* complaint on his desk and tapped it slowly with his index finger, deep in thought.

Whenever someone asked David what he did, he said he was "an alternate-investment professional." That was accurate and ambiguous enough for almost any occasion.

David monitored numerous information sources, looking for investment opportunities and pressure points. One of those sources was a service that notified him of any lawsuit involving a California legislator. From time to time, he had questioned whether the service was worth what he paid. Those cases occasionally had useful tidbits, but they rarely told him anything important that he didn't already know.

Until today. *Estate of Bell v. Anderson* was a revelation, a life changer. It could represent the greatest investment opportunity that had ever come his way. If the claims in it were true, that is. "Eric."

"Yes, Mr. Klein?" Eric Sturm said as he materialized in front of David's desk. He could move surprisingly quietly for a man of his size.

David handed him the complaint. "Look into this. I need to know whether there's anything to this case. In particular, I'm interested in finding out more about the Mind's Eye system described in there."

"Yes, Mr. Klein."

"And keep it low profile. We can't let anyone know we're interested in this."

"Yes, Mr. Klein."

# CHAPTER 5

Jo made sure she was in the courtroom early for closing arguments in *Estate of Lee v. Harrington*. She wanted the best possible seat, one that gave her good views of both the jurors and the lawyers. After studying the courtroom the day before, she'd decided that meant sitting in the second row of the gallery, halfway between the lectern and the jury box. Someone else had sat there the day before, and Jo wasn't going to allow that to happen again.

At first she had the courtroom to herself, except for the bailiff seated to the side of the judge's raised bench.

Dr. Harrington's legal team walked in a few minutes later. Julia Strickner led them single file down the aisle, like a grim mother duck trailing a line of overgrown ducklings in gray suits. They arranged themselves around their usual table with a minimum of conversation. A couple of the ducklings shot furtive glances Jo's way, but none of them was bold enough to make eye contact.

When Mike Webster walked in, he not only made eye contact with Jo, he smiled and gave her a slight nod, as if he vaguely recognized her. He may have—she had been in the courtroom for parts of the last three days, though she had been tucked away in a crowded corner where she would have been easy to overlook.

Webster was accompanied by Napoleonette—the nickname Jo had given the woman who sat behind him in the first row every day. Napoleonette had a pretty face, and her figure turned most of the male heads in the courtroom, but she clearly had short-woman's complex. She was about five foot three, but always stood perfectly straight and wore three-inch heels to court every day. Her pile of glossy black hair added at least another inch and a half.

Napoleonette was very red today. Red nails, red shoes, red purse, red lipstick. She had even switched her cell-phone case to red polka dots on white. She probably thought she was adding a splash of color to her otherwise conservative white blouse and black skirt. Instead, she looked like she had accidentally walked through the set of a slasher film.

Jo wasn't quite sure what role Napoleonette played. She looked nothing like any of the other lawyers, but she was comfortable in the courtroom. More comfortable than any of Strickner's ducklings, in fact. Jo would have guessed that Napoleonette was a paralegal or some other subordinate of Webster's, but she treated him like a peer. No—that wasn't quite right. A peer probably wouldn't touch his arm so much when they spoke or make frank comments about his socks like the one Jo had overheard outside the courtroom yesterday. Jo didn't think they were lovers, but they were closer than mere colleagues. It was almost as if they were brother and sister, though they looked nothing alike. Jo frowned slightly. She should find out more about Napoleonette.

The gallery gradually filled with the Lee family and their support-ers; Dr. Harrington and his; and a smattering of people whose relation-ship to the case wasn't clear.

The judge and clerk appeared through a door behind the bench and everyone stood up. They remained standing while the bailiff brought in the jury. Then the court got down to business.

Webster went first. Jo half listened to what he said, but she mostly watched him and the jury. His adrenaline level was up—Jo could hear it in his voice and see it in the way he moved. But he was intense and confident rather than nervous and jittery. He engaged with the jurors, and they responded to him. An older man in the corner of the jury box nodded several times. Several of the jurors smiled at the small jokes Webster scattered through his argument, and they all looked genuinely sympathetic when he recounted Mrs. Lee's description of the lonely, tense life she lived now that her husband was gone. When he asked the jury for a verdict of at least ten million dollars, several jurors wrote down the number on their notepads. And when Dr. Harrington made a faintly audible sound of disbelief, Jo thought she caught quick looks of irritation on two jurors' faces.

By the time Webster sat down, Jo knew the jurors liked and trusted him. And they were open to giving him and the Lees a lot of money.

Strickner took Webster's place at the lectern. She started with the same basic mix of nerves and confidence that he had displayed. She seemed to be doing well—until Jo started watching the jurors closely. They were mostly keeping their faces politely blank, but they weren't giving her the same subtle positive signals that Webster had gotten. In fact, Jo thought she spotted microexpressions of anger and disgust from two or three jurors.

Then Strickner first hit her main argument, that Dr. Harrington never knew that Daniel Lee was suffering symptoms consistent with a cerebral aneurysm and that he therefore could not possibly be found guilty of malpractice. She made the point well, and it sounded reasonable to Jo. But the jurors reacted like Strickner had just insulted their mothers. Several of them gave open signals of rejection—leaning back and looking away from Strickner or tightening their faces into near-frowns. The rest were more subtle, but no less negative.

Strickner looked confused but seemed to realize she had a problem. She switched to well-faked empathy for the Lee family, which mollified the jurors a little. But then she circled back and said that the Lees' tragic loss should not be blamed on Dr. Harrington, who'd had no reason to believe Daniel Lee's life was in danger. The jurors' hostility came back instantly. Jo wondered how much money Strickner was costing her client every time she tried that argument.

Strickner moved on smoothly and seemed to do well enough with the rest of her points. But she was going to lose. Badly. No question.

Jo slipped out when Strickner sat down. She had seen all she needed.

Back at her office, Jo dialed Webster's firm.

"Law Offices of Michael Webster," said a bland female voice. "Can I help you?"

"Yes. I would like to retain Mr. Webster."

# CHAPTER 6

Valeria D'Abruzzo and Mike Webster sat side by side in their firm's conference room, waiting for the receptionist, Janet, to bring in the prospective new client. Val was Mike's firm manager, paralegal, investigator, and proofreader. She used to also be the receptionist, secretary, and maid, but she had managed to delegate those jobs as the firm grew from two people (her and Mike) to the present seven.

Val stifled a yawn. She was looking forward to this meeting, but she had only gotten an average of four hours of sleep a night during the trial—though that was probably more than Mike had gotten, and he wasn't yawning.

After Val and Mike had returned from court yesterday, Janet told them she had scheduled a meeting with Dr. Johanna Anderson for nine the next morning. It seemed that Dr. Anderson wanted to hire Mike. Which was odd. Mike Webster was a plaintiffs' attorney who had never represented a doctor in his life, something that was clear to anyone who spent five seconds on the firm's website.

So even though Val was tired from a long day in court, she had done some research on Dr. Anderson. CourtLink showed a newly filed complaint against Dr. Anderson, which Val pulled off the San Francisco

Superior Court website. It was a medical-malpractice case filed by Mike and Val's old firm, Masters & Cromwell. Tim Cromwell had signed it himself, so the firm must have thought this would be a high-profile case. Which was also odd. The lawsuit seemed like an obvious loser to Val. Dr. Anderson was a psychologist who had allegedly committed malpractice by using an unproven new technique to treat a mentally ill and unemployed ex-con who then committed suicide. Val wasn't a lawyer, but she had seen lots of lawsuits and was pretty sure that this one had major causation and damages problems. The plaintiffs (the ex-con's parents, acting as executors of his estate) would probably lose, and even if they won, they wouldn't get much. So why was Tim Cromwell involved?

She had no trouble answering that question once she ran Accurint background reports on Dr. Anderson and the dead ex-con, Seth Bell. His father, Warren Bell, was a state senator who had spearheaded efforts to repeal California's MICRA law, which sharply limited the sizes of judgments in medical-malpractice cases. Tim was doubtless happy to do a favor for Senator Bell. That explained why Masters & Cromwell would be willing to take a case they would almost certainly lose money on, but not why Tim would get personally involved. Dr. Anderson's backgrounder cleared that up. She had made the covers of several professional magazines for a new technology-assisted treatment technique called Mind's Eye—the same technique that allegedly had contributed to Seth Bell's death. She also had testified as an expert witness against Masters & Cromwell in two big-money cases, one of which the firm had lost. Tim Cromwell had been the lead lawyer on the loser. So beating her in a case that focused on Mind's Eye would be personally sweet for Tim.

Val pulled up one of the articles profiling Dr. Anderson and got a surprise when she saw the accompanying picture: Dr. Anderson was the woman who had watched part of the Lee trial. Val had figured she might be a reporter for a legal newspaper or be doing research for a defense firm that had a trial coming up against Mike. This was the first time Val could recall a potential client going to the trouble of watching Mike in action. *She must want him pretty badly.*

Janet opened the door and ushered Dr. Anderson in. The psychologist was tall, skinny, pretty, midthirties, and dressed like she had a personal style consultant at Nordstrom. Probably Mike's type, in other words. Val leaned back so she could watch his reaction out of the corner of her eye. *Yep.* Very subtle, but Val knew Mike well enough to recognize that look.

Mike and Val both rose. "Thank you for coming in," Mike said, shaking Dr. Anderson's hand warmly. "I'm Mike Webster, and this is my colleague, Val D'Abruzzo. I'm going to apologize in advance, because I'm waiting for a jury to come back with a verdict. I'll have to go over to the court as soon as they do, even if our meeting isn't finished."

"Jo Anderson," she replied as she shook Val's hand. "I understand about the jury." She turned back to Mike. "Congratulations on your win, by the way."

He paused for a beat. "Uh, I don't know the verdict yet."

Dr. Anderson smiled. "I do. I'm a psychologist, and I've spent over a decade learning to read nonverbal cues. I was in the courtroom yesterday. The jurors never said a word, of course, but they were practically shouting that they were going your way. I'd be surprised if it took them long to reach a verdict—or if they awarded much less than the ten million you asked for."

Mike stared for several seconds, then grinned and ostentatiously rapped the wooden tabletop. "I hope you're right."

Val leaned forward. "Wow, I didn't know you could be that definitive without using Mind's Eye on the jurors."

Dr. Anderson gave Val an appraising look, then smiled. "Apparently, I'm not the only one who's been doing some research."

Val smiled back but said nothing.

"So, what can we do for you, Dr. Anderson?" Mike asked.

"Please call me Jo. As you may already know"—she flicked a glance at Val—"I am being sued for malpractice. In a nutshell, I am accused of causing—or at least failing to prevent—the death of a mentally ill young man."

Mike nodded. "The treatment allegedly caused him to commit suicide by drowning himself in a lake, right?"

"I see I chose the right lawyer. But then, I already knew that from seeing you in court and watching the jury yesterday."

Mike wrinkled his forehead and smiled. "I'm flattered, Jo, but I actually don't think I'm the best lawyer for you. I do plaintiffs' work. You need a defense-side lawyer. I'm sure your malpractice carrier will hire someone who can handle the case. And if they don't, I'll be happy to give you a referral."

She gave him a sardonic look. "To someone like Julia Strickner?"

He smiled diplomatically. "There are lots of good defense lawyers in San Francisco."

She grinned. "Okay, refer me to someone good enough to beat a top-notch plaintiffs' lawyer. You, for example."

Val knew no one had beaten Mike in court, and she suspected Jo knew that too. *Nice move.*

Mike returned the doctor's grin. "I'll have to think about that. Who's your insurance carrier? That may dictate who you can hire."

"I don't have one. My company is essentially self-insured."

"Well, whomever I refer you to will want to know about the case. Tell me about it from your perspective. In particular, I'd be interested in hearing about your treatment of Seth Bell."

"Certainly, but I can't go into too much detail. I want to protect Seth's privacy as much as possible. His parents are suing me, but that's not his fault."

Mike's eyebrows went up slightly, and Val could tell he was impressed. "Of course. Tell me whatever you feel comfortable revealing."

"Thank you. Seth was one of several patients referred to me by the California Department of Corrections and Rehabilitation. I have developed a new therapy method that the department thought could be very helpful to a lot of troubled young men and women. I think you've already heard of it." She nodded in Val's direction. "It's called Mind's Eye. How much do you know about it?"

"Not much," Val replied. "Just that it combines a bunch of technology. I also read that a functional MRI machine is really important."

"That's right," Jo said with a bright smile. "A modified fMRI machine is a key piece of Mind's Eye. In essence, I connect patients to an EEG, the sensors from a polygraph machine, and a couple of other devices. Then I put them in an fMRI machine." She paused. "Do you already know what that is?"

"It basically measures blood flow in the brain, right?" Val said.

Jo nodded approvingly, like a grade-school teacher whose student just gave the right answer. "Yes. A normal MRI machine does the same thing. What makes an fMRI special is that it doesn't just give a static picture. The difference between MRI and fMRI is like the difference between a snapshot and a movie. Plus, I can see the fMRI output in real time while I'm actually talking to the patient. I don't need to wait while it's processed.

"The blood flow in the brain tells me which areas are active—and that gives me insights into what my patients are thinking and feeling, whether they're lying or under stress, and so on. The EEG and the other sensors do the same thing in different ways. I also use a separate program to track tiny involuntary facial reactions called microexpressions. Taken together, these can provide a remarkably clear picture of what's going on inside someone's head."

"But is it possible to take them all together?" Mike asked. "How can you keep an eye on all of those different things and still do therapy? And wouldn't you have to be an expert with each one?"

"Excellent questions. The key is an algorithm that combines the outputs from all of those devices into one easy-to-read display on a computer screen. It's a tremendous help during therapy. It's like having a window into my patients' minds."

"Hence the name," Mike said, tugging thoughtfully at his chin. "I can see why Corrections would be interested."

"There are many applications. For example, we're hoping that Mind's Eye will help them identify which prisoners truly are no longer threats to society and are ready for parole, and which are acting. Or which defendants claiming to be insane really are. Or which prisoners are violent and should be isolated."

"Or which ones might be suicidal," added Val.

Jo paused for a second. "Yes. Now you understand why winning this case is so important to me. It's not just about money or my reputation; it's about the fate of Mind's Eye and the thousands—maybe tens of thousands—of people it could help."

"Very impressive," Mike said, "but I have one question: What happened to Seth Bell? Why didn't you see that he was suicidal?"

"That was two questions," Jo said, a smile tugging at the corners of her mouth. "I—"

Mike's cell phone chimed. He snatched it out of his coat pocket and looked at the screen. "I'm sorry, but the answers are going to have to wait. That was the court clerk telling us that the jury is back."

# CHAPTER 7

Ten minutes later, Mike and Val were walking down the hall toward Judge Williams's courtroom. Mike's stride was strong and forceful, while Val had to scurry to keep up. Mike usually moved at a more leisurely pace to accommodate her shorter legs and higher heels, but he was in a hurry. Val couldn't blame him under the circumstances, but she felt like a hobbit trying to run on stilts.

They reached the courtroom and found Susan Lee waiting for them outside the doors, trying to entertain her youngest, who was not happy to be there.

Mike reached the door first and held it open. "After you," he said to Susan.

She hesitated and looked down at her grumpy infant, who was quiet for the moment. "Should I bring him in?"

"Absolutely," Mike replied. "I want you in there in case the jury goes the wrong way and I need to poll them. Seeing the two of you might make some of them change their minds. If you'd feel more comfortable standing in the back of the courtroom with him, that's fine."

They went in and found the defense team and Dr. Harrington already there. Julia Strickner glanced at them as they walked down the center aisle, then turned to the court clerk. "Okay, everyone is here now," she said in a slightly exasperated voice, as if she had been waiting for an hour.

The clerk nodded to the bailiff, who disappeared through a door at the side of the jury box. For several minutes, the courtroom was silent, except for faint hushing sounds coming from Susan Lee at the back of the courtroom and occasional grumpy sounds from her baby.

Then the judge appeared through his door beside the bench. "All rise," the clerk ordered as the judge climbed the dais behind the bench.

They got to their feet, and the door by the jury room opened again. The bailiff stepped out and stood to one side as the jurors filed in and took their seats in the jury box. They kept their eyes down as they shuffled to their places, deliberately avoiding eye contact with anyone in the room. Val wondered what Jo Anderson would have said about their body language.

"Please be seated," intoned the bailiff.

"Ladies and gentlemen of the jury, have you reached a verdict?" Judge Williams asked in a formal tone.

An older woman in the back row cleared her throat and stood up, a piece of paper in her hand. Even from across the courtroom, Val recognized the CACI medical-malpractice verdict form. "We have, Your Honor."

"Please read it."

The woman looked down at the verdict form. "On Question One, yes, Dr. Harrington was negligent in the diagnosis or treatment of Daniel Lee. On Question Two, yes, Dr. Harrington's negligence was a substantial factor in causing harm to Daniel Lee. On Question Three-A, the past economic loss to Daniel Lee's estate is zero. On Question Three-B, the future loss to his estate is eleven and a half million dollars."

By his second glass of champagne, Mike Webster was feeling philo-sophical. The fatigue of chronic insomnia mixed with the elation of victory and the alcohol in his blood to create a sort of exhausted joy. The unease—almost fear, really—he always felt after a big win was just a vague haze in the back of his mind, unable to dim the pleasure of the moment. Mike relaxed bonelessly in his chair and watched the bubbles rise in his glass as it sat on the conference-room table. Then he picked up the glass in an impromptu toast. "Today is a good day."

"A good day," echoed several members of the firm as they lifted their glasses and drank.

"And the day we get paid will be even better," added Mike's senior associate, Camy Tang.

"To the day we get paid," said the junior associate, Brad Simpson, raising his glass.

Mike chuckled and raised his glass, as did the rest of the group.

Mike put his glass down. "You know, I'm not sure about that."

"About what?" Val asked.

"About the day we get paid being better." He leaned forward. "I mean, getting a boatload of money is great, but that's not why we do this job, is it? Not the main reason, anyway. It's about justice. We spent the last two weeks in Judge Williams's courtroom fighting for justice for Susan Lee and her kids, and today we won. That's sweeter than any payday."

Val raised her glass. "To justice for 'the fatherless and the widow'—and to Mike, who went and got it for them."

Most of the people around the table sipped their champagne with polite smiles. Mike recognized the look and didn't really blame them—they knew their boss was prone to pompous sermonizing. It was mostly crap to them, though they wouldn't begrudge him a little bloviating right after a big win. But Val's dark eyes shone as she drank to him. She gave him a wide, sweet smile with no hint of her usual Brooklyn edge, and he found himself smiling back. She really believed every word of that crap, just like him.

# CHAPTER 8

Someone coughed discreetly in the doorway.

David Klein looked up from his monitors, which were filled with a 32-column, 1,657-line Excel spreadsheet. "Come in, Eric."

The big man entered. He had not been invited to sit, so he stood in the middle of the office. "My report on *Estate of Bell v. Anderson* is ready."

"Go ahead," David said, gesturing toward one of his guest chairs.

Eric sat down and smoothed his slacks. He knew firm protocol well enough not to put anything in writing unless expressly instructed to do so. "I have been able to confirm most of what the complaint says. Seth Bell was a patient of Dr. Johanna Anderson, and he did commit suicide on March 3. His—"

"What about Mind's Eye?" David interrupted. "Is it like the complaint describes?"

Eric nodded. "I think so. You told me to be discreet, so I haven't talked to any experts, but I found several articles in medical journals that talk about it. They all say it's like the complaint describes."

"*Exactly* like?"

"Yes, Mr. Klein."

David drummed his fingers on the desk's leather blotter. He tried to estimate what the Chinese or Russians would pay for Mind's Eye. Something in ten figures, certainly. Possibly eleven.

"Who's funding her?" He hadn't specifically asked Eric to look into this, but a good analyst would have thought to do it anyway.

"The Oceanview Fund," Eric replied. "They've put twelve million into Mind's Eye so far. She's burned through a lot of that, but they've told her not to worry. They're very bullish."

"Oceanview?"

"Yes, Mr. Klein."

The Mind's Eye opportunity had just become interesting on an entirely new level.

"Are they taking stock or secured debt?" David asked, not really expecting an answer this time.

"Stock," Eric replied without hesitation. "She set up a company called Mind's Eye, Inc. She owns fifty-five percent and Oceanview owns forty-five."

David's eyebrows went up. "You were able to find out all of that without tipping anyone off?"

"I was able to piece it together from UCC filings and an interview Dr. Anderson gave. She said they plan to make money by licensing Mind's Eye to hospitals worldwide, which was why Oceanview has been buying stock in her company. So they have stock. If they also had secured debt, they would have made UCC filings. They didn't."

"Nice work."

"Thank you, Mr. Klein."

The idea that had been forming in David's head took clearer form. He wondered whether Oceanview was thinking the same thing he was. He decided it was possible but unlikely. They pitched themselves as white-knight investors and generally—but not always—played well within the rules. And if they had been thinking what he was, they certainly would have taken secured debt rather than stock, particularly only a 45 percent interest.

Would Oceanview try to stop him? They had already sunk twelve million dollars into Mind's Eye, and Eric thought they were willing to dump in more. On the other hand, they were risk averse for venture capitalists, and they mostly cared about hitting their profit benchmark. Besides, he had leverage over Oceanview that he could use if push came to shove. And he really hoped they gave him an excuse to shove.

"Eric, it's time that we started taking a few more risks and investing a little more money." He gave Eric a series of precise instructions, then had him repeat them. Eric did so perfectly. He did not take notes.

Eric showed no hesitation and asked no unnecessary questions. At the end, he simply said, "Yes, Mr. Klein."

But David had already turned back to his spreadsheet, indicating the meeting was over.

# CHAPTER 9

Jo couldn't do much about the Bell case until she heard back from Mike Webster. Fortunately, her programmer had arrived back in the States yesterday and had made a jet-lagged visit to her office to fix the problem in the Mind's Eye operating system. So Jo could at least put the lawsuit out of her mind and focus on her work. Or try to, anyway.

Today's referral from Corrections was Jack "Hammer" Adams. Jack had been in and out of prison since he was twelve, mostly for weapons or controlled-substance-related offenses. Most of those were nonviolent misdemeanors, though he had picked up two felony convictions during his career.

A month ago, Jack faced a third felony charge—and the threat of a life sentence under California's Three Strikes law if he was convicted. The DA's Office had offered to let him plead to another misdemeanor, but only if he underwent a psychological evaluation and, if recommended by the evaluation, therapy. He had never been diagnosed with a mental disorder, but the transfer memo from Corrections reported that both the DA and prison officials thought that Jack "showed signs of paranoia and schizophrenia." He might or might not be a paranoid schizophrenic, but he certainly wasn't stupid: he took the deal on the spot.

Jo had just finished giving Jack's file a final skim when her nurse, Shaun Hammond, stuck his head in her doorway. "Mr. Adams is here."

Jo nodded and followed Shaun out the door. His enormous back was like a moving wall in front of her. Shaun had been a defensive end at Cal until a knee injury ended his career. He had planned to go to medical school and specialize in sports medicine, but he was forced to readjust his goals when he discovered how hard the premed program at Cal was. He had then vaguely planned to open a sports-medicine clinic of some sort. Once Jo met him, however, she had persuaded him to come work for her. Or rather, Jo's venture-capital money had persuaded him. Jo paid him far more than an ordinary nurse or physical therapist would make. But then, an ordinary nurse or therapist didn't double as a walking security system, which was an important trait when dealing with a clientele that contained a lot of ex-cons.

Jack Adams was a small man of about forty with furtive, intelligent eyes. He got up slowly and showed a slight limp as he crossed the lobby. Jo decided that the "Hammer" nickname must be a joke.

"Good morning, Mr. Adams," Jo said with a professional smile. "I'm Dr. Anderson and this is my assistant, Shaun. Please step this way."

Adams silently followed Jo down the hall and into the Mind's Eye room. Shaun came in behind them.

Adams stopped in the doorway, looking uneasily at the massive fMRI machine and the array of devices set out in front of it. "I thought you were just going to do an evaluation."

"That's right," Jo said.

"So what's that for?" Adams asked, pointing at the fMRI machine. "I've done evaluations before. I never had to go in something like that."

"This is a new technique," Jo replied. "It's perfectly safe. All we're going to do is put some electrodes and a blood-pressure cuff on you. Then we'll do the evaluation."

Adams continued to hesitate. "I don't know."

"Don't worry," Jo said in a soothing voice. "Shaun will set you up with a light sedative to help you relax and lie still in the machine."

Taking his cue, Shaun placed a massive hand on the small of Adams's back and guided him toward the examining table. "Right this way, Mr. Adams."

Adams stiffened slightly, but gave Shaun a cowed look and allowed himself to be maneuvered onto the table.

Jo smiled and went into the control room to wake up the Mind's Eye computer and run a diagnostic to make sure everything was still functioning as it should. It hadn't crashed since her programmer wrote the latest patch, but she was still nervous about the software. Integrating the inputs from half a dozen devices, each with its own operating system, made Mind's Eye's software inherently unstable. But it seemed to be working fine for the moment.

By the time she finished, Shaun had Adams fully prepped and in the machine. An fMRI machine requires a tremendously powerful magnetic field around a person's head, so the machine uses enormous magnets that completely surround the patient. Jo therefore couldn't directly see any part of her patients except the bottoms of their feet, so she had a small camera mounted inside the machine that provided a view of their faces. She had installed a small monitor, allowing patients to see her as well.

The camera also fed into a powerful facial-recognition program on her computer. The software had been designed to scan thousands of faces in airport terminals and train stations, looking for terrorists and criminals. Jo's programmer had reconfigured it to scan a single face dozens of times per second. It then analyzed those scans to identify microexpressions—the fleeting, involuntary expressions that are an excellent indicator of what people are really feeling, regardless of the emotion they are consciously trying to convey. The program wasn't quite as good as Jo's brain, but it was much faster and missed nothing, whereas it would take Jo's full attention, going through the video later at half speed or less, to make sure she caught everything. Much better to have something that was 95 percent accurate, but instantaneous and integrated with her Mind's Eye display.

She tapped a key on her keyboard. "Do you see a green circle on the screen in front of you?"

"Yes."

"Good. I need you to focus on that as completely as you can for the next few minutes. Empty your mind of everything except the green circle. Can you do that?"

He nodded, causing spikes on several readouts.

"Please don't move," she said. "I need you to stay completely still to get accurate readings."

"Sorry."

"Don't worry about it. Just focus on the green circle. I'll put on some white noise if you like. What's your preference—light jazz, nature sounds, classical?"

"Uh, classical would be good."

She tapped another key and the soothing strains of "Clair de Lune" started drifting through the speakers inside the fMRI machine. Then she waited silently until his pupils dilated and his respiration, pulse, and blink frequency all dropped.

After about five minutes, he was ready.

"Good. Now I'm going to ask you some questions designed to make sure all this technology is working right. What is your full name?"

"Jonathon James Adams."

The Mind's Eye display showed what Jo expected: brain-activity patterns consistent with truth telling, emotionally flat, no indications of concealment or stress. There was an underlying matrix of anxiety and defensiveness, which was a little surprising now that Adams was both sedated and hypnotized.

"What day of the week is it?"

"Wednesday."

Same readout from Mind's Eye. "What city are we in?"

"Oakland."

No change. Good.

"Okay, now lie to me. Tell me that your eyes are brown."

"My eyes are brown."

Multiple indications of dishonesty popped up on Jo's screen. She had them color-coded red so they'd be easy to spot in contrast to the green indicators of honesty, and that part of the display was now largely red.

"Now tell me that we're in Paris."

"We're in Paris."

Same result.

Satisfied that Mind's Eye was properly calibrated and that she had a good picture of Adams's base mental state, Jo moved on to the meat of the evaluation. "Thank you. Do you sometimes hear voices that other people don't seem to hear?"

"No." He was lying. It was a lie he had rehearsed, so only about half of the dishonesty indicators turned red.

"Are you sure about that?"

More signs of dishonesty, accompanied by a flash of anger breaking through despite the calming effects of the sedative and hypnosis. "Yes."

"Do you ever see connections or patterns that other people don't appear to notice? For example, do you sometimes see secret meaning in the way cars are parked on the street or how a stranger glances at you?"

More lies coming. "No."

Jo paused and tried a different tack. "Why do you think you're here?"

"Because the DA wanted me to get evaluated."

"Why do you think the DA wanted you to get evaluated?"

"You'd have to ask the DA."

"I didn't ask why the DA wanted this evaluation. I asked why you thought the DA wanted it. So, what do you think?"

Another flash of anger, stronger this time, but he kept his voice even and his face mostly expressionless. "I really have no idea."

A clear lie. The dishonesty indicators were pure crimson.

"I'm sorry, but I think you do, Mr. Adams. These instruments are very good at identifying inaccurate statements. Please try answering the question again."

He was silent for a moment, but his brain and body spoke eloquently. He was still angry, but he was afraid now too. He had probably walked in thinking he could BS his way through this. And he had just discovered he was wrong.

"Well, maybe he thought I might have some, you know, issues," Adams admitted.

"Like what?"

"I, uh, sometimes get really down, like I don't want to live anymore and I don't have any energy. Some days I can't even get out of bed."

Jo chuckled. "That's not true, but you're hoping I'll recommend antidepressants, which you can then sell. Not going to happen. What's the real answer to my question?"

She watched with satisfaction as his fear level spiked. That had been partially informed guesswork, but Adams was now convinced she could read his thoughts.

Adams laughed nervously. "I guess maybe I sometimes talk to myself, and I'm kind of suspicious."

A quick glance at the display told Jo he wasn't lying this time, and his words matched the memo from Corrections. But he also had brain activity and stress patterns consistent with concealment. *Interesting.*

"I think you have more to tell me."

His fear levels went up again, as did his anger. He lifted his head and glared at the camera. "Okay, maybe I do sometimes hear voices talking to me. And sometimes I do see, you know, patterns and stuff that other people don't understand."

"Please don't move. It interferes with the readings."

He lay still, continuing to glare.

Jo took a closer look at his readings. He had broken completely free of the hypnosis early in the session, and the sedation didn't seem to be having much calming effect. It was probably just slowing his mental reactions some, which was remarkable given how effectively he was verbally fencing with her. His anger levels had also been unusually high throughout, even though Jo's questioning had been fairly innocuous.

A thought occurred to her: maybe it wasn't her questions that were making him angry. Maybe it was *her*.

"Mr. Adams, tell me about your relationships with women."

He froze. She didn't need to look at the Mind's Eye screen to know she'd hit a nerve. "What do you mean?"

"I think you know what I mean." She had no idea what he was hiding, but she could see it there. It roiled the currents of his emotions and thoughts like a whale swimming just below the surface of a calm sea.

"I . . . I need to talk to my lawyer."

# CHAPTER 10

Val was in the middle of a spreadsheet when Mike walked into her office and shut the door. "So, I've been thinking about Jo Anderson's case. Should we take it?" He sat down and stifled a yawn, watching her expectantly with bloodshot eyes. Did the guy ever get enough sleep?

She pulled out her notes on Jo Anderson and flipped through them to give herself time to think. Jo had rubbed Val the wrong way, but then any woman who was five foot eight, skinny, blonde, and country-club pretty would do that. And she hadn't liked the way Jo acted when they met with her. It wasn't anything specific, just a vaguely superior and calculating air that got under Val's skin. But Val knew she had a chip on her shoulder when dealing with highly educated people. All too often they stopped taking her seriously the moment they realized she had only a high school education. It didn't occur to them that they should be *more* impressed that she'd gotten where she was without a college degree, not *less*.

Val pushed down her instinctive dislike of Jo and tried to make herself be fair. "The case does sound interesting," she admitted.

Mike nodded. "I agree."

"And it sounds like you should be able to win this one," Val continued. "Unless she's completely making up this Bell guy's medical history, the plaintiff will have trouble proving causation." She ticked off the points in the defense's favor, holding up a perfectly manicured finger for each one. "He was mentally ill. He was very drunk. He died almost a week after his last Mind's Eye session. It's going to be hard for the plaintiff to prove that anything she did or didn't do caused his death."

"So you think we should take the case."

She shook her head. "It would involve hourly work, which we don't do. And if we did, there's no way we'd take her insurance company's rates. And at the rates we *would* take, she could easily hire any blue-chip defense firm she wanted. Besides, we really don't have the bandwidth. You know that. We were ignoring ten other cases while the Lee case was in trial. We can't take on another one. Not now."

Mike nodded slowly. "All true, but I'm thinking of taking the case anyway."

"Why?"

He shrugged. "There's something about this case I like?"

She arched her eyebrows. "You mean someone?"

He laughed. "No, I meant that I love what she's doing with Mind's Eye. She could help a lot of people. Isn't it great that she's starting with ex-cons? A lot of those guys have serious mental-health issues, and nobody ever helps them. Except now she is." He nodded in agreement with himself. "That's what I like about the case."

Val suppressed an eye roll. "How about referring her to Colin or Emily? They both do a lot more defense work than we do, and they're both good." Not as good as Mike, but no reason to bring that up. "Either of them can give the case the attention it deserves. You can't. You've got more stuff on the front burner right now than a food truck during lunch rush."

Mike drummed his fingers on the table, a pensive look on his face. "Yeah, maybe you're right. I'll give her their names. Whoever she picks can owe me a referral down the road, hopefully when I'm not so swamped." He shook his head slightly. "I would've enjoyed working with Jo Anderson, though."

Val smiled with relief. "Me too," she lied.

# CHAPTER 11

Jack Adams had spent a long day at San Francisco's Asian Art Museum. He had little interest in art, Asian or otherwise, and he hadn't actually set foot inside the museum. Rather, he'd spent the last ten hours standing on the sidewalk on the south side of the museum with a dozen competitors in one of San Francisco's open-air drug markets.

He yielded his spot shortly after seven thirty, when the night guys started showing up. Then he started across the Tenderloin, the garbage can of the city. Ninety-five percent of San Francisco was tech companies, expensive restaurants, and apartments that only bazillionaires could afford. Jack wasn't allowed there, of course. The cops pushed him and the rest of the trash into places like the Tenderloin and kept it there.

Jack's feet hurt, and standing in the sun had sucked all the energy out of him, but the night had turned cold and clammy. He shivered in his thin jacket and quickened his pace along the dark street, picking his way among mounds of rags that swore and sprouted makeshift weapons if he stepped on them.

He felt pretty good. Business had been brisk. He had over $300 in his pocket, enough to get food, pay for a night in his favorite SRO hotel, buy product for tomorrow, and still have a little left over. Speaking of leftovers, he had enough unsold pot for a bowl or two after dinner.

He took a different route to the SRO than he had before in order to avoid anyone who might be waiting for him along the way. He also avoided mailboxes, because most of those were booby-trapped. He wasn't sure about FedEx drop boxes, but stayed away from them to be safe.

He couldn't avoid being followed, though. Halfway to the SRO, a large man appeared out of the shadows beside him. He wore a black hoodie that obscured his face. Jack's hand slipped into his jacket pocket, where he carried a folding knife with a razor-sharp five-inch blade. If the big man in the hoodie noticed, he didn't give any indication.

"They're watching you," the man said without preamble. His voice was strange—faint and artificial, like the sound from one of those mechanical voice boxes that people with throat cancer used.

Jack said nothing. He had learned not to respond to strange visitors with messages.

"This time they're not just watching," the man continued. "They'll come for you. You need to disappear."

Jack nodded slightly but said nothing. He kept walking, hand on his knife, eyes flicking back and forth between the street and the man.

"This will help." The man held out an unmarked envelope, grasping it in a black-gloved hand.

Jack hesitated. This was new. None of the others had offered any kind of concrete help. They usually just gave him messages and warnings before disappearing into the shadows.

"There's a thousand dollars in here. And the home address of the woman who sent them after you. If you kill her, they'll stop hunting you."

"You know who sent them?" Jack whispered, startled into speech.

"We know many things," the buzzing metallic voice said.

"Who is it?"

"Her name is Dr. Johanna Anderson."

Of course. It made perfect sense. She put him in that machine that opened his brain like a can of tuna and plucked out his secrets. Now he was useless and she would have him killed. No witnesses that way. Rage boiled in him. He took the envelope.

Without saying another word, the big man turned down an alley and vanished in the shadows.

# CHAPTER 12

Jo took the news well, which relieved Mike. She had spent a lot of time and effort researching him, so he worried that she might not be willing to take no for an answer. That could have gotten ugly, which would have been unfortunate.

But Jo hadn't tried to force the issue. She graciously thanked him for his time and for the referrals. And when he mentioned how intrigued he and Val were by the Mind's Eye system, Jo invited him to her office for a demonstration. He accepted and arranged to come there the next evening after work.

He wondered what to make of the fact that her invitation hadn't included Val. Maybe it was nothing more than an oversight—but maybe the demonstration was an excuse for Jo to spend some time alone with Mike. That was an interesting possibility. She hadn't worn a wedding ring when she came to the office, and he had idly wondered whether she was unattached. He'd know soon.

The next day, Mike slipped out of the office early (which meant six for him) and drove over to Jo's office. It was in Oakland, so he left himself extra time to find a garage where he could park his BMW M6, but once he reached her neighborhood he decided it would be safe to leave it on the street. Jo's office was in a luxurious office complex overlooking Lake Merritt. It also had a private garage, which made the issue moot.

Jo buzzed him into the lobby and he walked up to her second-floor office suite. She was waiting for him at the door with a glass of white wine in each hand. Well, that cleared up his uncertainty about her intentions.

She handed him one of the glasses as he walked in. "I give most patients a mild sedative before we begin, but a glass of good chardonnay works just as well. I hope you don't mind."

He sipped the wine. It *was* good. "Not at all. This is starting out a lot better than most of my trips to doctors' offices."

She smiled. "Come on in. I'll give you a tour while you drink your wine."

She guided him through a small waiting area to an equally small conference room. What the room lacked in size, it made up for with a spectacular view of Lake Merritt. The sun had set, and the deepening twilight turned the lake into an expanse of dark glass surrounded by a necklace of pearly lights. The room was decorated more like a cozy café than an ordinary conference room. A large, low table dominated the room, surrounded by overstuffed chairs and a comfortable-looking leather sofa.

Jo sat down at one end of the sofa and patted the seat next to her. As Mike sat down, she placed her wine glass on the table and picked up an iPad.

"This is where the treatment process usually begins," Jo explained. "For some patients, I have a referral memo or other document that tells me what I need to know about their background and what issues they may need help with, but otherwise I start with an initial interview. So, Mr. Webster," she said with a grin and a wink, "tell me about your childhood."

He grinned back. "Shouldn't I be lying down on the couch? Isn't that how we're supposed to do this? Also, where's your cigar?"

"This is a nonsmoking building," she replied, "but if you'd like to lie down . . ." She leaned across him and pushed a button hidden in the cushions of the opposite armrest. An electric motor whirred softly somewhere in the sofa, and the side Mike was sitting on leaned back until it was almost horizontal. The bottom of the sofa rose up to become a footrest.

Jo slipped her shoes off, turned sideways so she could face him, and tucked her feet under her. "Better?"

Mike chuckled, then yawned. "Very relaxing. Feel free to poke me if I start snoring."

"Do you sometimes have trouble sleeping?"

"Now that you mention it, I do. I'll be exhausted all day, but the moment my head hits the pillow, I'm suddenly wide awake. I start thinking about everything that happened during the day or worrying about stuff I have to deal with tomorrow. It's like I can't turn off my brain. Sometimes it only lasts for an hour or so, but sometimes I'm up all night."

"Have you tried cutting out coffee and other stimulants?" she asked.

"Oh, yeah. I went cold turkey for a whole week. I was so out of it that my insurance company should've boosted my malpractice premiums. But I still couldn't sleep at night."

She tapped a note into her iPad. "Regular exercise also helps with insomnia, but I can see that you're already doing that."

"Thanks. Yes, an hour in the gym, six times a week."

Another note in the iPad. "Okay, I think I know enough now to give you a Mind's Eye demonstration. Let's go into the examination room."

She got up and put her shoes on. Mike felt around in the armrest cushions and found the control. He brought the sofa back into a sitting position, got up, and stretched. "That is great. I've got to get one of those for my TV room."

She led him into another area that looked like every medical examining room in America: linoleum floor, white Formica counters, white cabinets above and below, lots of expensive-looking machinery. An enormous cylinder took up much of the space. A bench with a white hospital sheet protruded from one end of it, next to a dark tunnel in the middle of the cylinder. On the bed lay a skullcap with lots of wires, a blood-pressure cuff, and some other things Mike didn't recognize but which looked like they were supposed to be attached to a human body somehow.

Mike paused in the door. Jo noticed his hesitation and grinned impishly. "It looks a little like a mad scientist's lab, doesn't it? But don't worry—I'm not at all mad right now."

He laughed. "How reassuring."

Her grin turned into an understanding smile. "Seriously, if you'd rather not go in the machine, I totally understand."

"No, no. That's fine." He gulped down the last of his wine and put the empty glass on a counter. "I really would like a demonstration. Let's go."

She spent the next ten minutes attaching sensors to him. Then she had him lie down on the bench of the cylindrical machine. Mike steeled himself and did his best to act relaxed. He hated being stuck in enclosed spaces, but he wasn't about to wimp out in front of her.

She pushed a button on the machine and the bed slid into the cylinder. His heart raced as his head entered the mouth of the tunnel, and he made a conscious effort to breathe normally. He closed his eyes so he couldn't see the wall of metal a few inches from his face.

The machine hummed to life. He noticed cool jazz music playing faintly in the background. A light shone on his eyelids. He opened his eyes and found himself looking at a monitor showing a smiling Jo.

"How are you feeling?" Jo's voice asked through unseen speakers. "It looks like you might be a little stressed."

"I'm fine. So, what do we do now?"

"We're going to engage in a little relaxation exercise that should help clear your mind. Please lie still and focus on the green circle you'll see on the screen . . ."

Half an hour later, the bench slid out of the machine. Mike sat up, feeling refreshed but just a little groggy, like he had just woken from a light nap. He couldn't remember precisely what had happened while he was in the machine. He had a vague recollection of talking about his law practice, his bedtime ritual, and some vacations he had taken.

"I think we made good progress," Jo said. He turned to find her standing next to him, looking down at her iPad. "I was able to identify the thought patterns that have been causing your insomnia. When you go to bed tonight, I want you to picture hiking in Kauai, the part where they filmed *Jurassic Park*. If thoughts of work start creeping in, just keep going back to Kauai, okay?"

"Did we talk about that?" He shook his head to clear it. "Did you hypnotize me or something?"

She shrugged. "I don't like that term because it makes people think of a mind-control trick. What we did really was just a relaxation technique that cleared your thoughts. 'Guided meditation' is a good way to think of it. Your memory of the session may be vague due to the combined effects of the wine and meditation. You may also feel a little sleepy, but that should wear off quickly."

He stretched and got to his feet. "Yes, I think it already has. I feel great." He really did—fully alert, but still refreshed and relaxed.

She smiled and patted his arm. "I'm glad to hear it. Let me know how you sleep tonight."

That night he fell asleep as soon as his head hit the pillow, and he dreamed of hiking to the top of a Hawaiian volcano with Jo.

# CHAPTER 13

*November*

The phone on Jo's desk rang. She pushed the hands-free button. "Jo Anderson."

"Dr. Anderson, this is Jason Nguyen at the DA's Office. I'm calling about your evaluation of Jonathon—'Jack'—Adams. Do you have a few minutes?"

"Certainly. What can I do for you, Mr. Nguyen?"

"Thank you. I'm particularly interested in your comment at the end of your report of the evaluation. You said that we 'should investigate Mr. Adams's connection to any unsolved crimes against women.' What made you say that?"

Jo hesitated for a moment. Adams had signed a consent form that allowed Jo to share her "evaluation of the patient's mental health" with the DA and the Department of Corrections. Did that give her permission to disclose everything he said? She decided to fudge. "Well, I saw and heard some things during the evaluation that caused me to think that he might have a history of violence against women. Since there was nothing like that described in the memo I got from Corrections,

I thought he might be connected to some unsolved, or possibly unreported, crimes." She paused, considering just how close to the line she could skate. "Also, he invoked his Miranda rights at the end of the evaluation. That's the first time I've ever had that happen."

"Did he give you reason to believe he'd committed any specific crimes?"

"No."

"Okay. How about specific types of crimes—assault, rape, murder?"

"No, nothing specific. I could tell he was hiding something, but not what it was."

"I see. Did he give any indication that he, ah, might currently be a threat to women?"

"Men who commit crimes against women typically don't stop. If he hurt women in the past, he's very likely to hurt them in the future."

"Okay. Do you have anything more concrete than that?"

"Just that he seemed hostile during the evaluation."

"Hostile to you personally?"

"Yes."

"Do you, uh, live alone?"

Her stomach clenched in a knot. "I live in a secure building."

"Okay, that's good. I didn't mean to alarm you." He paused. "Um, one last question: Did he give you any indication that he might be traveling or moving to a new address?"

The knot in her stomach tightened. "No. Are you saying you don't know where he is?"

"I'm sorry, but I just can't comment on an ongoing investigation."

# CHAPTER 14

Val hated proofreading briefs. Unfortunately, she was good at it. So every time an important brief needed to be filed, Val would read through it, muttering under her breath at every typo or grammatical mistake.

She knew it was important work. Mike was fond of quoting a favorite saying of a judge he knew: "Sloppy brief, sloppy brain." Any lawyer who couldn't get the rules of English right couldn't be trusted to get the much more complicated rules of law right. And if the judge didn't trust a lawyer, that lawyer usually lost. So no sloppy briefs ever went out the door of the Law Offices of Michael Webster. Val took pride in that fact, but man, did she hate proofreading.

Making matters worse, Brad Simpson had authored today's brief. Brad had graduated from Harvard Law School near the top of his class, and Val had no doubt that he was brilliant (Mike certainly thought he was), but even Brad admitted that he wasn't "a detail guy." His briefs were like elephants: very impressive, but a real pain for the person who had to clean up after them.

So Val was not in a particularly good mood when she heard Mike's voice drift in through her door. His office was right next to hers, so she got to share in most of his conversations if both their doors were open, as they were now. She got up to close the door, but stopped when she heard what he was saying.

". . . happy to take your case if you're still looking for a lawyer."

He paused while whoever was on the other end of the line spoke.

"Great! Since this is a defense case, I'll be charging you hourly. My normal rate is eight hundred dollars, but I'd be willing to discount that to five hundred for this case. I'd also delegate as much as possible to my associates and other professionals, whose rates are significantly lower."

Val walked into his office and looked at him with eyebrows arched and hands on her hips. Mike noticed her and held up a finger.

"There will be a five-thousand-dollar retainer, which will need to be replenished as we work. Also, you'll be responsible for expert-witness fees and other costs, but we'll consult you before spending more than five hundred dollars."

Another pause.

"Terrific. Val will be in touch with you about the retainer and getting you set up in our computer system."

"What's going on?" Val mouthed to Mike.

He grinned and gestured toward one of his guest chairs. Val remained standing.

"Sounds good. Hey, thanks again for last night. I slept like a rock. You really should let me pay you."

Another pause.

"Well, at least let me take you out to dinner tonight." He turned to his computer and pulled up his calendar. "Have you ever heard of Kiss Seafood? It's a terrific little place in Japantown. The *omakase* is fantastic . . . Excellent, see you there at seven thirty."

He hung up the phone and looked at Val. "What?"

She glared at him openmouthed for a second. "What do you mean 'what'?"

"You're looking at me like I just shot your dog."

"Did you just take Jo Anderson's case?" she demanded.

He looked sheepish but unapologetic. "Let me explain, and please sit down. I feel like you're about to reach over and clock me in the head with one of those spike heels."

"They're not spikes," she snapped, but she sat down. She took a deep breath and reminded herself that he was the boss, even though he always treated her like an equal. "So would you mind telling me what happened? Why are we now taking her case? And I don't mean to pry, but why are you taking her out to dinner? I thought it wasn't okay for you to date clients."

"There's no rule that says I can't date clients, but that doesn't matter because this isn't a date. It's a client-development dinner. Remind me to give you the receipt so we can write it off as a business expense."

"You taking Jo Anderson to a restaurant called Kiss is a business expense?" Val arched her eyebrows skeptically. "I thought it was payment for, um, something she did for you last night."

Mike laughed. "That did sound a little bad, didn't it?"

She held up a hand. "That's fine. It's none of my business what you and your lady friends do. Unless you want me to include the bills in our tax returns."

"If you must know—and apparently you must—she gave me a demonstration of Mind's Eye last night. It was awesome. I was completely blown away. You know how I have trouble sleeping some nights?"

She nodded. "You mean like every night?"

"Not last night." He was excited, talking with his hands. "She asked me a few questions, put me in Mind's Eye for half an hour, and I was out like a light as soon as I went to bed. Eight solid hours of sleep. I can't remember the last time that happened."

"That's great, but why does that mean she's now a client? Did a massive hole suddenly open in your schedule?"

"Sort of. I'll be a lot more productive now that I'm getting enough sleep, so I think I've got time to take on another case. Besides, this shouldn't take much time. It can't be worth much, so I'm guessing Tim took it as a favor to Senator Bell. He'll do a little work, settle for a few thousand dollars, and declare victory."

Val wasn't so sure. She wanted to press the issue, but she'd worked with Mike long enough to know he'd never back out once he'd agreed to represent a client, even if he later decided it was a mistake. She shook her head. "Maybe, maybe not. And who knows how productive you'll be in a week. You had one good night. That's it. What happens when your insomnia comes back?"

"I don't think it will."

She shrugged. It had been a done deal as soon as he offered to represent Jo. No use in beating a dead horse. She was still annoyed, though. "Your funeral."

# CHAPTER 15

The man with the strange voice had been right. The SFPD had shown up at several SROs asking for Jack. They also had plainclothes cops and snitches asking for him at the Asian Art Museum and other drug markets.

Fortunately, Jack had taken the man's advice. He used part of the thousand dollars from the envelope to buy a pup tent, sleeping bag, and trail food. Then he found an out-of-the-way corner of Golden Gate Park where he could camp without being seen.

He practiced with his knife for at least an hour every day and did calisthenics in the evening and morning. He ran too. His limp was pure affection. People saw it and underestimated him physically, which he had used to his advantage more than once.

The man had also been right about Dr. Anderson. The address in the envelope was an expensive-looking apartment building in Pacific Heights. The kind of place that could honestly advertise "spectacular ocean views" for pretty much all of its units.

Sure enough, Dr. Anderson lived there. One morning, Jack had bought a cup of coffee at a coffee shop across the street from the building and nursed it through the morning rush hour. At eight o'clock sharp, Dr. Anderson walked out the front door and down a landscaped path to where a valet had a silver Audi waiting for her.

Jack had left a few minutes after she did. He didn't like the location. Too much money, too few street people. Jack felt out of place and knew he looked it. If he stuck around too long, even in a coffee shop, cops or private security would notice him. He was sure even the few homeless people he saw were undercover agents, and they were probably looking for him.

He had also checked out Dr. Anderson's office on two different days. The setting was much better. During the day, a wide variety of people walked around Lake Merritt or simply hung out, making it easy to wander around and plan. And by the time Dr. Anderson left her office at seven, the area was dark and shadowy, so there were plenty of places to hide.

The problem was that Dr. Anderson didn't walk out of her office building, she drove. Her building had an underground parking garage with a guard at the only exit, making it virtually impossible to get to her. He would need to get into the building, past security, and down into the parking garage to even have a chance. No way that would happen.

So he went back to his tent, exercised, practiced with his knife, and imagined what he would do to Dr. Anderson. He turned the problem over in his head, considering different angles. He half expected the big man in the hoodie to reappear and tell him what to do, but it never happened.

Then an idea appeared in his mind. It wasn't great, but it might work. He made another scouting trip and came back more confident. Sometimes the simple, old-fashioned ways were the best.

And then he made his move.

# CHAPTER 16

Jo loved Kiss. It was a tiny place that seemed to have been teleported from Tokyo, complete with the husband-and-wife team that ran it. He was the chef and she was everything else—greeter, waitress, manager, etc. There were only three small tables and the sushi bar, twelve seats total, each of which was taken. The entire restaurant, including the open kitchen, would have fit in Jo's living room. The food was simple, plainly presented, and excellent.

Mike and Jo sat at a table for two, leaning in so they could hear each other without broadcasting their conversation. "So, why are you a lawyer?" she asked.

He flashed that insouciant smile she had noticed the first day she saw him in the courtroom. "There wasn't much else I could do with majors in rhetoric and philosophy, which I discovered after waiting tables for a year. So I was off to law school and the rest is history."

"Yes, it is," she agreed. "Maybe that's why you *became* a lawyer, but it's not why you're one today."

"It beats waiting tables."

"I'm sure it does, but that's not your only other option, is it? I'm guessing you could quit if you wanted to."

He looked down and poked at a piece of *toro* with his chopsticks. "Maybe. I haven't really run the numbers."

"So why don't you? Why aren't you off traveling the world or writing the great American novel or something?"

He plucked the *toro* off his tray and popped it into his mouth. He chewed slowly, looking around the restaurant. After half a minute, he swallowed and looked back at her. "My dad was a pastor. The Reverend Charles Webster. His church was in a building south of Market. The congregation was mostly longshoremen and bar workers. And a lot of vagrants and prostitutes showed up for the early service because they knew there would be free coffee and donuts afterward. There was never much money. The rent was cheap, though, and we made ends meet by living in an apartment upstairs from the church. It was a bad neighborhood but a great way to grow up. The church was never big or rich, but it was *alive*. It made a difference in the lives of a lot of desperate people. And I got to be part of that, twenty-four-seven, until I went to college.

"Then the dot-com boom happened in the late nineties, and SoMa became the hot place to found a startup. Suddenly, the land under the church was valuable, and the owner decided to evict us and the church."

"Did the lease let them do that?"

"Nope, but the church couldn't afford a lawyer, so the landlord bulldozed right through them. Literally. When I came home from college for Christmas break, the church had been leveled and they were laying the foundation for an artsy office building."

"What happened to your father and his congregation?"

Mike sighed and played with his food. "They tried to find another place, but rents were skyrocketing all across the city. A lot of the church members were being forced out of their apartments for the same reason. So eventually the congregation sort of fell apart. My parents moved to Oakland and they lived off my mom's salary until Dad got a job with the post office. They were okay, but the church was gone and it shouldn't have been. And if they'd had a decent lawyer, it wouldn't have been. It would still be there today, giving donuts and good news to broken people."

A little thrill went through Jo. Last night on the Mind's Eye display she had seen a hint of what drove him, and now she knew for sure. "So you're that decent lawyer, in more ways than one."

He smiled modestly. "Well, that's the goal, anyway. I love seeing something wrong and being able to make it right."

"Like you did in the Lee case."

"Exactly," he said, his eyes an intense sapphire. "There's nothing quite like bringing justice to widows and orphans. They'll be able to keep their house now, and Susan Lee can stay home and be a mother to three kids who were robbed of their father. Cases like that are what get me up every morning—which is a lot easier now, thanks to you." He lifted his drink and nodded to her.

She smiled and nodded back. "How did you do it?"

"Do what?"

"Win the Lee case. The doctor and his lawyer thought they had it in the bag up until closing arguments. What were they missing?"

He shrugged. "They probably drank their own Kool-Aid. It happens to a lot of lawyers and their clients. They get so wedded to their theory that they can't see the other side's case, but the jury does." He flashed that beguiling grin again. "But we've been talking a lot about me. Let's move on to a more interesting subject. How did you wind up in psychology?"

He was being evasive, but she didn't press the issue. If anything, it was reassuring to know that her lawyer would do what it took to win, even if that meant making moves he didn't want to talk about. "Well, I didn't take philosophy or rhetoric. I was a geeky premed student."

"So why are you a psychologist and not a doctor?"

"The same reason you're a lawyer, more or less. I wanted to . . . to heal *situations*, not just people. I saw abused women and children, people slowly killing themselves through addiction, young men who couldn't break out of patterns of violence. I didn't want to just patch up their bodies and send them out again. I wanted to fix what was really wrong."

"Like you did with me."

She waved a hand. "I didn't really fix anything. All I did was spot the thought patterns that were making it hard for you to sleep and teach you a simple technique for avoiding them. I didn't address any deep-seated problems."

He looked her in the eyes. "Did you see any?"

She paused, calibrating her words carefully. "Well, since you're asking, I think I did. I wasn't trying to map the landscape of your mind, but I couldn't help noticing some of its more prominent features. In particular, I saw some signs of anxiety. You compensate for it very well, but I'm pretty sure it's there. I think it's the root cause of your insomnia, and I'm guessing that it's causing other problems. For example, your blood pressure is on the high side even though you're in good shape."

He ate in silence for a moment, absorbing what she had said. Then he nodded slowly. "Maybe you're right," he acknowledged. "Do you think you could fix that?"

"Not quickly." She fished crabmeat out of a claw, which took some skill with chopsticks. "Anxiety is a serious and complicated issue. It would probably take multiple sessions just to identify what's causing your anxiety. Then we would need at least a few months to treat it. I'm guessing it would require a multipronged approach: talk therapy, Mind's Eye, and possibly some medications, at least in the beginning."

"Fine with me," Mike said without hesitation. "When can we start?"

She hesitated and put down her chopsticks. "It's not quite that easy. It would be . . . awkward for me to formally take you on as a patient at the same time you're representing me in court."

He frowned. "You're right. I'm imagining how that would play if it came out while you were on the witness stand." He winced at the image. "Forget I asked."

"No, no," she said quickly. "I can't *formally* have you as a patient, but there's no reason we can't chat in my office—and you'll need to have good firsthand knowledge of Mind's Eye in order to represent me, won't you? If anyone asks whether you're my patient, I'll say no. Beyond that, our conversations will be protected by the attorney-client privilege, right?"

"They will, but . . ." He shook his head. "I can't ask you to do that. It's not fair to you. If I'm not your patient, neither I nor my insurance carrier can pay you, so—"

"Which is fine," she cut in.

"Not from where I sit. You're going to be paying me tens—probably hundreds—of thousands in legal bills, but I can't pay you a dime? That's not right."

She reached across the table and put her hand on his. "That's very nice of you, Mike, but I really don't mind. I want my lawyer to be at his best when he's representing me. If that means I give him some free therapy, I'm happy to do it." She gave him what she hoped was a winning smile. "And if it makes you feel any better, you can take me out to one of your favorite restaurants after every session to have a client debrief or whatever you lawyers call it."

To her relief, he relaxed and smiled back. "Deal, but only if I get to bring the wine for our next 'chat' in your office."

Jo was tired but effervescent when Mike dropped her off at the curb outside her apartment building. It had been a great evening. Everything had gone exactly as she'd hoped. No, it had gone better.

She floated along the path through the landscaped strip that provided a buffer between her apartment building and the street. It was amazing how a few strategically placed flowerbeds, trees, and bushes turned a few yards of greenery into a barrier between the noisy stress of the outside and the comfortable quiet of her front lobby. She wondered how much of the effect was noise reduction and visual screening and how much was purely psychological.

A movement caught the corner of her eye. She started to turn, but something grabbed her throat. She tried to scream, but all that came out was a strangled gargle. Heavy masculine breathing in her ear, then a yank at her neck and she fell over backward.

A blow to the side of her head dulled her senses. She felt herself being dragged off the path and into the darkness.

# CHAPTER 17

Mike felt good as he pulled away from the curb. He had thought about parking and escorting Jo to the door, but decided against it. Walking her up would have raised the stakes too much. If they kissed or Jo invited him upstairs, then the evening would have been clearly a date. If neither happened, that would signal that dinner had been platonic and professional. Better for both of them to leave things pleasantly ambiguous. And better for him if he didn't have to explain to Val tomorrow that maybe the dinner at Kiss had been a date after all. It had been the right decision—the perfect end to a perfect evening.

He looked in the rearview mirror, hoping to catch a last glimpse of Jo walking to the door. He didn't see her.

Odd. It had only been a few seconds, and she hadn't exactly been sprinting for the door. But maybe she had already gone inside. He looked again and noticed something lying on the path. A woman's shoe. He couldn't be sure, but he didn't think it had been there when he dropped her off. And it was the same pale yellow as the ones Jo had worn to dinner.

The only free parking spot on the block was next to a fireplug, so that's where he stopped. He got out and stood on the curb, feeling stupid. The shoe was probably just trash. But maybe it wasn't.

He headed back toward the apartment building. He instinctively kept out of the light, allowing his eyes to adjust to the darkness and making him less visible.

Fifty yards from the path, he saw a flicker of motion in the bushes. A man, crouched over something that Mike couldn't quite make out. The man was between two bushes, completely invisible from the street and the building but silhouetted against one of the path lights from Mike's perspective. The man moved, and Mike saw two things at the same time: a flash of steel and blonde hair splayed on the ground.

Mike broke into a run, making as little noise as possible. The hard lessons of his childhood and youth flooded back to him. *Surprise wins more fights than strength. Hit from behind whenever you can. Know where your opponent's hands are and what's in them. Never hesitate once you commit to a fight. Don't stop until your opponent runs or is completely beaten.*

The man was focused on his victim and didn't hear Mike until he was only a few steps away. But the man moved fast. He was almost to his feet and half-turned by the time Mike was in range.

Mike's eyes flashed over his opponent as he hurtled toward the man. The guy wore a black sweatshirt and pants, black gloves, and a black ski mask. He was small and slender. His left hand was empty, but his right hand was coming up and held a large knife.

Acting on instinct, Mike ignored the knife. He could probably land the first blow before the knife could reach him. Even if he didn't, his opponent would only be able to land an awkward slash with little cutting power behind it.

Mike aimed a punch at the man's right temple, putting his momentum behind the blow. It was a risky tactic because if he missed, his inertia would carry him past his opponent, leaving him off balance with his back turned. But Mike didn't want to fight a man with a knife and maybe the skill to use it. And if he landed a solid punch to the temple, he would almost certainly knock the man out.

He missed. His opponent moved faster than Mike expected, and Mike's fighting reflexes had slowed slightly from nonuse. Instead of hitting the man in the temple and rendering him unconscious, Mike's fist smashed into the guy's cheekbone and upper jaw.

The man's head snapped around and he fell to his knees. Landing the punch killed enough of Mike's momentum to keep him on his feet. He skidded to a stop and turned to deliver a kick to the head of his downed opponent, or at least stomp on his knife hand. But the man was already rolling to his feet, so Mike had to settle for a solid kick to the ribs. The man grunted in pain but managed to get to his feet despite the blow.

Mike stepped in, wary of the knife but determined to keep the initiative. His opponent was hurt, but still armed and potentially lethal. And he seemed to know how to fight, which was worrying. But the man chose to run instead.

For an instant, Mike thought about chasing his opponent. The man wasn't moving fast. He favored the side Mike had kicked and seemed a little disoriented—but Mike remembered both the knife and the fighter's reflexes. Besides, the man was unlikely to come back.

Mike turned and looked down at the woman on the ground. It was Jo. She wasn't moving. The elegant dress she'd worn to dinner was torn and muddied, but there was no blood.

Mike kneeled next to her and checked for pulse and breath. Both were strong. He sat back on his heels and looked around to make sure Jo's assailant was truly gone. Once he was sure they were safe, he called 911. Then he waited for sirens.

As the adrenaline ebbed from his blood, he became aware of a sharp pain in his right hand. He gingerly felt the bones in the back of his hand, then quickly stopped when the pain spiked. He'd probably cracked one of his metacarpals with that punch. That was one of the risks of punching someone in the head.

Jo coughed and opened bleary, unfocused eyes. She tried to get up, but Mike laid a hand on her shoulder. "Hold on. Let's wait until the EMTs can take a look at you. They're on their way."

Jo's eyes cleared, then went wide as her memory returned. Her eyes went from Mike to her shredded dress. She clutched it together convulsively. Mike looked away and wished he had a jacket to offer her.

"I'm sorry. I should have walked you to the door."

"Thank you," Jo croaked. "Thank you for coming back."

She started to cry. Mike held her until the ambulance and police came.

# CHAPTER 18

"I'm disappointed, Eric." David Klein pressed his lips together and shook his head slightly. "I really am."

"So am I, Mr. Klein." Eric stood in the middle of the office again, and this time David didn't offer him a seat.

David liked the fact that Eric didn't try to justify his failure or shift the blame to Adams, even though Adams was clearly blameworthy. But David wasn't going to let his subordinate off the hook. He picked up a pen and played with it absently, spinning it through his slender, pale fingers. Eric shifted his weight from foot to foot but didn't ask to sit.

"So what do we do next, Eric?" David asked after a minute of silence.

"It's going to be harder to get to her now," Eric replied. "I don't think we should go through Adams again. He didn't kill her when her guard was down; there's no way he will when it's up." He paused, looking for a hint from his boss as to whether he was heading in the right direction. David kept his face expressionless. "So I thought we might, ah, hire a professional this time."

David sighed and shook his head. "Too risky. Adams was fairly safe. If we'd played on his paranoia properly—and you did do a nice job there, at least—he would take an anonymous envelope of cash and do whatever the strange faceless man told him to. No risk that he could be traced back to us. A hit man will be different. He'll ask questions. He'll want to know who he's working for. Otherwise, he risks getting set up. If he's caught, he knows who to sell to the police. And we can't have that, can we, Eric?"

"No, Mr. Klein."

"So think of something better."

"Um, how about stealing the machine?" Eric suggested tentatively. "We could send in a team disguised as movers over the weekend and have them cart the whole Mind's Eye apparatus out of the building. Then we smuggle it out of the country and sell it."

David gave him a withering look. He began to question his judgment in taking Eric on. "That's what you call a better idea. Seriously? Do you really think that's more likely to work than killing her and buying her stock out of her estate?"

"But couldn't Oceanview outbid us at the estate sale?" Eric asked hesitantly.

"Not going to happen," David said definitively. "We may have to buy them out to shut them up, but that's small change in this deal. So come up with a better idea or start polishing your résumé."

Eric's shoulders slumped slightly. "Yes, Mr. Klein." Then he snapped back erect. "I have an idea."

"Well?"

Eric described his idea, interrupted by occasional sharp questions from David. As the analyst fleshed out his plan, David became increasingly convinced that it could work and the risk level was acceptable—or at least justified by the astronomical potential returns.

When Eric finished, David sat silently for a minute, staring into the middle distance. Then his gaze returned to Eric, who was sweating slightly even though the room was cool.

"I like it, Eric. But you're wrong about one thing."

"What's that, Mr. Klein?"

"Adams. He still has a role to play after all."

# CHAPTER 19

Characteristically, Val was at her desk by eight thirty. Uncharacteristically, Mike wasn't. Val made a mental note to give him a little grief about that.

Val turned on her computer and went through the morning mail while it booted up. Then she turned back to the monitor and went through the e-mail that had accumulated overnight.

Still no Mike. She glanced at the clock in the corner of her screen: 9:02. Last night must have been more interesting than he'd claimed it would be.

She went to work on billings. Mike liked to say that the most important writing that lawyers did went into their bills. "Bills should sing," he instructed his lawyers. "They should read like poetry. Clients should read our bills and *want* to pay them. They should think, 'Wow, I can't believe my lawyers did so much great work in so little time. What a bargain!'" Brad Simpson's bills did sing—but all the songs seemed to come from the old Talking Heads album *Stop Making Sense*. For example, one entry read, "Research & draft partial PBJ (6.0)." What was that? Did he spend six hours researching and drafting a partial peanut-butter-and-jelly sandwich?

She heard Mike's door close at 9:23. Grateful for the interruption, she put down Brad's bill, walked over to Mike's office, and knocked on his door.

"Come in," he said, his voice rough and tired.

She opened the door, walked in, and sat in her usual chair. He looked terrible—bleary eyes with bags you could take grocery shopping. And it looked like he had shaved in the dark.

"Wow, what happened to you? Did that 'client-development dinner' with Jo Anderson end with a client-development walk along the beach at sunrise?" She glanced down and noticed a splint on his right hand. "Or did it end with you two getting in a fight?"

He was normally a good sport, but today he didn't even crack a smile. "Actually, the night ended with both of us in the hospital."

Val sucked in a breath and wished she could take back every word she had just said. "I'm so sorry. What happened?"

"Some guy attacked Jo after I dropped her off. I came back and stopped him." He kept his voice even, but Val could hear the anger in it. "I just wish I'd been faster."

"Is she okay?" Val asked. "Are you?"

"I'll be fine. I'll have to learn to do everything with my left hand for a few weeks, but that's okay. As for Jo . . ." He shrugged. "She's still in the hospital, but I think physically she'll recover soon. It may take a while for the invisible wounds to heal, though."

Val nodded soberly. She tried to choose her next words as delicately as possible. "Did the police get a DNA sample?"

"Yes, but not the way you're thinking. The guy didn't get a chance to rape Jo, but he did leave behind a nice DNA sample. Two teeth, to be specific."

"You rock. Did you know that? You absolutely rock."

He shrugged and sighed. "I don't know. I wish I'd rocked about three or four minutes earlier last night. Or better yet, walked her to the door." He took a deep breath and looked up. "But anyway, we have a case to work up. We need to get Seth Bell's medical records from Jo's office and figure out who else might have records we want to see—the prison system, other doctors or therapists, any hospitals that treated him. We should also start thinking about expert witnesses."

She nodded. "I'm on it. And you could use coffee. Philz Turkish?"

He yawned hugely. "Yeah, that would be great. Thanks."

Val went out to get the coffee herself rather than dispatching the firm secretary, Tina. She needed time to think without her phone ringing and e-mail chiming.

She played the conversation with Mike over in her mind several times as she walked to Philz, feeling more like an idiot each time. Why hadn't she noticed his hand before she opened her big mouth? It was right there on his desk, and the splint was huge. So how could she possibly not see it? And when she *did* see it, why did she have to keep joking?

Simple. She'd been sure she knew what happened last night—at least in general terms—and she was just itching to zing him about it. So she walked in and zinged him before she bothered engaging her brain.

She winced and replayed the conversation again as penance. *When you assume . . .*

Well, she was done assuming—at least about Mike and Jo. Mike was a hero. More than that, he was a good boss, a good friend, and an all-around good guy. Yes, he was also a ladies' man, but he wasn't a player. As far as Val could tell, he always treated women well, even if he rarely had exclusive girlfriends and couldn't stay in a long-term relationship to save his life. Besides, he certainly treated *her* well, so why should she care about his dating life?

As for Jo, she was a victim and deserved sympathy and kindness—even if she rubbed Val the wrong way. Jo had been horribly victimized last night, of course, but she'd probably been a victim before she ever walked into their office. Seth Bell's parents had victimized her with what was very likely a bogus lawsuit, and for some reason Masters & Cromwell was playing along. She'd come to the Law Offices of Michael Webster looking for protection, and that was exactly what she deserved—and not just from Mike.

Val picked up Mike's coffee and strode back to the office. She was actually looking forward to working on Jo's case by the time she got back. But then, she'd look forward to almost anything that gave her an excuse to take a break from deciphering Brad Simpson's bills.

# CHAPTER 20

Jo sat in her hospital bed, drinking chamomile tea and checking e-mail on her phone. She remembered nothing concrete about last night after leaving Kiss with Mike—just bits and pieces. Not being able to breathe. Mike's face wearing a concerned look. Police and doctors asking her questions. Then she'd fully awakened in the hospital this morning.

Her neck hurt, she had a tender lump near her left temple, and her brain felt a little fuzzy. Otherwise she was physically fine, except for a few minor abrasions and bruises. But was she emotionally fine?

Based on several studies Jo had read, she should feel depression, fear, and possibly guilt. But she felt none of those things. All she felt was deep anger and hatred for her attacker. He and men like him were animals, vermin that walked on two legs, hardly human. She had seen inside enough minds like that to know what lay there: uncontrollable rage, cold amorality, complete lack of empathy, twisted fantasies. They were broken beyond fixing, even with Mind's Eye. They should be killed or locked away forever where they couldn't hurt anyone.

She took a deep breath. It was a good thing that she wasn't currently treating any prisoners or ex-cons with predatory tendencies.

The phone by her bed rang. She picked it up. "Hello?"

"Hi. There's a Mike Webster here to see you. Shall I bring him in?"

Just the thing to break her out of this dark mood. "Yes, please."

After she hung up, she belatedly thought to look in a mirror. She braced herself and walked into the bathroom. The results weren't as bad as she feared—no makeup, and her hair was flat and a little disheveled. But other than that, she looked as presentable as she could after a night in a hospital bed.

There was a light knock at the door. Jo tucked her hair behind her ears and sat back down on the bed.

"Come in."

The door opened and Mike walked in, awkwardly carrying an enormous floral arrangement that was mostly made up of orange roses and white lilies.

"How lovely!" Jo said as she took the vase from him with both hands. The fresh, sweet scent filled the room, wiping out the stale hospital smell. "Thank you."

As she put the flowers on the bedside table, she noticed a large splint on his right hand. "Your hand—did you break it last night?"

He nodded. "The ER doctor called it a boxer's fracture."

She looked at his hand. The part that wasn't covered by the splint had small scabs on the knuckles. "I'm so sorry. Does it hurt?"

He shrugged and held up the damaged hand. "It aches a little, and I'll need to wear this thing for a week or two, but it's nothing compared to what happened to you."

"Oh, I'll be fine." She paused for a heartbeat. "Thanks to you."

"I'm just glad I was there."

"So am I."

They looked at each other in silence for a moment, and Jo wondered where the conversation might go next.

Someone knocked at her door.

"Come in," Jo called.

The door opened and a pleasant-looking woman in her midfifties walked in. Jo recognized her: Kate Hampton, a psychologist on staff at the hospital. Jo didn't know her personally but had heard her speak at a couple of professional-education events. Dr. Hampton specialized in treating women who had been raped or abused.

"Oh, I'm sorry," Dr. Hampton said when she saw Mike. "I can come back later."

"That's okay," Mike said, starting toward the door. "I was just stopping by." He turned to Jo and smiled. "See you soon." And then he was gone.

Once Mike had left, Dr. Hampton took a seat across from Jo. "It's a pleasure to meet you, though I wish the circumstances were different. How are you doing?"

Jo took a sip of her tea, which was now lukewarm. "I'm not sure, to be honest."

"What do you mean?"

"I'm angry at my attacker and want to see him caught, but other than that I don't feel anything—no panic, shame, or depression. Those emotions may come in the future, of course. The next time I need to be alone in the dark, for example, I'll need to—" Jo broke off and gave a little laugh.

"What is it?"

"I just realized that I was applying assault-survivor protocols to myself. I suppose that's a coping mechanism. I'm shifting into professional-psychologist mode in order to distance myself from the trauma I experienced."

Dr. Hampton smiled warmly. "An astute observation, Dr. Anderson. Right now it's easier to be a psychologist than a woman, isn't it?"

Jo looked down at her mug and noticed that she was gripping it so hard that her knuckles were white. She relaxed her hands with effort and put the mug on the bedside table. "Yes, it is," she said softly.

# CHAPTER 21

Jack Adams tongued the empty hole in his mouth where two molars used to be. The entire right side of his face throbbed with pain, and it hurt to move his jaw at all. The jaw felt like it was broken—and maybe a couple of ribs too—but he didn't dare go to the hospital. Instead, he self-medicated with pot and tequila and stayed curled up in his tent as much as he could.

He knew he was in danger. He saw signs everywhere: three men walking dogs in Golden Gate Park forming a perfect triangle, three Coke cans lying next to the same garbage can, three planes in the sky at the same time. It all meant something, but his brain was too muddled to puzzle out what. He heard voices on the wind. He couldn't quite catch what they were telling him, but it sounded ominous. He was being warned, though he couldn't tell where the danger was coming from.

They were after him, of course, particularly after his failed attack on Dr. Anderson. But who would they send? Where would they attack him? Was it safer to hide or to run?

He wished the big man with the hoodie and the metallic voice would come back. He had money and answers. He had shared both with Jack before. Maybe he would do it again.

Jack felt marginally safer in his tent, so he stayed there as much as possible. He needed to go out sometimes, though, even if just for more food, booze, and pot. He also hoped he might find the man in the hoodie.

As it turned out, the man in the hoodie was looking for him too. After two days in the tent, Jack went to one of his fellow drug dealers to replenish his pot stash. When their business was done, the man said that "a friend" had been looking for him. Jack was immediately suspicious and asked for a description of this alleged "friend." It was the man in the hoodie, who had come by the drug market earlier in the day. The man said he would be back the next evening at eight.

Jack stayed in his tent all the next day, except for a few furtive bathroom breaks. Then he went down to the Asian Art Museum, the back of his neck tingling the whole way. Now was the time of maximum danger. If they were setting him up, this was when they would strike. So he arrived two hours early and hid in the bushes until eight, watching for anyone who might be setting an ambush. Worryingly, three pigeons all pecked at the same half-eaten bagel on the sidewalk. Otherwise, the coast looked clear.

At eight o'clock, the big man walked up, scattering the troika of pigeons as he came. He wore the same hoodie he'd had on last time, and once again it hid his face.

Jack stood up from his hiding place, grunting as his ribs shot a jolt of agony through his chest. The man saw him and waited while Jack gingerly stepped through the bushes and approached him.

"Walk with me," the man said in that low artificial voice. He started off in a ground-eating stride without waiting for a response from Jack.

Jack hurried after him, struggling to keep up. His ribs sent a shock of pain with every step, but he forced himself to match his companion's pace.

The man turned a corner, then another, walking along the outer wall of the museum. Then he sidestepped into a tiny alcove in the museum's wall. He motioned to Jack, who stepped in beside him.

"The cameras can't see us here," the man said, "but we only have a few minutes."

Jack nodded. "What should I do?"

"You failed the first mission we gave you." The anger in the man's voice came through, despite the voice-altering apparatus.

"It won't happen again."

"You must follow instructions exactly and immediately if you want to regain our trust."

"I will," Jack insisted, bobbing his head vigorously.

"Very good." The man reached into his pocket. "Before you can do anything else, you need to heal. Our first instruction is that you take these pills."

He handed Jack three whitish pills and a bottle of water.

Three. Jack hesitated, warning bells clamoring in his head. "What are these?"

"Medicine," the man said. His head snapped to the side and he stared into the deepening darkness. Jack followed his gaze but saw nothing.

The man looked back at him. "There is no time." His voice was an urgent metallic hiss. "Take them, now!"

Jack looked down at the pills in indecision. What if the man was tricking him somehow? What if the pills were poison?

"Forget it, we'll find someone else. Give me those back!" The man snatched for the pills.

Jack reflexively pulled them back and popped them in his mouth. They tasted like no medicine he had ever taken before, but he swallowed them anyway.

# Chapter 22

Jo sat in her office, trying to concentrate. She had been discharged from the hospital yesterday, but canceled all her appointments for today as well because she knew she would not be at her best. It had been the right decision, but it left her too much time to brood. Her mind spun dark visions of what might have happened if Mike hadn't come back. And what might still happen if the police didn't catch her attacker. *Who was it? Jack Adams? Another patient?*

She sat at her desk, alternately fretting and getting irritated at herself for fretting. Her e-mail chimed. It was a message from Val D'Abruzzo, titled "Bell v. Anderson." So, what did Napoleonette want? Jo opened the e-mail and read it. Val wanted Seth Bell's medical records and any insurance policies that might cover the case.

Jo sighed and got to work. At least it kept her mind off the attack. The insurance-policy part of Val's request was easy: Jo had no insurance for Mind's Eye. Or at least not in the sense Val meant. Jo's malpractice carrier had been skittish about Mind's Eye and insisted on exorbitant malpractice premiums for minimal coverage. So Jo's financial backer, Oceanview, had given Jo financial guarantees that allowed her to self-insure.

The medical records took a little more effort. Seth Bell's file contained background materials from the Department of Corrections and Rehabilitation, copies of prescriptions for a light sedative and antipsychotic drugs, typed notes from Seth's earlier sessions, and several pages of illegible scribbling from later sessions.

First, she pulled and copied the physical file. Then she pulled up the typed notes on her computer. Oddly, the file showed that it had been accessed last week, and Jo didn't recall having looked at it since Seth's death.

Her phone rang. The caller ID showed the San Francisco District Attorney's Office. She picked it up. "Hello, Johanna Anderson."

"Dr. Anderson, this is Jason Nguyen. We spoke last week about Jonathon Adams."

Jo's heart skipped a beat. "Yes, I remember."

"I've got some news about him."

"Did he attack someone?"

"He did." Nguyen hesitated. "In fact, he attacked you. We just received the results of the DNA tests on the teeth from the crime scene. It was him."

"Have you arrested him?" Jo asked urgently.

"That, uh, won't be necessary. He died, probably sometime last night. The police found his body outside the Asian Art Museum this morning."

# CHAPTER 23

*December*

Mike looked across the conference-room table at Dr. Adrian Goff, who was at the Law Offices of Michael Webster to interview for a job as an expert witness in *Estate of Bell v. Anderson*. Val sat beside him, taking notes and observing.

Dr. Goff taught at Stanford, where he specialized in neuropsychology. He had written dozens of papers and articles on the subject, including several on the use of technology in talk therapy. He hadn't discussed Mind's Eye specifically, but he had analyzed several of its elements in depth and had written in general terms about "exciting new techniques by pioneering clinicians."

Dr. Goff also matched the popular image of a trustworthy professor. He was in his midsixties, had slightly unruly gray hair, and wore reading glasses, which hung on a brass chain around his neck. He even spoke with a slight Austrian accent. There was a vague air of tweed about him, even though he wore a pin-striped navy-blue suit.

"Did you have a chance to review the complaint?" Mike asked.

Dr. Goff gave a sharp, Teutonic nod. "Yes. I have also reviewed the media accounts of Dr. Anderson's technique, which is quite groundbreaking."

"It's pretty impressive, isn't it?" Mike agreed.

"It truly is. To combine all of these devices together into a single integrated system is a remarkable achievement."

"Why is that? Explain it to me like you'd explain it to a jury."

"Because they all do different things, and most of them are quite complex. To put it in layman's terms, it's like an iPhone. It may sound simple in concept to put a computer, a telephone, and a music player together into one device, but actually doing it was a tremendous technological breakthrough."

"But Dr. Anderson didn't create a single device," Mike said, testing him. "She simply connected existing devices."

"No, she didn't simply connect them; she turned them into an integrated system. That is not easy. I know. We have had difficulties integrating even two devices in a lab. She has integrated half a dozen and made them usable in a clinical setting. Perhaps a different analogy would help. The Apollo missions took existing technology—pressure suits, rockets, early computers—and combined them into a system that could do far more than its parts on their own. A system that could put a man on the moon."

Writing awkwardly with his left hand, Mike jotted "iPhone + Apollo" in his notes. They were good analogies, the sort of things that would stick with jurors and help them understand a complex case. And Goff had come up with them on the fly. That spoke well of his skill as an expert witness.

"So it would be fair to compare Mind's Eye to a moon shot?" Mike asked.

"It would seem so," Goff said, "though these media accounts are mostly public relations. No one has undertaken a close, unbiased examination of Mind's Eye."

It was a fair point. Now that Mike thought about it, the articles he had seen were mostly flattering stories with a PR feel to them. They'd probably started life as press releases from Jo's company or her backers.

Mike rubbed his temples to ward off an incipient headache. "Based on what you've written, am I correct that it's appropriate to use fMRI technology?"

"Yes."

"And EEG?"

"Yes, we have performed several experiments using those together in a research setting."

"We've read your paper," Mike replied. "Very intriguing. Also appropriate to use FACS or microexpression analysis?"

"Those are not the same thing, though they are related. And yes, both are appropriate."

Mike jotted down a note to read up on that point. "Thanks for the clarification. Would the same be true of traditional polygraph technology? Would that also be appropriate?"

"It could be, particularly if you were treating a patient who may be inclined to dishonesty—which I understand Dr. Anderson's patients often are."

"How about a light sedative and guided meditation or hypnosis?"

Dr. Goff shrugged. "I personally don't use hypnosis, but the APA—that's the American Psychological Association—says it can be an appropriate tool, and I have no reason to disagree with them. It's not uncommon to sedate fMRI patients, as being inside the machine can cause stress and even trigger panic attacks."

"Thank you. Since all of those tools are appropriate for use in therapy, it would also be appropriate to use them all together, correct?"

"I . . ." Dr. Goff paused and stared into the middle distance for a full minute, arms crossed on his chest. "It would depend on the case."

"So it could be appropriate if a patient was dishonest and delusional, for example?"

"It could." Dr. Goff nodded slowly. "Yes, it could," he said more decisively. "I would need to know more about the patient and see the treatment records to say anything definitive. I would also need to study the system in use in order to understand its effects. Ideally, I would like to see recordings of each therapy session."

"Of course," Mike said. "We're already gathering those." He turned to Val. "Do we have an ETA from Jo?"

"She e-mailed this morning and said she's hoping to get them to us by the end of the week." She hesitated, a troubled look in her expressive eyes. "Is it okay if I ask a question?"

"Sure," Mike said. Val had excellent instincts, and Mike had learned to give her free rein if she asked for it.

"I also have no objection, Ms. D'Abruzzo," Dr. Goff said.

"Thanks." She favored the professor with a dazzling smile, which he returned.

Mike repressed a chuckle. Val could certainly turn on the charm—one of the reasons she was such an effective investigator.

"Dr. Goff, you seemed to kind of hesitate when Mike asked you about using all of those things together. Why was that?" Val asked.

"A perceptive question. I hesitated because . . . well, each of those tools is powerful by itself. And based on what Dr. Anderson says in interviews, together they are significantly more powerful than the sum of their parts. It would seem that the Mind's Eye system gives Dr. Anderson more control over her patients than any therapist in history."

"You don't trust her?" Val asked.

He shook his head. "That's not it. I have no reason to mistrust her personally. It sounds like she is doing very interesting work and is helping people who probably could not be helped by traditional therapeutic methods. Mind's Eye is very likely a tremendous advance in the world of psychology—but it is an advance that is taking place entirely outside the controls and safeguards of the research lab. It is as if"—he gestured vaguely as he searched for words—"as if Dr. Anderson were Steve Jobs or one of those other Silicon Valley inventors, building a revolutionary computer in her garage. But instead of fiddling around with circuits and processors, she's fiddling around with the human mind."

# CHAPTER 24

After Val showed Dr. Goff to the door, she went in search of Mike. He wasn't in the conference room or his office. She ultimately found him going through drawers in the office kitchen.

"Looking for something?"

"Do we have any aspirin?" he asked without looking up.

"I've got Advil in my office. You can have some of that."

"Thanks, I've got a nasty headache. It came on in the middle of that meeting."

He followed her into her office and gulped down twice the recommended dosage. "Thanks," he said again. He dropped into one of her guest chairs and she sat down behind her desk. "So what did you think of Goff?"

"Straight shooter, smart, articulate, knows his stuff. Jurors will trust him—though that might not be a good thing, if Tim Cromwell gets him talking about how Jo is messing with people's brains in her garage."

Mike sighed, put his head in his hands, and rubbed his temples. "Yeah, I know. He went off the rails there at the end. I'm inclined to hire him, but we'll need to work with him on that. It seems like he's jealous of Jo or something."

That wasn't how it had seemed to Val. "Jealous?"

"Yeah, he's been working in the same basic field as her since she was in preschool—but she's the one who invented Mind's Eye, not him. Wouldn't a guy like that want to be the one who's the Steve Jobs of psychology?"

"Uh, yeah, I guess. But we do have some bad facts," Val pointed out. "This is a new technology, like he said, and that other guy committed suicide too."

Mike stopped rubbing his temples. "What other guy?"

"The one who broke your hand with his face. Adams, right?"

"He committed suicide? I thought the police figured he died of a drug overdose."

"That was just the detective's guess, since Adams was a junkie and he died near a drug market. Now they have toxicology results. Didn't you check your e-mail this morning?"

"Yes. I had about fifty new messages, and half of them were from you. I confess that I didn't read all of them in the half hour between when I got in and when we met with Dr. Goff."

"Well, one of those unread e-mails has a medical examiner's report attached to it. Adams had enough cyanide in his body to kill an elephant."

Mike sat back. "Huh."

"So now we have two suicides by Mind's Eye patients, out of about ten patients, right? And Jo has only been using Mind's Eye for around two years. I'll bet you ten—no, twenty—bucks Tim will have a PowerPoint slide that shows Mind's Eye has a ten percent annual fatality rate."

Mike started rubbing his temples again. "I don't know. Seems pretty clear to me that two is just a coincidence."

Val arched her eyebrows in surprise. "Are you serious?" She took a twenty out of her purse and slapped it down on the desk in front of her. "This'll be the easiest money I ever made."

# CHAPTER 25

David Klein clipped on his Bluetooth headset and dialed. He liked to be able to pace when he negotiated by phone. He loved the game—and he had just played his first card by calling the closely guarded personal cell-phone number of Senator Warren Bell.

"Hello?"

"Hello, Senator Bell. This is David Klein with Horizon Finance. We met at a fundraiser last year at Larry Ellison's home." That was the second card. It was also a lie. David had been at the fundraiser, but he hadn't talked to anyone except his partners and Ellison, whom he was advising on a hostile takeover.

"Yes, of course." Senator Bell's voice was warm and intimate. "What can I do for you, David?"

David strolled around his steel-and-glass coffee table, playing with a hand-grenade paperweight. "You and your wife can sell me the rights to the lawsuit against Dr. Anderson and her company."

"Excuse me?"

"You and your wife are the executors and beneficiaries of the estate of your son, Seth Bell," David explained in a slow, patient voice, as if he were speaking to a child. "That estate filed a lawsuit against a Dr.

Johanna Anderson and a company named Mind's Eye, Inc. I would like to buy the rights to any judgment that results from that lawsuit."

The line was silent for several seconds. "I'm sorry, but I don't think we can do that."

"Yes, you can," David said evenly. "I can arrange for an opinion letter from a top law firm if you like."

"I meant that I don't think it would be appropriate." Bell's voice was noticeably cooler now, and more cautious. "I'm sorry."

David had expected that response and played his next card. "It would be at least as appropriate as your vote on SB 216 last year." David had it on fairly good authority that Bell's vote on that bill had been purchased.

"I don't know what you're talking about." Senator Bell's voice was edgy and uncertain. *Good.* David was getting him off balance, and off-balance men were easy to push around.

"Of course you do, Senator. But that's not the point. The point is that there's nothing stopping you from selling that lawsuit, and I'm willing to buy it for a very generous price."

"I . . . Thank you for your offer, Mr. Klein, but I have to go. I'm late for a meeting."

"Really?" David strode over to his desk and looked at his leftmost computer monitor, which showed a map of Sacramento with Senator Bell's cell phone as a pulsing red dot. The senator was headed right where David's intelligence had said he would go. Time to play another card. "Who are you meeting down on Stockton Boulevard at this time of night? I'm sure that's totally appropriate too, right?"

Several seconds of silence. "I might have a few minutes for you. How much are you willing to offer for the lawsuit?"

David grinned and spent five minutes pushing hard. When he was done, Senator Bell had agreed to sell his right to any judgment in *Estate of Bell v. Anderson* for fifty thousand dollars. He had also promised to get his wife to sell her rights for another fifty thousand. David's lawyers had warned him that the deal ultimately might not be enforceable in court, if the Bells decided not to assign their judgment to him at the end of the case, but David had little doubt that he'd be able to enforce it outside of court if he had to.

Phase one of Eric's plan was a success. Now for phase two.

# CHAPTER 26

Mike emerged from the fMRI machine feeling as relaxed and refreshed as he had last time. It was a welcome change from the way he had felt when he walked in Jo's door. He had carried a load of stresses and nagging worries, like an armful of jagged rocks that he could neither hold comfortably nor put down. But after half an hour of talking to Jo on the sofa and another half hour of Mind's Eye, those rocks had been reduced to a handful of smooth pebbles that he could slip into his pocket and forget about for the evening.

Jo still wouldn't accept payment, insisting that Mike was a friend, not a patient. But she hadn't resisted when he offered to take her out to dinner again.

Tonight they were at another of Mike's favorite spots, a Greek restaurant called Kokkari. They spent a few minutes making small talk, discussing the menu, and ordering. Their drinks and appetizers arrived a couple of minutes thereafter. Then their server left and they were alone.

Mike watched Jo in silence for a moment as she sipped from a glass of sauvignon blanc and sampled the stuffed olives. She was a striking beauty—tall, graceful, sophisticated. It was a pleasure just to look at her and appreciate her effortless elegance, particularly now that he knew how much more there was to her than met the eye.

She put down her glass and smiled. "You certainly seem a lot less tense than you did a couple of hours ago."

"Absolutely. I feel much better. Are we making progress in finding the root cause of my anxiety?"

"I've been considering that. When you're stressed, what are you usually thinking about?"

"Work," he said without hesitation.

She nodded. "That's what I'm seeing on Mind's Eye too. But you don't want to quit your job, right?"

He shook his head. "We talked about that last time. I love my job. Every day, I get to go out there and bring justice to an unjust world. And I get paid lots of money to do it. How great is that?" He grinned and winked. "Or am I repressing or suppressing, and I really hate being a lawyer?"

She laughed musically. "If you're doing either of those, you're doing a remarkable job. Good enough to fool Mind's Eye, and you'd be the first person to accomplish that. No, I'm pretty sure you genuinely love being a lawyer. But it also causes you so much stress that you can't sleep without help. Normally, people relieve stress by doing things they enjoy and are good at, but not you. Why is that?"

He thought for a moment, then shrugged. "I don't know. Why don't you take a look inside my head and tell me?"

"I wish I could. I can't tell much more than what you're feeling and whether you're telling the truth. But we'll do some more digging next time. In the meantime, I want you to think about it. Ask yourself: Why does the thing that gives my life meaning also fill me with nerve-tearing stress? Answer that and we'll know what's eating away at you."

# CHAPTER 27

Jo started some chamomile tea, turned on Miles Davis's *Kind of Blue*, and got ready for bed. By the time she was in her pajamas—it was a chilly night, so she went with flannel—the tea was ready. She got her mug and wandered around her apartment, not quite ready to go to bed, but too tired to be productive.

Her thoughts turned back to the evening that had just ended. She had enjoyed her dinner with Mike. The restaurant had been excellent and so had the company. Mike was a natural conversationalist with a good sense of humor. He also tended to see the world basically the same way she did, so they shared a lot of the same tastes and opinions. For example, they both liked the outdoors, agreed on the best drive-through food (In-N-Out), and had the same general taste in music (he mentioned Miles Davis, which made Jo think to put on *Kind of Blue*). And she had to admit that he wasn't hard on the eyes.

Mike had walked her to the door tonight. Jack Adams was dead, of course, but she still felt nervous walking past the spot where he had hidden. So it was nice to have Mike beside her, even if it did raise the question of what would happen when they reached the door. She knew that she should say good night to him then and there and go straight in, but she wasn't entirely sure he would make it easy.

But he did. When they reached the door, he gave her arm a warm squeeze and thanked her for the evening. Then he turned and went back to his car, and Jo went inside. To her surprise, she had been disappointed. If he had kissed her, it would have caused all sorts of problems for both of them. But an irrational part of her still wished he had done it.

She laughed at the memory. *You're not fourteen anymore,* she told herself.

No, she was thirty-four, and smart thirty-four-year-old women didn't act on hormone-driven impulses. They thought things through and made smart decisions. They looked at the facts and acted rationally.

*Speaking of looking at the facts . . .*

She walked over to her home office and pulled up the video and data feeds from her latest Mind's Eye session with Mike. She fast-forwarded through, looking for the segment she wanted to watch again. There it was.

Mike's handsome face looked out at her, his expression slightly slack and glazed—the typical look of a Mind's Eye patient. "What makes you happy?" her voice asked.

"Lots of stuff. Being with friends, a good run in the hills, a walk along the beach with a pretty woman." He smiled sleepily, and the data feed showed that he was happy and relaxed, probably revisiting memories of the things he'd just listed.

She took a sip of her tea and listened to herself say, "Okay, what makes you happiest, Mike?"

He thought for a moment, brows furrowed as he struggled to concentrate. "Fixing things. Seeing a situation that's wrong and making it right. The people who come to me, they're desperate. They've lost someone important, they're dying of cancer, or something like that. They're victims of the medical industry." He paused, belatedly realizing that she was part of that industry. Embarrassment and concern swelled on his data feed. "No offense."

She smiled now, and she could hear the smile in her recorded voice. "None taken. Please go on."

"I can't undo the damage some incompetent doctor or drug company did, of course, but sometimes I can fix people's lives. Or at least help, anyway. A lot of my clients need money, and I can usually get them that. But more than that, they need justice. They need to see the people who ruined their lives held accountable. By the time clients walk in my door, they've been through hell. They went through a terrible medical disaster, and while they were still reeling from it, they got the runaround from bureaucrats and lawyers. They've been brushed off, stonewalled, and lied to. Lots of times, they've been told that what happened was their fault. And of course no one *ever* apologized to them, no matter how bad the screwup was. They feel absolutely helpless, like those doctors and executives are untouchable—like they can carelessly kill people and no one will ever make them pay.

"Then, after all that, my clients get to go to a courtroom and watch a judge and jury tell the doctors and executives to their faces that they're guilty. What happened is their fault, and it's going to cost them millions of dollars." He paused, eyes bright. "There's nothing like that moment. I'm on a mountaintop."

She'd heard basically the same thing from him at their first dinner. She hadn't picked up any hints that he was lying, though she couldn't help thinking that it sounded a little too good to be true. But it was true. She could see it right there on Mind's Eye. He believed every word he was saying. In fact, he was getting an endorphin rush just thinking about those "mountaintop" moments. She had never seen anything like it. Granted, most of the men she treated were criminals, but she had put a number of test subjects under Mind's Eye before she started using it in therapy.

She clicked the "Pause" icon and stared at the screen, deep in thought. So, what would a smart thirty-four-year-old woman do in a situation like this?

# Chapter 28

"Estate of Bell v. Dr. Johanna Anderson and Mind's Eye, Inc.," the clerk announced.

Tim Cromwell and Mike walked up to the lectern and stood on either side of it. Tim Cromwell was four inches taller than Mike's five foot eleven, and, despite being over sixty, Tim could still use his height well on the basketball court—a fact Mike knew from firsthand experience during his years at Tim's firm.

"Timothy Cromwell for the plaintiff."

"Michael Webster for defendants."

"We're here for our first case-management conference," said Judge Archimedes Stavros. Archie Stavros had been on the bench for nearly thirty years, and both Mike and Tim knew him well. "You gentlemen both know the drill. Give me your thirty-second overview of the case, and then let's talk scheduling. Plaintiff first."

Tim stepped to the lectern and spoke in a smooth, practiced tenor. He had a notepad in his hands but didn't bother looking at it. "Your Honor, this case is about a reckless psychologist who used dangerous and untested new technology on a mentally fragile young man, Seth Bell, even though she knew he was suicidal. Tragically, Mr. Bell took his life as a direct result of the treatment he received at the hands of the defendants. Thank you."

Tim stepped back and Mike took his place. Tim's description of the case annoyed him, even though he knew Tim was just giving standard plaintiff's spin. "Your Honor, as Mr. Cromwell just conceded, Mr. Bell was mentally fragile and suicidal before he ever met my client. Those problems caused his death, not the revolutionary and highly therapeutic technology developed by Dr. Anderson. Thank you."

Mike stepped back and Judge Stavros said, "All right, so we've got a standard but big-ticket med-mal case here, which doesn't surprise me, seeing you two in front of me—though I am surprised that you're standing on opposite sides of that lectern. Be that as it may, what are your plans for discovery, motion practice, and trial? Mr. Cromwell, you first."

Tim stepped back to the lectern. "This may be a standard malpractice case from a purely legal perspective, Your Honor, but the facts are not at all standard. As my friend Mr. Webster just admitted, the technology at the heart of this case is revolutionary. We expect to prove that it was also extremely unsafe. We therefore will need to take discovery from a number of third parties who were involved in the development of Mind's Eye or its component elements. We will also need to take discovery from the Department of Corrections and Rehabilitation, in whose care Mr. Bell unfortunately spent some years as a result of his mental infirmities." He looked down at his notepad. "We expect to issue at least thirty discovery subpoenas and take at least fifty-two percipient-witness depositions, several of which will likely take place in Europe or Asia. Then there will be expert depositions, probably half a dozen for each side. We also anticipate significant motion practice related to both substantive matters and discovery disputes. We'll also need a protective order, of course. As for trial, plaintiff believes it is too early to set a trial date."

Mike stared at Tim in disbelief as he nonchalantly stepped back from the lectern. The pretrial plan he'd just described would suck up thousands of hours of billable time and cost millions. That made no sense at all for a case that was worth less than a million. Much less.

The judge turned to him. "Mr. Webster?"

Mike stepped up. "I agree that we should have a protective order, but other than that I strongly disagree with what my friend Mr. Cromwell just said. There are no more than five or six relevant witnesses, all of whom are located in California. The discovery Mr. Cromwell just described is excessive and, frankly, abusive. If he attempts to take even half of it, we'll file a motion to quash."

"And if Mr. Webster attempts to block our reasonable discovery efforts, we'll file a motion to compel," put in Tim. Court protocol called for him to keep his mouth shut while Mike was at the lectern, but Judge Stavros ran a pretty lax courtroom, and Tim's seniority gave him certain privileges.

Mike started to respond, but the judge held up his hand. "It sounds like Mr. Cromwell is right about the active-motion practice, in any event. We're not going to set a trial date or any other deadlines today, but I think this case is going to require active management. I'm going to recommend that it be single-assigned. All right, let's go off the record and discuss logistics."

Ten minutes later, Tim and Mike walked out of the courtroom. As soon as the doors closed behind them, Mike turned to Tim. "What was that? Are you seriously planning on thirty subpoenas and fifty depos?"

"Fifty-two," Tim corrected. "And yes, that's exactly what we're planning on." He smiled and patted Mike on the shoulder. "You and I are going to be spending a lot of quality time together over the next couple of years, Mike."

"That's insane! You'll spend ten times more than this case is worth." A thought occurred to Mike and he frowned. "If you think you're going to shake loose a big settlement by running up my bills, you're wrong."

Tim shook his head. "My client isn't going to settle. The Bells have already told me that. They want the full truth to come out, which is why we're doing all those depos. Then they want a verdict, not just a check. You understand."

Mike nodded unhappily. This was going to cause major scheduling problems. He forced a grin. "Let's see if they feel the same way when I get a defense verdict."

Tim's smile broadened. "I've never had the chance to beat one of my former partners before. This is going to be great fun. And we're going to get paid to do it. This will be a litigator's dream, right?"

# CHAPTER 29

Val saw Mike walk by on his way to his office and followed him in. "So, how did the CMC go?" she asked.

He hung his coat on a hanger on the back of his door. "In a word, weird."

"What happened?"

"Tim says he plans to send out thirty subpoenas and take fifty-two depos, including some overseas. He also plans on lots of motion practice. And he claims his clients won't settle. I may need to clear a lot of room in my schedule for this. Camy's too."

"How?" Val demanded. "Are you going to hire another lawyer?"

"We might have to, but before we do that, we should do a little investigating."

"By 'we,' you mean me, right?"

Mike chuckled and sat down behind his desk. "Well, if you want to be technical about it, yes, you. Unless you don't think you can handle it."

She flicked her hand dismissively. "Please. Have you ever given me a job I couldn't handle?"

"That's my girl," he said with a needling grin.

"Girl?" Her eyebrows went up and she crossed her arms. "Thanks for reminding me that you're overdue for your mandatory antidiscrimination training. I'll sign you up for the next available all-day seminar in Fresno. But after that, what do you want me to investigate?"

He turned serious. "Here's what's bugging me: this case isn't worth much. You know that. I know that. Tim didn't deny it. So what's with the scorched-earth litigation? Tim says his clients want a verdict, not just a check. I can understand that, but I can't understand why that means taking fifty-two depos, thirty subpoenas, and a bunch of motions. There are maybe three or four significant fact witnesses on each side, plus a couple of experts. That means a dozen depos max, and only one or two third-party subpoenas. We could do all that and have this case ready for trial in six months. All that other stuff Tim wants to do is just file-churning."

"He must be getting paid hourly, not on a contingency fee," Val said. "Otherwise, he'd only be getting a third of the judgment or settlement, and there's no way that would pay for all that work."

"Right. He said as much when we were talking outside the courtroom. So Seth Bell's parents are willing to blow millions of dollars just so Tim Cromwell can do lots of unnecessary discovery. That makes no sense."

"Okay, so what do you want me to do?"

"First, let's do some digging into the Bells' finances. Are they so rich that they can throw millions at this case without noticing? Second, I want to know more about the Bells generally." He thought for a moment, then shook his head. "There's something about this case I'm missing. What is it?"

She nodded. "I'm on it. By the way, speaking of something missing, we got Seth Bell's medical records from Jo Anderson this morning, and it looks like the video is missing for some of Bell's sessions, particularly the later ones."

"Did you ask her about it?"

Val nodded. "She says the hard disk must have filled up. The system kept trying to save data, but there was no room. She makes it sound like a totally innocent and understandable IT screwup. You can guess how Tim Cromwell will make it sound."

"Yeah." He paused for a moment, rubbing his temples. "I doubt he'll get anywhere with it."

"Are you sure about that? It just so happens that the data for the key Mind's Eye sessions is missing, and the jury will have to rely on Jo's description of what happened. You really don't think Tim will be able to get anywhere with that?"

He glared at her. "No, I don't. Jo is a good witness and her story sounds perfectly reasonable to me. Tim is just going to annoy the jury if he pushes on this issue."

Just like Val was annoying Mike, she realized, though she had no idea why. He usually appreciated it when she probed his case for weaknesses. Not today, though. He was rubbing his temples again—maybe his headache was back.

"Anything else?" he asked.

She wanted to suggest hiring a computer-forensics expert to take a look at Jo's hard drive. If Jo's story held up, great. They would then have an expert witness to support her at trial. But if it *didn't* hold up, they needed to know that now, before Tim Cromwell could figure out the truth and catch her lying under oath. So hiring an expert was the rational thing to do—but she got the feeling that Mike was not in the most rational frame of mind.

"Nope, that's it. Want some Advil from my stash?"

"That would be great."

She turned and started to leave.

"Hey," he called after her. "Don't actually sign me up for any seminars in Fresno, okay?"

She gave him her sweetest smile and walked out the door.

# CHAPTER 30

*February*

David Klein decided it was time to start phase three.

True, he didn't really need to start it now. Phase two could easily run for weeks—even months—before phase three was really necessary. But there wasn't any need to wait.

Besides, David admitted to himself, he *wanted* to start phase three. He had been looking forward to it for a long time. Years, to be honest.

He picked up the phone and dialed. He'd had the line swept for bugs that morning, so he was reasonably confident that it was clean. He couldn't be sure about the other end, of course, but the odds that Mordecai Xi's phone was bugged were very slim.

"The Oceanview Fund, Mordecai Xi's office," said a female voice he recognized. "How may I help you?"

"Hello, Kim, it's David Klein. Put me through to Mordecai."

"David." The line was silent for several heartbeats. "I'll see if he's available."

"I'm sure he is. Tell him the password is Phoebus."

"Rebus? Will he know what that means?"

"Phoebus. And yes, he will most definitely know what it means."

"One moment."

Muzak played for thirty seconds.

"David," Mordecai's voice boomed. "Good to hear from you. It's been a long time."

"Too long," David replied, matching the false heartiness of his former boss. "When was the last time we talked?"

"I, ah, can't remember."

David did. It was in Mordecai's office. Mordecai had called him in on the pretense of wanting to discuss a new deal. In fact, it was a ruse to get David out of his office while security searched it. When they were done, they came for him in Mordecai's office and escorted him out of the building.

"How very careless of you. I hope your memory is better when it comes to the Phoebus deal. Did you ever remember where you misplaced those fronting agreements?"

"I can't say that I, ah, recall the agreements you're talking about," Mordecai said warily.

David smiled. Mordecai couldn't be sure that David was the only one on the line and wasn't recording their conversation, so he was playing it safe. Or as safe as he could, under the circumstances. "That's very interesting. I'll bet the SEC and FBI could refresh your recollection once I send them copies of the agreements."

"What do you want?" His voice was flat and hard, all the bonhomie gone. He was caught and he knew it.

David's smile broadened. The Phoebus deal had made over three hundred million dollars for Oceanview, but it had also been illegal. A Russian oligarch who had been barred from doing business in the US had used an Estonian front company to do the deal. He controlled the front through two undisclosed agreements, which Mordecai had discovered just before closing. He went through with the deal, made three hundred million, and became an accessory to securities fraud, wire fraud, and several other felonies. Then he had the poor judgment to fire David, who had the original agreements and proof that Mordecai had seen them before he signed his name to the deal.

This was turning out to be just as much fun as he had hoped. "I want two things. First, you cut off all funding to a company called Mind's Eye, Inc. and anyone associated with it."

"I can't do that. We've already got over twelve million invested in them. If I cut them off, there will be questions from the board."

"You can't do it? I was hoping you'd say that, Mort. I'm going to enjoy reading about your trial in the *Journal*. I've got the anonymous e-mail to the feds all teed up and ready to go. Hitting send in three, two—"

"Hold on! Fine, I'll make it happen. Why do you care about Mind's Eye?"

Mordecai's tortured squirming was exquisite, like the writhing of a loathsome insect as it roasts, pinned by the white heat of a magnifying glass. David savored the moment, trying to lock every detail in his memory. "Because I do."

"Give me a couple of days to get the signatures I need."

"Speaking of signatures, that was only one of the things you're going to do for me."

A weary sigh. "What else do you want?"

And now for the perfect finish. "A fronting agreement giving me control of all Oceanview's shares in Mind's Eye, Inc. And you have to sign it."

# Chapter 31

Val had arranged to meet her brother, Angelo, at the SoMa food-truck park. They hadn't picked a precise spot, but she was pretty sure she knew where to find him. And there he was: at the Bacon Bacon truck. He was already halfway through a greasy monstrosity of a sandwich that sprouted strips of bacon the way a centipede does legs. It was a messy meal, but he had somehow managed to keep his suit spotless so far. There was probably a course on that at the police academy.

She got a veggie wrap from the ÉireTrea truck and joined him on a bench. "Hey, Angy." She gestured toward his meal. "How many pigs you think it takes to make one of those things?"

"I'd eat here three times a day if Peg would let me," he replied before going in for another bite. Peg was his wife. The family liked her, but there had been some grumbling among the older relatives about the unwisdom of "mixed marriages" because Peg was Irish, not Italian.

"Maybe she'll feel different if you take out a big life-insurance policy and name her as the beneficiary."

He grinned. "That's my big sis, always lookin' out for me. How you been?" His strong Brooklyn accent always made her a little nostalgic.

She had worked hard to get rid of hers when she'd joined Masters & Cromwell, but he was proud of his and had intentionally kept it.

"Can't complain. Staying busy."

"Datin' anyone?"

She arched an eyebrow at him. "Why do you care?"

He shrugged a meaty shoulder. "Who says I do? Mama asked me to find out. Every time I talk to her, it's 'Angelo, is yaw sistah seein' anyone? I *worry* about her. She's almos' thirty.' Or 'Angelo, you should introduce her to some nice Catholic men.' So, want me to introduce you to some nice Catholic men?"

Val felt her blood pressure rising, but she couldn't help laughing at her brother's pitch-perfect imitation of their mother. "No. I can find a man just fine on my own if I want to."

He gave her an appraising look. "Or maybe you already did. Maybe you got your eye on a guy, but he hasn't asked you out. Like that young chemistry teacher when we were in high school. You ignored all the other guys while you were crushin' on him."

She rolled her eyes. "How about we find something else to talk about?"

"Up to you. What do you want me to tell Mama?"

"Tell her I'm dating an ax murderer. But it's okay 'cause he's Catholic."

He snorted. "Yeah, that'll totally make her leave us alone." He took a swig from a large cup of Coke. "How about I tell her you been real busy, but I'll set you up with one of my friends next month or so?"

She sighed. His friends tended to be good, solid men to whom she had absolutely no attraction. "Fine."

"So now that we got that outta the way, what's up?" he asked around another bite. "Didja just wanna grab lunch or was there somethin' you wanna talk about?"

"Now that you mention it, I've got a little work project I'd like to bounce off you."

"I thought you might. Tell me about it."

"Part of it is pretty straightforward: Mike wants me to figure out how much a state senator and his family are worth."

"*State* senator?"

"Yeah."

"You're already done. Form 700."

"Form what?" she asked.

"Form 700. It's a financial-disclosure thing. Every state official has to fill it out. It lists every investment they own and anyone who paid them money, other than the state. And you can get any state salary online too. Those'll give you most of what you wanna know."

"Unless they're leaving stuff off this Form 700 thing," Val observed.

"Which would be dumb. Any senator who gets caught doin' that is in for a world of hurt. He'd only risk that if he was bein' bribed or somethin'."

Val pulled out her phone and typed "Form 700" into her to-do list. "Thanks. The second piece of this project is a little harder. Mike wants me to do some general poking around in the backgrounds of the senator and his family. See what's there."

"There's Accurint," Angy said, "but I'm guessin' you already know 'bout that."

She nodded. "That picks up most stuff. CourtLink should catch any lawsuits or bankruptcies. And there's lots of places I can go for criminal records."

Angy held up a thick finger. "Unless they were expunged."

"Why would that happen?"

"Mostly because the perp turned eighteen, but there are other reasons."

She drummed her fingers on the bench, but took care not to chip her nails. Seth Bell could have had a juvenile record. In fact, he probably did.

"Do expunged records completely disappear? Or is there a backup copy somewhere?"

"They're *supposed* to completely disappear," Angy said as he used the last crust from his sandwich to wipe up stray crumbs of bacon from the wax-paper wrapper. "But lots of times that doesn't happen. For most juvie perps, there are lots of copies of their records floatin' around. The local PD'll have one. So will the DA. So will any place they stayed. The court'll have a copy too. If the perp got picked up in a different jurisdiction, there'll be more copies there." He popped the crust in his mouth and chewed contemplatively. He swallowed and added, "And one of the cops who worked the case might have kept some stuff too. Sort of a background file if they thought the kid was likely to reoffend."

"Thanks. How would I figure out whether any of those places has the records I'm looking for?"

"*You* wouldn't," Angy replied as he wiped his fingers and beard with a fistful of paper napkins. His suit, dress shirt, and tie were still magically spotless. "None of those people are supposed to have the records, so if you start askin', any copies will just disappear. But if—speakin' purely hypothetical here—a cop does the askin' for you, things might be different. People might be a little more open to a brother in blue."

"If a hypothetical cop did that, I'd owe him a big thank-you."

"And Field Club–level tickets for the next Giants-Mets game?"

She laughed. "Hypothetically. And all the chili dogs and garlic fries he can eat."

"Sweet. Officer Hypothetical is on it."

"One more thing—I might need someone to do some computer forensics work. Basically, I need to ask some questions about a hard drive. I may also need some files analyzed to see if anyone edited or tampered with them. Can you give me a referral?"

He nodded. "Sure. I know a coupla guys who do that. I'll send you their names. If you use 'em, tell 'em I sent you, okay?"

"Of course. Thanks, Angy."

"No problem." He balled the sandwich wrapper and napkins, shoved them in his cup, and threw it in a trashcan. "Hey, I gotta go, but it was good seein' you."

She gave him a warm hug and a kiss on the cheek. "Likewise. You take care of yourself, Angy. Stay safe."

He chuffed. "That'll be easy. Too easy for my taste. I'm doin' mostly financial-crimes stuff now. So unless I die of boredom or paper cuts, I got nothin' to worry about."

# CHAPTER 32

The first three hours of Mike Webster's day went more or less as he expected.

At nine, he arrived in the office to find twelve e-mails from one of Tim Cromwell's associates waiting for him. Three more arrived while he read the first twelve. All had some form of discovery attached to them. There were document requests demanding every scrap of paper or byte of data related to the development of Mind's Eye, deposition notices for everyone in Jo's office, subpoenas for Jo's contacts in the Department of Corrections and Rehabilitation. All told, there were over two hundred pages of discovery. In short, an aggressive first wave of the discovery tsunami Tim had promised.

Responding to all of this would be a lot of work. Many of the requests were overbroad or otherwise objectionable, but a lot of them weren't. Mike and his team would need to go through each item in each request and respond to it separately. They would also need to start gathering all the documents and information called for by the legitimate requests, which would need to be reviewed and prepared for delivery to Tim and his team. All of that would take weeks of dull, complicated work.

He gave Tim's handiwork a quick skim and then forwarded the whole mess to his senior associate, Camy Tang. He had assigned Camy to handle defensive discovery, so she would take care of responding to all the discovery requests the other side dumped on them. Mike had assigned himself offensive discovery, which meant he was in charge of writing all the discovery requests *they* would dump on Tim. Camy had greater attention to detail than Mike, so she was better suited to defensive work. Also, offensive discovery was generally more fun, and one of the perks of owning the firm was that Mike got to delegate the less fun stuff.

Mike's offensive discovery plan was the opposite of Tim's. Mike would focus only on critical witnesses and facts, at least at the outset. He would take as few depositions and ask for as few documents as possible. Then, when he had the key elements of his case in place, he would push the judge to cut off discovery and set a trial date. If Tim wasn't ready because he had been screwing around with minor witnesses and dragnet document requests, tough. Judge Stavros probably wouldn't force Tim to go to trial if he really wasn't ready—but he might force Tim to cut back his demands to stuff he really needed for preparing his case.

By noon, Mike had fired off his responding discovery salvo. It consisted of two depo notices (for Seth Bell's parents) and two document requests (for the contents of Seth's cell phone and computer, if he owned either). And it only took one e-mail to send.

At exactly noon, his phone rang and everything changed. "Mike, it's Jo." Her voice was tense and oddly tentative, as if she was getting ready to confess a crime. "I got a call this morning from my financial backers at the Oceanview Fund. They've cut me off, effective immediately. No warning and no explanation."

"Wow." His mind whirled as he tried to grasp the implications of what she'd just said. "So . . . how long do you think it will take to find a replacement?"

"I've been on the phone ever since I got the news from Oceanview. No one is interested, not with that lawsuit hanging over me and the company."

He began to suspect where she was going. "What does this mean for you financially?"

The tentativeness in her voice increased. "This was a total shock, so I don't have much cushion. I also don't have a lot of income yet. I'm going to try to get my landlord to cut my rent, but I'm not very optimistic. If that doesn't work, I'm going to have to lay off my receptionist."

"Anything else?"

"Well, I don't think I'll be able to pay you for a while."

# CHAPTER 33

Val came back from lunch to find Mike in a black mood. He was pacing in his office, muttering, and scowling out at the spectacular view of the San Francisco Bay.

She stopped in his doorway. "What is it?"

He stopped pacing and turned to face her. "Jo's financial backers. They just cut her off. No warning. No explanation. She's in deep trouble."

"Wow." She paused for a minute as the information sank in. "Any idea why they did it?"

He shook his head. "I don't know anything about them, but this makes no sense. They've been huge fans of Mind's Eye from the start, and the only thing that's gone even a little wrong is this lawsuit."

"Think that could be it?" Val asked. "They're pulling out 'cause they're spooked by the Bell case?"

"No. If they were worried about it, I would have heard from them. They'd hire their own lawyer to do an independent analysis of the case. Then they'd get Jo's permission to ask me a whole bunch of pointed questions. After that, their lawyer would give them an evaluation of the case and tell them whether it was a serious risk. They'd never decide to just walk away from a twelve-million-dollar investment without even talking to the guy who's handling the case."

Facts came together in Val's mind like puzzle pieces clicking into place. "This totally explains what Tim is doing. He's running up Jo's bills at the same time her money is getting cut off. She can't afford to defend the case, so she'll either default or go BK long before trial."

The storm clouds in Mike's eyes thickened and he nodded. "I had the same thought. I really hope it's not true. Tim has always been a good guy. If he's part of a scheme to win by bankrupting Jo . . ." His voice trailed off and he shook his head. "He said his client decided on the scorched-earth litigation tactics, not him. I'm going to give him the benefit of the doubt, at least for now."

Val nodded vigorously. "Oh, I agree. I wasn't thinking Tim was behind this—I was thinking it was the Bells. They're just using Tim. And somehow they got to Jo's money men."

Mike nodded and tugged at his lower lip. "Seth Bell's father is a senator. It's possible that he did something behind the scenes to make Oceanview—they're the money men—cut Jo off."

"So, what do we do?"

He looked a little surprised. "What do you mean?"

"Well, I'm guessing Jo isn't going to be able to pay us. Most firms withdraw when their clients stop paying them—especially small firms like ours."

He looked at her like she'd slapped him. "Are you suggesting we should withdraw?"

"No. I'm your firm manager, so it's my job to talk to you before we make an expensive decision—even if it's the right decision. This is a really expensive decision. You're talking about footing Dr. Goff's bills, which will run nine hundred bucks an hour, and he's only really qualified to talk about Mind's Eye. We may need another expert to testify about how schizophrenia and depression make people suicidal. So we're looking at four or five hundred thousand in expert fees. Maybe more.

We may also need to hire a PI to help with some of the digging we'll need to do. Then there's lost time for you and Camy. We've already had to turn away good cases so you could work on the Bell case. We were probably going to take a hit on that because you were only charging a blended rate of four hundred an hour, and you could have made at least twice that on other work. Now you're talking about doing the Bell case for free. That's probably at least another half million in lost billings. All told, if you decide to represent Jo pro bono, you're costing the firm around a million. I'm not saying we should withdraw—that's your call, not mine. I'm just making sure you know what it will cost if we *don't* withdraw."

"A million?"

She nodded.

He thought for a moment, then nodded. "Yeah, that's probably about right. We're not withdrawing, though. Maybe we'll take stock instead of cash or maybe we can work out some kind of payment plan with Jo—or maybe we will do this pro bono and take the million-dollar hit. If she doesn't have the money, she doesn't have it."

"I'll run an asset check on her and make sure she doesn't have it," Val interjected. Mike could be impetuous when he was full of righteous anger, and she had learned from hard experience that she needed to keep an eye on him when he was like this and make sure he didn't do anything stupid. Like agree not to charge a client who might have ten million stashed away in a Caribbean bank account, for example.

"I hate this kind of sleazy gamesmanship." His face darkened and he started pacing again. "It makes my skin crawl. This is the same basic tactic that that landlord used to destroy my parents' church. He had his shock-and-awe legal team and the church didn't have the money to fight back. No money, no justice." He slammed his fist into his hand. "That is not going to happen here! Not. Going. To. Happen."

A thought struck Val. "Your parents' church."

"Yeah, what happened was—"

"No, no. I know the story. What happened to them was terrible, but you just made me think of something. The landlord wanted to get rid of the church because it was sitting on valuable land, right?"

"Right."

"So what is Jo sitting on that's valuable?"

He stopped pacing. "Mind's Eye. If Jo and her company go bankrupt, Mind's Eye gets sold to pay their debts. The Bells buy it. If they have a big enough judgment against Jo, they might not even have to pay anything. They would just bid their judgment when Mind's Eye is auctioned off by the bankruptcy estate." He paused. "How's that backgrounder on their finances coming?"

"You'll have it by the end of the week."

# Chapter 34

*March*

Mike loved deposing witnesses. In some ways, it was even more fun than cross-examining them at trial. For one thing, it was very hard to surprise witnesses at trial. Every e-mail or scrap of paper that could be used at trial had been disclosed weeks in advance on pretrial exhibit lists. Every other witness who could testify had also been disclosed. Then some junior lawyer had combed through all of that evidence to create a witness-prep binder, which the witness had read through at least once. And then a senior lawyer had done at least one mock cross-examination to spot and address any weaknesses in the witness's testimony. By the time Mike actually got to cross the witness on the stand, the witness had canned answers for at least 90 percent of Mike's questions. Making matters worse, Mike couldn't use any evidence that the judge decided not to let in, which—as the Lee trial nearly demonstrated—could be devastating.

But during a deposition, Mike could use whatever he wanted, regardless of whether he had disclosed it to the other side. And with very rare exceptions, no judge would stop him.

Today, for example, Mike was deposing Senator Warren Bell. They sat in a conference room at Mike's office, Bell and Tim Cromwell on one side of the table, Mike and Camy on the other. A court reporter sat at the end of the table, transcribing Bell's testimony, which was also captured by a videographer behind Mike. In front of Camy lay a carefully organized stack of exhibits. With luck, Bell had seen less than half of them before, and his lawyers had seen less than that.

Once the preliminaries were over, Mike pulled out his first surprise. He could have waited, but he liked to rattle witnesses early in their depositions. "Senator Bell, do you recall signing the complaint in this case?"

"Yes."

"Did you read it before you signed it?"

"Yes." Bell's tone was even and his patrician face wore a look of slightly strained patience, as if he were dealing with an obnoxious reporter.

Mike nodded to Camy, who handed copies of the complaint to Bell, his lawyer, and the court reporter. "Please mark this as Exhibit One," Mike said to the court reporter. He turned to Bell. "Please read the last sentence of paragraph twenty-four into the record."

"'Seth, like many young men, had some difficult years, but he was never suicidal.'"

"What exactly did you mean by 'difficult years,' Senator?"

"Seth had substance-abuse issues that caused him a lot of problems."

"But they never caused him to become suicidal?"

"No."

Mike nodded to Camy again. She distributed copies of a newspaper article, which the court reporter marked as Exhibit 2. When Bell saw it, sharp creases of anger appeared around his mouth and eyes.

"Please read the title and date into the record," Mike said.

Tim Cromwell raised his hand. "Objection, no foundation has been laid showing that this exhibit is authentic."

Bell hesitated, as if waiting for a judge to materialize and rule on Tim's objection.

Mike smiled. "Go ahead and answer."

Bell looked at Tim, who gave a grudging nod. With few exceptions (an objection based on the attorney-client privilege, for example), witnesses have to answer deposition questions even if their lawyers object.

Bell picked up the article. "The title is 'Assembly Member Bell's Son Rushed to Hospital After Suicide Attempt,' which is false, by the way. The date is August 15, 2000."

"Thank you. Was it true that Seth was rushed to the hospital after being found unconscious in a running car in the garage of your home?"

"He was not trying to commit suicide."

"That's not what I asked. Please answer my question."

Bell put the article down. "Yes, that is true."

"Thank you. Were you home at the time of this incident?"

"I don't remember."

"You don't?" Mike said, putting a trace of disbelief in his voice. "Maybe the last paragraph will refresh your recollection. Please read it into the record."

Bell glared at Mike, but read. "'Bell was at the Democratic National Convention in Los Angeles and unavailable for comment. His office issued a statement asking that his family's privacy be respected during this difficult time.'"

"If you weren't at home at the time, how do you know Seth wasn't trying to commit suicide?"

"Because he told me. He said that he drove home and fell asleep with the engine running."

"When did he tell you that?"

"When I got home from the convention."

"Which was several days after the police concluded, presumably after speaking with Seth, that he had attempted suicide, correct?"

"Objection, assumes facts not in evidence," Tim said. "You can answer," he added to his client.

"That's what the article says," Bell said, dismissively gesturing at the piece of paper. "I have no idea what the police concluded or whether they spoke to Seth. You'd have to ask them."

Mike moved on to the next point in his depo outline. "Was Seth ever diagnosed with any mental illness?"

"Yes, he was diagnosed with schizophrenia and depression."

"Was he taking medications for either of those conditions?"

"Yes. He had medications and he took them. They controlled his problems."

"Was he taking them in the weeks before he died?"

"Yes."

"He didn't live at home at that time, did he?"

"No."

"Then how do you know that he was taking his medications?"

"Because he told us he was whenever we asked."

"When did you ask?"

"Whenever I spoke to him."

"How often did you speak to him?"

"I don't remember."

"When was the last time you spoke to him before he died?"

Bell shifted uncomfortably in his seat. "I don't remember."

"Was it more than a week before his death?"

"I don't remember."

"More than a month?"

Bell shrugged with one shoulder and looked down at the table. "That's possible."

"What was Seth's phone number?"

"I . . . His mother would usually hand the phone to me when she was done talking to him."

"So you don't remember the number?"

He shook his head.

"I'm sorry, you're going to need to answer verbally for the court reporter."

"The answer is no."

"Do you remember his street address?"

"We would usually meet somewhere, not at his apartment."

"So the answer to my question is . . ."

"No, I don't know the address."

"How about his e-mail address?"

"Well, an old guy like me doesn't use e-mail much," Bell said with an obviously forced smile, "so I don't remember his e-mail address either."

"All right." Mike checked off another item on his outline. "Did you ever ask Seth whether he was drinking or using illegal drugs?"

"Yes. He said he wasn't."

"Did you believe him?"

Bell was silent for several seconds. "He never gave me reason to disbelieve him."

Camy handed Mike two documents. One was the blood-work section of Seth Bell's autopsy report. It showed near-poisonous levels of alcohol, antidepressant levels consistent with abuse rather than treatment, traces of marijuana and cocaine, and no sign of the antipsychotics Seth was supposed to be taking. The other document was a copy of Seth's 2005 conviction for vehicular manslaughter and driving while intoxicated.

Camy looked inquiringly at Mike, but he shook his head slightly. He had everything he needed in order to show at trial that Bell was in denial about his son's substance abuse. Rubbing his face in it during his deposition wouldn't accomplish anything.

"Senator Bell, please read paragraph forty-six in Exhibit One, the complaint."

Bell picked up the complaint and flipped to the right page. "'Seth was a gifted computer programmer who was working on a degree in computer science at the time of his death.'"

"Thank you. Was Seth employed at the time of his death?"

"No."

"Did he ever hold a job in computer programming?"

"No."

"Did he ever hold a job in any field?"

"I think he worked in the prison store while he was incarcerated."

"Any job other than that?"

"Not that I'm aware of."

"Was he enrolled in computer-programming classes at the time of his death?"

"I thought he was enrolled at San Francisco State University."

"Is that what he told you?"

"He told his mother, who told me. I may have misheard or misremembered."

"Are you aware that my firm subpoenaed Seth's records from SFSU?"

"Yes, and I'm also aware that there were none." Bell's eyes flashed with anger. "As I said, I may have misheard my wife or misremembered where she said Seth was studying."

"Would you be surprised to learn that we had contacted every school in the Bay Area that offers classes in computer programming and that none of them had any record of Seth being enrolled?"

"Yes," he said, practically hurling the word at Mike.

"Because he told your wife that he was studying computer programming, correct?"

"Correct."

Mike leaned back in his seat and regarded Bell silently for a moment. "Senator, from where I'm sitting, it doesn't look like you're going to be able to prove that Seth's death was the result of something my clients did and not his preexisting mental illness. But even if you do, you can't recover economic damages because Seth had no income. You also can't recover for medical expenses because none were caused by the malpractice you allege. To be honest, you'll probably lose this case, and even if you win, you won't recover enough to pay Mr. Cromwell's bills. So why did you file this case? And when you answer, remember that you're under oath."

"Objection, calls for attorney-client communications," Tim said. "Senator, don't reveal anything we said or wrote to each other."

"That's fine," Mike responded. "Just tell me what led you to hire a lawyer as good—and expensive—as Mr. Cromwell for a case as bad as this."

Bell's face darkened. "I brought this case because my son deserves justice. Perhaps this is hard for someone like you to understand, but this case isn't about money. I have spent years fighting for the victimized and disenfranchised, and now I'm fighting for my son. My wife and I sued to vindicate Seth's memory and honor. He didn't kill himself, he was killed by your client's recklessness. She experimented on him, used him like a lab rat. We filed this case to hold her accountable for what she did."

"You wanted to make clear to the world who was to blame for Seth's death."

"Exactly," Bell said, glowering at Mike.

"Because before you filed this case, the world blamed you, didn't it?" Mike reached into Camy's pile of exhibits and pulled out two scathing articles written a week before the case was filed. One was titled "Warren Bell's Orphan Son" and the other "An Inconvenient Boy." Both chronicled Seth's "abandonment" by his parents, particularly his father, who had indeed made a political career as the champion of the vulnerable and disenfranchised. Perhaps, the reporters speculated, if Warren

Bell had paid more attention to his own vulnerable and disenfranchised son, Seth might still be alive.

Mike handed copies of both articles to the court reporter. "Please mark these as Exhibits Three and Four." He then slid copies across the table to Bell. "Read the dates and titles of these for the record."

A vein stood out on Bell's forehead when he saw the articles. He looked at Mike with undisguised fury, got up, and stormed out of the conference room, dropping the articles in the garbage can as he walked through the door.

# CHAPTER 35

To Val's surprise, Mike strode into her office at twelve thirty.

"Why are you back?" she asked. "I thought you were going to be at the Bell depo all day."

"So did I. But he got mad and walked out in the middle. Tim tried to talk him into coming back, but he was too ticked off. He said he wouldn't answer any more questions from me unless the judge ordered him to."

Val laughed. "You are a charmer. What happened?"

"I hit a nerve when I brought up 'Warren Bell's Orphan Son.' He likes to portray himself as a compassionate guy who's always looking out for the vulnerable, including the mentally ill. I'll bet he really thinks of himself that way. Except he wasn't looking out for Seth, and the papers called him on it. He must have really hated that. It made him look bad to the public—and to himself. So he had to find someone to blame for Seth's death. That's why he sued Jo. And that's also why he stomped out of his depo when I pointed out what he was doing."

"Can he do that?"

"Nope. So I sent Camy to start working on an *ex parte* motion." He grinned. "If Bell wants an order, we'll get him an order. I told Camy to put in a request for sanctions. If Bell has to write a check to us for a few thousand dollars, he may think twice before pulling another stunt like this."

"Hey, speaking of money, I just got Senator Bell's Form 700," she said, holding up a document. "Very interesting."

"Form what?" Mike's stomach rumbled audibly. "Let's discuss it over lunch. Chinese?"

"Love to, but I'm on a diet." She could still fit in her regular wardrobe, but a couple of her skirts were getting a little too tight.

"Why are you dieting? You look great."

She smiled at the compliment. "You're sweet, but I really shouldn't."

"Fine. Just come with me and you can watch me eat while we talk."

"What fun."

She grabbed her purse and the Form 700 and met him at the elevator. Five minutes later, they were at Yan's Kitchen. Mike ordered General Tso's chicken for himself and got a pot of green tea for them to share.

"You're sure you don't want anything?" he asked. "My treat."

She looked longingly at the menu, but shook her head. "Thanks, but no."

The waiter left and Val glanced around to make sure they could have a semiprivate conversation. "So, what happened at the depo?"

"It was going pretty well. I scored some points that will be useful when I cross Bell at trial. I also was close to getting him in the right frame of mind—he stepped in it twice when he said one thing and then Camy handed him an exhibit that showed something else. By the end, I don't think he knew what we were going to pull out of the exhibit pile next. Nice job, by the way. You gave me ammo that Tim had no idea even existed."

She shrugged one shoulder modestly as their waiter arrived with the tea. "Camy gave me a lot of help. So what made him walk out?"

Mike sighed and looked down at his cup. "I may have pushed a little too hard. He's a sanctimonious, grandstanding piece of work, a whited sepulcher with a fresh coat of paint. I rubbed his face in it a couple of times, and he walked out after the second. Which was too bad—I was just getting to the questions I really wanted answered."

"The financial stuff?"

He took a sip of his tea and nodded. "The more I think about it, the less it adds up. I mean, the Bells are worth about five million, so they *could* do this, but *would* they? Let's say Tim's costs for this case are double ours. That's two million. The Bells could pay that, but it would hurt. They'd have to sell investments, maybe even the place in Tahoe that you found. That could make sense from a purely dollars-and-cents perspective if they can get their hands on Mind's Eye as a result. Possibly. But it would be risky and ugly. Think about how it would play out. The Bells spend two million to force Jo into bankruptcy. Then they have to pay more to bankruptcy lawyers to get Mind's Eye. And if anyone bids against them when Mind's Eye is auctioned off—a hospital chain or medical-device company—the Bells could lose. They'd be out over two million with nothing to show for it except a worthless judgment. And the press would probably cover the whole thing, which won't help Senator Bell's political career."

The waiter arrived with Mike's food. It looked and smelled delicious.

When he left, Mike concluded, "So in a nutshell, this makes less sense to me today than it did about a week ago. I was hoping I might be able to shake some more-or-less straight answers out of Bell, but he walked out too soon."

"You might find some answers in here," Val said as she slid the Form 700 across the table. "Bell just filed this yesterday. It's his annual financial-disclosure form."

Mike picked it up and started reading. He seemed to completely forget about Val and his food, which sat on his plate, tempting her.

After five minutes, she couldn't take it anymore. She took her chopsticks out of their paper sleeve, snapped them apart, and rubbed the loose splinters off of them. "You mind?"

He grunted and waved at his food without taking his eyes off the document. She took one bite. Then she took another. And another.

By the time Mike put down the Form 700 a few minutes later, his plate was half-empty. "I thought you didn't want to eat."

"I don't," she said around a mouthful of chicken. "This is your fault for taking me here and leaving this sitting in front of me. Now start eating before you do any more damage to my diet."

He complied, finishing off the remains of his meal in two minutes. He pushed his plate aside and put the Form 700 on the table between them. It was open to a schedule disclosing outside income sources for Bell and his family.

Mike pointed to an item titled "Sale of intangible property." It showed that the Bells recently received $100,000 from someplace called Horizon Finance. "What's this?"

"I thought that might get your attention. Horizon Finance is a San Francisco outfit. As far as I can tell, they're basically a private-equity fund that works with gray-market investors—Russian and Chinese companies with US tax problems, Iranians who aren't allowed to invest here, and that sort of thing. I don't think they specialize in tech startups or real estate or anything—they just go wherever the money is. But a lot of that is guesswork. There's very little public on them—bare-bones website, no SEC filings, virtually nothing. I had to spend a couple of hours trolling in the deep web to find anything at all."

She handed him the thin results of her research. He flipped through it in a few minutes and handed it back. "So any clue what these guys bought from the Bells for one hundred grand? I've got a guess, but I'd like to hear yours first."

Val fiddled with a chopstick. "I see a couple of clues, but not much more. First, 'intangible property' is weirdly cryptic. I mean, doesn't that usually cover copyrights or patents or something like that?"

Mike nodded. "It's basically anything you can own but not touch."

"Okay, so if they sold a copyright, wouldn't the form say 'sale of copyright' or something like that?"

"I don't see why not."

"And if they sold a patent, it would say 'sale of patent,' right?"

"That's what I'd expect."

"But instead it says 'intangible property,' which seems deliberately unclear. Like they're hiding behind legalese."

Mike nodded again. "I agree. Go on."

"Second clue: they sold it to Horizon. These guys are big-ticket opportunistic investors. They're not looking to buy the copyright for Senator Bell's autobiography or something like that. They're looking for a big score. If they don't see a potential profit of a hundred million or more, they're not interested."

"That fits pretty much every private-equity guy or investment banker I ever met," Mike said. "Any other clues?"

Val took a sip of tea and thought for a moment. "Nothing except what you just pointed out: The Bells aren't really in a position to try that bankruptcy strategy we were talking about. Horizon is, though. That would be right up their alley. I'm guessing that they somehow heard about this case and bought a piece of it. In exchange, they're bankrolling the lawsuit."

Mike refilled their teacups and took a sip from his. "If that's what's going on, why did Bell put it on his Form 700? What if some reporter goes through the same analysis you just did?"

"Yeah, it could get a little awkward," Val acknowledged. "But I'm guessing it could get more awkward if he didn't put it on. I think he could go to jail for that if anyone figured it out. Enough people probably know about this that there's a decent chance it would come out sooner or later. So it was better for him to just drop something murky in his Form 700 and hope no one decides to dig."

Mike nodded. "I had the same gut reaction, though I hadn't thought through it in as much detail." He picked up his cup in both hands and stared absently at the contents, idly sloshing the tea back and forth.

Val could almost hear the wheels whirring in his head, so she drank tea in silence until he was done thinking.

He looked up after a moment, a predatory smile on his face. "Okay, let's have some fun with our new playmates at Horizon Finance."

# CHAPTER 36

Sitting in his corner office at Horizon Finance, David Klein frowned at his subordinate. "In retrospect, I'm confused by your last report, Eric."

Eric stood in front of David's desk, hands clasped behind his back. "I'm sorry, Mr. Klein. What would you like me to clarify?"

"You told me Johanna Anderson wasn't able to pay her lawyers—or am I misremembering?"

Eric cleared his throat. "No, Mr. Klein. Our source was quite clear on that point."

David swiveled his chair around to face his bank of monitors. One of them showed the transcript of Senator Bell's deposition. He pointed an accusing finger at the screen. "She had not one, but two lawyers at Bell's deposition, and they had clearly done a lot of prep work. How do you explain that?"

Eric shifted his weight from foot to foot. "I'm not sure."

"You're not sure," David repeated, drawing the words out. Eric stared at an empty spot on David's immaculate leather desktop as if it was the most fascinating thing in the world. "Billions of dollars depend on our ability to separate her from her lawyers. We're not doing it. And all you can say is that you're not sure why not?"

Eric's face was pale, but he didn't cringe. "If she's not paying her lawyers, then there are two possibilities. Either someone else is paying them or the lawyers are working for free."

"Self-evidently. And?"

"And we need to find out which before we act. If someone else is paying the lawyers, then we need to cut off that funding. If they're working for free, our next step is to make them stop."

"Good. Get on it."

"Yes, Mr. Klein."

# CHAPTER 37

*That was weird.*

Val had spent the morning sifting through 33,641 pages of records from the California Department of Corrections and Rehabilitation. At least they were on searchable DVD. Ten years ago, they would have come in seventy bankers boxes and gone into a conference room, where a team of junior attorneys would have spent weeks reviewing them page by page. Now Val could search them alone in a couple of days at her computer. Progress. Sort of.

The Corrections records were part of the mountain of documents produced in response to Tim Cromwell's flurry of subpoenas. They were on Val's computer because Mike had ordered copies of everything that any of the recipients of Tim's subpoenas produced. Mike didn't particularly want all of this stuff, but someone had to take at least a cursory look at it in case it contained any surprises. That someone was Val, and she had just found a surprise.

Tim Cromwell had subpoenaed all of Corrections' records related to Mind's Eye, most of which were utterly irrelevant—five copies of every invoice Jo sent, hundreds of pages of standard state-contracting forms, and so on. Over a thousand pages were completely blank because

Corrections had redacted everything on them but produced the blank sheets anyway.

Faced with so much dross, Val had almost immediately started doing keyword searches. One of those searches was *"new patient" /s intake.* That pulled up ten identical sets of forms—one for each patient in the cohort Corrections had sent Jo. All of the names and other identifying information had been redacted, except for Seth Bell's, of course. The dates hadn't been redacted, though. All of the forms were dated within a week of each other, except for Seth's. His was almost three months later. *Why?*

Val typed in a new search: *Seth /3 Bell.* Then she opened the earliest document that her search found. It was an e-mail from Jo to her contact at Corrections. The subject line was "Another patient?" The text read:

Tammy:

I've got an opening for another patient, and I'd be happy to take on another CDCR referral. I can give you the same discounted rates as the others. If you're interested, I suggest an individual named Seth Bell who lives in San Francisco. I believe he meets all the criteria for the program, but please check your records and confirm.

Best,

Jo

Val sat back and absently played with her hair. Corrections had picked all of Jo's patients except Seth. Why did Jo reach out and ask for him? Was he different in some way? Was it somehow related to his death?

They needed to know the answers to those questions before Tim Cromwell asked them on cross-examination. Sometimes the lawyers contacted witnesses to nail down these sorts of loose ends, and some-times Val did it.

Ordinarily, she'd send an e-mail to Mike and Camy and let them decide whether to handle it themselves or delegate it to her. But Val suspected that Mike would want to ask Jo about it, probably during one of their dinners. Camy would defer to her boss, of course. And somehow Val doubted that Mike would make a serious effort to get to the bottom of this. But Tim Cromwell would. Besides, Mike and Camy were both out for the day, handling depositions.

"Better to ask forgiveness . . ." Val murmured to herself as she dialed Jo's office number.

The receptionist answered on the second ring. "Hello, Dr. Anderson's office."

"Val D'Abruzzo calling for Dr. Anderson. Is she available? I need to talk to her about her case."

"One moment."

Static-filled synthesizer music played for almost a minute, and Val began to wonder whether Jo would take her call. *She'd better,* Val thought—particularly now that she was getting legal services for free. But then Jo came on the line. "Hi, Val. What can I do for you?"

"Could you tell me how Seth Bell became your patient?"

"I thought you already knew—he came in through Corrections."

"That's not what the records from Corrections show."

"How strange. What do they show?"

"That you asked for him."

"I—" Jo was silent for a second. "I'm sorry, but I'm a little confused. I might have suggested Seth, but I'm certain he came in through the Corrections program."

"Why did you suggest him?" Val heard the irritation in her own voice and added, "Sorry, the other side is going to ask you tough questions about this, so we need to do it first."

"That's fine. You're testing my memory here, but I think I suggested Seth because he had an unusual diagnosis and he lived near my office. That would make him a natural fit for the program."

"What about Seth's diagnosis made it so unusual? And how did you know about him or his diagnosis?"

"I've got an appointment in a few minutes and I need to get ready. Could we talk about this later when I've had time to review the file? Please e-mail me any questions in advance, if you don't mind."

Val did mind, but there was nothing she could do. "That's fine. We'll be in touch."

She hung up and frowned at the phone. Jo's answers weren't particularly reassuring. Neither was her sudden need to get off the phone. If she really had an appointment she needed to get ready for, why had she taken the call?

Val glanced at the clock on her computer: 1:06. The call ended less than two minutes ago, so Jo must have had an appointment starting "a few minutes" after 1:04. How likely was that?

She picked up the phone and dialed again.

"Hello, Adrian Goff speaking."

"Hi, Dr. Goff. This is Val D'Abruzzo from Mike Webster's office."

"What can I do for you, Val?"

"I'd appreciate your professional opinion on a couple of questions."

"Of course. That's what you're paying me for. Fire away."

"Is schizophrenia combined with depression an unusual diagnosis, at least among mentally ill ex-cons?"

"Sadly, no. Those two conditions go together frequently, and both occur more often among current and former prisoners than in the general population."

As she suspected. "Thanks. Would it be hard to find depressed and schizophrenic ex-cons in Oakland?"

"I haven't done any demographic studies, but I think not. When I was in graduate school, I interned at a free clinic in Oakland. Many of our patients had criminal records, and I believe several suffered from both schizophrenia and depression. That was thirty years ago, however. Would you like me to look into the present makeup of the psychological-patient community in Oakland?"

Not at the rate he'd be billing while he did it. "No, thanks. One final question: Is it typical for therapists to start appointments at, say, ten minutes after the hour?"

He chuckled. "Not intentionally, though it is typical for psychologists to run late."

"But not to have appointments scheduled to start ten minutes after the hour, right?"

"That is correct."

"Thank you, Dr. Goff. You have been very helpful."

# CHAPTER 38

Mike wished he could deal with only one case at a time. Life would be so much easier. It would even be easier if he could limit it to just five cases. Instead, he had ten that were all active at the same time. Well, it was his own fault for biting off more than he could chew. He had delegated a lot to Camy and Brad, but there was still a lot left on his plate. For example, he couldn't assign them to handle a mandatory settlement conference when the judge had specifically ordered that "lead trial counsel shall attend." So he had spent the morning sitting in a conference room while a mediator fruitlessly tried to cajole him and defense counsel into settling a case their clients didn't want to settle.

Mike walked out of the mediator's office at quarter after one. As he got into his car, his phone chimed. He pulled it out and saw a text from Jo: `Have a few minutes to talk?`

He closed the car door and called her. "Hey, Jo. Got your text. What's up?"

"Thanks for calling so quickly. I was just wondering whether there was some sort of emergency in my case."

"No, not that I'm aware of. Why do you ask?"

"That's a relief. I got an odd call from Val a little while ago. She told my receptionist that she needed to talk to me, so I made time to take the call. Then she started grilling me about the details of how, when, and why Seth Bell became my patient. She seemed to think there was some urgent problem that we needed to talk about. She never explained what it was and I had to cut our call short, but it left me a little worried."

"I, um . . ." He paused, thoroughly confused. What the heck was Val doing? "Let me check with Val. She didn't say anything to me about this, and I'm a little surprised that she called you out of the blue. I'll talk with her and we'll sort this out."

"Thanks, Mike. I knew a quick call with you would clear things up."

"No problem. I've gotta go, but I'll call you later. Oh, and do you like Indian food? There's a curry place I'm thinking of for our dinner on Friday."

"I'll trust you. All of our dinners so far have been the highlight of my week."

"Mine too. See you soon."

"See you."

He spent the trip back to the office wondering how to handle the situation. His first instinct was to slap Val down hard. She had no business interrogating witnesses—let alone clients—without talking to him first. That was embarrassing at best and could cause serious problems at worst. What was she thinking?

He had a nasty suspicion that this wasn't about the case. It was about Jo. Val didn't like her, that much was obvious. She also didn't like the fact that Mike and Jo were getting close. Bringing that up—even hinting at it—was likely to hit a nerve with Val.

But he hadn't heard Val's side of the story. She could be a little direct and that might rub people the wrong way, but she generally knew what she was doing. And she had never given him any reason not to trust her judgment before this.

As he pulled into the parking lot, he decided to use as light a touch as possible. He needed to make sure this sort of thing didn't happen again, but he really didn't want this to blow up into a fight. He and Val had had a few fights early in their relationship, and none of them had ended quickly or easily. If Val felt she had been unjustly attacked or that he had wronged her and was refusing to apologize, she wouldn't let go of it. Ever.

So even if he were right about her dislike of Jo driving her actions, it would do no good to bring it up. Better to make this a purely professional issue—but still be firm.

Five minutes after Mike walked into the office, Val appeared in his doorway. "I need to talk to you about the Bell case. Do you have a few minutes?"

"Sure."

"Good." She closed the door, sat in one of his office chairs, and recounted what she'd found in the Corrections records and her calls with Jo and Dr. Goff. "So we need to get to the bottom of this. Tim Cromwell will destroy her in her depo if she doesn't have better answers by then. And I really don't like the fact that she wasn't being honest with us."

Mike sighed and rubbed his temples to ward off the headache he could feel coming. "Okay, first things first. You know better than to question witnesses without even giving me a heads-up, and that's especially true when the witness happens to be a client."

"I'm sorry, Mike." She didn't sound particularly sorry, but at least she wasn't arguing with him. Yet.

"You should have known that Jo would call me and that I'd be caught totally flat-footed. That wasn't fun, and it didn't make us look particularly competent."

She winced. "Sorry about that"—and this time she actually seemed apologetic. A hopeful sign.

"You also shouldn't be running our expert's clock without my okay. What's Goff's hourly rate?"

"Nine hundred an hour for consulting."

"And his minimum charge is half an hour. So you just cost me at least four hundred and fifty dollars. Don't do that without asking."

She nodded.

"Okay, now let's look at each of those quote-unquote lies. First, Jo said Bell had an unusual diagnosis, right? Did you check to see whether any of the other patients Corrections sent to her had the same diagnosis?"

Val sat up straight. "No, but Dr. Goff—"

He held up a hand. "You asked him about whether Bell's diagnosis was rare in the general population, not whether it was rare among Mind's Eye patients. But Jo was talking about Mind's Eye patients, not the general population.

"Second, you asked him whether there were likely ex-cons with Bell's diagnosis living in Oakland, but that doesn't contradict what Jo said. According to you, she said Seth Bell lived near her office. Was that false?"

"He lived in San Francisco, at least fifteen minutes from her office."

"So is it a lie to say he lived near her office?"

She looked down. "That depends on how you define 'near,' I guess."

"Precisely. And finally, Jo said she had an appointment 'in a few minutes,' which was suspicious because it was only a few minutes after one and therapists typically schedule their appointments on the hour or half hour. But what exactly does 'a few minutes' mean? Isn't it possible that Jo meant that she had an appointment at one thirty and needed twenty or twenty-five minutes to get ready for it?"

"Twenty or twenty-five isn't a few," Val objected.

"So what? She wasn't under oath. Have you never been slightly disingenuous when you're trying to get off the phone with someone who is being rude?"

Val's eyes flashed. "I wasn't being rude!"

"Think about it from Jo's perspective. Someone from her lawyer's office calls her out of the blue and says she needs to talk. Then that someone starts asking pointed questions about old paperwork. There's no emergency. The person on the other end of the line was just curious—and maybe suspicious. Some people might find that a little rude, no?"

"I was just doing my job."

"Well, in the future, check with me before doing this part of your job, okay? No more calling witnesses without getting my permission first."

She reddened and pressed her lips into an angry line. For a second, Mike thought the fight he had been hoping to avoid would start. But Val simply jerked a nod and walked out.

# CHAPTER 39

Jo's last patient left at five, and Shawn left at five thirty. Once he was gone, Jo got the office ready. She dimmed the lights in the therapy room, put some cool jazz on the office sound system, and checked the temperature of the bottle of chardonnay in her personal fridge. It was Mike's turn to bring wine, but it couldn't hurt to have a backup bottle in case he didn't.

Once she was satisfied with the office, she went to work on herself. She took her blazer off and hung it on her chair. Her hair clip came out and she dropped it in her purse. She went in the bathroom, touched up her makeup, and ran her fingers through her hair to get rid of the kinks that came from having it up all day.

She gave herself a critical appraisal in the bathroom mirror. The sapphire blouse set off her eyes, and the gold earrings went well with her blonde hair and light tan. Satisfied, she went back to her office and waited.

At six, the door buzzer sounded. She opened the door and Mike came in. She gave him a quick, ambiguous hug and took the bottle of wine he handed her.

"Great to see you," she said. "How was your week?"

He smiled, but she could see the stress in his face. "Wine first."

"That bad?" She went into the client meeting room and he followed. She retrieved a corkscrew and two glasses from the table and opened the bottle. It was a good sauvignon blanc, which he knew she preferred to chardonnay (his favorite type of white wine). *How thoughtful.* She poured a glass and handed it to him.

He took a sip. "Ah, much better."

"So, shall we talk about dinner or your week?" she asked as she poured herself a glass.

"My week actually wasn't that bad. It was a little busier than usual, but no big deal—particularly now that I'm able to sleep most nights, thanks to you."

"I'm glad I was able to help. Tonight I was thinking we might talk about how your job relates to your father."

His eyebrows went up. "My dad?"

"You love them both, but they both cause you stress. Did you ever wonder whether there might be a connection?"

"Between my job and Dad?" He paused and looked into the middle distance for a moment. "No, I don't think I did. But you're right that they do kind of make me feel the same."

"Do you have any idea why that might be?"

He took a slow sip from his glass, then shook his head. "Can't say that I do." He tapped his head. "But I'm guessing that it's all in here somewhere, waiting for you to find."

"Ready to go in the machine?"

He drained his glass and set it on the table. "Ready as I'll ever be."

She knew he still felt uneasy in the fMRI machine, but he never hesitated to go in. She wished all her patients were as willing to confront their fears.

Ten minutes later, he was in the machine and had slipped into a light trance.

"Okay, Mike," she said into the microphone, "let's talk about your father. Do you love him?"

"Yes." Mind's Eye showed he was telling the truth. She also caught a strain of underlying affection when he thought about his father.

"Do you respect him?"

"Yes." Also an honest answer.

"Did you want to be like him when you were growing up?"

"Yes." Still truthful, but with a hint of unease.

"Does the thought of being like him make you uncomfortable?"

"Yes." The unease flared strongly.

"Why is that?"

He was silent for a moment, but she could see his mind working hard. "Because . . . because he failed."

"How did he fail?"

"I'm not really sure. It just sort of happened. He used to have the church and Mom. He was happy, accomplishing a lot. And now he's alone in a studio apartment down in San Diego. It's really sad.

"And you know the worst part? He didn't do anything wrong. He wasn't embezzling from the church or cheating on Mom or drinking or anything like that. There's nothing you can point to and say, 'That's why this happened to him.'"

"Why is that the worst part?"

"Because it's so wrong, so unfair. He did everything right and then it all fell apart."

Jo studied the screen. It showed anger and honesty, but also something else lurking in the background—something that looked a lot like fear. He thought that his father's fate was unjust, but it also frightened him. *Why?*

"Did something about what happened scare you?"

He looked confused, and the display matched that. "Not really. Or at least not now. I'd love it if some greedy landlord or developer tried a stunt like that on me."

Jo frowned at the screen. Mike was telling the truth, but not all of it. Maybe he didn't know the whole truth. "Is there anything else you'd like to tell me about your father? Or anything that you wouldn't like to tell me, but that maybe you need to?"

He thought for a moment. "Nothing I can think of." Again, an honest answer—but she still saw something hiding in there. She couldn't put her finger on it, and apparently he couldn't either.

Jo decided to try a different angle. "You mentioned your mother. What happened to her?"

"She left," he said shortly. Mind's Eye showed anger, resentment, and hurt. The hypnosis was essentially gone, but he was relaxed and compliant, so she didn't worry about it for the moment.

"Please tell me what happened."

"I was away at school, so I don't know all the details, but I think she got frustrated with Dad after he lost the church. He used to be, you know, a pillar of the community, an important guy doing important work. But that was gone and then he was just a middle-aged man with some useless degrees and a dead-end job in the post office. She wanted him to find something better—or at least better paying—but he couldn't. So she got a job in sales. She was good at it, and pretty soon she was in management. Her company was headquartered in New York, so she traveled out there a lot. The trips got longer and longer. She rented a little apartment out there so she wouldn't have to live out of hotel rooms. That should have been a warning sign, of course. There were lots of warnings, but Dad didn't see them. He trusted her and he was happy for her success."

Jo heard the bitterness in his voice and saw it on the screen. "Then what happened?"

"She stopped coming back. She called Dad one day and told him that she wanted a divorce. She's been in New York ever since."

"How did that affect your father?"

"He put up a good front, but I know it hurt a lot. She didn't want to try reconciliation, which I think hit him particularly hard. He aged ten years in the month after she asked for a divorce. He never spoke badly of her, though."

"Do you think she's a bad person?"

"I think she's a person, so she's got good and bad in her. This was a bad episode, but she had lots of good ones. Even during the divorce, she wasn't all bad. She made more than Dad, so she sent him money for a while even though no one made her do it. She's human, like everyone else. We're all broken, and none of us can be completely trusted."

Jo could see the last line resonate powerfully in his mind. It was the lesson he had learned from his parents' divorce, and it had taken root deep into his soul. *How deep?*

"What's the longest relationship you've had with a woman?"

His tension level shot up. "Depends on what you mean. I've had a relationship with my mom for almost forty years."

She chuckled. "Let's exclude relatives."

"In that case . . . I don't know, maybe a couple of months."

She frowned at the screen and scrolled back through the last couple of minutes of Mind's Eye output. His defenses were up now. He wasn't lying, but he was hiding the truth in a thicket of carefully chosen words. "You've come out of the meditative state. Let's see if we can get you back into it."

"Does that mean I get another glass of wine?"

She smiled. "I'd have to take you out of the machine and then get you all set up again when you were done with your wine. We'd be late for dinner."

"Well, we can't do that. You should stock Mind's Eye 2.0 with those little airline bottles."

"Excellent idea." She changed the screen in the fMRI to the hypnosis sequence. "Okay, see the green circle?"

Five minutes later, he was back in a hypnotic state. "Do you remember when we were talking about relationships a few minutes ago?"

"Yes," he said, his voice even and colorless.

"You said that the longest relationship you'd had with a woman who wasn't a relative was a couple of months."

"Yes."

"What about Val D'Abruzzo?"

She watched the screen carefully as she mentioned Val's name. Mike's reaction was instant and . . . complicated. He had strong positive feelings toward Val, but they didn't fall into a clear category. There was also a surface strain of irritation, probably from a recent conflict—Jo could guess what caused that. And she thought she caught an overlay of repression, as if he didn't like to think about his relationship with Val too much.

"Oh, that's different," he said. "We've been together for ten years, but that's professional. We've never dated or anything."

That was mildly comforting, though the screen revealed more than a purely professional relationship. "Is it different?" Jo asked. "We were talking about relationships and trust, not romance. Can you trust Val in a way that you can't trust other people?"

He hesitated, and she could see the conflict going on in his head. "I never thought of it that way."

"Now that you're thinking of it that way, what *do* you think? Is Val really more trustworthy than the rest of the world?"

"I don't . . . I guess not. It's just that we've been together for a long time and she's never let me down."

"Like your mother never let your father down. Until she did. Everyone is human, even Val."

"Everyone is human," he repeated.

# CHAPTER 40

This was bad.

Five minutes ago, the managing director of Horizon Finance had walked into David's office and handed him a document. He said only three words: "Deal with this." Then he turned around and walked out. No instructions, no deadline, no description of the consequences of failure. None of that was necessary. A visit from the managing director bearing a physical document told David everything he needed to know.

The first part of the document was a report on visits to Horizon Finance's website. The site wasn't designed to *convey* information. Anyone who needed to know about Horizon learned through in-person meetings and word of mouth. Rather, the website was designed to *collect* information. The site was hard to find and had virtually no content. It was little more than an empty facade on an obscure side road of the information superhighway. Very few people found it by accident, and those who did never stayed for more than a second or two. Anyone who lingered or tried to poke around behind the facade was there because they were investigating Horizon. And that was something Horizon needed to know. To that end, Horizon had installed a very powerful tracking program behind the seemingly empty facade. Commercially available programs like Google Analytics could be spoofed or evaded by anyone with sufficient technical expertise. Horizon's program could not. One of their investors, a tech company affiliated with the Chinese military, had designed it, and it had never failed yet.

The traffic report that the managing director had just handed to David had several redacted entries—even David wasn't entitled to know everything—and one unredacted entry showing three separate visits last Tuesday by someone from the Law Offices of Michael Webster. One of those visits had included attempts to find hidden directories and pages.

The second part of the report the managing director had handed David showed search-engine traffic targeting Horizon. Horizon couldn't monitor all traffic on all engines, but they could install cookies on all but the most secure computers. Once a computer had a cookie on it, Horizon could follow its searches. And it turned out that whoever had visited their site from Mike Webster's office had then gone to the SEC, Morningstar, Bloomberg, and a number of investor chat rooms and forums.

Worryingly, several searches probed connections between Senator Bell and Horizon. Following that trail, David did some searching of his own—and discovered Bell's Form 700.

David stared at the form in stunned fury. *How could Bell have been so incredibly stupid?* His first instinct was to put a contract on Bell. The brainless senator would die what would appear to be an accidental death, and David wouldn't have to worry about him again. All the better if it was a painful death.

But then David's instinctual self-discipline kicked in. He forced himself to look at the situation rationally. Without Bell, Horizon's chances of getting Mind's Eye were reduced. Horizon's agreement with Bell might not be enforceable in court, which probably wasn't a problem while Bell was alive because David had extrajudicial leverage over Bell—but he wouldn't have that leverage over Bell's estate. Further, if Bell's wife had even the slightest suspicion that Horizon Finance or

David Klein bore any responsibility for her husband's death, she might not react well.

Also, after thinking about Bell's actions for a few minutes, David had to admit that they weren't quite as stupid as he first thought—at least not from Bell's perspective. Bell was a politician and thought like one. One of the easiest ways for him to get into trouble was to fail to disclose money that he got from a lobbyist or business. Based on his conversation with David, Bell could easily have concluded that David was a lobbyist or some other type of political operative. He almost certainly had no idea what David really was. So publicly disclosing his deal with David was the prudent thing to do based on what Bell knew and who he was. If anyone had acted stupidly, it was David—a fact that would not escape the managing director if David wasn't able to control the situation.

David got up and paced, trying not to think about what could happen if things went wrong. Much better to work on a plan to make things go right.

He dialed Eric's extension. "Eric, our timetable has moved up. I need your plan for dealing with the Webster firm by the end of the day."

# CHAPTER 41

Val and Angy sat outside Val's favorite bakery, drinking coffee and munching enormous cookies that were so good they almost justified the amount of time she'd have to spend in the gym working them off. Angy was off duty today and dressed in jeans and a ratty old Mets sweatshirt. He'd dressed in essentially the same outfit whenever possible since he was ten years old, and it was easy to look at him and see nothing more than a twentysomething guy who was dressed like a vagrant and loafing on a weekday. In most cities, a casual observer would assume he was unemployed. In San Francisco, most people probably figured that he was a semiretired tech millionaire. He certainly got better restaurant service dressed like this than when he was wearing his off-the-rack suit—he called it his "cop suit," since cops were the only ones in the Bay Area who wore cheap suits and always kept their jackets on (to conceal their guns).

"Any luck finding those expunged criminal records we talked about last month?" Val asked.

"Not yet, but there are still plenty of rocks to turn over. I'll let you know." Angy took a sip of his coffee. "Any luck freein' up time in your schedule to go out with one of my Catholic friends?"

"Not yet. I'll let you know." Val suspected that her brother hadn't been looking too hard for Seth Bell's records, but she decided to take his hint and drop the subject. For now. "So, how's work treating you?"

He shrugged. "Good, I guess." He broke a piece off his cookie and popped it in his mouth. "Kinda boring, to tell the truth," he said around the bite of cookie.

"Why's that? I thought you liked investigating financial crime."

He swallowed. "I do, but the feds grab all the good cases. I'm thinkin' of joinin' the FBI just so I can work on somethin' bigger than crooked payday lenders."

Val gave him what she hoped was a mysterious smile. "I am."

"You are what?"

"Working on something bigger than a crooked payday lender."

Angy's thick black eyebrows went up. "Really? I thought Mike only did med-mal and personal injury and stuff like that."

"Yeah, but there's some sort of financial firm pulling strings in one of our cases. Mike has me investigating. I'm guessing they're dirty. Really interesting stuff."

"Huh." He held up his cup for a refill. The server hurried over with a fresh pot less than five seconds later. When she was gone, he turned back to Val. "So, tell me about this interestin' case you're investigatin'."

Val hid her excitement. Horizon Finance was proving to be a tough challenge. They managed to keep everything useful about themselves locked down, and she was having a hard time picking those locks. Angy had tools she didn't, so getting him interested could be a big help. "Sure. There's a company that I think paid the other side in a lawsuit we're working on."

"Paid them for what?"

"To drive our client into bankruptcy. The client has some technology that these guys would like to get, so they're trying to push up our client's legal bills. Also, her financiers cut her off, and we think these guys might have been behind that too."

"Extortion?"

Val shrugged nonchalantly. "Could be. That's one thing I'm looking at. There's other stuff too. Like I said, an interesting case. Tough to find anything on these guys, though."

"I'm not surprised. Sophisticated financial criminals try not to leave a trail. There's an old sayin' on Wall Street: 'Never write what you can say. Never say what you can nod. Never nod what you can wink.' The smart ones live by that."

"What about all those smoking-gun e-mails and texts I read about in the *Wall Street Journal*?"

"Those are the stupid ones. Here's a not-so-old sayin': 'E-mail is forever.' The smart ones know that. Don't count on your guys sendin' moronic e-mails to each other. Still . . ." He stroked his beard thoughtfully. "How much money are we talkin' about? How big are these guys?"

"That's one of the things I haven't been able to find," Val said. "I'll bet they're big, though. They seem to be sort of a private-equity fund for foreign bad guys."

She could see his interest level go up.

"Where are they?" he asked.

"They're in San Francisco, so you'd have jurisdiction."

"What's their name?"

"Horizon Finance, LLC."

He froze for a second, then looked down into his coffee cup for several seconds. "Thanks."

*That was interesting.* "You're already looking at them, right? What for?"

"No comment, and I really mean that." He fidgeted with his cup. "Sorry. I can't talk, but if you find anythin' that's, you know, interestin', I'd appreciate it if you passed it along. Maybe we can help each other without talkin', you know?"

# CHAPTER 42

*April*

Mike waited in the gallery of Department 301, Judge Charlotte Spink's courtroom. They had been single-assigned to Judge Spink, so she would be handling everything in their case from now on, including Mike's request to force Senator Bell to sit for another deposition. She would also hear Tim Cromwell's competing motion to require Jo to turn over the Mind's Eye hard drive. Tim had filed his motion the day after Mike filed his and set it for hearing on the same day and time Mike had chosen. That was not a coincidence, of course. Faced with a discovery dispute, most judges sought a compromise, even if one side was clearly right—a practice known in the legal community as "splitting the baby." So Tim had given Judge Spink something to compromise on.

Mike had arrived early to see whether Judge Spink appeared to be in a compromising mood. Fortunately, she didn't. He watched as she dispatched the three motions scheduled in front of his with quick, decisive rulings—all of which sounded right to his ear. *Good.*

"Estate of Bell v. Anderson," the clerk called.

Mike and Tim stepped up and stood on either side of the lectern.

"All right," the judge said. "The defendant's motion was filed first, so let's handle that one first. I am inclined to order the deposition to go forward, but deny sanctions—this time. But if the deponent walks out again, it will cost him. Any argument, Counsel?"

"Not from me, Your Honor," Mike said.

Tim cleared his throat. "If I might have a moment, Your Honor."

"Of course."

"Senator Bell will appear for his continued deposition, but we ask that the court grant a protective order preventing further abusive questioning."

"If you want a protective order, file a motion asking for one. And to prevent unnecessary motion practice, let me tell you that I didn't see anything abusive in the transcript of Mr. Webster's questioning. Aggressive, yes, but not abusive. He's entitled to be aggressive. Anything else?"

Tim shook his head. "Not on this motion, Your Honor." He didn't seem particularly upset or surprised by Judge Spink's negative response to his impromptu motion for a protective order. He was probably just putting on a show so he could tell Senator Bell that he had tried.

Judge Spink nodded. "Okay, next up we have the plaintiff's motion to compel. I'm inclined to grant this one too."

That was an unpleasant surprise. "Your Honor, the plaintiff has made no showing that there is any information about Seth Bell contained on that hard drive that hasn't been produced," Mike objected. "This is nothing more than a fishing expedition."

"And we've got a big one on the line," Tim Cromwell replied, holding up a magazine article. "In this article, Dr. Johanna Anderson says that the Mind's Eye system 'automatically records every session,' so where are the recordings of Seth Bell's sessions? We have some of them, but not the later ones. We are entitled to those."

"As I explained to Mr. Cromwell, the hard drive was full," Mike responded. "As a result, some sessions weren't recorded."

"And we are entitled to test that explanation," Tim Cromwell retorted. "The only way to do that is by examining the hard drive to determine whether it has any additional records related to Seth Bell—or whether there's evidence that such records were destroyed."

"The problem is—" Mike began, but the judge raised her hand.

"All of this was in your briefs," Judge Spink said. "I read them. Do you have anything to add?"

"Your Honor, that hard drive is packed with confidential patient information and other material that is protected by law," Mike said. "It cannot simply be turned over to the plaintiff. At the very least, it should only go to a neutral third party for review. Moreover, Dr. Anderson needs that drive to treat patients, so it should also be copied first. The copy would go to the expert."

"That sounds reasonable to me." The judge turned to Tim. "Counsel?"

"So long as the third party is acceptable to my client, and Dr. Anderson bears the cost, plaintiff agrees."

"The plaintiff is the one that brought this motion," Mike retorted. "They should bear the cost."

"The cost will be split equally between the parties," Judge Spink said. "Unless either of you objects, that is."

"Plaintiff does not object," Tim said instantly.

Mike still couldn't believe she had granted Tim's motion, and wanted to object, but he knew it would be counterproductive. "No objection, Your Honor."

# CHAPTER 43

David Klein watched his screen, waiting until Senator Bell had left his office. Bell had bought a new cell phone after the first time David called him, a Blackphone loaded with security. Getting the number and GPS tracking data for that had been expensive and difficult, but worth the money and effort. Calling Bell on his ultra-encrypted new toy would send a useful message.

But was it the right message?

David drummed his fingers spasmodically on his desk. Eric's plan wasn't great, but David hadn't been able to think of anything better. Several other options had higher odds of success, but they had far higher costs if they failed. Eric's idea, on the other hand, had much less in the way of downside risk.

The dot representing Bell moved, heading to the capitol parking garage.

"Elvis has left the building," David muttered to himself. He waited until Bell was in his car and driving out of the garage. Then he dialed.

Bell must have had a pretty good idea who was calling even though his phone would only show a string of zeroes. He probably didn't want to talk to David, but he was smart enough to answer. "Hello?"

"Senator Bell, you listed our payment to you on your Form 700. That was a mistake."

"I had no choice," Bell said. "The law is quite clear, I—"

"It was a mistake," David repeated. "Don't make any more mistakes."

"Such as?" Bell asked warily.

"For one, no more disclosures about your relationship with us."

"What about the lawyers' bills? You're making me the middleman for paying those, and that will show up if anyone ever looks at my finances, which does happen from time to time."

That actually was not a bad point. "All right, instruct Cromwell to send all future bills to P.O. Box 9896 in San Francisco, 94105. Are there any other potential leaks we need to resolve?"

"No, there are no other problems I can think of," Bell said.

"If you think of any in the future, you will also need to think of solutions. We will not tolerate another leak." David kept his voice even and calm, with just a slight emphasis on the word "not."

"Okay. I need to get to a meeting, so if there's nothing else, I—"

"You are sitting in your car, driving down L Street toward your condo. Anyone you are meeting there can wait while we finish talking."

The line was silent for several seconds while Bell absorbed the fact that Horizon Finance could still track him. David smiled.

"What else do we have to talk about?" Bell asked.

"Your deposition," David replied. "We understand that you have been ordered to go back for a second session. Is that correct?"

"Yes."

"Thanks to your foolish disclosures on your Form 700, we expect that you will be asked about your relationship with Horizon Finance."

"I wouldn't say we have a relationship," Bell said. "We've had one business transaction, but that's all."

"Excellent answer. Now here's how you're going to answer the other questions you're likely to get about Horizon Finance." David took a deep breath and relayed Eric's script.

*This had better work.*

# CHAPTER 44

Mike stood next to Jo on the bow of a ferry heading to Alcatraz. She had commented during their last dinner that she had lived in the Bay Area her entire life but had never gone to any of the tourist spots. So Mike was taking her on a tour of the Rock. When they got back, he would treat her to chowder in a sourdough bowl at the Boudin Bakery. Then they'd finish the evening with sundaes at Ghirardelli Square. He had a gift-wrapped cable-car pencil sharpener in his pocket to give her as a memento.

A chilly, wet breeze blew in their faces. Mike felt Jo shiver beside him. He glanced back at the enclosed area of the boat, where the other tourists sat or stood. "Do you want to go inside?"

"No, I'm fine. I like the view better out here."

He took off his jacket and draped it around her shoulders. She started to object, but he said, "I'm also fine, and I'm wearing more layers than you are. You tourists often don't realize how cold it is on the Bay."

She smiled and pulled the jacket around her. She looked somehow different in it—small and vulnerable. Mike felt a sudden surge of protectiveness. He wished he could put his arm around her and draw her in to warm her.

She caught his eye. "Penny for your thoughts."

"Doesn't the money usually go the other way with psychologists?"

Her smile widened, but she said nothing.

"I was just thinking about how you're different right now from the way I usually see you. When we're at your office, you're an in-charge professional. When we go out to dinner at one of my favorite restaurants, you're the elegant lady who waiters remember the next time I eat there alone. But right now you're just a tourist who forgot her coat."

She rolled her eyes. "I must look charming."

"You do." It was true. She was always beautiful, no matter what she wore, but "charming" didn't really apply to her usual look. Polished, sophisticated, impressive—those applied. When he'd seen her in the past, she always looked like she was on her way to an embassy dinner or a C-level meeting. Now she stood in front of him, shivering in a borrowed jacket and trying to keep the breeze from blowing her hair into her face—and she looked charming.

She squeezed his arm. "You're sweet."

"Just honest." He paused. "You know, we've talked a lot about my relationships, but not yours. So if you don't mind me asking, why are you single?"

"Bad luck, I suppose."

He looked at her, askance. "I have trouble believing that. Let's try one of the questions you asked me—and if you don't give me a straight answer, I'll have to feed you wine and stick you in a machine."

She laughed. "Sounds terrible. What's the question?"

"What's the longest relationship you've had with a man? And no, relatives don't count."

"Not even husbands?"

He blinked. "You were married?" he asked stupidly.

Her face grew serious. "I was, a long time ago. We met in college at UCLA and got married after we graduated." She sighed and shook her head. "We were children and we acted like it. I'd prefer not to go into the gory details—and believe me, every failed marriage has gory details, even the ones where people manage to be friends afterward."

"Did you manage to be friends?"

"No."

She was silent for so long that he thought she must have decided the topic was closed. Then she said, "It was ugly and no one was completely innocent. It tore me apart. I almost dropped out of my PhD program because I thought I couldn't help other people with their lives if mine was such a mess."

"I'm glad you didn't."

She squeezed his arm again and left her hand on it. "Thanks."

"What kept you going?"

"I told my mentor that I was thinking of quitting, and he talked me out of it. He told me an old joke: What's the definition of psychology?"

Mike shrugged. "I give up."

"Two crazy people talk to each other and one of them gets better."

He laughed. "I'd hardly call you crazy."

"Wait until you know me better." She smiled mischievously and winked at him, then grew serious. "His point was that you don't have to be problem-free to treat other people's problems. Damaged people can help other damaged people. That spoke to me. I buried myself in my studies and internships. I worked or studied every waking hour—not that I had much choice."

"And here you are, helping damaged people."

"Trying to, anyway."

They stood in silence for a moment, watching the island approach. The fortresslike prison loomed toward them out of the middle of the Bay, foreboding and beautiful at the same time.

"You never quite answered my question," Mike said. "Was your marriage your longest relationship?"

She nodded. "We were together for three years and two months, including the time we dated."

"How about since then?"

She took a deep breath and blew it out. "To be honest, I haven't had any real relationships since then. With anyone. My parents died while I was in grad school, and my only sister died a long time before that. I have patients and I have work, and that's been about it." She glanced up at him with a small, ironic smile on her face. "I'm with people all day long, but I'm really alone."

They had reached the island, and before he could respond to Jo, the crowd surged around them, carrying them ashore. Then came a guided tour of the prison with anecdotes about some of its more colorful occupants. The rest of the group listened attentively, and a few filmed the tour with their phones. Others took selfies in Al Capone's cell.

It really was an interesting and entertaining tour, but Mike only paid attention intermittently. His real focus was on the woman by his side.

What was she to him? Client, therapist, friend, and more. How much more? He wasn't sure what the answer was, but the question scared him—and thrilled him. He felt like he was standing at the top of a cliff, getting ready to jump off. Cold black water lay below him, but maybe he could fly.

He looked over at Jo. She stood listening to the tour guide, wearing his jacket, alone in the crowd. Except for him.

# Chapter 45

*May*

Val had mixed feelings. She had just finished reading the report from Kjeldaas Consulting, the neutral third-party expert who reviewed the copy of the Mind's Eye hard drive. Jo was the firm's client, so Val was at least theoretically pleased and relieved that Kjeldaas found no evidence that Jo had destroyed data or withheld files relating to Seth Bell. But Kjeldaas said nothing about whether Jo's story held water. Val still needed to know that.

She walked into Mike's office. "Got a minute?"

"Sure." He waved at a guest chair. "What's up?"

"Did you read K—, Kje—, uh, the computer guy's report?"

He nodded. "Nice to see Tim's evidence-spoliation argument go down in flames."

"Yeah. This guy sure seems to know his stuff, huh?"

"He does."

"Not too expensive either."

"No." Mike cocked his head. "Why? Do you want to hire him for something else?"

"I was just thinking—he already has the hard drive, and we never got an expert opinion on the drive being full."

"What do you mean?"

"Remember Jo's explanation for why some of Seth Bell's sessions didn't get recorded? She said the hard drive must have been full. We should check that out. Maybe we could hire this guy to do it."

Mike shook his head. "His contract is with us and Tim jointly. He'd have to send his report to both of us."

"So hire him under a new contract."

"Then he wouldn't really be neutral anymore, would he? If we have to call him at trial to talk about his report, the first question he'll get on cross-examination will be 'Isn't it true that Dr. Anderson is paying you to testify here today?'"

"No, because she's not paying for anything," Val retorted, then instantly regretted it. She needed Mike to see this as tying off a loose end in their case, not her pursuing a vendetta against Jo.

He sighed. "We've been over this. The asset search you ordered made it pretty clear that she can't pay our bills without selling everything she and her company own."

It was true. Val had argued that Jo should at least pay something, but Mike had shot her down. Rehashing that wouldn't accomplish anything.

"I was just kidding," she said. "I see your point about what would happen on cross. So should we hire a different expert? I got a couple of referrals from Angy. They're reasonable and they look pretty good."

"Angy is great and I'm sure his referrals are too, but we don't need another expert, particularly since—as you pointed out—we'll be paying the bills ourselves. Let's wait and see whether Tim raises the hard-drive thing. If he does, we can revisit this, okay?"

She kicked herself for that snarky remark about Jo. "Okay."

She got up and went back to her office. The mail had arrived while she was talking to Mike, and it sat in a bin on the floor beside her desk.

On the top was a small package from Kjeldaas Consulting. She opened it. It contained the copy of the Mind's Eye hard drive and a note from Mr. Kjeldaas saying he was returning it to Jo's attorneys now that his assignment was complete.

Val held the hard drive, looking at it and tapping it slowly with a perfect red nail. Mike would expect her to send it to Jo or have it wiped. But if she did that, she'd never be able to test Jo's story.

She shut her door, searched her e-mail for a phone number, and dialed.

"Hello, Hutchinson Holdings," a woman's voice said. "How can I help you?"

"I'd like to speak to Edward Hutchinson, please. Angelo D'Abruzzo referred me."

# CHAPTER 46

*June*

Senator Bell sat across the table in Mike's conference room. He wore a navy-blue suit, a striped red tie, and a look of dignified disdain.

Once they were on the record, Mike gave him a genial smile. "Welcome back, Senator Bell. You realize that you're still under oath?"

"Yes."

Bell probably expected Mike to pick up where he had left off, but that wouldn't accomplish much. Mike didn't really care what Bell had to say about the articles discussing Seth's alleged abandonment by his family. Bell's tantrum last time spoke louder than any canned answer he might be prepped to give now. Better to rattle him again.

Mike held out his hand to Camy, and she gave him four copies of Bell's Form 700. "Senator Bell, why did Horizon Finance pay you and your wife one hundred thousand dollars?"

If Bell was surprised, he gave no sign. "The answer to that question is confidential."

Tim Cromwell leaned forward. "We're designating this portion of the deposition confidential under the protective order. Go ahead, Senator."

Bell nodded. "Horizon Finance paid us a license fee for certain intellectual property."

"What property?"

"As I mentioned last time, Seth was involved with computers. He came up with an idea for a game. My wife and I licensed that idea to Horizon Finance."

Mike frowned. "Why would a finance company want to buy an idea for a computer game?"

Senator Bell shrugged. "You'd have to ask them that. I believe that they have an interest in a company that develops computer games."

That was hardly unusual for a Bay Area private-equity firm. Still, Mike wasn't convinced. "Tell me about the game."

"Seth called it 'House.' At the beginning, players would answer a questionnaire about what they feared most, loved most, and so on. Then the game would create a haunted house where the players would face their worst fears and fight to save what they loved most. At the end, it would be revealed that the house was really their own mind."

That sounded like the plot of *Rooms*, a book Mike had read a few years ago. "You're sure Seth invented this game? He didn't get the idea from somewhere else?"

"I don't know where he got it from. All I know is that Horizon Finance wanted to buy it."

"How did you find out about this game?"

"Seth told me about it. Then, after he died, we found his notes in his apartment."

"Okay. How did you learn that Horizon Finance might be interested?"

Bell hesitated for a moment, then said, "I mentioned it to some people who work in Silicon Valley. One of them must have mentioned it to someone at the company Horizon has an interest in—or maybe one of them worked for that company. I don't remember exactly."

"Do you remember generally?"

"Not beyond what I just told you."

"Who were these people you talked to about the game?"

"I just said I don't remember."

Mike arched his eyebrows. "You don't remember any of them?"

"Not at the moment, no." Bell turned to Tim. "I'm not a lawyer, but it seems to me that we're getting pretty far afield."

Tim nodded. "What bearing does this have on the case, Mike?"

"Well, for one thing, it goes to damages. You're claiming lost income from Seth's allegedly bright future as a programmer. I'm entitled to test your evidence on that point."

"We won't use this transaction as evidence of Seth Bell's earning capacity," Tim responded. "Senator Bell signed an NDA with Horizon Finance, so we can't."

Mike turned to Bell. "Is that true?"

"It is."

"Who signed the NDA for Horizon?"

"I believe the name on the signature line is David Klein. I also believe he is one of their directors."

Mike turned back to Tim. "You'll stipulate to exclude all evidence regarding the sale of House to Horizon Finance?"

Tim nodded. "Yes. With that stipulation, are we done with this line of questioning?"

Mike thought for a moment. "Almost. Senator Bell, is Horizon Finance paying your legal bills in this case?"

That question finally rattled Bell. He froze and flushed. "Why does that matter?"

"Just answer the question."

Bell licked his lips. "No. No, they're not."

Tim stirred in his seat and looked uncomfortable, but said nothing.

"Are you sure about that, Senator?" Mike asked. "Remember that you're under oath."

Bell's face darkened further. "Yes, I'm sure."

Mike looked at him in silence. Faced with a lull in conversation— even a conversation as unnatural as a deposition—most people will talk compulsively. But Bell just stared defiantly back at Mike.

After half a minute, Mike gave up and moved on to another topic, but he put an asterisk in his outline next to the section about Horizon Finance and wrote "FOLLOW UP."

# Chapter 47

Val's desk phone rang. She pushed the speakerphone button. "Hello, Val D'Abruzzo."

"Good morning, Miss D'Abruzzo. This is Edward Hutchinson. Would now be a good time to discuss my evaluation of the hard drive you sent me?"

Val snatched up the receiver, taking Hutchinson off the speaker. "Sure, now is good. What did you find?"

"You had asked whether the hard drive was full, so that a program that automatically saved data to the hard drive wouldn't save because there was no space."

"Yes, and?"

"The hard drive isn't full—but I can't tell whether it was on the dates you gave me for the missing videos and data files. There are a lot of deleted files and file fragments, which makes it look like someone did clear space on the hard drive at least once."

So Jo had been telling the truth—or at least there was no way to tell whether she hadn't. "Okay. Thanks for the fast turnaround on this project. Please send me your invoice and a short report—an e-mail is fine."

"I'll do that today. But there are a couple of other things you might want to know."

"Oh? What?"

"First, the software logs all activity, which is a pretty typical feature. When something goes wrong, the programmer needs to be able to pull up a record of everything that happened. Any attempted video and data saves would have been logged. There were no attempted saves on the days you gave me."

Val's ears perked up. "I was told that the program automatically saved video and data from each session. Are you saying that's not the case?"

"No, it does—if the automatic-save feature is activated. That's the second thing I thought you would want to know. The program also logs when the autosave feature is activated and deactivated. Someone deactivated the autosave feature for a few hours on each of the days you asked about."

# Chapter 48

Mike was tired when he walked out of the Bell depo. He had slept well last night, but the depo had been a grueling experience. Bell had fought him on every point, and, aside from the question about Horizon Finance paying Tim's bills, Mike got very little useful testimony out of him.

He walked back to his office, looking forward to a little mental downtime clearing out his e-mail and surfing news sites on the net. Instead, Val popped out of her office as he reached his door. There was a fierce look in her eyes that told him he wouldn't be getting any downtime for a while.

"Mike, we have to talk."

He sighed. "Sure, come on in."

She followed him into his office and closed the door behind her. She didn't sit down.

"You know how the video and data files are missing for six of Seth Bell's twelve sessions?"

So she was still fixated on that. He suppressed a groan. "Yeah, because the hard drive was full. We've been over this."

"No. They're missing because Jo turned off the autosave feature in Mind's Eye. She intentionally didn't save those sessions."

His mental exhaustion started to blossom into a headache. "That makes no sense. Why would she do that?"

Val folded her arms. "We'd better ask her, dontcha think? And if she doesn't have a really, really good answer, I don't see how we can keep representing her."

"That's my call, not yours," he snapped. "I'll ask her about it, but before I do that, I need to know more. For example, how did you find this out?"

"I had an expert look at the Mind's Eye hard drive," she said, looking down at him defiantly.

Irritation added to the building pain of his headache. "The expert report said nothing about the autosave being turned off."

"Not the report from that neutral expert with the weird name," she said impatiently. "They were only hired to answer a couple of questions, remember? I'll bet they never even looked at the autosave thing."

"So who did?"

"A guy named Edward Hutchinson."

"Who's he?"

"An expert I hired."

Mike did his best to hold back the anger burning in his chest. "When exactly did I authorize you to hire him?"

She lifted her chin. "You didn't. I said *I* hired him, not the firm. If you want me to pay his bill, that's your decision."

He could hardly believe his ears. "Wait, you hired an expert on your own dime? You're that invested in destroying Jo? I'm starting to seriously question your judgment."

"And I'm starting to seriously question yours!" she fired back. "I hired this guy because we needed to and I knew you wouldn't do it. You can't bear to hear anything bad about your precious Jo."

He felt like someone was driving ice picks into his temples. He closed his eyes and rubbed them in silence for a moment. Then he took a deep breath and opened his eyes.

"In light of our friendship and your long years of service, I'm going to overlook that outburst," he said, keeping his voice calm with effort. "All cases have bad facts. If they didn't, no one would ever litigate. I don't need you going out and digging up more. So please stop. All you're doing is building Tim Cromwell's case for him."

Her eyes flamed. "No, all I'm doing is trying to find out the truth! That used to matter to you. You used to care about justice, not just winning."

Before he could reply, she turned and stormed out.

# Chapter 49

Val sat in her office, staring at her computer screen without seeing it. It had been an hour since she walked out of Mike's office, but she hadn't calmed down. If anything, she was more upset. And worried.

Mike wasn't acting like himself. At all. His judgment really was off, at least when it came to this case. Maybe it was just that Jo had him wrapped around her little finger—but that was also not like him. Val had known him for ten years, and she had seen plenty of women—lots of them better than Jo Anderson—try to land him. But Mike Webster had a Teflon heart—the harder a girl tried to attach herself to it, the faster she'd slide off. And then there were those severe headaches he had been getting recently.

So what was going on? Having been involved in hundreds of medical-malpractice cases, Val had no trouble thinking of worst-case scenarios. A brain tumor was an obvious one—those often led to headaches, personality changes, and impaired judgment. An aneurysm like the one that killed David Lee could produce at least some of the same symptoms. So could brain injuries, and she was pretty sure she'd read that some diseases could too.

Or was it possible that Mind's Eye was causing Mike's headaches? It was a new technology, and it did focus on the brain.

She was Googling whether fMRI scans could cause brain cancer when Mike knocked on her door.

"Got a minute?" he asked.

"Of course," she replied, turning away from her monitor.

He took a seat. She noticed that he had left the door open, which surprised her a little. Was he sure that everything they were about to say could be shared with the whole office?

"During the depo, I asked Bell about the Horizon Finance thing. He spun out a story about the money being for some computer game that Seth developed. He stuck to it during the depo, but I don't completely buy it. I'd like to send a subpoena to Horizon. Could you draft something that asks for all records they have about this case or Seth Bell? Make sure to include a request for any bills from Masters & Cromwell and any record that they've been paying those bills."

So he wasn't going to try to clear the air? He was just going to pretend they'd never fought?

"Okay, I'll get you a draft by the end of the day." She jotted a note to herself. "Is there, uh, anything else you'd like to talk about?"

He looked very tired. "Not particularly."

He started to get up, but she said, "Just a minute."

She walked around her desk and shut the door. She stood still for a second, praying that she would get this right. Mike's life could depend on it. She turned to face him, leaning against the door.

He eyed her with wary surprise, then cleared his throat. "I'm not going to make you pay that Hutchinson guy's bill. I know you were just trying to help."

"Thanks, but that's not what I want to talk about." She paused, choosing her words carefully. "Mike, I'm worried about you. You've been having some pretty bad headaches recently, haven't you?"

"I have."

"Well, remember what happened to David Lee?"

"Of course, but he had other symptoms. I just have headaches."

She hesitated. Should she mention his personality changes and judgment issues? No, too risky. She wasn't fast or diplomatic enough to do that without saying something that was likely to trigger another fight. In fact, he knew her well enough to guess what was causing her hesitation, and she could see him starting to react.

"But you've never had headaches like this," she rushed out. "I mean, have you? I don't remember it."

He paused for a heartbeat, looking her in the eyes. "Maybe not."

She released the door handle, which she realized she had been holding in a death grip. "Could you see a doctor about it?"

A brief look of annoyance flashed across his face, but then he gave her a half smile. "If it'll make you happy, sure. I'm set to have my regular MRI on Friday, and I'll ask the doctor if she sees anything unusual."

"Jo's not a neurologist."

"If she's not qualified, I'm sure she'll give me a referral."

"What if Mind's Eye is causing your headaches?"

"How?"

"I don't know—but a neurologist might."

"I'll ask Jo about it. If there's a risk, I'm sure she'll tell me."

"But I—" she began to protest, but stopped when she saw the warning in his face. "I'll get to work on that subpoena."

"Good." He got up and she reluctantly opened the door.

He paused before walking through and smiled at her. "Thanks for looking out for me."

She smiled back. "Sorry, I can't help myself."

# Chapter 50

*July*

When the news came, David was deep in the financials of a potential junk-bond investment. It looked like a good prospect. The company held valuable oil rights in the Dakotas, but it had overextended itself during the fracking boom and it went belly-up when oil prices plunged. The company's credit rating dropped from A to CCC, driving up its borrowing costs and putting further financial pressure on it. It defaulted on its bonds and went bankrupt. That's where it was right now. The owners were trying to put together a reorganization plan that would allow them to keep their bloated payroll. But if Horizon could get enough of the bond voting rights, they could crush the owners, fire the workers, and sell the oil rights to—

A man cleared his throat loudly.

David whirled around to see the managing director sitting in one of his guest chairs, his left ankle on his right knee. He was a small, lithe man who could have been anywhere from fifty to seventy. He moved with unnatural silence when he wanted to, and rumor had it that he had been an assassin in his youth—before he discovered that finance was equally suited to his gifts and personality, but better paying and less dangerous.

He tossed a document on David's desk. "This was just hand delivered to our office." The managing director spoke with a faint and unidentifiable continental European accent, though he went by the unlikely name of Bill Johnson.

David looked down at the document. It was a subpoena from the Law Offices of Michael Webster. His heart and brain shuddered to a stop. "I'll . . . I'll take care of this, Mr. Johnson," he forced out.

"That's what you told me last time," the managing director observed with unnerving calm, "and yet the problem was not taken care of."

"We'll do better this time."

"I'm sure you will. I will be personally supervising this project from now on."

That was a disturbing development. "What . . . what would you like Eric and me to do?"

"You will develop a plan that both terminates Mr. Webster's efforts to obtain information from or about the firm and ensures that we obtain Mind's Eye at a cost of no more than thirty million dollars. You will present this plan to me one week from today."

"Yes, Mr. Johnson."

The managing director rose with fluid grace and walked out without another word.

David didn't move for twenty minutes, his mind entirely absorbed by the problem in front of him. He considered and rejected a dozen possible solutions before settling on a plan. The first step was simple—almost crude—but relatively likely to succeed.

He summoned Eric. "I need you to come up with a plan to kill Mike Webster. Present me with three proposals within forty-eight hours."

"Yes, Mr. Klein."

# CHAPTER 51

"So, what should we talk about tonight?" Jo asked.

Mike looked into his glass and swirled his wine absently, then leaned back into the cloudlike cushions on Jo's sofa. "Let's start with something easy: headaches."

Jo tilted her head slightly to the side. "Headaches?"

"I've been getting them a lot recently. Bad ones. Val noticed and was worried, so I thought I'd mention it to you. Have you seen anything unusual in any of our sessions?"

"No. I haven't been looking, but I think I would have noticed something big enough to cause headaches. I'll check tonight, but I wouldn't worry. There are lots of things that can cause headaches—a minor change in diet, a new chemical your office cleaner is using, even the fact that your sleep habits have changed for the better."

"Can Mind's Eye cause headaches?"

"It never has before, and I can't see why it would."

"Thanks."

"If you're worried, I can give you the names of some good neurologists, though you'll need to go through your GP to make sure your insurance covers the visit."

"That would be great, thanks. Just to be safe."

"Of course. I'll send you an e-mail. It was good of Val to suggest that you talk to me." Jo paused. "Has she expressed concern about anything else?"

Mike took a slow sip from his wineglass while Jo watched him expectantly. "Now that you mention it, she has. According to Val, it looks like the autosave function on Mind's Eye might have been turned off for some of Seth Bell's sessions."

Jo stared at him in surprise for a moment, then frowned. "That's odd. Why does Val say that?"

Mike felt a familiar throbbing start between his temples. "We got the copied hard drive back from that neutral expert, and Val had another expert look at it. He said the autosave had been turned off during Seth Bell's later sessions. That's why there's no video or data files for them." He paused. "By the way, I'm getting another one of those headaches. It's right in here." He pointed to the bridge of his nose. "Right behind my eyes."

She looked at him with concern. "I'm sorry to hear. Want some Tylenol?"

"Thanks, I would."

She disappeared into her office and came back a few minutes later with a small bottle of Tylenol, which she handed to him. He gulped down two pills and handed it back.

"Thanks," he said. "So, any thoughts on what Val said?"

"Well, I can assure you that I didn't turn off the autosave feature—but that doesn't mean it didn't get turned off. The software is very buggy. I sometimes think my programmer puts in bugs just so he can bill to fix them. I wouldn't be at all surprised if there was some glitch that randomly turned autosave off and on. This isn't the first time I've lost sessions. I just assumed the hard drive was full—which is another recurring problem." She sighed and took a sip of her wine. "The joys of running a biotech startup. Did Val say anything specific that I could pass along to my programmer?"

"She didn't, but . . . um, I might not have given her a chance. I'll ask her about it."

Jo smiled wryly. "We're lucky to have Val diligently checking our case for weak spots."

The sofa was very comfortable, but Mike squirmed. "Yeah. Listen, I'm sorry about that. She's terrific, but she can be a little stubborn and she has strong opinions."

"Including about me," Jo observed with a smile.

Mike's face heated, and he was grateful for the dim lighting. "I've talked to her, and I can assure you that—"

Jo reached over and put a hand on his thigh. "It's not your fault, Mike. It's not even really hers. Think about her situation."

"I'm, uh, not sure what you mean."

"How long have you been with Val?"

"Ten and a half years. We celebrated our anniversary a couple of weeks before I met you."

"Your anniversary," Jo repeated. "You're close, yes?"

"I guess so."

"You're not just professional colleagues, you're friends. Am I right?"

"You are." He wanted to say more but wasn't quite sure what.

She leaned her chin on her fist, looking at him silently for a few seconds. "Did it ever occur to you that Val might think your relationship was special?"

"We . . . Well, I guess maybe it is special in a way—but we're just friends," he hastened to add.

"But you're close friends. Friends who celebrate anniversaries."

"That was only a work anniversary. We . . ." His voice trailed off as he remembered taking Val out to dinner that night. They exchanged gifts and drank a bottle of very good champagne over the course of the evening. Val had toasted "the ten best years of my life," and he had returned the sentiment.

"Okay, I guess we are pretty close," he admitted.

"And now you and I are becoming close. Can you see how that might feel threatening to her, even if you two are 'just friends'—and how she might react to that threat?"

In truth, he would've preferred not to see it. But he knew it was there. Val hadn't liked Jo from the start, and her dislike had only grown stronger as Mike and Jo became closer. Val was jealous, and it was getting to be a real problem. It was affecting Val's judgment to the point where he wasn't sure he could trust her on this case.

He sighed. "Everyone is human."

# CHAPTER 52

*August*

Mike went over his notes one more time before heading to court. Horizon Finance had responded to Mike's subpoena with a slew of objections. They admitted having documents related to Seth Bell's alleged computer game, but argued that they didn't have to produce those. They claimed they had nothing related to *Estate of Bell v. Anderson*.

"We're sure the Bells can't be paying Tim Cromwell's bills on their own?" he asked Val.

She nodded firmly. "Not without selling stocks or homes, which they're not doing. I've been over their finances half a dozen times. Either Tim is doing this for free or someone else is paying him."

"He's not doing it for free," Mike replied. "He told me that flat out, and I don't see any reason why he'd lie." He frowned in thought for a moment. "And we're sure Horizon Finance must be doing it?"

She held up a manicured hand and waggled it equivocally. "Sure? Not really. But I can't think of any other alternatives."

That would have to do. He looked at his watch. Time to leave. "So, are you coming down to the courthouse to watch the festivities?"

She looked away. "Um, sorry, I can't. I've got plans for lunch, and I need to leave by eleven thirty."

"What plans?" he asked in surprise. She was dressed up, and he had assumed it was because she was going to court with him. Apparently not.

"I'm having lunch with a friend of Angy's at the Tadich Grill. We're meeting at eleven forty-five and I don't want to be late. Sorry."

Mike sighed heavily and looked at the floor. "I'm deeply hurt that you won't be in court today, but have fun. At least he's taking you someplace nice."

"I really am sorry," she said anxiously. "Do you want me to try to reschedule?"

"No, no. I'm kidding." He grinned broadly to show that he meant it. "Seriously, enjoy yourself."

She still looked uneasy. "Are you sure?"

"One hundred percent sure. Okay, maybe ninety-nine percent. Camy will be there, so there wouldn't be anything for you to do except watch and pray that I don't screw up."

"I can do that while I'm eating my salad," she said with a relieved smile. "And if you do screw up, I won't have to see it."

"See? This lunch date is a win-win," he replied as he stuffed his notes and the briefs into his briefcase.

"I do pray for you whenever you're in court."

Mike looked up from his packing. She was watching him with a tentative, almost shy smile. He realized that she was reassuring him. She was about to go out on a date rather than come to court with him, and she wanted to make sure he knew that she still cared about him.

He smiled back. "I know. Why do you think we always win?"

He slung his bag over his shoulder and headed to court.

◆　◆　◆

"Estate of Bell v. Anderson," Judge Spink's clerk announced.

Mike took his place at the defense-side table, with Camy beside him. Horizon Finance's lawyers were at the plaintiff table this time because they were opposing Mike's motion. Interestingly—and encouragingly—Tim Cromwell wasn't sitting with them. He was in the middle of the front row of seats, distancing himself from Horizon physically—and possibly from their legal position as well.

The judge nodded to Mike. "Go ahead, Mr. Webster. As usual, I've read the papers, so no need to repeat what's in them."

Mike stood and stepped up to the lectern. "Thank you, Your Honor. We are cognizant that third parties like Horizon Finance have reduced discovery burdens, but that doesn't mean they have none. Horizon is refusing to produce a single document in response to our subpoena."

"Because they claim they have no discoverable documents," the judge observed. "They say that everything they have relates to this computer game, and all of that is confidential trade secrets." She looked at Horizon Finance's lawyers. "Isn't that correct?"

Their lead lawyer, a gray-haired eminence from Bay Area silk-stocking firm Dana & Enersen, half stood. "It is, Your Honor."

Judge Spink turned back to Mike. "Why should I order that produced?"

"I don't believe that's all they have, Your Honor."

Her white eyebrows went up. "Really? What else do you think they have?"

Mike decided to gamble. "Well, for starters, I believe they have bills and possibly correspondence from Masters & Cromwell, which represents the plaintiff in this case. That all needs to be either produced or described in a privilege log."

Horizon Finance's lawyer got to his feet. "That's simply untrue, Your Honor. As stated in my client's subpoena response, they have no documents related to this litigation."

Mike glanced back at Tim Cromwell, who looked like he had just swallowed a mouthful of lemon juice. "Mr. Cromwell is here, Your Honor. Let's ask him."

The judge looked at Tim. "Counsel?"

Tim got to his feet with obvious reluctance. "Mr. Webster is correct, Your Honor. Horizon Finance has been receiving and paying our bills for several months. They also have received a number of e-mails and other correspondence regarding this case."

Mike resisted the urge to pump his fist in the air. He had gambled on two things: his ability to read Tim's body language and Tim's honesty. Both gambles had paid off.

The judge turned back to Horizon Finance's lawyers, storm clouds gathering on her grandmotherly face. "Counsel, this sounds directly contrary to what you just told me. Please explain."

Mike stepped away from the lectern and the Dana & Enersen lawyer took his place. "It is contrary, Your Honor," he admitted. "There must have been some miscommunication between my client and me. We'll get to the bottom of this as quickly as we can."

"You'd better," responded Judge Spink. "In the meantime, I'm granting the motion to compel. The parties are to meet and confer regarding the mechanics and timing of the production. And to avoid any future 'miscommunications,' I'm going to warn you now that if there are more problems, I will be open to the appointment of a special master with authority to inspect Horizon Finance's records personally."

She stood and the clerk said, "Court is adjourned."

As Mike walked out, he texted Val: Nicely prayed.

# CHAPTER 53

Congrats! Val texted back. Tell me about it this p.m.

She put down her phone and smiled apologetically. "Sorry, my boss texted."

"I understand," Ryan Daley said with a smile. He had a nice smile. It went well with his nice face and nice personality. He worked with Angy on the financial-crimes team, so he was probably pretty smart too.

When she'd finally run out of excuses and agreed to a blind date with one of Angy's friends, Val had dreaded what he'd send her way. His single friends tended to be single for good reasons. So Val set the date for lunch on a workday. That meant it could go no longer than an hour, she wouldn't have to be alone with her date, and he wouldn't try to slow dance with her.

But then Angy set her up with Ryan. His Facebook page seemed surprisingly normal and his pictures were suspiciously good looking. Val had steeled herself for a guy with WMD-strength halitosis or an unintelligible stutter, but Ryan had neither. So what was wrong with him? Half an hour into their lunch, she hadn't discovered the answer to that question.

Not that Val was actually interested in him. She wasn't really looking for a guy at the moment. Even if she were, she wouldn't start a relationship with a guy she had met under maternal duress. That would only encourage Mama. She could almost hear her mother's voice twenty years from now: "You really should listen to me, Valeria. Remember how you wouldn't listen to me about men for years? And then at last you listened, and what happened? You finally got married. So you should listen to me when I say . . ."

Val shivered.

With an effort, she refocused her mind on the here and now—and discovered that Ryan had just asked her a question. Something about favorite movies. That could mean he was fishing for a second date, so she answered carefully. "I mostly like classic movies—stuff with Humphrey Bogart, Spencer Tracy, and Lauren Bacall."

"Oh, then you'd probably like this film festival too." He paused, and she was afraid he was about to ask her to go to it with him. What should she say? She started frantically scrambling for an excuse, kicking herself for not having listened to his question more carefully. But instead of asking her to go with him, he said, "Would you like me to send you a link to their website?"

Wait—he wasn't asking her on a second date? Come to think of it, he hadn't seemed particularly interested in her so far. He had been friendly and polite, but he hadn't said or done anything indicating romantic intentions. She wasn't interested in him, but that was supposed to be a one-way street. She was a little hurt—and confused—to find that he seemed to feel the same way. She was back down to 120 pounds, which meant she could fit comfortably into her regular wardrobe, and she had turned enough heads on the way to lunch to know that she looked good in the outfit she had picked.

"That would be great," she said, flashing her best smile.

They spent the next half hour arguing and agreeing about movies. Then they moved on to TV shows, followed by music. Before Val knew it, it was one thirty.

"Whoa, I need to get back to the office!" she exclaimed when she realized what time it was.

"Go ahead, I'll take care of the bill," Ryan said, reaching for his wallet.

"Thanks. I had a great time. I'm glad we met and got to know each other."

"Me too." He looked as though he was about to say something more, but stopped.

"What is it?"

He took a deep breath and blew it out slowly, looking down at his empty plate as he did so. He appeared to reach a decision and looked up again. "Okay, I'll be straight with you. You deserve it. I just hope you won't be mad." He looked away again. "You're great and I really am glad we met, but . . . well, I'm actually interested in someone else. But the thing is, she's not Catholic. My parents really didn't like that, and they kept bugging me to at least get to know some Catholic girls before things get too serious. I knew Angy was Catholic and he said he had a sister, so I—What?"

Val couldn't stop laughing. "I'm sorry," she gasped. "I . . . I'm gonna absolutely kill Angy."

"What? Why?"

She told him the story, and soon they were both laughing. Then they spent several minutes trading entertaining but unworkable ideas for vengeance on one Angelo D'Abruzzo.

Val said, "Listen, it really has been great, but I do need to head back to work."

Ryan nodded and gave her a warm smile. "Me too. I'm glad we got that thing cleared up. I hope we run into each other again. Let's stay in touch."

"We have to," Val replied. "We still haven't figured out what to do about Angy."

# CHAPTER 54

*October*

Jo looked at the Mind's Eye monitor, trying to decide what to do next. Mike's face looked back at her, relaxed and slightly vacant. This was the part of the session where she usually tried to explore the root causes of his anxiety, but she had made no progress in the last half dozen sessions.

She decided to change gears. "Mike, let's talk about your father, about what happened to him. I think something about that scares you. Do you know what it is?"

He was silent for a long moment, staring at the camera with glassy eyes, but the Mind's Eye display showed something rising to the surface of his consciousness. "Failing," he said at last.

A glance at the display told her that she was close. "What do you mean?"

His mental wheels turned for several seconds. "He failed, so I'm afraid I will too."

"Why does his failure mean that you might fail?"

"Because . . . because he was such a good man, better than me, but he failed anyway. He didn't do anything wrong, but he failed anyway."

"Good people sometimes fail," Jo observed. "They make mistakes or things just don't work out. What was different about your father's fate?"

"He did everything right. He worked hard, he was a great pastor, he married a good woman and treated her well. And everything fell apart anyway."

Now she understood. Finally, after months of digging around in his mind, she had found the root of his anxiety. "Are you afraid the same thing will happen to you?"

"Yes."

"Do you have this fear often?"

"Always. It's there in the back of my head all the time. Whenever we have a big win, I wonder whether it's the last one. Will I lose a couple of cases and see my business pipeline go dry? Or will some judge who's in the defense lawyer's pocket try to get me disbarred because I bent some little rule?"

"Does that sort of thing happen often?" Jo asked.

"It happens," he replied. "Plaintiffs' attorneys who are too effective make enemies. Sometimes those enemies manage to take them down for bending a rule here or there—ticky-tack little stuff that isn't wrong and that everyone does. But these guys get hit with a sledgehammer for no reason other than that they sued and beat the wrong people. They lose their licenses, maybe even go to jail. Google Bill Lerach and you'll see what I mean."

He was becoming animated as he talked, rising out of his hypnotic state. Rather than break the flow to put him back under more fully, Jo decided to press ahead. Besides, if he came out of hypnosis now, he'd probably remember their conversation fairly clearly, which could be beneficial. "Tell me more about the fear. What are you afraid will happen?"

"That I'll wind up where Dad is now, just with more money." He drew a ragged breath. "I'll be old and alone somewhere, sitting on a park bench and wondering where it all went wrong."

"Is that what your father is doing?"

"I guess so."

"When is the last time you talked to him?"

"I called him on his birthday last month."

"How long did you talk?"

He thought for a moment. "I don't know. Maybe five minutes."

"When was the last time you *really* talked? You know, sat together for an hour or two talking over dinner or went for a long walk together?"

He shifted uncomfortably in the fMRI machine, sending jagged spikes through the sensor outputs, but Jo didn't want to distract him by telling him to hold still. "Maybe ten years," he said. "I helped him move out of that apartment in Oakland and we talked some then."

"Why haven't you talked since then?"

"I'm afraid to talk to him," Mike said. His eyes glistened as he spoke. "He was so defeated when he left for San Diego. I can't bear the thought of seeing him like that. I looked up to him so much. I admired him more than anyone, and then . . ." His voice wavered and he broke off. He closed his eyes and two tears ran down his temples. He swallowed and took a deep breath. "I guess I'm terrified of seeing what he has become."

"And what you're afraid you might become," Jo said softly.

He nodded.

It was time to gamble everything. Heart pounding, Jo got up and ran into the fMRI room. She pushed the button that slid out the bed Mike lay on. When he emerged, she grabbed him in a tight hug. He hugged her back fiercely.

"You'll never have to be alone," she whispered in his ear.

He kissed her.

# CHAPTER 55

Mike sat behind his desk, staring at his phone. He had pulled his dad's number up from his contact list. Now he sat there, looking at it. It looked back at him, challenging him to call. He wanted to, but what would he say? He couldn't imagine a conversation much different from the same one they'd had five or six times a year for the past decade:

*How are you doing, Dad?*

*Can't complain, Mike. How about you?*

*Everything is good up here. Happy birthday / Merry Christmas / Happy Easter / etc.*

*Thanks, Mike. Same to you. I hope you're having a great day.*

*I am, thanks. Say, I've got to get going, but it's good to talk to you.*

*Likewise, son. Thanks for calling.*

*Bye.*

*Bye.*

What exactly would that accomplish?

He sighed and put his phone away. He needed to do a lot of thinking—soul searching, really—before he dialed that number. And that was something he simply didn't have time for. He'd do it after Jo's case was over. Trial was only a month away. Maybe he would take a couple of weeks off and go down to San Diego. He and Dad could have those dinners and long walks Jo was hinting at last night.

But for now, all of his mental energy and time were sucked into trial prep. True to his promise, Tim Cromwell had showered Mike and Jo with document requests, subpoenas, and deposition notices. Responding to it all—even in the most minimal fashion possible—took all of Camy's time and most of Mike's. Even Brad had gotten roped into helping fight running skirmishes with Tim's minions over privilege logs, production of metadata, and other discovery friction points. It was good experience for Brad, who had been too junior to get much time in court until now, but it meant that there was essentially no one to handle the other cases in the office. That meant unhappy clients and reduced firm income, neither of which was healthy for the Law Offices of Michael Webster. In an ominous sign, the firm had suffered operating losses for the last three months in a row—the first time that had ever happened. Even with Jo's help, Mike was having trouble sleeping again.

Jo . . .

That was something else Mike needed to do some soul searching about. He had never had a serious romantic relationship in his life. To be honest, he didn't really know how something like that was supposed to work. He'd had lots of unserious romantic relationships, of course. He had the two-month fling down to a science. But he went into each of those with the knowledge that they'd run their course in a season or less. They would follow their natural arc, from the nonthreatening first date to the effervescent long weekend to the bittersweet-but-sensitive breakup. But what happened if there was no arc? If he and the woman he was with were seriously considering spending their lives together? How did that work?

He remembered his parents' relationship during their good years. They'd seemed to love and care for each other, but they always had full lives—overfull, really. Mom was always at the center of a whirlwind, with ten things going on at once. Dad was in his study working on a sermon or meeting with the elders or out leading a mission or something. Maybe their early years together had been full of candlelight, wine, soft jazz, long dinners in cozy little restaurants, passionate kisses atop the Eiffel Tower at night, and walks along the beach at dawn. But Mike doubted it.

Maybe their marriage broke up because they didn't know how to be together when they weren't doing something. Or maybe that wasn't what happened—but it didn't really matter, because Mike had no interest in a union like that. At least not now. Maybe in ten or fifteen years he'd want what amounted to little more than a permanent female roommate, but not yet.

So what did he want from Jo? What did she want from him? Where was this supposed to go? He didn't know what he was supposed to do next. Sweep her away for a surprise weekend in Italy or Hawaii, like he had done for past girlfriends? Or go to the other extreme and apologize for kissing her and keep their relationship just on the platonic side of the line—at least until the case was over? Or something in the middle?

All he knew was that he couldn't imagine a future without her—which had never happened to him before. But the thought of maybe marrying her someday still filled him with deep unease. Why? Because of what had happened to his parents? Or something else?

He felt the warning signs of a migraine and sighed. Time to stop chasing his tail over this. All he was doing was giving himself a headache and wasting time he didn't have. Blowing off Jo's case so he could think about her was probably not the best way to her heart.

He turned around and picked up a fat three-ring binder from the floor. It held the depo prep materials Camy had put together for the next big deposition—which happened to be Jo's. She was the last major witness to be deposed because her depo had been delayed while the Kjeldaas firm examined her hard drive and issued their report.

Camy had put together a good binder. It included every excerpt from other depos that mentioned Jo, the Kjeldaas report, and every other document that was likely to be an exhibit at Jo's depo. For good measure, she had also run an Accurint report and several media searches. All told, a nice, thorough set of prep materials—but one that would take most of the day and evening to plow through before Jo came in for a dry run tomorrow. Oh, well. He probably wouldn't have slept much tonight anyway.

# CHAPTER 56

By the fifth hour of Jo's depo, Mike could feel his attention slipping. That was good news and bad news. It was good news because it meant that Jo was doing well. Mike always cautioned witnesses to listen carefully to each question and answer only what was asked. Don't volunteer anything. Don't help the questioner by answering the question he should have asked, but didn't quite. Don't let your answers get careless or chatty.

Jo was doing all of that. Her training as a psychologist probably helped. As she'd pointed out during their prep session yesterday, she had been taught to be a professional listener. Most people naturally focus on what they want to say in a conversation, not what the other person is saying. They tend to pick up certain words or phrases in what the other person says and then unconsciously fill in the rest—which is one reason two people can have very different recollections of the same conversation. But a psychologist needs to be able to consistently focus on what a patient is saying, then respond appropriately.

Whatever the reason, Tim Cromwell hadn't laid a glove on her all day. She parried all of his questions with ease. Better still, there had been no surprises. Camy had done her work well, and Tim hadn't shown Jo a single exhibit that they hadn't talked about while prepping. He made a mental note to send Camy a nice e-mail. Or maybe something more. She'd been working awfully hard and—

What was that?

He tried to pick up the thread of Tim's questioning. Something about ethics violations. He looked down at the live raw-transcript feed on the laptop in front of him, filled with typos and abbreviations:

Q. Are you aware that Psychs are govd by eth-ics rules?

Yes, of course.

Q. Is that true even for Psych studs?

I'm not sure. Its been some time since I was a stud.

Q. Well, when you were a Psych stud, were you govd by ethics rules?

I dont remember.

Q. Really? Do you remember that you were accd of violating Psych ethics rules as a stud?

No.

Q. [Exhibit 18 marked]

Mike looked up from the screen in time to take a document handed to him by Tim Cromwell's associate. It was titled "Findings of Disciplinary Commission."

Before Mike could read more, Tim said, "Does this refresh your recollection that you were accused of—and found guilty of—violating ethical rules while you were a psychology student?"

Tim's tone was carefully neutral, but Mike recognized the light in his eyes. Tim had just sprung his trap, and he thought he had caught Jo in it.

Jo looked at the document for a long moment, but didn't open it. "No."

Tim's mouth and eyebrows quirked in surprise. "But you have seen this document before, correct?"

"Yes." Jo's voice was low and tight.

"All right. Please turn to the last page and read the paragraph titled 'Conclusions.'"

"Aloud?"

"Yes."

Jo flipped to the end of the document, and Mike did the same with his copy. Then she read, "'The Commission concludes that Professor Burnside and Johanna Anderson both violated the University's Code of Conduct. They both violated Rule 3.12 by engaging in an inappropriate physical relationship. They both violated Rule 4.1 by failing to disclose this relationship to the head of the Psychology Department. They both violated Rule 7.2 by making false and misleading statements to the Commission during its investigation into this matter. Professor Burnside violated Rule 1.2 by granting preferential treatment to Johanna Anderson. Johanna Anderson violated Rule 1.3 by knowingly accepting such preferential treatment. The Commission recommends that Professor Burnside be suspended without pay for one year and that he be permanently barred from one-on-one contact with female students. The Commission further recommends that Johanna Anderson be removed from the University within the next six months.'"

Mike's head was spinning and pounding by the time she finished reading. How could this possibly be the same woman he'd come to know?

"Thank you, Dr. Anderson," Tim said. "Were you married at the time of the events described in Exhibit Eighteen?"

"I was."

"And was Professor Burnside also married?"

"I . . . I believe so."

"And you don't consider any of that unethical?"

"Objection." Mike paused, fighting through the red haze of pain that filled his head. "Vague and ambiguous. Misstates the witness's earlier testimony."

Jo took the hint. "That's right. Your earlier questions asked whether I had been accused of violating the ethics rules governing psychologists. I haven't. This"—she gestured to the disciplinary-commission findings—"had to do with whether a personal mistake I made broke the rules at the university where I was studying at the time. Those are very different. That's like me accusing you of violating the rules of legal ethics because you were caught shoplifting in law school."

"What you did was a little more serious than shoplifting, don't you think?"

"I made a mistake in my personal life over a decade ago," Jo replied, agitation in her voice. "I regret it deeply and the consequences were very painful—but it had nothing to do with Seth Bell, Mind's Eye, or this case." She turned to Mike. "Do I need to keep talking about this?"

"I object to this line of questioning. What is the relevance of—" He winced as a jag of pain shot through his head.

"Off the record," Tim said to the court reporter. "Mike, are you okay?"

"Sorry. I've got a nasty headache. Can we take a short break?"

"Of course," Tim said. "Five minutes?"

"Sure, thanks."

Mike stood and walked out of the room, followed by Camy and Jo. In the hallway, he stared at the floor, willing the pulsing pain in his head to ebb. They'd changed the carpet since he worked at Masters & Cromwell. The new one was hideous, and he wondered who had picked it. Old John Masters had always been colorblind and he now had glaucoma too, but he had always insisted on making office-decor decisions. Maybe he was responsible for this one.

"How are you feeling, Mike?" Camy asked. "Do you want me to take over, or should we reschedule the rest of the depo?"

Mike took a deep breath and looked up. Oddly, meditating on the horrific carpet had made his head feel a little better. "No, I'll be fine. Let's go back in."

He felt Jo's eyes on him, but he didn't meet her gaze. He couldn't. The thought that this woman—whom he had been on the cusp of falling in love with—did something like that . . . His stomach roiled. But now was not the time to try to sort this out. There was a deposition to finish.

He kept his eyes straight in front of him and strode back into the conference room.

# CHAPTER 57

Jo sleepwalked through her appointments the next day. She had three routine evaluations, which she handled on autopilot. She jotted down a few notes, but she was so distracted that she knew they were worthless and didn't even bother trying to write them up. She would need to go back and analyze the Mind's Eye recordings later, when she could focus.

She couldn't take her mind off her deposition yesterday. Or, more accurately, the ten minutes of the deposition spent on that old disciplinary report from her grad-school days. The rest of the deposition had gone according to the script she and Mike had worked out during her prep, but that ten minutes disturbed her deeply for two reasons. First, where had that report come from? She hadn't given it to Mike, so how did the other side get it? Not the university—schools were very protective of student and faculty disciplinary records. Professor Burnside? Unlikely. He had done everything he could to move on, including switching schools and wives. He would want to revisit this episode even less than she did. The only other copy she knew of was in a file cabinet in her office with the rest of her academic and licensing records.

The only thing more disturbing about the episode had been Mike's reaction to it. He hadn't even been willing to look at her. Worse, his microexpressions and body language strongly communicated disgust and shock. All of her hard work with him was on the verge of crumbling away.

After her last appointment, Jo retreated to her office to think. But she made the mistake of checking her e-mail first. It contained a message from Mike's senior associate, Camy Tang. Camy had forwarded the pretrial disclosures she and Mike had received from Tim Cromwell earlier in the day, which included a list of the witnesses Cromwell planned to have testify at trial. Shaun's name was on that list, which struck Camy as odd because Cromwell had never taken Shaun's deposition. Camy wanted to interview Shaun as soon as possible.

Jo could hear Shaun working in the fMRI room, getting it ready for the next day's slate of appointments. "Shaun," she called. "Could you come here for a minute?"

A few seconds later he appeared in her door, filling nearly the entire door frame.

"Shaun, you know that lawsuit involving Seth Bell's death? The other side's lawyers have listed you as a witness, so our lawyers would like to talk to you."

He shifted his weight from foot to foot. "Uh, okay."

Something in his manner was off. She turned her full attention to him. "Shaun, do you know why the other side would list you as a witness?"

He shrugged meaty shoulders. "Because I work here, I guess?"

He was lying.

Fear gripped her heart in a fist of ice. She could hardly breathe. She stared at him in silence for several seconds, and his face began to grow wary. "Is that the only reason?" she forced out at last.

"Uh, yeah," he said, edging back out of the door.

Sudden realization hit her. She had a spy in her office. "Shaun, did you send them copies of things you found in my files?"

"No." Lying again.

"For example, did you go into my personal files, find my school records, and send those to the people who are suing me?"

He shook his head in denial, but everything else about him was open admission.

"What else did you give them?"

"I . . . I didn't give them anything," he lied.

Fear and shock gave way to desperation-tinged anger. "Shaun, I just realized that you've worked here for almost a year, but we've never treated you to a Mind's Eye session. What do you say we give it a try?"

To her satisfaction, she saw a gleam of fear in his eyes. "Right now?"

"Sure, why not?" she said with false brightness. "It'll be fun!"

"Uh, I don't know." He took a step back. "I've got a lot of work to finish up and then I have to go. I've got plans."

Jo stood up and walked toward him. "This will only take a few minutes."

Despite the fact that he was more than twice her size, he continued to back away, hunching his shoulders slightly. "Sorry, maybe tomorrow."

She stopped and folded her arms. "Shaun, you have two choices. Either go into Mind's Eye now or lose your job."

He stared at her for several seconds, his mouth slightly open. Then he pulled himself fully erect. "I quit."

# CHAPTER 58

To Val's relief, Mike finally saw a neurologist two days after Jo's depo. The doctors Jo had recommended were outside the network covered by the firm's insurer, but Dr. Goff knew a good neurologist who was in-network. And since Mike was complaining of acute symptoms, she saw him on an emergency basis.

His appointment had been first thing in the morning, and he showed up at work shortly before noon. He headed into his office, and Val followed him in.

"Well?" she said.

He turned and grinned. "Well, I don't have a tumor or aneurysm— or at least not one big enough to be obvious in a quick read of an MRI. And if a tumor or aneurysm were causing my headaches, it would almost certainly be obvious."

Val felt tension go out of her shoulders. "That's great news."

He nodded. "Yeah, I was pretty happy to hear it. Dr. Lay is going to run some blood work and take a closer look at the MRI scans, but she's pretty confident."

"So what's the problem?"

He shrugged. "She's not sure. She doesn't think it has anything to do with Mind's Eye, but she was interested to hear that the headaches started a couple of weeks after I started seeing Jo. She's going to talk to Dr. Goff about it before my next appointment."

Val resisted the urge to make a snippy remark about Jo not needing a machine to cause headaches. "Anything she can do for you in the meantime?"

"She gave me a prescription for some painkillers, but that's it."

"Maybe you should try working on something else for a while. You mostly get headaches when you work on this case, right?"

He thought for a moment. "Now that you mention it, I guess that's true." He slung his coat onto one of his guest chairs. "Not that it's an option right now. I can't really stop working on Jo's case three weeks before trial."

"Is something about the case stressing you out?" *Or someone, particularly after her depo.*

"Oh, yeah."

"What?"

"Horizon Finance. Those guys are utter sleazeballs. Remember how Tim sandbagged us with that school-discipline report at Jo's depo? Well, we just found out where he got it. Camy talked to Jo while I was at the doctor, and it turns out that Jo's nurse was stealing documents. He quit when she confronted him last night."

Val stared in disbelief. "I can't believe Tim would pull a stunt like that! He could lose his license, couldn't he?"

Mike nodded. "I called him on the way in. He denied knowing anything about it. He said he got the report and some other documents from Horizon Finance. They told him that they got it all legally. He said he'll produce a copy of it to us."

"Do you believe him?"

"He sounded believable." He hesitated for a heartbeat. "Frankly, I *want* to believe him."

"Me too," Val replied. Tim had taken a chance by hiring her when she was a nineteen-year-old with no legal or secretarial experience, and he had always been nice to her when she was at Masters & Cromwell. She didn't like the idea that he might be engaging in this sort of conduct to win a case. It wasn't like him. Or at least she hoped it wasn't.

"But whether I believe him or not," he continued, "I'll bet Horizon is involved. Combine that with the fact that they're paying Tim's bills and lying about it, and I think they're the puppet masters pulling Tim's and the Bells' strings. And I'll bet that what we know so far is only the tip of the iceberg."

"I agree. We're gonna crush 'em in front of Judge Spink."

"I think we should do more than that."

"What do you mean?"

"You told me Angy wanted us to let him know if we found anything on Horizon. Well, we have."

"I'll pass it along to him."

"I'd like to meet with him too. I'd like to sit down with him and Jo so we can explain what's going on."

Val hesitated. "I don't know, Mike. Angy doesn't like it when lawyers try to leverage his investigations to help them in a private case."

"It won't be like that, I promise," Mike said. "It'll be just a free interview with a couple of witnesses—one of whom happens to be a crime victim—plus some free evidence. That's all."

"If that's all, shouldn't we just send him what we've got and say that you and Jo are available for interviews?"

"Well, I would like to see how he reacts," Mike admitted, "and maybe we can talk him into sharing a little about his case against Horizon."

"Which is exactly the type of thing he hates," Val retorted. "I really do think you're pushing a little too hard here."

"Oh, come on. I'll take him out to lunch wherever he wants, and I promise not to push. Okay?"

A free lunch would go a long way with Angy. "Okay, I'll ask. No promises, though. He's my little brother, and he has spent his entire life not listening to me. I think it's a point of pride for him."

"Hey, Val," Angy's voice said from her speakerphone.

"Hey, Ang. How's it going?"

"Good, good. Can't complain. How about you?"

"Oh, I could most definitely complain."

"Really? 'Bout what?"

"I think you know."

"And why d'you think that?" he asked.

"Tell me you had no idea that Ryan was only taking me to lunch because his mother wanted him to go on a date with a Catholic girl."

He laughed. "I'm many things, Val, but I'm not a liar."

"Yeah, you are many things. Want a list?"

"Ryan already gave me one. Can't believe he kisses his mother with that mouth. Guess I didn't set you up with a nice Catholic boy after all." He started laughing again. "Man, I wish I coulda been there to see you two figure it out. Musta been classic."

She couldn't help smiling at the memory. "Maybe, but you owe me one."

"Maybe," he said warily. "Why? D'you got somethin' in mind?"

"Just lunch. You pick the place, Mike foots the bill."

"So why is that me doin' you a favor?"

"Because Mike wants to talk to you about Horizon Finance. It'll be a two-way street, though. He's got some evidence and a victim for you to interview."

Angy groaned. "You know I can't talk about active investigations."

"So just tell him that nicely a few times while you eat free food and listen to what he has to say."

"I dunno, Val."

"Would you rather I find another way to make us even?"

"Okay, fine. Brenda's on Friday?"

"Deal."

# CHAPTER 59

Mike parked in the Civic Center garage, a cavernous subterranean parking lot located under the little park that served as a front lawn for San Francisco's ostentatious neoclassical City Hall, complete with gilded faux-Renaissance dome. The park's other sides were bordered by the California Supreme Court, the Asian Art Museum, and the Bill Graham (*no, not Billy Graham,* as locals often had to inform visitors) Civic Auditorium. The park was also kitty-corner from the San Francisco Superior Court, and a block from the federal courthouse and the San Francisco Opera and Symphony buildings.

However, the little park also sat on the edge of the Tenderloin, San Francisco's poorest and most crime-ridden neighborhood. A scattering of prostitutes and drug dealers, tired from a long night's work, lounged on the park's benches. Junkies and homeless people slept on the grass and surrounding sidewalks.

The three-block walk from the parking-lot entrance to Brenda's was therefore a walk through San Francisco society. Gray-haired pillars of the bar in two-thousand-dollar suits rubbed elbows with government lawyers in khakis and Kirkland shirts. Elegant society ladies and their tuxedoed husbands strolled up red carpets during rush hour on their way to charity events at the museum or opera, while the working classes streamed past on their way to their cars or trains. Streetwalkers threw come-hither looks or flashed leg at FBI agents in somber suits, then laughed. On one occasion, Mike had simultaneously stepped over a passed-out drunk and greeted a Supreme Court justice.

Brenda's didn't take reservations, so they put in their names and waited on the sidewalk until a table for four was available. Mike and Angy had always gotten along well and the weather was nice, so Mike didn't mind standing around for ten or fifteen minutes. He did, however, have to make a conscious effort to keep the conversation from drifting too far into the merits of superhero movies or the never-ending tribulations of the Oakland Raiders—subjects of great interest to Angy and him, but not Jo. Mike did not trust Val to make polite conversation with Jo, so that meant keeping to topics that interested all of them. Fortunately, that didn't prove difficult, as Jo promptly asked Angy if he had any interesting stories from his time as a beat cop in that neighborhood. He did, of course. Mike had heard most of them before, and Val had probably heard them all, but Angy was a good storyteller and they only had a quarter of an hour to kill.

The autumn sun gleamed in the pale gold of Jo's hair and turned her eyes a luminous sea blue. She gave a sparkling laugh in response to a funny line in one of Angy's stories. Mike remembered the feel of her mouth against his and the warmth of her body in his arms.

And then he remembered that she'd cheated on her husband. That she'd accepted favors from the professor she slept with.

He turned away, and found himself face to face with an approaching waiter.

"Your table is ready," the waiter announced to the group. He ushered them in and seated them at a table nestled in a corner, where they had at least a little privacy—though Mike suspected Angy had picked Brenda's in part to make it hard for them to talk much about anything confidential.

Mike waited until the server had brought their drinks and a flight of beignets before he brought up business. "Angy, Val mentioned that you might be interested in a certain company with the initials H.F. that is also of interest to us." He took a USB drive out of his pocket and slid it across the table. "Here are some documents that might be helpful. They were stolen from Dr. Anderson sometime over the past six months by an individual in her office. That individual then provided the documents to attorneys who are suing Dr. Anderson. So it looks like the company has been engaging in data theft, and possibly other crimes."

Angy looked at the USB drive but didn't pick it up. "Can you prove all of that?"

"Yes," Mike replied. "I've also included a memo outlining our proffer. Basically, Dr. Anderson can testify that those are her documents, that they could not have found their way out of her office unless they were stolen, and that her former employee quit when she confronted him about the theft and asked him to take what amounted to a lie-detector test. I can testify that the lead attorney in the case I mentioned told me that he got the documents from H.F."

"Okay," Angy said, voice and face neutral. He looked at Jo. "Anything you'd like to add?"

She leaned forward. "Not substantively, but I did want to let you know that I'm trained to identify microexpressions and read body language. When I asked Shaun—that's my former employee—whether he had taken any of my documents, his nonverbal reactions made it quite clear that he had. I would be happy to discuss my specific observations with one of your experts if that would be helpful."

Angy nodded. Then he took a bite of crawfish beignet, chewed it slowly, and took a long sip of watermelon iced tea. He put down his glass and picked up the USB drive. He examined it like an archaeologist looking at an artifact, turning it over slowly and carefully in his hands. Mike watched with forced patience, waiting to see whether the fish would take the bait.

At last, Angy dropped the drive into his shirt pocket. "This is interesting, thanks. I'll let you know if I have any questions or would like to bring either of you in for a formal interview. Anything else?"

Mike shook his head. "Just let us know if we can be of further assistance. For example, if there are any particular documents that you're looking for, you can tell Val and I'll see what we can do."

Angy's thick eyebrows went up. "You're the lawyer, not me, but I thought that violated the Fourth Amendment."

Mike grinned. "Not precisely. The Fourth Amendment doesn't let you use civil discovery to avoid getting a warrant. But if you happen to want evidence that we want too, then that's perfectly kosher. And I'm positive that we'll want anything you do."

"Thanks, Mike," Angy said. "I'll talk to the DA's Office. So, did I ever tell you about the time Jerry Brown's car got stolen about two blocks from here?"

He had, but it was a good story. Moreover, it was a clear hint that Angy was done talking business. Which was fine—Mike had gotten everything he could reasonably hope for. "What happened, Angy?"

By the time Angy had finished the story, the bill had come. Mike paid it and they left.

None of them noticed a slight, fastidious man in his midthirties sitting by himself near the door. He watched them leave and sent a text as soon as they were out the door. Then he paid his bill with cash and left precisely one minute later.

# CHAPTER 60

Jo walked next to Mike and started asking him questions about the case, so Val fell in step with Angy. "Thanks, bro," she said.

"Nothin' to thank me for," he replied. "That wasn't bad at all. In fact, it was actually kinda useful." He patted the pocket containing the thumb drive. "And a free lunch at Brenda's is always worth it." He looked over his shoulder at Mike and Jo, who were a couple of steps behind them and deep in conversation. "By the way, I got somethin' for you. Remind me to give it to you the next time we get together."

"Sure. What is it?"

He hesitated and glanced back again. Jo and Mike were a little closer now. "You'll see. So where are you parked?"

"Civic Center garage. How about you?"

"Same."

It turned out that Jo had parked there too, and since they had all arrived within ten minutes of each other, they were all on the same level. They took the elevator down, carrying on separate conversations as they went. Mike and Jo talked litigation strategy, while Angy and Val debated whether to fly back to New York for Christmas or try to persuade the rest of the family to come to California.

"The thing is, Mama hates to fly," Angy argued. "She'll wanna take Amtrak, and she won't wanna go alone. So Joey or Lisa will hafta go with her, and they can't take that much time off work."

"But what if we upgrade her to business class?" Val asked. "I'll pay for it."

"Then we'll hafta upgrade Papa too, and he'll wanna get his money's worth in free booze."

"Even if someone else is paying?"

"*Especially* if someone else is payin'," Angy said as they stepped off the elevator. "He'll feel like he's wastin' a gift otherwise. We'll hafta take him off the plane in a wheelchair."

Val rolled her eyes. "Seriously? I think you just want to go back to Brooklyn. Why you're nostalgic for that place in winter is beyond me. It's cold, but there's hardly ever any snow. And—"

A tall man stepped out from behind a dirty concrete pillar. He wore a hoodie and a ski mask. His right hand held a gun. Without saying a word, he pointed and fired.

Val froze.

Angy shoved her between two cars. She stumbled and fell as more shots boomed. The noise was deafening in the enclosed space of the garage, like repeated lightning strikes five feet away.

Val tried to scramble to her feet, but Angy fell on top of her. For an instant, she thought he was trying to shield her, but then she realized that he wasn't moving.

Her heart stopped. "Angy!" she screamed.

No response.

There was a gun in Angy's hand. She was shaking, but she grabbed the pistol and peeked over the trunk of the car to her right. The man in the ski mask jogged along the aisle of cars in a crouch. One arm hung limp. He glanced between the cars as if hunting someone.

She tried to aim and pulled the trigger. The gun roared and bucked in her hand. The rear window of the car the man was passing shattered. He spun around and Val ducked back behind the car.

Her ears rang, but she could hear shouts. She couldn't see what was happening because the cars blocked her view and she didn't want to risk standing up. The man in the ski mask looked toward the voices, then turned and ran for the stairwell at the far end of the garage. He reached it and disappeared. A moment later two police officers flashed past, chasing him.

Val turned back to her brother. The front of his immaculate dress shirt was covered in wet red stains. There was a hole in his stomach and another in the left side of his chest where his heart was. His eyes were half-open and glassy. He wasn't breathing.

"Angy!" she screamed again.

He didn't move.

She kneeled over him and started frantically pumping his chest like she had seen paramedics do on TV. Blood welled out of the holes as she pushed, but nothing else happened.

Strong hands pulled her away. She struggled to get free, get back to her baby brother. But there was someone else kneeling over him now. A police officer. She turned and saw that another officer was holding her. She realized he was talking. ". . . everything we can. An ambulance is on the way."

She stopped struggling and stared. Everything seemed to be happening in slow motion at a distance. A policeman crouched over Angy, doing something, but the rear end of an SUV blocked her view. She could only see her brother from the waist down now. His legs sprawled out clumsily from between the cars.

She turned away and started to hide her face in her hands—then realized they were covered with Angy's blood. Mike stood a few feet away, talking to another officer. His face was an expressionless mask of shock. A third policeman was talking to Jo.

"Are you injured, ma'am?" the officer who had been restraining Val asked.

She struggled to focus, then took mental inventory of her body. Her left knee hurt. She realized that she had landed on it when Angy shoved her between the cars. She flexed her leg carefully. It seemed to operate fine. She shook her head. "No," she heard her voice say. "I'm not injured."

"Good. All right, ma'am. I need you to tell me everything you can about the man who attacked you."

"He . . . he just appeared and started shooting. It was like he was waiting for us. He . . ."

Suddenly it was too much. She broke into great racking sobs and couldn't say anything else.

# CHAPTER 61

David Klein drove south on Van Ness, cursing the traffic. He always cursed it, but never before with the desperate intensity he used now. Every few seconds, his eyes went to the rearview mirror, looking for the telltale flashing red and blue lights. So far, nothing. He'd heard a few sirens, but that was to be expected in this neighborhood.

The car in front of him stopped suddenly, forcing him to hit the brakes yet again. Eric groaned from the backseat. David felt a flash of anger. Clearly Eric had at least partially failed. Otherwise he wouldn't be bleeding all over the Lincoln Navigator David was driving.

How badly had Eric failed? David glanced over his shoulder. Eric lay on the seat with his eyes closed. He had one arm raised and pressed on the inside of the bicep with his free hand. Bright-red blood flowed around his fingers. So he'd been shot in an artery. David was no doctor, but he knew that was bad. Better get the full story now before shock set in.

"What happened?" David asked.

"What?" Eric said, his voice weak and unfocused.

"Tell me what happened," David ordered. "Start from when I texted you from the restaurant."

"Okay. I . . . I went down to the third floor in the garage. I kept my face turned away from security cameras. Then I hid behind a pillar between the elevator and Webster's car. I heard them coming, and I waited until they got close, like you said. Then I stepped out—but . . . but there were four of them, not two. Webster and his assistant were there, but so was Dr. Anderson and another guy. I . . . think he was a cop."

David's knuckles whitened on the steering wheel. He had seen the four of them leave together, but he knew they had driven separately and therefore assumed that they had parked separately. Stupid. But stupider of Eric not to have put eyes on his target before he pulled a gun.

Eric's voice had trailed off, so David prompted him. "Then what happened?"

"I, uh, shot . . . shot at Webster."

"Did you hit him?"

"Not sure, but don' think so." Eric's voice was growing weaker and he was starting to slur. "No blood an' . . . an' he hid in some cars wi' Annerson."

"Who shot you? Webster?"

"Un-unh. Cop, so I shot him."

So Eric had missed Webster, but hit a cop. Fabulous. "Did you kill him?"

"Yeah, I think."

"Did you kill anyone else?"

"No. Wen' lookin' for Webster, but the girl started shootin' at me an' I hear' people comin', so I ran."

This story just kept getting better. "Did anyone see you?"

"Don' . . . don' thin' so. I . . . ." His voice faded again.

David pulled onto 101 South. Traffic thinned out some and he was able to drive at a decent speed. He managed to relax a little. His nerves were still taut, but no longer like piano wires. He could think now, and he had information to work with. He could make decisions.

First decision: what to do with Eric. He obviously needed medical attention, but bringing him into a hospital with a bullet wound would mean an instant call to the police. Since Eric had managed to both shoot a cop and leave three witnesses alive, David doubted it would take long for the SFPD to put two and two together. So hospitals, trauma centers, and so on were all out.

Stash him at Horizon Finance and find a friendly doctor? If David pulled off to the side of the road and put a tourniquet on Eric's arm, he might last long enough for that to work. But it was a risky move. The managing director had stopped by David's office a week ago to warn him that law enforcement was investigating Horizon Finance. He didn't say which agency because that wasn't information David needed to know. What he did need to know was that Horizon could be under surveillance at any time. The building itself should be safe, but the phone lines couldn't be relied on once they left Horizon's offices. And the building entrances might be watched. So the risks of bringing Eric to Horizon outweighed the likely benefits.

Come to think of it, there weren't many benefits to keeping Eric around. He had made some good decisions, but too many bad ones. Maybe it was best to cut Horizon's losses and move on. David glanced at the backseat. Eric's face was pale and gray, and his breath came in uneven gasps. His injured arm hung down, oozing blood slowly but steadily. A large, dark puddle filled the footwell.

David drummed his fingers on the wheel for a moment, then decided to let the problem of Eric solve itself.

While that happened, he moved on to his second decision: what to do with the car and the other evidence. The Navigator had been stolen from a dealership that was closed for the week, then fitted with fake plates. That made it an ideal getaway car, but one that needed to be disposed of fairly quickly. That was straightforward, particularly now that Eric's corpse would be part of the evidence that would be disposed of at the same time. David had arranged to have a car waiting for him in a secluded little canyon in the middle of the desert outside Los Angeles. He would park the Navigator there, douse it in gasoline, and let it burn out. Someone would report it eventually, but all that would be left would be a smoking shell and Eric's carbonized remains. The police would probably assume it was the work of a Mexican drug gang, do a halfhearted investigation, and let the case go dormant. Eric would be a John Doe cold case.

That left David's final and hardest decision: what to do with Mike Webster. Webster was proving to be an increasingly difficult problem. At first, he had been a mere annoyance, a lawyer who needed to get out of the way so that David could force Johanna Anderson into bankruptcy and then pluck Mind's Eye from her hands. Then Webster started asking questions about Horizon and became a serious nuisance. And when he managed to expose the answers to those questions as lies, he became a threat. And threats to Horizon Finance needed to be eliminated. The first attempt to eliminate Webster had not gone well, obviously, but that had been due in large part to poor execution by Eric.

He started to draw in a deep breath, and he almost gagged. Blood and other substances emitted by dead bodies stink. David had never been around a fresh corpse, particularly of someone who died violently, and this was a deeply unpleasant surprise.

He sighed and rolled down the windows. He had a long drive ahead of him. Oh, well. At least he'd have plenty of time to come up with a more effective way to deal with Mike Webster.

# CHAPTER 62

Mike didn't have time for this. Any of it. Trial was eight days away and he needed to clear his decks and focus all his time and energy on getting ready. Today he had to submit any motions *in limine*—special motions related to the evidence that would be put on at trial. Preliminary jury instructions and witness lists (Mike had included David Klein out of spite) were due tomorrow. Then he had to spend the next week working on his opening statement, responding to Tim's *in limines*, working with key witnesses, and doing the dozens of other things that had to get done before trial.

He did not have time for repetitive, hours-long police interviews. Or reliving what had happened, over and over, like an endlessly replaying video in his head that he couldn't stop. And he particularly didn't have time for the waves of grief and guilt that threatened to drown him when he thought of what happened to Angy, the wife and children he left behind, the look on Val's face as the cop talked to her, the—

*No, stop it.* Following those mental ruts one more time wouldn't do Angy, Val, or anyone else any good. He needed to concentrate on winning this case first. Once that was done, he could work through his emotions in Mind's Eye or with a bottle of wine. He could also think of something to do for Angy's family, though everything that occurred to him felt like either an empty gesture or payment of blood money.

He turned back to the half-edited *in limine* motion on his screen. Brad had done a good job on the first draft, but he had a penchant for unnecessary rhetorical flourishes. Quoting from *The Iliad* might have scored Brad points in a mock Supreme Court brief for a law-school moot court competition, but it would get him laughed at in a routine motion seeking to exclude tax returns at trial.

He recognized Val's knock at his door. He swiveled away from Brad's opus. "Come in."

It was the first time he had seen her since the day Angy died, three days ago. Mike had told her to take as much time as she needed, and he hadn't expected to see her for a while. But here she was.

She looked different. She wasn't dressed in black and her makeup wasn't streaked with tears, but a cloud of mourning followed her into his office.

He got up, walked around the desk, and gave her a hug. She hugged him back, fiercely and wordlessly. They stood together for nearly a minute, holding each other.

They separated, and Val took her usual seat in his left guest chair. Her eyes were dry, but they held an enormous weight of pain. "Angy's funeral is on Sunday in Brooklyn," she said without preamble.

Mike nodded. "I told you before, take as much time as you need. Oh, and I'd like to send flowers." He regretted the flower comment immediately—it was an afterthought and sounded like it.

Val looked at him like he'd insulted her mother. "Send flowers?" she asked incredulously. "You mean you're not going?"

He shook his head. "Your place is with your family. My—"

"Place is paying your respects to Angy," she finished for him. "He died saving your life! How can you not go to his funeral?"

He sighed. "I'd love to, Val, but the Bell trial is coming at us like a semi. I just don't have time to take a couple of days off to fly across the country for Angy's funeral. I wish I did, but I don't."

She glared at him. "The only reason Angy is dead is because *you* insisted on that lunch meeting. I tried to talk you out of it, but you wouldn't listen. You basically asked me to twist his arm to get him to say yes, and like an idiot I did it. You owe him for that, and you owe me. Go to Brooklyn and show him the respect he deserves from you."

That was both true and deeply unfair. He pushed back the urge to defend himself—she had just lost her brother, and no one could expect her to be completely rational. He spread his hands helplessly. "I can't just abandon a client on the eve of trial."

Her large expressive eyes filled with fury. "This client deserves to be abandoned! She's been bad news from the start. She manipulated you into taking her case and then she got you to represent her for free. Plus, she lied to us over and over."

Mike felt the tightness in his head that warned of an impending headache. Great, just what he needed. "I know we've had some differences of opinion about Jo, but I really don't think she's a liar. She—"

"Seriously? She lied to you about the missing video files from Seth Bell's sessions. She lied to me about why he was in her Mind's Eye program. And based on your reaction at her depo, I'll bet she wasn't honest with you about her divorce. Want me to go on?"

This conversation was the verbal equivalent of running a nail file over an exposed nerve. He took a deep breath and let it out slowly, making an effort to relax the muscles in his neck and shoulders, just like Dr. Goff and the neurologist had recommended. "As I said, we've had some differences of opinion about Jo. But this isn't just about Jo. It's also about Mind's Eye. If I lose this trial because I'm not prepared, there's a good chance that Horizon Finance gets it. Who knows what they'll do with it or who they'll sell it to. We can't risk it falling into their hands, can we?"

"I don't feel that great about leaving it in *her* hands," Val shot back. "Look what she's done to you. She's hypnotized you or something. You're completely blind to anything bad about her. Snap out of it!"

The pulsing pain between Mike's temples went up a notch in intensity. As did his temper. "If anyone needs to snap out of it, it's you. You're the one who's completely blind. You're blind to anything good about her or Mind's Eye."

"There *is* nothing good about her! I've got news for you, Mike: just because a woman is built like Barbie and looks good on your arm and laughs at your jokes doesn't mean she's a good person. Even if she happens to be smart too."

His head felt like it was being crushed in a vise, and the pain added fuel to his growing anger. "You're jealous. You've been jealous of Jo since she set foot in this office. I see it in your face and hear it in every snarky remark you make about her. You can't stand the way she looks or the way she talks, and it drives you nuts that I see something in her. You're being irrational, and we both know it."

Val's face went pale. "So now I'm just a jealous irrational woman, is that it?"

"You've been through a very difficult experience and I understand why you're upset," Mike said through a migraine haze, trying to keep his voice calm. "Take as much time as you need to work through it, but when you come back, I expect you to act like a professional."

She gaped at him. "As much time as I need," she repeated. Her face went from white to furious red. She stood. "As much time as I need?" she said again, her voice rising. "How about forever!"

She turned and stormed out of his office, slamming the door behind her. The noise echoed in his skull. He wanted to go after her and really let her have it, but getting into a screaming match in the middle of the office would do no good. Better to let things cool down and then try to make peace before she left for Brooklyn.

He took some Advil and worked on those muscle-relaxation techniques again, doing his best to ignore the sound of her slamming things in the office next to him. He'd seen her mad before, but nothing like this. He dimmed the lights, put on some soothing music, and did mindless work until the noise next door stopped.

Half an hour later, blessed silence reigned. Better still, the combination of Advil, music, and muscle relaxation had reduced his headache to a faint buzz in the back of his head. Time to go talk to Val.

He took a deep breath and thought through what he should say: He valued and respected her deeply and was sorry if he'd implied otherwise. It was wrong of him to let things degenerate into an argument, particularly at a time like this. He wished her a safe trip and would appreciate it if she would pass along his heartfelt condolences to her family. He would do so in person as soon as he could do it appropriately. Something like that.

He steeled himself and opened his office door. The office staff all looked at him, and several whispered conversations ended abruptly when his door opened. He ignored their stares and walked into Val's office. It was empty. Not just unoccupied, but empty. All of Val's personal items had vanished. Nails and faint rectangles on the walls showed where her pictures had hung for a decade.

She was gone.

# CHAPTER 63

The day before Angy's funeral, the trees lining the street between the D'Abruzzos' apartment building and the church had been in full fall finery. But overnight, a storm had come through, stripping the branches bare and clogging the street drains with grimy clots of red and yellow leaves. Skeletal branches waved in a cold, wet wind under scudding gray clouds.

Val shivered as she trudged behind Angy's coffin, one hand balled in her coat pocket and the other clutching a copy of Psalm 51. The priest and the mourners were reading alternate verses as they walked.

*"Hide thy face from my sins, and blot out all my iniquities,"* Father Cavallini said in a reedy, age-cracked voice, black vestments flapping. He spoke as loudly as he could, but he walked in front of the coffin and was hard to hear.

*"Create in me a clean heart, O God, and put a new and right spirit within me,"* Val and the other mourners replied.

*"Cast me not away from thy presence, and take not thy holy Spirit from me,"* the priest called faintly.

*"Restore to me the joy of thy salvation, and uphold me with a willing spirit,"* the mourners said with leaden voices.

They turned and entered the church, a tall building of red brick and cement that had somehow both intimidated and comforted Val as a child. She, Angy, and Joey had all been baptized here. They'd all gone to Sunday school and catechism here. Joey had fallen in love with a local girl and they'd had the wedding here. And now Angy's funeral was here.

Val slid into the dark, varnished pew next to Peg, who took her hand and held it tightly. Mama sat on her other side, holding her other hand while cuddling Peg's two-year-old, Anthony, on her lap. Papa sat beside Mama with his arm around her, and Joey sat next to Papa with an arm around him. None of them was crying at the moment, probably because they were all comforting each other.

Angy's coffin lay in front of the altar, surrounded by candles and covered by a white pall. For the first time, it looked right. Seeing the coffin at the funeral home had been deeply depressing—the long line of mourners filing past it and looking in at Angy's artificially peaceful face, the canned music, the faint antiseptic smell. It had all created a miasma of death that clung to Val for hours after she left.

Then Angy's coffin arrived at their house on the day of the funeral and sat in the middle of the living room, surrounded by a stiff police honor guard and clergy solemnly intoning somber words and sprinkling holy water. That had been utterly horrible. The living room was where they'd opened Christmas presents as children, sat around the fireplace drinking hot chocolate after skating in Prospect Park, and greeted Nonna and Nonno when they came back from one of their cruises bearing gifts for their grandchildren. That room held ten thousand good memories, but now they were all tainted by the image of Angy's coffin surrounded by grim men.

But seeing the coffin here felt right. Angy's death was still wrong, of course, but at least he was dead in the right place. Everywhere else, the focus was on Angy's deadness and the family's "loss"—she must have heard that word a thousand times over the last two days. But here the focus was on the aliveness of Angy's soul. He was gone, but he hadn't just vanished into a black pit called Death. Angels had come down to that grimy parking garage in San Francisco, Father Cavallini said. Beings of unimaginable celestial splendor had tenderly lifted Angy from the bloody concrete and carried him to paradise.

Val had heard similar sentiments many times since Angy's death, but always as quick little asides, as if the speakers were embarrassed. A formulaic "He's in a better place" or "Angy is with God now," followed by questions about how the family was doing, the funeral arrangements, the hunt for Angy's murderer, and so on. Father Cavallini wasn't the least bit hurried or embarrassed when he talked about heaven. He spoke of it rhapsodically and with the authority of a native citizen—which Val supposed he practically was after sixty years in the priesthood.

Then Father Cavallini came down from the pulpit, sprinkled more holy water on the coffin, and walked around it with the thurible, filling the pews with the smell of incense. He said more prayers, ending with one Val hadn't heard before: "O God, whose attribute it is always to have mercy and to spare, we humbly present our prayers to thee for the soul of thy servant Angelo, which thou has this day called out of this world, beseeching thee not to deliver it into the hands of the enemy, nor to forget it forever, but to command thy holy angels to receive it, and to bear it into paradise; that as it has believed and hoped in thee it may be delivered from the pains of hell and inherit eternal life through Christ our Lord. Amen."

The funeral ended a few minutes later. The pallbearers took the coffin out to the waiting hearse for the short drive to the cemetery. Val followed, driving her parents' car, with Mama in the passenger seat and Peg wedged between two car seats in the back. To Val's surprise, Mama was informing Peg that she and Papa were moving to California to help Peg with Anthony and his baby brother, Patrick, who had slept through the service in his car seat and was currently getting a bottle. And to Val's greater surprise, Peg didn't object. In fact, she seemed genuinely grateful for the offer and even said how wonderful it would be to have more family nearby, particularly now that she would be going back to work.

Peg and Mama also stood together during the committal at the cemetery and afterward, when shivering mourners paid their last respects before heading for the parking lot.

The cemetery office had an urn of stale but hot coffee, which Val visited several times, returning with steaming cups to keep her parents warm. On the way back from one of her trips, she heard a familiar voice at her shoulder. "I understand that your parents may be joining you in California."

She turned to see Father Cavallini, now wearing a long wool coat over his vestments.

"Yes, Father. They were talking about it on the way to the cemetery."

"Do you think it's wise?"

Val smiled, guessing that the old priest had been hearing Mama's side of more than one of her disagreements with Peg. Mama had a tendency to use the confessional to confess other people's sins, then ask forgiveness for getting mad at them. "Peg and Mama haven't always seen eye to eye, but I think this will be good for them. Peg tends to be independent, but now she needs help. Mama mostly needs to be needed, and now she is. Besides, Papa and I will be there to break up any fights."

The priest chuckled. "Hopefully, there will be few. I will miss your parents, but it would be good for the two halves of your family to be reunited. And I know Paolo will not miss New York winters."

"Very true," Val replied. She paused for a moment, then asked the question that had been gnawing at her. "Do you think that's what God intended? To bring our family together? Is that why he let Angy die?"

Father Cavallini sighed. "God never intends evil, but he does work in it. He didn't intend for your brother to be murdered any more than he intended any sin, all the way back to the Garden of Eden. God didn't let Angy die to bring your family together, but he can create some good out of Angy's death if we let him."

Val sat on the plane back from New York. It was a red-eye, and everyone around her was asleep or pretending to be. She had tried sleeping for about half an hour, but failed. Now she leaned her head against the side of the cabin, watching the dark landscape slide by beneath her. And thinking.

Ever since she left San Francisco, her thoughts had been on Angy and her family. She had left behind a tangle of unanswered questions. Now she was flying back to them at five hundred miles per hour, and she had no more answers than she did when she left.

Her mind circled back to Father Cavallini's words in the cemetery. *God never intends evil, but he does work in it.* Angy's death was indirectly bringing Mama and Papa to California. It had also triggered the chain of events that made her quit her job. Was that also God's work?

She mulled that over. She had been with Mike for a decade and didn't regret a minute of it. But she had gotten stuck. Her life hadn't really moved forward in all that time. And it wasn't just her job—pretty much everything in her life was the same as it had been ten years ago: apartment, friends, even the restaurants she went to. Did she want to be living the same life thirty years from now? Wasn't it time for a change?

It was. She hadn't realized it before, but it definitely was time for a change. For one thing, she needed to get out more. She had fallen into a comfortable routine. She got up every morning, spent long hours at work, and went home. If it wasn't too late, she might get together with friends or go to a yoga class. On Saturdays, she slept in and went shopping in the afternoon. On Sundays, she went to church in the morning and spent the afternoon with Angy and his family. That was it. Week after week, month after month, year after year.

Val's routine didn't bring her into contact with many eligible men, and she didn't seek out any. It was her own fault. For years, she'd been holding on to a stupid daydream, and it kept her from dating real men.

For as long as she had known Mike, he had been searching for the right girl—or so Val told herself. He dated one after another, but it never lasted for more than a few months. Clearly, he was looking for companionship that they couldn't provide. But Val could. She had been by his side for years. He relied on her and respected her. They were good friends—and every now and then, something in his voice or the way he looked at her said they might be more. Sometimes—particularly during the early years of their relationship—she'd dreamed about the day that Mike would suddenly wake up and notice her right there under his nose. The woman of his dreams, and he'd had her all along.

*Right.*

That was a fantasy for a nineteen-year-old girl infatuated with a handsome single boss ten years her senior. But as Mama regularly reminded her, she was twenty-nine now. It was time that she acted like it.

What did that mean? More importantly, what future waited for her at the end of this flight? Mike and her job were both gone.

Should she try to land a job with another firm? That would be hard. Most places required a college degree and a paralegal certificate, and she had only a high school diploma. The best she could hope for was a legal secretary position, which would put her right back where she'd started ten years ago. And she would probably be stuck there forever—she could hardly count on another Mike Webster plucking her out of a secretary's chair and making her his firm manager/paralegal/ investigator. Plus, most paralegals got paid less than half of what Mike gave her.

So what was she going to do? *Become a lawyer,* she realized.

The thought stunned her, but she knew she could do it. She had worked on a hundred cases from start to finish, and she knew the inside of a courtroom better than most attorneys. She had brainstormed legal strategy, interviewed witnesses, done basic legal research, and even ghostwritten first drafts of some simple briefs.

It would be a lot of work. She had picked up a dozen business and finance courses in community college over the years, but she only had about half of what she needed for a college degree. Then there would be three years of law school, four if she only went part time. But it was doable, especially if she went to school full time, which she could probably manage with a part-time job and the money she had saved while working for Mike.

Valeria D'Abruzzo, Esq. *Wow.* Angy would be proud.

# CHAPTER 64

*November*

Mike was trying to be patient. He really was. But trial began in less than forty-eight hours, and he simply did not have time to be teaching people their jobs.

He plopped a stack of binders on the desk of Eileen, the secretary shared by Camy and Brad. They landed with more force than he'd intended, causing both Eileen and her desk paraphernalia to jump. "I can't use these witness binders. They need to have numbered tabs and a table of contents. They're also too thick. The depo transcript excerpts are full size. Swap them out for the condensed versions."

Eileen looked at him fearfully. "I'm sorry about that. I'll fix it right away. Umm, where are the condensed versions?"

"You'll need to create those."

She hesitated. "How should I do that?"

Mike took a deep breath and reminded himself that Eileen was Brad's aunt and was very diligent, even though she wasn't particularly technically savvy. "There's a function that lets you print four pages of transcript on each page," he explained. "Eight pages if you print on both sides."

"Oh. Val always did that, but, um, I'll see if I can figure it out."

Mike would have shown her if he knew how to do it, but he didn't. He simply knew that it could be done, because Val could do it. And he was pretty sure that Eileen couldn't. Left to her own devices, she would fiddle with the program all day and fail. "Camy," he called. "Can you come out here and help Eileen with the witness binders?"

"Sure," she called back. "Should I take a break from working on the research for the *in limine* oral argument?"

He gritted his teeth. "No, I—"

"I'll take care of the binders," Brad announced as he popped out of his office and hurried to his aunt's rescue.

Mike turned and walked back into his office to work on his opening statement. This was at least the tenth such incident in the week since Val left. Camy and Eileen had wasted most of an afternoon looking for a clean copy of Seth Bell's childhood hospital records because no one knew where Val had saved it. Then Camy realized that no one had ordered the transcript of their last hearing in front of Judge Spink, so they needed to get it on a rush basis at triple the usual cost. And so on.

Now Mike sat in front of his computer, Googling "how to put video clips in PowerPoint"—and feeling his blood pressure steadily rise when he couldn't get any of the answers to work. And he had a nagging suspicion that even if he could figure it out, the result would look amateurish. One more thing that Val had always handled for him—and that consequently he had never learned to do for himself. He could ask someone else in the office to learn so he could get back to working on the substance of his opening. But then he'd be taking them away from equally—if not more—critical tasks.

He leaned back and rubbed his eyes. He had known that Val was important to the firm, but he hadn't quite realized just how important. Losing her was like losing the electricity in the office: there were some obvious ways that it made life harder, but there were also a thousand ways that you didn't realize until you stumbled over them.

And it wasn't just the firm. He missed Val personally—particularly at a time like this. She'd been his sounding board for every opening statement and closing argument. When he was buried in trial prep, she'd show up with takeout from Yan's Kitchen without needing to be asked. She knew how and when to break the tension by waltzing into his office to give him grief about his tie or shoot the breeze for a few minutes. He was a better—and happier—lawyer when she was around. So why did she have to leave with no warning at the exact moment when he needed her most?

His blood pressure went up another notch at that thought. He didn't think Val had intentionally sabotaged him or the firm, but she could hardly have done more damage if she had acted maliciously. She had stormed out without giving a single thought to what she was doing to everyone in the office. Maybe she felt that he deserved to be punished. Fine. But why was she punishing Camy, Brad, and poor overwhelmed Eileen?

Part of him wanted to call Val and let her know the chaos she had caused. She would probably feel guilty, and she might even come back to help them get ready for trial. But he knew he couldn't do that to her. She was still grieving for Angy. Moreover, she still had qualms—justified or not—about working for Jo. He wouldn't use guilt to force her to do something she thought was wrong.

Part of him also wanted to call Jo and ask whether she had time for a glass of wine and maybe a short Mind's Eye session. He needed to talk to someone, and Mind's Eye really took the edge off of his stress. Besides, he hadn't really talked to her since Angy died almost a week and a half ago. They'd had a few mostly-business conversations—always with Camy on the line—about the upcoming trial, but that was it. Mike felt a little guilty about that. But he simply didn't have time for wine and therapy between now and the trial. And he wasn't ready to have her looking into his mind, not until he knew what she would see there.

Thinking of Angy's death reminded him of yet another problem: the police investigation. The lead homicide detective investigating Angy's murder was treating it as a mugging gone bad. That seemed wrong to Mike. The killer never even demanded their wallets. And Mike and Angy had just finished a meeting about Horizon Finance when they were attacked. Wasn't it at least possible that Horizon was behind Angy's murder?

Mike had argued all of this to the detective but got nowhere. Muggings happened regularly in the Civic Center garage. Ergo, the killer was probably a mugger. Any investigation of Horizon Finance would be the responsibility of the Financial Crimes Unit, not the Homicide Unit. Mike got the sense that there was some sort of bureaucratic turf battle going on. If the investigation of Angy's death potentially involved Horizon, then the Homicide Unit would have to cede control to the Financial Crimes Unit—or something like that.

Whatever the cause, the SFPD seemed intent on their mugging-gone-bad theory, and the lead detective simply dug in his heels when Mike pointed out that it didn't fit the evidence. That bothered Mike. Angy deserved justice, and Mike feared that he wasn't going to get it. Further, if it was Horizon, there was a chance they would take another shot at killing Mike. A good chance.

And there wasn't much he could do about it. He didn't have the time or skills to investigate Angy's murder on his own. He couldn't go into hiding without handing a default victory to the Bells and Horizon. Maybe he could hire a bodyguard, but that was about all. Yet he had a sneaking suspicion that even that wouldn't be much help. Horizon didn't seem like the type of organization that would try the same thing twice—particularly if it hadn't worked the first time.

Dissatisfied, he turned back to the half-finished mess on his computer, hoping that inspiration would strike before Horizon Finance did.

# CHAPTER 65

Val braced herself and dialed Ryan's number.

"Hello, Ryan Daley speaking."

"Hi, Ryan. It's Val D'Abruzzo. Angy's sister."

"Sure, I remember." Pause. "I'm really sorry about Angy. I miss him every day."

"Yeah, me too." She could feel her throat starting to swell, so she took a deep breath and hurried on before she started crying again. "I'd like to do anything I can to help with the murder investigation. I don't want to get in your way or anything, but I've done a lot of investigating. If there's any way I can be useful, please let me know."

"Thanks, Val. I'll pass that along. But I work in Financial Crimes, not Homicide. Those guys generally handle investigations on their own to make sure things are done according to their rules and the case will hold up in court."

She had expected that, but she had to at least make the offer. Now on to the main reason for her call. "Okay, I understand. Speaking of financial crimes, there's something I wanted to make sure you knew. Angy met with my boss and me right before he was killed. We talked about a company called Horizon Finance. Angy was investigating them, and we gave him a bunch of documents on a thumb drive. I wanted to make sure those got to whoever took over after Angy died."

"I'm working on that too," Ryan replied. "This is the first I've heard of a thumb drive full of documents. When did you give it to Angy?"

"About ten minutes before he was shot." The image of Angy holding the thumb drive and drinking watermelon iced tea flashed through her mind, followed by him sprawled on the garage floor. She wiped her eyes and forced out, "It must have been in his pocket when he died."

"Which means it's probably sitting in an evidence locker waiting for someone in Homicide to look at it." Ryan muttered something under his breath that Val didn't catch. "That could take a while. I hate to impose, but would it be possible to send me a copy of what was on that drive?"

"I, uh, don't have access to them anymore. They're at the firm where I used to work. But I'll bet that the firm would be willing to give you a copy." She gave him Mike's number and e-mail. Then she added, "I pulled together most of those documents and I helped write the cover memo that was also on the drive. If you'd like me to come in for a witness interview or something, I'd be happy to walk you through what we found."

"That would be great. Hold on a sec, let me just check to make sure the drive didn't make its way up here somehow." He put down the receiver, and the line was silent for half a minute. Then he was back. "No drive, but I did find something interesting. There was a package sitting on Angy's desk with 'Val' written on it in his handwriting. Any idea what that might be?"

She remembered him saying he had something for her as they walked to the garage. "None. Could you send it to me?"

"Sure. On its way."

# CHAPTER 66

David couldn't sit still when he was nervous. So he stood in front of one of his ceiling-to-floor windows, absently watching construction crews at work on a new building on the other side of the street. Six months ago, there had been a well-maintained 1980s-vintage, twenty-story office building on the same spot. David hadn't heard about any problems with the old building, but it vanished over a long weekend and a new one with identical dimensions now rose in its place. Most likely, the owner had decided that the increased rent that could be charged for a new building outweighed the cost of building it. It would then merely have been a question of tapping one of the many streams of easy money flowing through Silicon Valley to finance the construction.

It was probably a foolish investment. The rents in the old building had all been over a hundred dollars per square foot, so the rents in the new one would have to be truly breathtaking to cover the cost of demolition and construction. Even a slight dip in the Silicon Valley economy could put the owner in bankruptcy, particularly if someone reported rats in the building or something like that. If whoever was financing the building also ran into trouble, it might be possible to pick up the building for a deeply undervalued price if the market was right.

David made a mental note to do some background research and keep an eye on the situation. Spotting good investments early had made his career at Horizon Finance. And he strongly suspected his track record was the only reason he was still at Horizon after the string of setbacks he had suffered on the Mind's Eye project.

When he had reported Eric's spectacular failure in the Civic Center garage, he had half expected that Mr. Johnson would call security and have David removed. However, one of David's other projects had come through with a nice profit, so he was able to report that at the same time, which he had hoped would be enough to buy him another chance. It was. The managing director had given David a long look and said, "Well, the immediate problem has solved itself. Be careful that you don't become a problem yourself."

The memory of that admonition sent a fresh jolt of nervous adrenaline into his blood.

Since that meeting, David had been honing what had been his backup plan. Hopefully, it would pay off. There wouldn't be time to try anything else, with trial looming. But just in case, David had started making very personal plans. A new identity, someplace far away. A Cayman account. Maybe Horizon would come hunting him and maybe they wouldn't bother. Hopefully, he'd never find out.

There was a deferential knock at the door. He glanced at the clock on his phone: 10:29. His new associate was punctual. *Good.*

"Come in," he called.

The door opened and a young Asian woman stepped in. She was petite and fresh-faced, and she could probably have passed for thirteen with the right clothes, hairstyle, and makeup. But her black eyes held a hard, calculating look that no thirteen-year-old ever had, and she carried herself like a panther.

"My name is Irene Yang," she said, her voice soft but confident. She had a faint trace of an accent. "I have been assigned to you."

She handed him her résumé. Straight As from Berkeley; a year at private-equity powerhouse Hellman & Friedman; trained in gymnastics and various martial arts since the age of three.

He walked over to his desk and dropped the résumé in his shredder. Then he sat and turned to face her. "Hello, Irene. I'm glad you're here. We have a lot of work to do, particularly on this Mind's Eye matter."

She nodded. "Mr. Johnson briefed me. I've already followed up on some of the leads Eric Sturm left behind."

So she was taking assignments directly from the managing director. That meant she was reporting back to him as well. And that meant she was a spy. Good of her to let him know. Maybe that was a message from the managing director. Maybe not.

"Good," he said. "Any developments?"

"Yes. I've investigated a dozen of the cases Webster tried. The results are promising."

Maybe that was why Mr. Johnson had taken Eric's failure in stride. "Give me the details."

As she reported her findings, he gradually relaxed. The results really were promising. Very promising. His hunch had paid off, and she had found exactly what he had hoped she would.

When she finished, he nodded casually. "As expected. Run down those last two cases and make sure there are no loose ends. This needs to be airtight, and there's no reason it shouldn't be. When we spring this on Webster, there can't be any way for him to wriggle out of it—and he's an excellent wriggler. Understood?"

She nodded. "Yes, Mr. Klein."

# CHAPTER 67

Mike's desk phone rang. He didn't recognize the number.

He hesitated for two rings. The opening statement was still a mess and he had less than twenty-four hours to get it in shape. The last thing he needed was another distraction. On the other hand, he vaguely recalled that the 553 prefix was associated with the SFPD.

He picked up the phone on the third ring. "Hello. Mike Webster speaking."

"Mr. Webster, my name is Ryan Daley. I work in the Financial Crimes Unit at the San Francisco Police Department. Do you have a few minutes?"

"Sure. I've got a trial starting tomorrow morning, but I can certainly spare a few minutes. What can I do for you?"

"Thanks, I appreciate it. I promise to keep this short. Did you give Angelo D'Abruzzo a thumb drive containing documents related to Horizon Finance?"

Mike sat up a little straighter. "I did. Do you think Horizon might be involved in Angy's murder?"

There was a long pause. "I can't comment on an ongoing investigation. Would it be possible for you to make another copy of that thumb drive? He had the original at the time of his death, so it's now evidence in a homicide investigation."

"Sure. I—" All the semi-related problems floating in his mind clicked together. How to win the trial. The SFPD's misguided investigation of Angy's murder. How to deal with Horizon Finance. There might be a solution to all of them. It was risky, but it could work. He ran through it again. Yes, it could definitely work. It could also definitely get him killed.

"Hello? Mr. Webster, are you still there?"

"Yes, I—" His phone might be bugged. He also needed a little time to think this through. "I can bring you a copy of the thumb drive this afternoon. Are you free at, say, three o'clock?"

"Yes."

"Great. I'll stop by your office then."

Mike spent the next four hours churning out a terrible opening statement. The words weren't that awful, but everything else was. He had no PowerPoint, no video clips or models, not even a foam board he could point to. He had none of the props and extras that modern juries expected, and he had no time to get them together before he went to meet with the police. He'd have to figure that out tonight. It was more important that the meeting go well. If it did, it would more than make up for a subpar opening tomorrow morning.

At 3:35, Mike was watching Ryan Daley fiddle with the thumb drive, unconsciously doing exactly what Angy had. He held the drive in both hands, slowly revolving it as he considered Mike's proposal. He had a good poker face, and Mike wished he had Jo here to help him read it.

At last, Ryan shook his head. "It's a really interesting idea, but I don't think we can do it."

"Why not?"

He sighed. "I can't do anything that looks like I'm stepping on a homicide investigation."

So it was a bureaucratic turf issue. That just made a risky idea riskier. "So don't," Mike replied. "Just keep up your routine surveillance of Horizon Finance. If you happen to come across evidence related to a homicide investigation in the process, great. You can refer it to your homicide team."

Daley's eyebrows went up. "If all we do is surveillance, you'll be completely on your own."

He shrugged. "I know."

Two small buckets of long-cold Chinese takeout sat on the island in Mike's kitchen. They were his favorite—General Tso's chicken with brown rice—but he had barely touched them. Tomorrow would be a big day. This would be the first time that opening statements in a big case would be the second-most important thing he had on his calendar.

And the most important thing on his calendar tomorrow might be the last thing he ever did. He was about to poke Horizon Finance very hard. This was an organization that had probably killed Angy, and Mike didn't think they'd have any qualms about killing him too.

He picked up his phone and checked the time: 10:03. Well, that was okay. Dad was a night owl. He pulled up his father's number and dialed.

"Hello?" Dad's voice said after the first ring.

"Hi, Dad. It's Mike. How are you doing?"

"Can't complain, Mike. How about you?"

"I . . . Could you pray for me tomorrow, Dad?"

The line was silent for several seconds. "I pray for you every day. What's special about tomorrow?"

"I've got a big trial and some other stuff going on. I can't really talk about it now."

"Are you in trouble?"

"I'm sorry. I really can't talk about it yet. Just pray for me, okay?"

"Of course."

"Thanks. I love you, Dad."

"I love you too."

# Chapter 68

Jo sat next to Mike at the counsel table closest to the jury box, which currently held a dozen prospective jurors. More filled the gallery of the courtroom.

She felt utterly helpless. These strangers were going to sit in judgment on her. They were bored, disinterested, annoyed that their daily routines had been disrupted. They knew nothing about her, about psychology, or about Mind's Eye. Yet they held her professional life in their hands.

And the man sitting beside her held her personal life in his hands. What would he do with it? A month ago, as he kissed her and held her to him, she thought she knew. But then Cromwell threw her affair in Mike's face, casting it in the ugliest possible light. She saw the agony and betrayal in Mike that day. She wanted to talk to him, to explain. She had hoped to get a few minutes alone with him after they met with Val's brother, but they were attacked in the parking garage. After that, Mike had vanished into a whirlwind of trial preparation, particularly after Val quit. Jo wasn't sad to see her go, but her abrupt departure had thrown Mike's office into an uproar and eliminated any free time he might have had for Jo.

The few times she talked to him over the past two weeks, he was cordial but distant. She knew he was under a lot of stress, but she could also sense that he was withdrawing from her. But how far? How much damage had been done? If only she could get him into Mind's Eye, she would know in minutes. She could also help him, soothe him. But for now all she could do was sit next to him and try to help him win the trial.

Judge Spink read some preliminary statements about the jury-selection process and had the group in the box take an oath to give honest answers during jury selection. She then gave a short, neutral summary of the case, agreed on in advance by Mike and the lawyers for Seth Bell's estate. After that, she asked questions aimed at ferreting out bias and weighing the validity of various requests to get out of jury duty.

When the judge was done, Tim Cromwell spent nearly half an hour asking questions of his own. He had a smoothly genial manner, but Jo could tell that the jurors were getting irritated by the time he was done. Jo didn't blame them—they'd been sitting there for over an hour already.

She watched the juror candidates closely throughout and jotted down notes on which jurors seemed inclined to one side or the other. She handed her notes to Mike, who glanced through them without comment or reaction.

After Cromwell sat down, Mike stood and asked five minutes of perfunctory, almost distracted questions. This might have been a conscious decision, an attempt to score points with the jurors by wasting less of their time than the judge or his opponent. If so, it worked—about half the jurors reacted positively to him when he finished and sat down.

Jo doubted that Mike was just making clever tactical decisions, however. He had been very preoccupied all morning, and it seemed as though he could hardly keep his mind on the trial. He would have seemed bored if not for the little signs that he was under incredible stress and trying to hide it: his breathing was shallow and rapid, he kept his arms close to his sides to hide sweat rings in his armpits, his muscles were taut inside his suit, and so on. His combination of distraction and agitation reminded Jo a little of one of her first prisoner referrals, a death-row inmate whose execution date had just been set.

Once the two sides had agreed on twelve jurors, Judge Spink had the jurors swear another oath (this time to be faithful jurors) and gave them a second round of instructions. Then she took a brief break while the plaintiff's team got ready for their opening statement.

While Cromwell's minions scurried to set up, Mike stared down at his notepad. Jo leaned close and whispered, "Is everything okay?"

Mike jumped slightly. "Yeah, sure." He stood up. "I think I'll go stretch my legs while we have the chance."

He walked out of the courtroom and Jo followed. "You're awfully tense," she said as she caught up to him in the hallway outside the courtroom. "Are you sure you're all right?"

"First-day-of-trial butterflies. It happens every time. It's a little worse today because I'm flying solo. I'll be fine."

That was true, but it wasn't the whole truth. "If that's all, then why are you so distracted in there?"

He glanced up and down the hall, which was neither crowded nor empty. "Sorry, I can't talk about it now."

"How about a glass of wine and a chat at my office when we're done here?" she asked, her voice low enough that she wouldn't be overheard. "I found an excellent Australian sauvignon blanc you'll love, and it's been a while since our last Mind's Eye session."

"I know," he said, looking a little guilty. "I'd love to, but I'm going to be busy after court today." She could see the tension—and now fear—spike in him. It wasn't the trial that had him on edge, she realized. It was what he'd be doing after he left the courthouse.

"And you're scared to death of what you're going to do," she replied.

He gave a tight little smile. "I hope you're the only one who figures that out."

Foreboding and compassion filled her heart. "What are you doing tonight? Is there anything I can do to help? I—"

She broke off as Tim Cromwell approached. "The clerk wants us back, Mike. It's game time." He gave Mike a friendly clap on the back and walked toward the courtroom.

"Thanks, Tim," Mike said to Cromwell's retreating back. He turned to Jo. "Thanks for asking, but I'm going to have to do this on my own. I'll tell you about it when I can." He gave her arm a quick squeeze and followed Cromwell through the heavy double doors of Judge Spink's courtroom.

There was nothing Jo could do. She walked in and took her place at Mike's side just as the bailiff brought the jury in. Everyone in the courtroom sat once the jurors took their seats, except Tim Cromwell. He stood in the middle of the courtroom, a smile on his pleasant, aristocratic face.

"Ladies and gentlemen, thank you for being here," Cromwell began, walking casually to the side of a projection screen that had appeared during the break. "I realize that you have better things to do than listen to two lawyers bloviate, as my friend Mike Webster likes to put it. I think I speak for both of us when I say that we truly appreciate your time and the sacrifice you're making."

Jo couldn't help admiring Cromwell's performance. He moved around the courtroom with comfortable grace and spoke with unaffected warmth, as if he were in his living room telling a story to friends. His appearance also subtly conveyed likability and trustworthiness. He wore a plain navy suit, pale-yellow shirt, and a crimson tie with a conservative pattern. His shoes were well-polished black wingtips. His hair had been recently cut by a skilled barber, but didn't look styled. Nothing about him was either extravagant or shabby. He looked and sounded competent, friendly, and reliable. The kind of man you'd trust enough to buy a used car from.

The jurors felt the same way. Cromwell was making eye contact with each of them as he spoke, systematically working his way across the jury box. As he did, Jo noted little smiles and positive body language from several of them. They were ready to believe him.

Cromwell clicked a tiny remote and a picture of Seth Bell appeared on the screen. He was sitting at a restaurant table and smiling, his arm around his mother. It was a happy, natural scene, one that any family could identify with. Seth had been a good-looking man with a deceptively friendly smile. "This is Seth Bell. He died last spring after being treated by the primary defendant in this case, Dr. Johanna Anderson. As Judge Spink said, Dr. Anderson is a psychologist. There are standards of care for psychologists, and you'll hear about those. You will also hear that Dr. Anderson did not use standard treatment methods on Seth. Instead, she used a dangerous and experimental technique, something she calls Mind's Eye."

Mike stood. "Objection, argument. Also, Mr. Cromwell is conflating standards of care and standard treatments. Those are two separate things."

Judge Spink nodded. "Sustained."

Mike sat down and Cromwell continued without missing a beat. "You are going to hear Dr. Anderson testify that she is the only person in the world who uses Mind's Eye. You're also going to hear her admit that she has been using it for less than two years. Finally, you will hear her admit that Mind's Eye patients have a ten percent annual fatality rate. I will leave it to you whether Mind's Eye is dangerous and experimental.

"This is the equipment she uses for Mind's Eye." He clicked the remote again. Jo expected to see a picture—which Mike had fought to keep out and lost—of the fMRI machine, EEG cap, and other Mind's Eye sensors arranged to look vaguely like medieval torture devices. But instead the screen showed an image of the lake at Shadow Cliffs where Seth had committed suicide.

"Uh." Cromwell clicked the remote again. Seth's death certificate came up. He clicked a different button. Shadow Cliffs again. "Sorry about this." He clicked again. This time, PowerPoint vanished and the Facebook page of one of the jurors appeared.

A junior lawyer sitting in front of the laptop frantically typed on the keypad and the screen abruptly went blank.

Cromwell grinned sheepishly at the juror whose Facebook page had been on display. "Sorry, we lawyers always do background research."

A couple of jurors glanced at Mike, who did not have a laptop in front of him.

Several members of Cromwell's team huddled over their laptop. One of them looked up at her boss and shook her head.

Cromwell turned to the judge. "Your Honor, could we have a five-minute recess while we solve this technical problem?"

The judge agreed and the courtroom cleared.

Jo wanted to talk to Mike, but he pulled out his phone and hurried to an empty corner. He put the phone to his ear and started talking in hushed tones, his eyes warily scanning the area around him for possible eavesdroppers. Jo sighed and sat down on a bench, hoping that whatever was looming toward him went well.

Five minutes stretched to ten. Then twenty. After thirty-three minutes, one of Cromwell's people called them back in.

The goodwill that Cromwell had built with the jury had dissipated. When they came back into the courtroom, they were both annoyed and distant. Cromwell apologized for the delay and picked up his opening statement where he had left off. He moved through the rest of his speech with polished efficiency. He laid out the evidence that Jo had been negligent both in using Mind's Eye and in not spotting "red flags" warning of Seth's impending suicide. He had no further tech disasters, and the video clips and other visuals he used were all slick and professional. The jurors listened politely, but the rapport Jo had noticed earlier was gone. *Good.*

When Mike's turn came, he strode up to the lectern holding nothing but a yellow notepad. "Ladies and gentlemen, I join Mr. Cromwell in thanking you for your service and your time. Both are valuable, and I will waste neither. You've had a long day and I know you'd like to get home, so I'll be brief."

He scored some points with his promises to be brief and not waste their time. But Jo had known enough lawyers to worry that he might not be able to keep either promise.

"Unlike Mr. Cromwell, I don't have a PowerPoint or any videos to show you. All I have is a story that happens to fit the evidence you will see and hear in the next few days. It's mostly the story of Seth Bell. You may have noticed that Mr. Cromwell didn't talk much about Seth in his opening. He focused on Dr. Anderson and the supposed dangers of her treatment methods. He's a very clever lawyer, so I'm sure there's a reason he did that, and I think I know what that reason is.

"Seth Bell was a deeply troubled young man. That picture you saw was a bright moment in his life, but there were many dark ones. He was diagnosed with paranoid schizophrenia and depression at the age of seventeen. He attempted suicide for the first time that same year."

"Objection, argument," Cromwell said.

"I'll rephrase, Your Honor," Mike responded. "Seth was found unconscious in a closed garage, sitting in a car with the engine running. He survived, but after that there were drug and alcohol overdoses. He did time in prison, and both his prison and parole medical records noted that he had suicidal thoughts and substance-abuse problems. In fact, it was those preexisting problems that brought Seth Bell to Dr. Anderson's office.

"Seth had been receiving psychiatric treatment and counseling for his problems for years, but with little success. His problems were substantial, complex, and deep rooted. That was why he was a good candidate for Dr. Anderson's Mind's Eye program. As you'll hear, the California prison and parole system refers difficult patients to her, patients who haven't responded well to regular treatment techniques. Seth Bell was one of those patients.

"Did Seth have 'red flags for suicide,' as Mr. Cromwell said? Of course he did. Seth had had red flags for suicide since he was seventeen. As you'll hear, Dr. Anderson was trying to remove those flags. Trying hard. Tragically, her efforts were no more successful than the more traditional techniques tried by Seth's earlier therapists.

"There weren't any new or different flags during his last session with Dr. Anderson. He didn't announce that he was planning to kill himself or anything like that. In fact, you'll hear Dr. Anderson testify that Seth seemed to be in relatively good spirits when he left her office.

"This story ends on a cold spring day last year, over a week after Seth's last session with Dr. Anderson. Seth started to drink early that day. Even though he had been repeatedly warned not to mix his medications with alcohol, he drank. And drank. We're not sure when he started, but by the time he boarded the ferry from San Francisco to Alameda shortly after one o'clock in the afternoon, he was staggering. You'll see security-camera video showing that and also showing him continuing to drink while he was on the boat. Cameras on a BART train show him still drinking four hours later. He passed out or fell asleep on the train, then started drinking again when he woke up. He stumbled out of the station at the end of the line at six and caught a cab to Shadow Cliffs Regional Park. That's the last time anyone saw him alive. The next day, the police pulled him out of a lake in the park. His blood-alcohol content was point-three-two percent, which is near lethal levels."

Mike paused and made eye contact with each juror for a fraction of a second, just as Cromwell had. Jo wondered whether he had learned that trick from his former boss. If so, he had learned it well. The jurors responded positively, as they had throughout his opening.

"The evidence will show that Seth Bell did not die because of anything Dr. Anderson did or didn't do. She tried to help him. She was the last in a long line of mental-health professionals who tried to help him. They all failed. In the end, no one could save Seth Bell from his own demons. Maybe he killed himself or maybe he simply slipped and fell into the lake. Either way, that is a tragedy, but it is not malpractice. At the end of this trial, I am going to ask you for a not-guilty verdict, and I'm confident you'll agree that's the only verdict the evidence will support.

"Thank you, and have a good evening."

He sat down, having spoken for less than a third of the time Cromwell talked, not counting his half-hour-plus of technical difficulties. Jo noted microexpressions of surprise and pleasure from the jurors, in addition to the more general positive responses she had noted earlier.

Round one to the defense.

Everyone in the courtroom stood silently while Judge Spink dismissed the jury. She left, and a buzz of conversation and activity filled the courtroom. Jo turned to congratulate Mike, but he was already gone.

# Chapter 69

Mike parked outside Horizon Finance and looked up at the building, a glassy block checkered with dark and light squares. It was after six, but it looked like about two-thirds of the occupants were still there. Ryan had thought David Klein would probably be among them, and Mike hoped he was right.

He took a deep breath and tried to say a quick prayer, but he was too nervous to do anything other than repeat "God, please help me" over and over.

Waiting wouldn't make things any better. He got out of the car and strode across the parking lot, feeling unseen eyes on him. His nerves calmed as he walked, just like they always did when a big court hearing actually started. The anticipation was over.

He pushed through the glass doors and walked into the lobby. Two fitter-than-usual security guards immediately locked eyes on him from behind a large steel desk. They watched silently as he approached.

"I'm here to see David Klein of Horizon Finance," Mike announced. "My name is Mike Webster."

One of the guards nodded. "Please wait over there, sir," he said, gesturing to a cluster of chairs about twenty feet from the security station.

Mike took a seat and watched as one guard picked up a phone and had a brief conversation that Mike couldn't hear. The other guard watched Mike steadily but without obvious malice. He looked like a trained attack dog waiting for the command to either kill or ignore a possible target.

The first guard put down the phone. "This way, sir." He gestured for Mike to go through a windowless door to the side of the lobby.

For an instant, Mike was unsure what to do. Were they going to kill him in there? Should he run? Or was this some sort of routine screening process? And if he did run, what were his chances of getting out of the parking lot alive?

Well, if they were going to kill him, they'd probably get the chance eventually even if he got away tonight. He walked through the door.

He found himself in a utilitarian room that held little more than a TSA-style body scanner and an X-ray machine. "All metal or electronics in here," the guard said, handing Mike a plastic bin. "Shoes and jacket off too," he added, handing Mike a second bin.

Mike put his cell phone, keys, and belt in the first bin and sent them through the X-ray machine, followed by the second bin with his shoes and jacket. He then stepped into the scanner and assumed the hands-above-the-head position.

The machine did its thing and the guard motioned for Mike to step out. The guard then frisked Mike thoroughly. "Okay," he said when he was done.

Mike put his shoes and belt back on. He reached for his phone, but the guard shook his head. "Uh-uh. You can pick it up on your way out."

Mike shrugged and walked out, relieved that at least he was leaving the room under his own power.

The guard followed him out and pointed toward the bank of elevators. "Second elevator on your right, sir."

Mike stepped into the elevator. It was a smooth box on the inside with no buttons or controls other than a red knob labeled "Emergency Call." It whisked him straight up to the fifteenth floor.

The doors opened, revealing a blandly anonymous corporate lobby—black granite tiles, short gray carpet, a table with two empty vases. Over the table, six-inch-high brushed-steel letters spelled "Horizon Finance, LLC."

A large man with a crew cut waited behind the reception desk at the end of the lobby. He wasn't wearing a uniform, but he was cast from the same mold as the security guards downstairs. Mike walked up to him. "Mike Webster to see David Klein."

The man nodded and picked up a phone receiver. "Mr. Webster is here."

A moment later, a petite young Asian woman appeared. "This way," she said, then turned and walked back the way she had come without waiting for a response.

Mike followed her, looking around as he walked. He passed rows of cubicles lined with rows of monitors, an open kitchen with several types of complicated coffee machines and baskets of snacks, and a foosball table. It looked like a dozen other tech or VC offices he had been in. But for the Pentagon-level security, he would be starting to doubt his assumptions about Horizon.

The woman led him to a large corner office, just like Ryan had described, and stopped at the door. She gestured for him to go in, then shut the door behind him.

A man slouched behind an oversized desk to Mike's left, his feet up. David Klein. Klein regarded Mike with cold, intelligent brown eyes. He was a few years younger than Mike—maybe thirty-three. Longish, gelled brown hair swept back off his high forehead and was tucked behind his ears. His complexion was pale to the point of being vampiric. He wore a white dress shirt that had been expertly tailored to make him look wiry rather than skinny.

Mike walked over to Klein's desk and started to sit in one of his guest chairs.

"I didn't say you could sit," Klein snapped.

"I didn't ask," Mike replied. He sat down and rested his left ankle on his right knee. He leaned into the corner of the chair, so that he faced both the window and Klein. He could see the dim outline of a half-finished building across the street. "You need to make a deal with me, David."

The corners of Klein's mouth quirked in a small, sardonic smile. "Why is that?"

"You want Mind's Eye. Desperately. You've tried everything to get it. You forced Oceanview to stop funding Dr. Anderson's company, hoping to push her into bankruptcy. That didn't work, so you tried underwriting the Bell lawsuit and running up my legal bills. That also failed. Then you tried to kill me, but you blew that too."

Klein's expression didn't change as Mike spoke. He sat there with his fingers steepled, watching Mike with a mixture of arrogance and annoyance.

"Now it's too late to take me out," Mike continued. "Any competent lawyer could win the case at this point, and it would cost ten thousand dollars, max. The only way you win and get your hands on Mind's Eye now is if I help you do it. So you need to make a deal with me."

"You're delusional, Webster," Klein said, his voice cold and disdainful.

"Really? I guess I'll be going, then." Mike started to get up.

"You don't want to do that."

Mike paused, halfway to his feet. "Why not?"

"Because *you* need to make a deal with *me*."

"Why?"

Klein smiled venomously. "Because if you don't, I'll get you disbarred."

Mike sat back down. He didn't like where this was going, but he had to hide it. "And how would you do that?"

"Oh, we've got quite a file on you, Webster. I'm sure the state bar would be very interested to know how you've put together such an impressive string of wins."

Mike shrugged with what he hoped looked like indifference. "They already know. I've spoken at half a dozen bar conventions in the past year. I gave away all of my secrets."

Klein's smile broadened, showing his teeth. He pulled his feet off the desk and sat up. "Not all of them. Did you mention how you managed to let jurors overhear you describing excluded evidence in the *Lee v. Harrington* case? Or how you did the same thing last year in *Smith v. Wong* and at least two other cases? How about the time you bribed a hospital employee to give you the personnel file of a doctor with an alcohol problem in *Pollard v. University Health Care*? And did you mention destroying inconvenient documents during any of your convention speeches?" He paused and gave Mike a predatory look. "Do I need to go on?"

Klein's words hit like hammers, shattering Mike's confidence. They had found out. Somehow, they had found out. He fought to keep his face and voice calm. "That's the best you've got? Those are all the legal equivalent of going seventy when the speed limit is sixty-five. At most, the bar would give me a tongue-lashing. More likely, they'll do nothing. There's no way they'd disbar me. No way."

Klein gave a harsh laugh. "We've already consulted an expert in legal ethics. You will almost certainly get disbarred. You might even go to jail."

Mike fought to stay focused. He had a plan and it should still work. He just needed to stick with it. "Get to the point. You said you wanted to make a deal. What is it?"

"Simple. You lose the Bell case. You also bill Anderson for every second of time you've worked. And we never call the state bar."

Mike stared out the window at the shadowy building across the street. With just a little push, he could get Klein where he wanted him. He was sure of it. But if he did that, Klein would destroy him. They would destroy each other.

Klein needed to be destroyed, and he needed to take Horizon Finance down with him. Mike knew that. He also knew instinctively that David Klein needed to be destroyed more than Mike Webster needed to keep practicing law.

There was no clever way out, or at least none that Mike could think of on the spur of the moment. Just a brutal choice. Best to get it over with fast, before he could think about the consequences.

"Let me get this straight," Mike said, still looking at the building and speaking slowly and clearly. "You are proposing that I intentionally lose a case and try to bankrupt my client so that you can buy her technology out of bankruptcy? Are you serious?"

Klein nodded sharply. "Of course I'm serious. And if you're serious, you'll take that deal before I change my mind."

*Gotcha!* Mike had won, though Klein didn't know it quite yet. But Mike wanted more. "Serious? You want to see me serious? You got it!" He leaned forward and let some heat creep into his voice as he spoke. "You tick me off, and it's going to cost you. If you want me to lose that trial, that will cost you ten million dollars. In advance. And trying to kill me will cost you another ten, also in advance."

Klein's pasty face flushed to deep crimson. "You're not getting a penny, moron. In fact, I—"

As Mike had hoped, Klein wasn't used to being talked to like this and didn't handle it well. "Add an extra million for insulting me. Payable now."

Klein looked at him incredulously. "You—"

"Go on, Dave," Mike said, making a shooing motion. "Turn around and make the wire transfer on your computer. I know you can do it."

Klein's eyes burned with rage. "If you're not very careful, you're going to wind up like your friend in the garage."

"I'll wind up like my friend in the garage?" Mike said, facing out the window. "You'll need to find a better triggerman to kill me, Dave."

Klein smiled savagely and nodded. "Trust me, we never make the same mistake twice."

Mike wasn't a criminal lawyer, but he was pretty sure he had enough now. "No, you always find new mistakes to make."

Mike stood and waved his hands over his head.

Klein jumped to his feet and stared at Mike as if he'd lost his mind. "What the—"

"This whole conversation has been recorded," Mike explained. "I just signaled the police that I'm in danger and they should move in."

"You're insane," Klein said, the anger in his face replaced by wariness. He reached under his desk for an instant. Then he picked up a paperweight and held it like a weapon. "Sit down and stay where you are. Security will be here any second."

Mike laughed and sat down. "You think we weren't recorded because I'm not wearing a wire, right?"

"Yeah," Klein said uneasily. "You were searched downstairs."

Mike nodded. "I was indeed. We figured you guys would check for that. So rather than put a wire on me, the police set up in that construction site across the street." He pointed to the half-finished building. "They've been filming us with high-resolution cameras. They probably were able to pick up some of what you said, but they got everything that I said. The lighting is pretty good in here and I've been enunciating clearly, so they won't have any trouble reading my lips. Also, you nodded helpfully in a couple of places."

Klein looked at the building across the street. "You're lying," he said uncertainly.

"We'll see who comes through that door—your goons or the cops."

As if on cue, shouting erupted on the street outside.

Mike went to the window and looked down. A group of men wearing black with "SWAT" in yellow letters on their backs swarmed into the building. Two security guards lay on the ground with their hands behind their heads, watched by one of the SWAT team members.

Mike heard Klein cursing in a shaky voice and turned to find him standing next to him, looking down. He was shorter than Mike would have guessed, and just as skinny as he thought. Klein weighed 150 pounds, tops.

"Dave, you just confessed to ordering a cop killing and committing a bunch of other felonies. You are in deep trouble. You are probably going to spend the rest of your years in prison, and the guards have all sorts of special ways to make life a living hell for cop killers." Mike turned around so that his back was to the window. "You're going to need friends."

At the word *friends*, Klein tore his eyes away from the scene on the street and looked at Mike with a mixture of terror, hope, and pleading.

"I said you need to make a deal with me," Mike continued, "and you really, really do. Here's the deal."

Mike spoke quickly for thirty seconds. Klein listened and nodded. As Mike finished, three heavily armed policemen burst through the door.

# CHAPTER 70

Val's cell phone rang. It was Mike's ring, a snatch from the song "9 to 5."

She pulled her phone out of her purse and stared at it. She wanted to answer, to talk to him, to make everything right, to just hear his voice. But she wasn't ready yet. She looked at the contents of Angy's last gift to her, spread out on her kitchen table. She couldn't tell Mike about that yet—but she couldn't *not* tell him if they were talking on the phone.

The phone stopped ringing. A few seconds later, a text message from Mike appeared: Call when you can.

"Oh, I will," she said to the empty room. She sighed and dropped her phone back into her purse. She went back to work on her research with renewed vigor.

Her phone rang again five minutes later. The number looked vaguely familiar, though she couldn't quite place it. She answered. "This is Val."

"Val, it's Ryan Daley. I have news for you."

"What?"

"We caught the guy behind Angy's murder."

She froze. She stood with her mouth open, staring at nothing. Then she had so many things to say that she couldn't get any of them out.

"Val? Are you there?"

"Yeah. I . . . That's great. Congratulations. Thank you." It was inadequate, but it was all she could put into words at the moment. "Who killed him?"

"A guy named David Klein from Horizon Finance was the mastermind. He says the actual shooter is dead. Angy shot him. We're checking it out."

Val sniffed and realized she was crying. "Thank you," she said again. "Thank you."

"Angy was a good man," Ryan said, his voice unsteady. "I'm glad we were able to catch the guy who killed him. And the evidence we've got is really solid. I don't think he'll be able to skate, no matter how good his lawyers are."

"That's great," Val said through her tears. "You guys rock."

"Thanks." The line was silent for a couple of seconds. "I can't say much about an ongoing investigation, but your boss rocks too. He's a really stand-up guy."

Mike? Did the documents on the thumb drive break the case open somehow? Or did he do something else? "He can be a really great guy," she said.

"No kidding. Hey, I've gotta go, but I wanted to let you know. We'll be in touch as the case moves along."

"Thanks. I really appreciate it."

She hung up. Then she pulled up Mike's text again. `Call when you can.`

She wanted to call, wanted it badly. To talk about Angy, about Jo, about the trial, about everything. "But I can't," she said aloud. "I'm not ready yet."

She would be soon, though. A few more days of research and running down loose ends. She had to wait until she had everything wrapped up in a neat package. Then she would call.

# CHAPTER 71

"The plaintiff calls Olivia Bell," Tim Cromwell announced.

Mike was both surprised and pleased. Senator Bell was the obvious first witness. He was a natural public speaker and he had been the lead spokesman for the family throughout the case. His wife, Olivia, was a brittle society matron, the kind of woman who is very good at cocktail-party conversation but can't handle anything more serious. Camy had taken her deposition, but Mike had skimmed the transcript and watched parts of the video. Whenever Camy asked a remotely hard question, Mrs. Bell retreated into vague answers and plastic smiles. She wasn't nearly as effective as her husband, so Mike took it as a backhanded compliment that she was testifying first. That meant Senator Bell had been so damaged during his depositions that Tim couldn't lead with him.

But Mike's sense of victory began to evaporate as soon as Olivia Bell took the stand. She wore a simple blue dress and a single strand of pearls. It was a good look for today. She projected reliability and respectability, not the society-wife image on display at her deposition. She had been well coached.

Tim used his direct examination of her to introduce Seth Bell to the jury. Through Olivia's maternal perspective, Tim painted a picture of Seth as a gifted and charming young man. Yes, he had had some substance-abuse problems and mental-health challenges. And yes, he had gotten into legal trouble on a few occasions, but he had been doing much better recently. He had made a real effort to turn his life around since he got out of prison, and it had been working. That was when the picture Tim had used in his opening was taken. Seth had just passed his fifth straight parole-required drug test, and he was moving out of his halfway house and into an apartment of his own. It had been a good day, and they had gone out to celebrate.

But then Dr. Anderson started treating him. His drinking started again. His bouts of depression became worse and longer. Everything started to go downhill. And then he came back to the town where he'd grown up, and he killed himself. She choked up when she talked about his death, and Mike heard a few sniffles from the jury box.

It was effective. Tim had done an excellent job of prepping her for trial. At her depo, Olivia Bell had come across as detached, almost embarrassed by her son's death. But today she had acted the part of the grieving mother to perfection. And Mike suspected that it really was little more than acting. As the spouse of a professional politician, she had doubtless learned how to display the right emotions at a public event and to give convincing recitations of canned answers to canned questions.

Mike hadn't planned to do her cross-examination today, so he wasn't completely prepared for it. In fact, he wasn't really prepared for her at all. He had been so busy and distracted over the past few days that he hadn't done any work getting ready for Olivia Bell. The last time he had even thought about her was three months ago when Camy reported on her depo.

Should he have Camy do the cross? She knew the witness better than he did—but she also hadn't done any prep. She was good on her feet, but not as good as he was. Besides, it wouldn't be fair to foist this on her with no warning. He rubbed his temples to try to ward off the headache that had been gathering steam during Mrs. Bell's testimony, then jotted down a quick cross-examination outline.

Tim finished his direct examination and sat down. Judge Spink looked at Mike. "Any cross-examination, Counsel?"

Camy looked at Mike inquiringly.

"I've got this," he said under his breath. "Yes, Your Honor," he replied to the judge.

He walked up to the lectern and looked at Olivia Bell. She met his gaze and gave him a wary smile.

He smiled back. "Mrs. Bell, did you ever sit in on Seth's therapy sessions with Dr. Anderson?"

"No."

"Before this case started, did you ever see any video or other record of those sessions?"

"No."

"Would it be fair to say that you don't know what transpired in those sessions?"

"I suppose so."

He paused. The cardinal rule of cross-examination is *Never ask a question that you don't know the answer to.* Given his lack of prep, that rule covered pretty much any other question he could think of. So he decided to do the next-best thing and only ask questions that he didn't care how she answered.

"Mrs. Bell, is anyone paying you to testify here today?"

She stared at him in surprise. "Excuse me?"

"Is anyone paying you to testify today?"

"No."

"Is anyone paying you to pursue this lawsuit?"

She gave him an exquisitely disdainful look, like he was a caddy who had just wrongly accused her of moving her ball. "Of course not."

"You're sure?"

"Yes," she said indignantly.

"No further questions."

# CHAPTER 72

After trial adjourned for the day, Jo came over to Mike, who was packing his briefcase. "Hi, Mike. Are you free for dinner tonight? My treat. I want to hear the whole story of how you took down that Horizon Finance guy."

"I'd love to, but I have to work tonight. I need to get ready for tomorrow's witnesses. Between Val leaving and the Horizon Finance business, I haven't been able to prepare the way I usually do. You may not have noticed, but I was basically winging it today."

Actually, she had noticed. So had the jury. They had liked Mrs. Bell, and they hadn't appreciated his attempt to insinuate that she had been bribed, particularly when his questioning didn't go anywhere. That was one of the topics she had hoped to delicately raise over dinner.

"Well, we can make it a working dinner," she said. "I've been watching the jury and the witnesses, and I could give you my thoughts on who's telling the truth, how the jury is reacting, and that sort of thing. What do you say?"

He stopped packing and looked her in the eyes. "I really would love to, but I just can't. The kind of prep I need to do involves reading transcripts and looking at documents and kicking around possible cross-exam questions with Camy. But if you could send me an e-mail with your thoughts on today, that would be fantastic."

She forced a smile. "I understand. I'll send you an e-mail tonight."

"Thanks." He flashed her the dazzling smile she had first seen so long ago, then turned back to his packing. A minute later, he hurried off with Camy.

Jo watched them go with a lingering sense of unease. She sighed. In a week, trial would be over and she'd know where they stood, for better or worse.

# CHAPTER 73

Shaun Hammond was a big man, too big for the chair in the witness box. He moved around in his seat, trying to get comfortable—and looking shifty and nervous in the process. Plus, the chair squeaked. Loudly. When Hammond repositioned his ample posterior or jerked his head to flip his blond hair out of his eyes, the chair sounded like an unoiled door in a haunted house.

Mike jotted "chair" on his notepad to remind himself to track down a chair like the one in the courtroom for future witness-prep sessions, particularly when the witness was built like a lowland gorilla who needed to cut back on the bananas. He wondered whether Tim Cromwell had made the same note. Probably not. Tim was in the middle of his direct examination and was likely too focused on Hammond's testimony to notice the sound effects. Mike decided he would mention it after the trial. He and Tim were unlikely to be on opposite sides of the courtroom again, so there was no reason not to give him a tip—and Tim had given him thousands when Mike was a young lawyer.

Hammond described the Mind's Eye system succinctly and in fairly neutral terms—which he had doubtless been coached to do in order to make the jurors view him as unbiased. He gave a quick overview of how

Jo's office worked, emphasizing his role. And then he gave the testimony Horizon Finance had paid him for.

"Was Seth Bell the only one of Dr. Anderson's patients who committed suicide?" Tim asked.

Mike stood. "Objection, lacks foundation. It has not been established that Seth Bell committed suicide."

The judge nodded and turned to the jury. "Ignore any facts assumed by Mr. Cromwell's question." She looked at Hammond. "You may answer the question."

"No. A patient named Jonathon Adams also killed himself."

Jo handed Mike a note that said: "Not patient; eval. only."

Mike nodded. He could have objected, but didn't. He could make that point more effectively on cross-examination.

"How many patients had Dr. Anderson treated with Mind's Eye as of your last day in her office?"

"Ten, including Adams and Bell."

"And how long had she been using Mind's Eye?"

Hammond leaned to the side and the chair groaned. "She had been treating patients with it for a little less than two years when I left."

"So two out of ten killed themselves in less than two years. That's more than ten percent per year." Tim's eyebrows went up. "I guess I was wrong in my opening statement."

Mike stood. "Objection. If Mr. Cromwell is going to testify, he needs to be under oath, and I get to cross-examine him. But I will stipulate that he was repeatedly wrong in his opening statement."

Tim held up his hands. "The last thing I want is for Mr. Webster to cross-examine me about my math skills."

That brought a smile from the judge and several jurors. If Mike had a hat, he would have tipped it. Not many lawyers could score points while being busted for breaking the rules.

Judge Spink turned to the jury. "Please disregard those last remarks. The comments of the lawyers are not evidence."

"Were you present when Dr. Anderson treated Seth Bell?" Tim asked Hammond.

"Some of the time."

"But not always?"

"No. Some of his sessions were in the evening after I had left for the day."

"Who monitored all those Mind's Eye machines if you weren't there?"

Hammond leaned back. The chair squealed in protest. "Nobody, I guess."

"Did those machines ever malfunction?"

"Sure. The software crashed about once a month, sometimes more. Other stuff went wrong too—wires would come loose and that sort of thing."

"Do you know whether anything went wrong when Dr. Anderson was treating Seth Bell by herself?"

"Well, I wasn't there, so I can't say for sure, but she did tell me that there was at least one malfunction."

"What was the malfunction?"

"The data feed didn't record, so the video and sensor data were all lost. First we thought the problem was that the hard disk was full, but then Dr. Anderson said there may have been a software glitch that turned off the recording."

"Is the data recording an important part of Mind's Eye?"

"Oh, it's critical. Without the data from a session, you can't track a patient's progress. And if something goes wrong—like it did with Seth—you can't go back and look at the sessions to figure out where the problem was."

"I see. Is it possible that other important parts of Mind's Eye also malfunctioned during Seth Bell's sessions?"

Hammond shrugged. The chair creaked. "Sure, but it's impossible for me to say what happened because I wasn't there."

"Why weren't you there?"

"Because Dr. Anderson always scheduled Seth's sessions for Monday, which was my day off. She usually saw patients on Tuesdays through Saturdays and did paperwork and stuff on Mondays."

"Did she treat other patients when you weren't there?"

Hammond nodded toward Mike. "She was always alone when she treated him."

The judge and jury all stared at Mike. He reflexively started to get up to object, then thought better of it, made a dismissive motion, and sat down. Judge Spink would probably sustain his objection, but she couldn't erase Hammond's testimony from the jurors' minds; it would merely make the jurors think Mike and Jo had something to hide.

"Mr. Webster?" Tim said, pointing to Mike.

"Yes. He started coming in after she got sued. Always after hours when Dr. Anderson was the only one there. I'd come in the next morning and find new data files with Mr. Webster's name on them."

Mike smiled as if Hammond's testimony amused him. In truth, he was fuming. And he had another headache, which didn't improve his mood.

Mostly, Mike was mad at himself. Tim was hitting him a little below the belt, but he should have seen it coming. Handled well—and that was generally the only way Tim handled things—Hammond would testify that Mike was a Mind's Eye patient before Mike could object. And the benefit of getting that fact before the jury was significant for Tim: jurors almost always side with the lawyer they trust more, and they weren't likely to trust Mike as much after hearing that he was seeing Jo for Mind's Eye treatments and who knew what else. It was an obvious move, in retrospect. He should have been ready for it.

Tim wrapped up a few minutes later, and Mike took his place at the lectern. "Mr. Hammond, you testified that Jonathon Adams was a patient of Dr. Anderson, correct?"

"Correct."

"But he wasn't, was he? Dr. Anderson only performed an evaluation on him, correct?"

Hammond shrugged. "She used Mind's Eye on him."

"Yes, but she didn't take him on as a patient. She only performed a one-time evaluation on him at the request of the Department of Corrections, correct?"

"We did an evaluation," Hammond admitted. "I don't know the details."

"In fact, there are a lot of details about Mind's Eye that you don't know, isn't that true?"

He crossed his tree-trunk arms. "I'm not sure what you're talking about. You'll have to be more specific."

"All right. You don't know that Dr. Anderson was able to cure my insomnia in just one session with Mind's Eye and lowered my blood pressure in five sessions, correct?"

Tim stood. "Objection. I may have been testifying, but Mr. Webster is giving an infomercial."

Chuckles from the jury box.

"If Mr. Cromwell didn't want the jury to hear about my experience, he shouldn't have asked about it on direct. Besides, I'm allowed to lead on cross."

"That's not leading," Tim replied, "that's—"

Judge Spink held up her hand. "Sidebar."

The two lawyers walked up to the bench under the reproving glare of the judge. She leaned over and spoke in a low voice so the jurors couldn't hear. "If you two don't cut it out, I'm going to put you both under oath, and you won't like the questions I ask."

"I understand, Your Honor," Mike said.

"You'd better," she said. "Both of you. You're manipulating the jury and evading the rules of evidence, and I don't appreciate it. Any more misconduct and you risk a mistrial and sanctions. Is that clear?"

"Yes, Your Honor," they said in unison.

Tim retreated to his chair and Mike went back to the lectern. "Mr. Hammond, are you familiar with a company called Horizon Finance?"

Hammond leaned forward and hunched over. His hair fell in his eyes again and he brushed it back with thick fingers. "I, uh, may have heard the name."

"Have they ever paid you money?"

"I don't believe so."

"So you don't remember?" Mike asked, a note of incredulity in his voice.

"I don't remember every place that has sent me money in my life."

Mike leaned forward on the lectern. "Let's make this more specific. I'm not asking about your whole life. I'm only asking about the past year. And I'm also only asking about Mind's Eye. Now, with those qualifiers, has Horizon Finance paid you any money?"

"No."

"So they're not paying you to testify today?"

"No."

"And they also didn't pay you to give them confidential information or records from Dr. Anderson's office?"

Hammond squirmed and looked down, drawing sounds of agony from the chair. "Uh, no."

"No further questions."

# Chapter 74

"I loved how you handled Shaun."

Mike looked up from his phone to see Jo smiling at him. He was sitting on one of the benches in the hall outside the courtroom, catching up on e-mail before heading back to the office for pizza and prep. He felt himself smile back. "Thanks. He got a little too cute and gave me a couple of openings."

She sat down beside him and put her hand on his arm for a second. "And you were exactly cute enough. I loved the infomercial."

"The judge didn't, but maybe the jury did."

"They did." She hesitated. "I think they're still leaning against us, though. Today didn't seem to move the needle much."

He sighed and nodded. "That's what I thought. Tomorrow is going to have to be better—which is why I need to get back to the office and start getting ready. Tim says he's planning to put on three witnesses tomorrow, including Senator Bell."

"I understand." She put her hand back on his arm and looked into his eyes. "I miss you."

"I miss you too," he said. He reached over and gave her hand a squeeze. "I'll be glad when this trial is over."

"Not nearly as glad as I'll be," Jo replied.

Camy came out of the courtroom, where she had been answering some questions the court reporter had. Jo slipped her hand off his arm and the two of them stood as Camy approached.

"All set?" Camy asked.

Mike nodded. "I can finish up my e-mail when we're back at the office. Let's go."

The three of them chatted about the trial as they rode the elevator down. Mike and Camy were going back to the office and Jo was headed home, so they caught separate Ubers when they reached the street.

Once in the car, Camy and Mike both pulled out their phones. Mike pulled up his inbox, but there was nothing really urgent that he needed to deal with. If he were being honest, he probably could have spent part of the evening with Jo. Of the three witnesses set to testify tomorrow, Camy would handle two. He had Senator Bell, but he didn't need to do a lot of work to get ready for that because he had taken both sessions of the senator's deposition. A couple of hours should do it.

So why didn't he make some time for Jo? Because he was afraid to, he realized. They had been hovering on the edge of something big and exciting and scary. And just as he was getting ready to take the plunge, he heard the story of her divorce, dragged out of her at her deposition. It was worse than his parents' divorce—and that had been bad enough to make him gun-shy about marriage for his entire adult life. Would Jo do the same thing to him that she did to her first husband?

It also troubled him that she hadn't told him voluntarily. The only reason he knew the truth was that Shaun Hammond was a treacherous sleazeball. What other secrets might be out there that Shaun hadn't found?

He felt a little like a shark-attack survivor who's finally gotten up the courage to go back in the water—and sees a gray triangle in the waves. *Is it a shark fin? A dolphin? Something else? Tough to tell, but maybe it's better to stay on the beach after all.*

And yet she had touched him deeply. She had reached into the broken places in his heart and mind and helped them begin to heal. Should he push her away? Could he?

He sighed and rubbed his temples, battling yet another nasty headache. He reached into his briefcase and pulled out the medication his neurologist, Dr. Lay, had prescribed for him. Only two pills left—he needed to give her a call tomorrow to see if she'd renew the prescription. He swallowed the pills dry and waited for them to kick in.

They arrived at the office. Mike dropped his bag in the conference room and went to his office to order pizza. The voice-mail light on his phone was blinking. He hit the speakerphone button and played the message back: "Mr. Webster, this is Steve Adelman with the state bar. We've received a complaint covering a number of incidents, and we'd like to talk to you at your earliest convenience."

# CHAPTER 75

"Dr. Anderson, you want the jury to believe that during your final session with him, Seth Bell didn't give warning signs that he was suicidal, correct?"

Jo struggled to focus on the exact words of the question. She had been at this for over two hours, and her brain was exhausted. Plus, she was sitting in an uncomfortable chair, but Mike had warned her that she needed to look comfortable and relaxed. No fidgeting, squirming, or hesitating. This was much harder than her deposition had been. "Yes, that's correct."

"You claim that if Seth gave those warning signs, you would have said something in your notes about the session, correct?"

"Yes."

"Because you mention anything significant in your notes, right?"

"Yes."

"Please look at the document marked Exhibit Thirty-Six."

Jo fished it out of the pile of paper on the table in front of her. Exhibit 36 was the notes from a session five months before Seth's suicide. "I have it."

"Do those notes indicate that Seth was delusional during that session?"

She looked over the notes. She knew she was being set up, but couldn't quite see how. "I don't see anything based on a quick skim."

"Read them carefully. Take all the time you need."

Face burning, she forced herself to go through the notes line by line. "I don't see anything about him being delusional during this session," she said five minutes later.

"Here's a clip from the session described in Exhibit Thirty-Six."

A large TV on a cart to her left came to life. Seth's face filled the screen. "Why aren't you taking your medication?" Jo's voice asked from off screen.

"Because it's poisoned," Seth said.

"Why do you think it's poisoned?"

"I saw them talking when I came in to pick it up last time. Before I came in, they were talking about me, how they were going to kill me."

"How did you know what they were saying before you came into the pharmacy?"

Seth licked his lips nervously. "I can hear what people are saying even when they think I can't. Sometimes I can hear them from a mile away."

The clip paused. Seth's frozen face stared out of the screen, eyes wide and lips wet. Looking crazy.

"Would you agree that Seth was exhibiting delusional behavior?"

"Yes, but I wouldn't have charted it."

"You said that you chart anything significant. Delusional behavior isn't significant?"

"Well, yes. But I would have documented it during my evaluation, not necessarily every time it happened."

"So you're changing your testimony and admitting that you don't put everything significant in your session notes, correct?"

"I . . ." She sighed and rubbed her eyes. "I screwed up there, didn't I?"

Camy put down her prep outline and smiled diplomatically. "It was a tricky line of questioning," she said. "You were doing great up until that point."

"You were," Mike said from where he lounged in a chair to the right side of the conference room, in a position that roughly approximated the jury's viewpoint. "Even that last part wasn't too bad. You were caught by a simple trap that catches lots of witnesses: you fell into a rhythm of agreeing with a series of accurate statements, and then you agreed with one that wasn't quite accurate."

Jo nodded. "When she asked whether I put anything significant in my notes, I should have said any significant *changes*. Seth had been delusional ever since I first met him. There was no reason to describe every single delusional statement he made."

"And you'd also want to note any suicidal ideation or behavior, even if it's not new," Mike added. "You want to track the language of the guidelines."

"Yes, of course. I'm sorry, I knew that. We talked about it during our last prep session." She sighed and felt very tired. "Could we take a break? I feel like my brain is full of cotton."

"Of course," said Mike. "Want some coffee or something? We've got a Philz, a Starbucks, and a Peet's all within a block."

She shook her head. "I would like to stretch my legs and get some fresh air, though."

"I wouldn't go for a walk by myself after dark around here," Camy said.

Jo smiled at Mike. "Would you mind accompanying me?"

He hesitated for a heartbeat, then smiled back. "Of course not." He turned to Camy. "Cook up something particularly nasty while we're gone. Do your best Tim Cromwell imitation."

Camy rubbed her hands and smiled gleefully. "With pleasure."

Five minutes later, they were strolling through Sue Bierman Park, a small oasis of green in the heart of San Francisco's Financial District. It was beautifully landscaped and reasonably well lit, but there were still plenty of shadowy spots, and Jo saw several apparently homeless men lounging in out-of-the-way nooks.

Jo felt a familiar surge of panic and resisted the urge to reach into her purse and clutch the can of mace that lived there. She would have felt uneasy in the park after dark even if the memory of Jack Adams's attack didn't still haunt her. But she wasn't going to let what Adams did define or limit her. Going for an evening stroll was a way to confront her fear. Self-therapy, sort of. Besides, it gave her an excuse to walk very close to Mike. She hoped he would put his arm around her, but he didn't.

"It's been a while since we were alone together," she observed.

He nodded. "It has."

"Since before my deposition, and that was over a month ago."

"That sounds right."

She took a deep breath and steeled herself. "I've been wanting to talk to you."

He turned and looked down at her. "About what?"

"What came out during the deposition. My divorce and . . . well, what led to the divorce. Did, um, did that bother you?"

Darkness hid his face, but she could hear the "yes" in his voice when he answered. What he actually said was, "It surprised me."

"I tried to tell you when we were on the ferry, but it's hard for me to talk about it. It's very painful, even now. I feel awful about it. Ashamed. Dirty. It's the one thing in my life that I really regret. My relationship with Dan Burnside wasn't the only thing that wrecked my marriage, but it was the big thing. When he started doing me 'favors' in the Psychology Department, I didn't know how to say no. And then the university started asking questions. He said they couldn't prove anything and that we should just keep our mouths shut and admit nothing. I foolishly agreed." She sighed wearily. "You know the rest of the story. I was wrong, I was stupid, and I paid a terrible price."

"We all make mistakes," he said, compassion in his voice. "I'm sorry yours cost you so much."

"Are they still costing me?" she asked, her voice shaking slightly. "With you?"

He stopped walking. "Everyone is human. I don't hold this against you. I just . . . I don't know. You've got your baggage; I've got mine. I've always had a phobia of serious relationships, and what happened to you is an example of why. I'm not blaming you or my mom or anyone, but I just have a really hard time putting myself in a situation where that kind of thing might happen to me—or I might do it to someone else."

She hugged him and he hugged her back. "I know you'd never hurt me," she said. "And I'd rather die than hurt you."

He said nothing, but he held her tight.

They stood like that for a moment, neither speaking. Then a small woman appeared around a bend in the sidewalk, preceded by two dogs that each outweighed her.

The spell broke and Mike released her. "We'd better head back. Are you ready for more?"

"Yes."

# CHAPTER 76

Mike was losing, and he knew it. The case wasn't a lost cause, but he was behind and running out of time. If the trial were a football game, Tim and his clients would be ahead by a touchdown in the fourth quarter.

Tim had done a good job with the witnesses he'd put on so far. Mrs. Bell had been a sympathetic witness and got his case off to a strong start. Shaun Hammond hadn't been particularly likable, but he had made Jo and Mike look bad, which was all Tim probably wanted.

Mike had hoped to score some points when Senator Bell took the stand, but he had done a lot better than he did at his deposition. Tim brought up Seth's earlier suicide attempts and the senator's failings as a father. Senator Bell had confessed his paternal mistakes and even got a little teary-eyed on the witness stand. Crocodile tears, Mike was pretty sure, but the jury didn't know that and there wasn't an effective way to tell them. Senator Bell then echoed his wife's testimony that Seth had been doing a lot better until Jo started treating him, but that he went downhill quickly after his first Mind's Eye session.

After Senator Bell, Tim put on Seth's parole officer and several of his friends. They all testified that Seth's mental state seemed to deteriorate after he began his Mind's Eye sessions. The parole officer was particularly damaging: she said that she had seen Seth the day after his last Mind's Eye session and that he had talked about an infatuation with a dead girl named Maggie or Maddie. He said he hoped to see her again soon.

Of course, none of that conclusively proved that Mind's Eye killed Seth or that Jo was negligent in failing to find out that he was seriously contemplating suicide. Tim hadn't put on any evidence that Seth's worsening problems were caused by Mind's Eye as opposed to some other factor—his increased drinking, for example. And the fact that Seth made comments to his parole officer that could be construed as suicidal didn't mean he had made similar comments to Jo. But taken together, all of that evidence had tipped the scales in Tim's favor.

Mike wouldn't have many chances to tip them back, so he had to make the most of his opportunities. His first chance would come in a few minutes when Jo testified. Then there would be a battle of experts. Mike had Dr. Goff, and Tim had a competing expert from the University of Michigan named Hiram Young. Dr. Goff had a good résumé, but Young made him look like a rookie with a mail-order degree. Also, Dr. Goff had never been a really enthusiastic defender of Jo or Mind's Eye. Dr. Goff thought Mind's Eye was fascinating, and he didn't think Jo had committed malpractice, but he wasn't entirely persuaded that Mind's Eye was ready to be used on actual patients. Worse, he had left Mike a voice mail yesterday saying that he had spoken with Mike's neurologist and that they agreed that Mike shouldn't use Mind's Eye until they had a chance to review the records of his past sessions. Mike could just imagine how that would play with the jury if it came out.

Mike did his best not to think about it. No need to borrow tomorrow's troubles. He would worry about Dr. Goff when his prep sessions started after court today. For now, he needed to focus on Jo's testimony. Her final prep session had gone smoothly and she was a good witness.

But Tim was an excellent inquisitor, and he had spent a lot more time in a courtroom than Jo had.

"We call Dr. Johanna Anderson next," Tim announced.

Jo got up from her seat beside Mike and took the stand. She had her hair back in a simple black clip and wore a cream-colored suit. The goal was to make her look professional, but not austere or threatening. Mike thought it worked.

Tim went through much of the same material he'd covered during Jo's depo, though in a more streamlined fashion. He covered Jo's contract with the prison system to treat prisoners and parolees, her initial evaluation of Seth as a schizophrenic with depression and substance-abuse problems, and other important but uncontroversial topics. Then he went to the meat of his examination. "Dr. Anderson, would you agree with me that your Mind's Eye system is unique?"

"The elements of it have all been in use for years, but as an integrated system, yes, it is unique."

"In fact, it's so unique that you have patented it, haven't you?"

"Yes."

"Would you also agree that Mind's Eye represents a major change from traditional methods of psychotherapy?"

"No. The psychotherapy methods I use are actually quite traditional in most respects. All Mind's Eye does is provide me with a new tool to understand my patients' mental and emotional state during therapy. It does not change the therapeutic methods I use."

The muscles around Tim's mouth tightened slightly. "All right, but you would agree that Mind's Eye is a major new tool for therapists, correct?"

"Yes."

"And you're the only one using that tool, correct?"

"I am the only one currently using an integrated system that incorporates all of the elements that make up Mind's Eye. There are other people using different parts of it."

"But most of those people are using those devices in a research setting, correct? They're not treating patients."

"I don't know. All of the devices that make up Mind's Eye have been used outside the lab for years, and most of them are being used in therapy."

Tim turned to the judge. "Move to strike everything after 'I don't know' as nonresponsive."

Mike started to stand, but the judge didn't wait for him. "Denied. The witness was responding to your statement that the people using those devices weren't treating patients."

Mike sat back down, resisting the urge to smile. Jo wasn't letting Tim get away with anything and it frustrated him. Tim didn't handle frustration well.

"Thank you, Your Honor," Tim said. He turned back to Jo. "Dr. Anderson, how is it that such a remarkable tool didn't allow you to see that Seth might commit suicide only a week after your last session?"

There was an edge of sarcasm in Tim's voice, but Jo didn't rise to the bait. Instead, she did the smart thing and focused on Tim's question, which had been sloppy. She made him pay for it. "Mind's Eye allows me to see many things, Mr. Cromwell, but the future isn't one of them. Unless Seth was severely depressed or considering suicide during our sessions, I wouldn't be able to tell that he might commit suicide later. Suicidal impulses can arise very quickly, particularly in patients who suffer from depression or have substance-abuse problems. Unfortunately, Seth was both depressed and a substance abuser. Further, it is not at all clear to me that Seth committed suicide. He became very intoxicated and drowned, but I do not know whether his death was intentional or accidental."

Tim's face darkened slightly. He switched to a different line of attack. "Dr. Anderson, have you ever been found guilty of a crime or rules violation involving dishonesty?"

She sighed and looked down. "Yes," she said softly.

"I'm sorry, I couldn't hear you," Tim said, even though her answer was clearly audible from where Mike sat beside the jury box.

"Yes," she said more loudly. "When I was in graduate school, I made a mistake in my personal life and I lied to cover it up. That violated the school's rules. That's the only time, and I've regretted it ever since. I—"

"Thank you, Dr. Anderson," Tim cut in. "You were found guilty of more than just hiding a personal mistake, weren't you?"

She looked at the jury. "Yes. I—I had an inappropriate relationship with one of my professors," she said in a confessional tone. "I was young and stupid and—"

The frustration in Tim's face grew. "And you accepted preferential treatment from him, isn't that true?"

Mike could have objected but decided not to. He remembered Napoleon's famous admonition, "Never interrupt your opponent when he is making a mistake." Tim seemed to think that Jo was faking her emotions and failing to give straight answers to yes/no questions. So he was trying to control the situation by cutting her off and communicating to the jurors that he didn't believe her, so they shouldn't either. Mike was pretty sure that was a mistake, and he was going to let Tim make it.

"That's what the school found," Jo said to the jurors, looking at the female jurors in particular. "Professor Burnside was a powerful man," she continued, her voice quavering slightly. "I was his student and I didn't know how to say no to him, so I . . . I . . ." Her voice trailed off and she wiped her eyes, leaving little black smears.

"So you accepted favors from him," Tim said, his voice cold and disdainful. "And you lied about that too, didn't you?"

She nodded and wiped her eyes again. "To my shame, I did," she said, her voice thick with unshed tears.

"No further questions," Tim said.

Mike took a quick look at the jurors. Yep, Tim had made a mistake. He had seriously dented his standing with them, particularly the women in the box.

Mike got up. "Dr. Anderson, would you like to take a break before we continue?"

She sniffed. "Thank you, I would."

"Your Honor, could we have a five-minute recess?" Mike asked.

"Of course," Judge Spink replied. "I suspect the jury could use a break too. Court is adjourned for ten minutes. Dr. Anderson, please do not speak to anyone, including your attorney, during the break."

Ten minutes later, they were back in the courtroom. Jo looked fresh and composed. Several of the jurors had smiled at her with compassion when they came back from the jury room.

Mike had five and a half pages of follow-up questions he could ask about the topics Tim had covered during his examination. But if he did that, Tim could go back into those areas on redirect when Mike was done. If Mike left those topics alone, however, Tim had to as well. Tim hadn't exactly covered himself with glory during his examination of Jo, but there was a good chance that he'd do significantly better if given another chance. Mike decided not to give him one, even though that meant dumping most of his questions as well.

"Dr. Anderson, several witnesses have said that Seth Bell's mental state deteriorated during the time you treated him. Do you agree?"

"I do."

"Do you know why that might have happened?"

Tim stood. "Objection, calls for a narrative."

He was right. "I'll rephrase the question," Mike responded. "Dr. Anderson, please tell us what factors you believe contributed to Seth Bell's worsening mental health."

"Based on my treatment of him, I believe there were two primary contributing factors. First, at the same time I started treating Seth, he moved out of the halfway house where he had been living since his release from prison. He moved into an apartment, where he lived alone. Losing the social support and structure provided by the halfway house destabilized him. Second, Seth stopped going to Alcoholics Anonymous after he left the halfway house, and he started drinking and using drugs again. Numerous studies have shown that substance abuse worsens the problems of people who suffer from depression or schizophrenia. Seth suffered from both."

"Any other factors?"

"No."

"Switching gears, your former nurse, Mr. Hammond, mentioned that a man named Jonathon Adams committed suicide after you saw him. Was Mr. Adams a patient of yours?"

"No. The California Department of Corrections and Rehabilitation asked me to do a psychological evaluation of Mr. Adams. I did, but that was all. I saw him only once professionally."

"Did you ever see him outside the office?"

"Yes. He attacked me outside my apartment building. I don't remember much of what happened. Fortunately, he was interrupted." She stopped there because Judge Spink had granted Tim's *in limine* motion barring any mention of the fact that Mike had saved her. The judge reasoned—probably correctly—that the full story wasn't really relevant to whether Jo committed malpractice, but would prejudice the jury in favor of Mike.

"Was Mr. Adams injured in the attack?"

"Yes. I believe the autopsy showed that he lost two teeth and suffered several cracked ribs when he was interrupted."

Jo smiled at Mike, who smiled back and rubbed his right hand where there was still a slight swelling in one of his metacarpals. If the jurors picked up on the nonverbal communication between lawyer and client, so be it. Tim frowned, but said nothing.

"Do you know whether the police pursued him?"

"They told me that they did and I have no reason to doubt them."

"How long after he attacked you did Mr. Adams commit suicide?"

"Just a day or two, I believe."

"In your experience, can physical pain or being pursued by the police make a person suicidal?"

"Yes."

"No further questions," he said to the judge.

The judge looked at Tim. He looked back silently for a few seconds, then stood slowly, his face clouded with indecision.

Mike could almost hear the debate going on in Tim's head: Mike's examination had gone well and the jury liked and sympathized with Jo even more now than they had when Tim had sat down. He probably felt confident that he could land a few punches, particularly now that he had had a chance to calm down and regroup. On the other hand, he could only ask questions about topics that Mike had gone into. Tim's options were therefore limited to Seth Bell's solitary lifestyle; his substance abuse; and Adams's evaluation, attack on Jo, and death. None of those would be particularly appetizing subjects from Tim's perspective. Further, Mike would get to ask still more questions when Tim was done.

"No further questions," Tim said at last.

# CHAPTER 77

Before she testified, Jo had thought the jurors were leaning toward the Bells. After she left the stand, she sensed that they were essentially undecided. That's where they seemed to stay during the remainder of Tim Cromwell's case—until they heard from his expert, Professor Hiram Young, PhD.

Jo had known Young by reputation only. He headed the clinical psychology program at the University of Michigan and had quite literally written the book on clinical psychology. That book, *Fundamentals of Therapy*, sat on most therapists' desks—including Jo's.

Young testified that Jo's use of Mind's Eye in therapy was unjustifiably risky. It was a powerful tool, and it hadn't been evaluated in a laboratory setting at all. Rather, Jo had tried it on a few volunteers to calibrate it. Then she put it straight into use. She was effectively testing it on prisoners through her arrangement with the California Department of Corrections and Rehabilitation. That was dangerous and highly unethical.

Young also criticized Jo's records of Seth's treatment, which he called "spotty and incomplete." He argued that her reliance on Mind's Eye's automatic-recording feature might have caused her to take less-than-thorough notes during therapy sessions. She might well have failed to properly document signs of impending suicide as a result.

On cross-examination, Mike pointed out that Young hadn't testified that Jo's use of Mind's Eye had caused Seth Bell's suicide. Young admitted that. He also said that he had read the depositions of the Bells and Shaun Hammond and that he based his opinions about Seth's treatment in significant part on what they said.

But Young vigorously disagreed when Mike tried to get him to concede that there was no evidence that Mind's Eye could have been a contributing factor in Seth's death. No, there was no research showing that use of an fMRI machine, an EEG cap, or the other elements of Mind's Eye exacerbated suicidal impulses. But that, he claimed, was like arguing that combining three or four powerful drugs was safe because each of them was safe individually. Medical professionals couldn't just assume that sort of thing—it needed to be thoroughly tested first, Young said. If a doctor chose to give a patient an untested drug cocktail like that, it would be clear malpractice. And if the patient then died, the absence of research into the possible dangers of the drug combination would not be a defense. It would be an indictment.

Jo watched the jurors as Young testified. They paid attention and, for the most part, seemed to find him persuasive. They leaned forward slightly when he spoke, smiled at his dry jokes, and even occasionally nodded when he made a point. Jo had worried about that precise outcome from the moment she'd heard that the Bells had hired Young. Young's decades as a professor gave him an air of authority and an easy, conversational style on the stand. And his credentials were impeccable. Mike's cross-examination did some damage to Young, but not much.

Tim had rested his case after calling Young. Since it was late afternoon, the judge had adjourned court early. Mike would start his case tomorrow morning.

Until that point, Tim had decided which witnesses would testify and in what order. He also got to question them first. Now that Tim had rested, Mike would take the lead. He'd call his first witness in the morning. That witness was supposed to be Adrian Goff, so that he could rebut Young as quickly as possible.

But Mike had said nothing to Jo about Goff since the trial started. Presumably Mike and his team were working with Goff on his testimony, but Jo had expected to be included in those conversations because of her knowledge of both Mind's Eye and Seth Bell. So she was surprised and a little worried when Mike hurried out of the courtroom without saying anything about Goff.

She called him when she got back to her office.

He picked up on the first ring. "Hi, Jo. What's up?"

"I know how busy you are, and I was just wondering whether I might be able to help. For instance, I could assist with Dr. Goff's preparation."

"Uh, yeah. Thanks, I appreciate the offer, but there's been a change of plans. I'm not planning to call him after all."

"What? Why not?"

"Well, I've been having some conversations with him over the past few days and, uh, his opinions have changed. I don't think putting him on the stand is a good idea."

Fear prickled her spine. "What would he say?"

"It's kind of complicated. I can explain it after trial. I'm sorry, but I don't really have time right now."

"I understand. Will we be putting on a different expert? I'd be happy to meet with him or her."

"Actually, I'm about to meet with a witness who may make expert testimony unnecessary."

"Really? Who's that?"

"It's still confidential and I'm not sure I can pull it off. I'd tell you if I could. You'll know tomorrow."

"Um, okay. I'll see you tomorrow."

She ended the call and stared at the phone. She couldn't tell from his voice alone whether he was being evasive or distracted—or possibly both. She wished she could have talked to him in person.

What was going on with Goff? It troubled her that Mike had been talking to him without her. And it troubled her even more that Goff apparently could no longer testify that she hadn't committed malpractice. What exactly had he said to Mike? The possibilities ranged from the troubling to the terrifying.

Speculating would just drive her crazy, so she did her best to put it out of her mind. The trial would be over in just a few days. She would know soon enough.

# CHAPTER 78

"The defense calls David Klein," Mike announced.

As the jury watched Klein walk through the courtroom, Mike snuck a glance at Tim. He was staring straight ahead with a sour look on his face. Mike couldn't really blame him. Tim hadn't had any reason to think that Mike seriously intended to call Klein until last night, when Mike gave him the list of witnesses that he planned to call the next day. Tim had complained vociferously to Judge Spink, but without much chance of success. As Mike noted in response, Klein's name had been disclosed in discovery—most notably by Tim's own client, Senator Bell. Further, Mike had listed Klein as a possible trial witness. If Tim hadn't taken the disclosure seriously, that was his problem. Judge Spink had agreed, leaving Tim nothing to do but fume.

Klein wore an orange prison jumpsuit—a small victory for Tim. Ryan Daley and a uniformed officer accompanied him into the courtroom and sat in the front row. Klein sat down in the chair in the witness box. The jumpsuit was too big for him and made him look even smaller and skinnier than he'd looked when Mike had visited Horizon Finance.

The bailiff swore in Klein, and Judge Spink nodded to Mike. "You may proceed, Counsel."

"Thank you, Your Honor. Mr. Klein, what company did you work for until last week?"

"Horizon Finance, LLC."

"What does Horizon Finance do?"

"It makes and manages investments for a select group of clients."

"What kind of clients?"

Klein shrugged. "The kind of clients who don't have access to normal financial-service providers. Iranian and Russian companies that are banned from investing in the United States, North Korean officials, corporations owned by the Chinese military. That sort of thing."

"What was your position at Horizon Finance?"

"I was a director."

"What did you do?"

"I managed an investment portfolio."

"Did you specialize in a particular type of investment—energy or technology companies, for example?"

Klein shook his head. "I focused on finding unusual or offbeat investments, the sort of opportunity that more traditional money managers usually miss."

"Does that focus relate to this lawsuit?"

"Yes."

"How?"

"I had a service that notified me of lawsuits involving certain politicians and executives. Those sometimes reveal, ah, pressure points that can be profitable."

"Was Senator Bell one of the politicians you monitored?"

"Yes. So I learned about this case. As soon as I read the complaint, I realized that the Mind's Eye system could be very valuable. Several Horizon Finance clients were connected to foreign intelligence and security services. Mind's Eye would be exceptionally useful for interrogations."

"How valuable did you think Mind's Eye might be?"

"If I had to put a price—"

"Objection, relevance," Tim said as he stood. "None of this has anything to do with whether Dr. Anderson's malpractice contributed to Seth Bell's death."

"It's very relevant to this case," Mike responded. "I can tie it up in just a couple of questions."

"All right," the judge said. "The objection is overruled without prejudice."

Tim sat down and Mike turned his attention back to the witness. "Mr. Klein, did Horizon Finance invest in Mind's Eye?"

"Yes, indirectly."

"How did Horizon Finance indirectly invest in Mind's Eye?"

"We purchased the rights to this lawsuit."

Surprised murmurs from the jury box.

"How did you do that?" Mike asked.

"Senator Bell and his wife agreed to sell the lawsuit to us."

Camy handed Mike a small stack of copies and gave one copy to Tim. "Mr. Klein, was that sale memorialized in a written contract?"

"Yes."

"Your Honor, may I approach the witness?"

"Yes," Judge Spink said.

Mike walked across the well, the open space between the lectern and the witness box. He handed one copy to Klein and another to the court clerk. Then he returned to his place behind the lectern.

"Mr. Klein, I've just handed you what has been marked as Defendant's Exhibit One. Is that the contract between Horizon Finance and the Bells for the sale of this lawsuit?"

Klein glanced through the document. "Yes."

"The defense moves to admit Defendant's Exhibit One into evidence," Mike said to the judge.

"One moment, Your Honor," Tim said. He huddled with his team and Mrs. Bell, who sat in the front row. After a couple of minutes, he stood up. "Your Honor, might I be heard at sidebar?"

"Certainly," Judge Spink replied.

Mike and Tim went up to the bench, and the judge leaned toward them. "We object to this exhibit," Tim said. "It was never produced in discovery and we didn't see it until less than twelve hours ago. We were severely prejudiced by this delay. The Bells were unable to discuss this document when they testified, and I won't have time to adequately prepare to cross-examine Mr. Klein about it—which is yet another reason why his testimony should not be allowed."

Judge Spink turned to Mike. "Any response?"

"Yes, Your Honor. We sent this document to Mr. Cromwell as soon as we received it. That only happened last night. The reason it wasn't produced during discovery is that Horizon Finance failed to comply with their discovery obligations yet again. So did the Bells, it would seem. That is not my client's fault. Further, Mr. Cromwell hasn't contested the genuineness of this document. That presumably means that the Bells knew about it, but chose to omit it from their testimony and document productions. If Mr. Cromwell wants to put them on the stand during rebuttal to talk about that, he can do so."

The judge looked at Tim. "All right, I'll give you the last word. Anything further?"

"No, Your Honor. The admission of Defendant's Exhibit One is improper because of the unfair prejudice to the plaintiff."

"Okay, thank you both." She straightened and turned to the clerk. "Defendant's Exhibit One is admitted."

Tim returned to his seat and Mike went back to the lectern. "How much did Horizon Finance pay the Bells for this lawsuit?"

"We paid them each fifty thousand dollars."

"How did you pay them?"

"By wire transfer."

Camy handed Mike another stack of documents, with a copy to Tim. Mike said, "Your Honor, may I approach the witness with Defendant's Exhibit Two?"

"Yes."

After Mike had distributed copies and was back at the lectern, he asked, "Is Defendant's Exhibit Two a copy of the wire-transfer confirmation?"

"Yes."

"You're sure that this wire transfer was payment for the lawsuit and not for a computer game?" The Bells hadn't mentioned the computer-game story during their testimony, but Mike wanted to be ready in case they tried it on rebuttal.

"Yes."

"Did Horizon Finance ever purchase the rights to a computer game from the Bell family or the estate of Seth Bell?"

"No."

"We move Defendant's Exhibit Two into evidence."

Tim rose. "Same objections as to Defendant's One."

"Overruled," Judge Spink said. "Defendant's Two is admitted."

"Okay, did Horizon Finance ever pay money to a gentleman named Shaun Hammond?"

Klein gave a crooked smile. "I'm not sure I'd call him a gentleman, but yes, we paid him."

"For what?"

"When we first learned about Mind's Eye and this lawsuit, we decided we needed an inside source. So we contacted Hammond and offered to pay him for documents and information."

"Did he agree?"

"Yes, enthusiastically. He gave us whatever he could get his hands on. He also wanted us to invest in a sports-medicine clinic he planned to open."

"How much did you pay him?"

"All told?" Klein paused for a moment. "About twenty thousand dollars."

"How did you pay him?"

"The amounts were relatively small, so we used cash."

"Did you also pay him to testify?"

Klein squirmed a little and glanced up at the judge. "Yes."

"How much?"

"Another ten thousand dollars."

"Did Horizon Finance spend any other money on its investment in this case?"

"Yes, we paid the legal bills of Masters & Cromwell."

"I renew my relevance objection," Tim said.

"Overruled," Judge Spink replied without hesitation.

"Tim Cromwell is my friend, so I'm not even going to ask how much his bills were," Mike said with a smile.

"They weren't cheap, I'll tell you that," replied Klein.

Ordinarily, Mike would have expected that exchange to draw at least a smile from some of the jurors, but they were all staring at Klein as if hypnotized.

"You said that this was all an indirect investment in Mind's Eye. How was Horizon Finance investing in Mind's Eye by spending money on this case?"

Tim stood. "Objection. Could I be heard at sidebar again?"

The judge agreed and they walked up to the bench. "Your Honor," Tim said, "we are getting pretty far afield here. This is a medical-malpractice case, nothing else. Mr. Klein's testimony regarding his company's investments is utterly irrelevant to the issues the jury needs to decide. Further, any probative value his testimony may have is outweighed by the unfairly prejudicial effect it is having on the jury."

"Mr. Klein's testimony demonstrates that the plaintiff's key witnesses were less than truthful on the stand," Mike said. "I'm sure that's prejudicing the jury against the plaintiff, but that's hardly unfair."

"Nothing he's saying now contradicts anything in the plaintiff's case," Tim said. "Nor does it have anything to do with the propriety of Dr. Anderson's actions or the safety of Mind's Eye. Mr. Webster's last question simply asks for Horizon Finance's investment strategy. That has no bearing on any issue in this case."

"That's a fair point," Judge Spink acknowledged. "I suspect the jurors can put two and two together by now, so I don't think the witness's answer will be particularly prejudicial—but I also don't think it will be relevant. Objection sustained."

Mike walked back to the lectern, smiling as if he were pleased by the judge's ruling. In truth, it didn't bother him particularly. As Judge Spink noted, the jurors had already heard that Horizon Finance was using the case to somehow get control of Mind's Eye. It probably didn't matter that they didn't hear precisely what Horizon had in mind. In fact, Tim's objection might even be helpful because the jurors would assume that whatever Klein had been about to say made the Bells look bad.

Mike glanced down at his outline. There were only two topics left, and he would have preferred not to ask about either. But he really didn't have a choice, because Tim was sure to bring them up if he didn't. Better to draw the sting by doing it first.

"Mr. Klein, based on your clothing and the entourage you brought with you today, it would appear that you are currently in custody. Why is that?"

"I have been charged with murder, wire fraud, and other crimes."

"Do those charges relate to Horizon Finance's efforts to obtain control of Mind's Eye?"

Tim stood. "Objection, relevance."

"Sustained," Judge Spink said.

"Why are you testifying here today?"

Klein looked a little confused. "Because you asked me to and the guards said I could."

"And why did you agree?"

"Because we made a deal."

"What is our deal?"

"I agreed to testify for you, and you agreed . . ." Klein hesitated for a second as if searching for the right words to express the deal they'd made in the seconds before he was arrested. "You said you would do what you could to help me during my upcoming discussions with the DA and the US Attorney's Office."

"Did I ask you to testify in any particular way?"

"You asked me to cooperate. Other than that, no."

"Did I ask you to say anything that you didn't think was true?"

"No. You said that I should tell the truth, the whole truth, and nothing but the truth."

"And have you done that today?"

"Yes."

"No further questions."

Mike sat down. Klein watched him apprehensively. Klein had been nervous ever since Horizon reported Mike to the bar. Once Klein heard about that, he assured Mike repeatedly—and somewhat desperately—that it wasn't his fault. His associate, Irene, had the investigative file on Mike. She would do whatever the managing director told her to. Klein couldn't control that, could he? A deal was still a deal, right? Mike had assured him that it was, but Klein hadn't seemed reassured. Not surprising. He probably was not used to trusting people he dealt with—or being trustworthy in return.

Tim took Mike's place at the lectern. "Mr. Klein, did you ever meet Seth Bell?"

"No."

"Have you ever met Dr. Johanna Anderson?"

"No."

"Do you have any training in the fields of psychology or neurology?"

"I took a psychology class when I was in college. Other than that, no."

"Other than what you've learned through this case, do you have any knowledge regarding Dr. Anderson's treatment of Seth Bell?"

"No."

"You testified that you have been accused of a number of crimes. Do any of those crimes involve dishonesty?"

Klein thought for a moment. "I suppose so."

"Which ones?"

"Wire fraud, mail fraud, banking fraud." He paused and looked off into space for a moment. "There might be others. Those are the only ones I can think of."

"Have you ever made a false statement under oath? That would include a false statement in a document that you signed under penalty of perjury."

"I'm not sure. It's possible."

"In light of your extensive history of dishonesty, why should the jury believe anything you've said today?"

Mike got to his feet. "Objection. He's simply harassing the witness now."

"Sustained," said the judge.

"Is it important to you that Mr. Webster keep his end of the deal you described?" Tim asked.

Klein's gaze flicked to Mike for a split second and he stiffened inside his baggy prison clothes. "Of course," he replied with poorly affected nonchalance. "It's always important to me that people keep the deals I make with them."

"Do you think he would be quite as helpful to you if your testimony today didn't support his case?"

"I think he would keep his word," Klein said warily, his gaze drifting over to Mike again.

"No further questions," Tim said.

"Any redirect, Counsel?" Judge Spink asked Mike.

"No, Your Honor," Mike said. Tim's questioning was hardly a surprise, and Mike was prepared for it.

"All right, the witness is excused," the judge said.

Klein left the courtroom, accompanied by one of the officers.

"The defense calls Ryan Daley," Mike said.

Ryan took the stand and was sworn in. "Officer Daley, are you a
member of the San Francisco Police Department?"

"Yes, sir. I work in the Financial Crimes Unit."

"Are you familiar with the matters discussed during David Klein's
testimony today?"

"Yes."

"Was his testimony untruthful in any respect?"

"Not to my knowledge."

"Are you testifying here today pursuant to an agreement?"

"Yes."

"Please describe that agreement."

"I don't know all the details, but as I understand it, the District
Attorney's Office agreed that I could testify here today if you would
help with their investigation of Horizon Finance."

"Does that agreement require you to testify in a certain way?"

"No."

"Does that agreement impose any limits or conditions on your
testimony?"

"No. I can't talk about the specifics of the case against Horizon
Finance because it's still pending. Other than that, there are no limits
on my testimony—except that I have to tell the truth, of course."

"No further questions."

Mike sat and Tim stood. "It seems that I'm the only one in the
courtroom who hasn't made a deal with Mr. Webster," he said with a
faint air of exasperation.

"It's not too late for you to come over to the light side," Mike said
from his seat.

That prompted chuckles from several jurors and a frown from Judge Spink.

Tim gave a thin smile and turned to the witness. "Officer Daley, is it unusual for a police officer to testify in a civil case when there is a criminal case pending on the same subject?"

"I don't know."

"Would it be fair to say that Mr. Webster's help is very important to the DA's Office?"

"I don't know."

He flipped through his notes for a few seconds. "No further questions."

Mike stood. "The defense rests."

# CHAPTER 79

Val took a deep breath and wiped nervous sweat off her palms. She picked up her cell phone and pulled up Mike's number. Then she put the phone back down.

She picked up her checklist and went over it one more time. She'd run down every loose end as best she could. Every witness had been called. Every piece of evidence that could be authenticated had been. She was done.

The documents from Angy's package lay in neat rows on her kitchen table. Each one had a small stack of backup material underneath it. She had built a good case. Mike would be proud—or at least he should be.

But proud was not the reaction she expected from Mike. Anger was more likely. Disillusionment and disappointment too. She just hoped she didn't get disbelief, not after all the work she had put in.

He shouldn't disbelieve her. He couldn't. The evidence was overwhelming.

So why was she afraid to call him?

Because the Mike she knew would have believed her months ago. He wouldn't have lied to himself. He wouldn't have blown her off and told her she was just jealous. He—

The memory of their last conversation plopped into her mind like a rude fat man on a subway seat, crowding out everything else. Anger, hurt, and regret coursed through her. Suddenly she was blinking back tears.

*No.* She was not doing this again. She was going to be professional and cordial when she called him. Anything else would undermine her credibility and give him an excuse to not take her seriously.

She took a deep breath, then another one. Then she said the Our Father slowly, focusing on the words, to calm down and put herself in the right frame of mind.

And then she called Mike.

# CHAPTER 80

Mike's cell phone rang. He put down his plastic fork and pulled the phone out of his pants pocket.

Val.

He swallowed hard, and a lump of half-chewed chicken and rice crawled down his throat. *Answer it? Don't answer it?* He stared at the phone in indecision for several seconds.

"I don't have time to talk to her," he told the empty conference room.

It was true. He'd love to have her back. He'd even be willing to apologize to make it happen. But he just didn't have time for a long, draining conversation right now.

He had a closing argument to write, and he only had tonight to do it. Tim had surprised him by wrapping up his rebuttal case in only one day. Then Judge Spink decided to do closing arguments tomorrow rather than work through jury instructions and other housekeeping matters. So instead of having several days to write and hone a closing, he only had a few hours. He couldn't spend that time on the phone with Val. He just couldn't.

Finally, the phone stopped ringing. He put it on the table, waiting for the voice-mail icon to pop up. Instead, it beeped to announce a new text: `Need to talk to you.`

`Busy writing my closing,` he typed back. `Tomorrow?`

`No. Can't wait. Has to do with closing.`

He groaned and rubbed his forehead in anticipation of the headache he felt coming. Maybe he could put it off with a little white lie. `Meeting with Jo & Camy over dinner. Call you later.`

`Liar. You're sitting in conference room alone eating takeout.`

He couldn't help laughing. Oh, well. Busted. Might as well talk to her and get it over with. He hit her speed dial on his phone.

"Lucky guess," he said as soon as she picked up.

"You always work on closings alone, and you always get takeout from the Chinese place downstairs."

"Actually, I'm working on a restraining order against you for bugging my office."

She didn't laugh. "We need to talk."

He sighed. "I know. I said some things I shouldn't have and I'm sorry. It's just that—"

"That's not why I called."

"Oh . . . Well, what's up, then?"

She took a sharp breath and let it out. "Jo's been lying to you."

His stomach muscles tightened. "How do you know?"

"I managed to get a look at Seth Bell's criminal records."

"So did I. Jo didn't lie about anything in there."

"Those are his *adult* records. I'm talking about his *juvie* records."

"How did you get those? I thought they would've been sealed when he turned eighteen, and destroyed five years after that."

"Just listen." She took a deep breath. "He killed Jo's younger sister."

Mike stared at the conference-room wall without seeing it. "Her sister?"

"Her name was Madeline Nordahl. He did it at Shadow Cliffs—the same place where he committed suicide." Val was talking fast, words shooting out at machine-gun speed. "They were in the same high school. He said they were drinking and doing drugs and having sex, and she accidentally overdosed. Her family didn't buy it and neither did the detective on the case, but Seth managed to get a pretty good plea deal. He did five years in a Youth Authority school in Stockton. After that, he was in and out of mental hospitals and prisons for the next fifteen years. Until Jo found him."

Mike couldn't get his brain to process what Val was saying. He wouldn't have been any more stunned if she tried to convince him that Jo was an alien wearing a human disguise. "So wait . . . How come CDCR let her treat him?"

"They wouldn't know. His juvie records were . . . well, the official records did get sealed and destroyed years ago. Plus, Jo's last name was different back then: she was Johanna Nordahl. She even looked different—brunette, glasses."

"Let me get this straight. You're not just saying she committed malpractice, you're accusing her of murder?"

"Mike, this guy raped and killed her little sister! You really think it's a coincidence that she picked him for Mind's Eye? That the video of her sessions with him just happened to not get recorded? That he killed himself after she'd been treating him? That she never mentioned that he'd murdered someone in her family? So yeah, I think Jo murdered Seth Bell. You got a better explanation?"

He shook his head, then immediately regretted it as a flash of pain arced across his brain. "That's a very serious accusation, Val. Do you have any hard evidence?"

"I've got his criminal records. If that's not good enough for you, I dug up news reports of Madeline Nordahl's murder and Johanna

Nordahl's wedding to Karl Anderson. I've also had off-the-record conversations with some people in law enforcement who authenticated Seth's juvie records. It all checks out. Oh, and one other thing: Angy got those records for me. It was one of the last things he did before he died."

"Can I talk to those witnesses?"

"No. They only talked to me because I was Angy's sister and I promised not to tell anyone their names."

"Uh-huh. Could you get me certified copies of the records?"

"No. They weren't supposed to still exist. People could get in trouble. Someone took a risk by even sending them to Angy."

"Okay, does that article about the murdered girl mention Seth's name?"

"Of course not. He was a juvenile."

"Is there anything else you can give me? Anything at all?"

"If you want me to come over, I can show you everything I just told you about. It's all there and all backed up as much as it can be."

"As much as it can be," he echoed. "But you can't leave it with me and there's no one I can call to corroborate it, right?"

She sighed. "Right."

"So I'm just going to have to trust you on this?"

"I guess you are." Val paused. "You used to trust me."

He rubbed his temples with the thumb and middle finger of his free hand. That headache was coming along nicely. "Look, let's not have the same fight we had two weeks ago. I don't have time to deal with this right now, but I'll withhold judgment until—"

"Mike, don't do this. Don't help her get away with murder. I'm begging you, please." Her voice was pleading now. She sounded like she might be on the verge of crying.

He winced and squirmed. "What do you want me to do? Withdraw from her case on the day before closing arguments? Call the police and say, 'A little birdie told me you should look into whether Johanna Nordahl Anderson had a motive to kill Seth Bell'?"

"Yes! It'll be tough, but it's the right thing to do. You know it is."

"No, I don't. Abandoning a client is not the right thing to do. And I wouldn't just be abandoning her; I'd be abandoning every patient in the future who wouldn't be helped by Mind's Eye because Jo lost this lawsuit." The more he talked, the more certain he became. "What if she said the same thing about you? Wouldn't you want me to insist on rock-solid evidence? Wouldn't you want me to give you a chance to respond?"

The toughness was back in her voice. "So now you not only want 'rock-solid' evidence from me, you want to lay it all out for her on a silver platter? Really?"

"It's only fair."

"It's your funeral." The phone went dead.

He dropped the phone back in his pocket and put his head in his hands. He remembered seeing an X-ray of a guy who got shot in the head with a nail gun. That's what he felt like right now.

He tried to work on the closing, but between his headache and Val's call, he couldn't focus.

Half an hour later, he had managed to write exactly three words: "Ladies and gentlemen." He gave up and shoved his notes away.

"My funeral."

# CHAPTER 81

Mike didn't sleep that night. He spent most of the hours between dusk and dawn wandering around the office or staring at his notepad. He prayed some and agonized a lot. He thought about what Val had said and the concerns Dr. Goff had raised a few days ago. But he also remembered Jo: the brilliant, compassionate therapist and inventor who helped him—and could help thousands—with Mind's Eye. Was she really a murderer? And was it even possible to turn Mind's Eye into a murder weapon?

He went through half a dozen Tylenol pills and another half dozen Tums tablets as he tried to sort out the truth. Eventually he gave up. He needed more information and more time—but he wouldn't have either before he had to give his closing tomorrow morning. He glanced at his watch and corrected himself—*this* morning.

At three o'clock, he finally decided what he needed to do. It wouldn't be pleasant or easy, but it was the only thing he could think of.

He finished his closing argument at five and went home. Then he lay in bed for an hour, staring at the ceiling. At quarter after six, he gave up and went to the gym. By the time he came home at seven thirty, he felt almost normal—except for an undertone of fatigue reminding him that he wasn't twenty-five anymore. Even that was almost gone by the time he finished a breakfast of espresso, orange juice, and oatmeal.

At quarter after eight, he walked out the door, ready to deliver what was almost certainly the last closing argument of his career.

Val was in the courtroom. Mike hadn't expected that. She sat in the back of the gallery, by the door. Silent entreaty filled her face. Their eyes locked for an instant, but he looked away quickly. This would be hard enough already.

He scanned the faces of the jurors, forced himself to smile, and began. "Ladies and gentlemen, thank you for your time and attention over the past week. I know that being forced to spend five days listening to Mr. Cromwell and me is not most people's idea of a good time. But it is only through the sacrifices of tens of thousands of citizens like yourselves that our legal system can function and thousands of other citizens can get justice from a jury of their peers. And now that you've heard and seen the evidence in this case, I think you know what justice requires.

"At the beginning of this case I told you what I expected the evidence would show. Well, now the evidence is in, and I think parts of it surprised everyone in this courtroom. But the bottom line remains the same: the other side had the burden of proof, and they didn't carry it.

"They needed to show that Dr. Anderson was negligent in her treatment of Seth Bell and that her negligence caused his death. They showed neither. All three of their key fact witnesses were dishonest with you. Seth Bell's mother, his father, and Shaun Hammond all sat in that chair"—he pointed to the witness stand—"and told you things that weren't true. Each of them said they hadn't been paid by Horizon Finance. And then David Klein and Officer Daley took the stand and told you the truth. They told you about Horizon Finance, a company with a client list that's a Who's Who of international bad guys. They told you that Horizon Finance paid over one hundred thousand dollars to Senator Bell, Mrs. Bell, and Mr. Hammond. They told you that Horizon Finance bought the rights to this case from the Bells and paid Shaun Hammond to steal documents and information from Dr. Anderson. Then Horizon Finance paid him to come here and testify. Why pay all of that money? So that when this case was over, Mind's Eye would be in the hands of Horizon Finance.

"All three of those witnesses took an oath promising to tell the truth, and then they lied to you about getting paid off by Horizon Finance. I don't think you should trust anything else they have to say about this case. As Thomas Jefferson said, 'He who permits himself to tell a lie once, finds it much easier to do it a second and third time.'

"None of the other fact witnesses that Mr. Cromwell put on the stand said a word about Seth's treatment. In fact, some of them hardly knew him at all. The most any of them said was that they saw Seth at some point between his final therapy session and his death and that he seemed depressed or unstable. That's it.

"You also heard Professor Young testify, but remember that he was an expert witness, not a fact witness. You heard him say that he relied on the Bells and Shaun Hammond for his facts—and you know how reliable they are. He even explicitly admitted that he had no idea whether anything Dr. Anderson did caused Seth Bell's suicide. Beyond that, what did he say? Just that he didn't like all the new technology Dr. Anderson uses. Well, Professor Young has been a psychologist for a long time, and sometimes people who have been doing something for a long time get suspicious about change. And remember that even he admitted that all of the devices that form a part of Mind's Eye had been in use for years with no ill effects."

Mike felt a headache beginning to form. "The only reliable evidence about what happened during Seth Bell's therapy sessions came from Dr. Anderson and her medical records. Dr. Anderson testified that Seth never expressed suicidal thoughts during his final therapy session. Her notes from that session, which she wrote the same day, are entirely consistent with her testimony. And none of the evidence that Mr. Cromwell put forward contradicted either her notes or her testimony.

"At the beginning of this trial, I said that Seth Bell's death was a tragedy, but not malpractice. That is exactly what the evidence has shown. I'm confident you'll agree and that you'll return a verdict of 'not guilty.' And with that, I commit Dr. Anderson's fate—and the fate of Mind's Eye—into your hands. Thank you."

He heard a muffled choking sound and a door closed behind him. He knew without looking that Val had just left the courtroom. She had heard what she came for. And he had done what he had to.

# Chapter 82

The jury had only been deliberating a few hours when Jo got the message she had been waiting for, a text from Mike that read: Jury back. Heading to court.

She had just started an evaluation, so she couldn't leave. She couldn't even respond to his text. Instead, she had to spend the next fifty-five minutes trying to keep her attention focused on figuring out how likely it was that a seventy-year-old check forger would reoffend if he were granted parole.

She rushed through her questions, barely listening to the geriatric fraudster's answers or looking at the Mind's Eye display to gauge his reactions. That would have to come later when she reviewed the tape. She finished in forty-five minutes and shooed him and his guard out of the office.

As the door closed behind them, the phone buzzed with a new text from Mike: Not guilty.

She let out a most unprofessional whoop.

The prison guard poked his head back in the door. "Are you all right, Dr. Anderson?"

She laughed. "You have no idea how all right I am."

An hour later, Jo stood in front of the mirror in her office bathroom, trying to stop smiling for long enough to get her makeup right. She felt giddy, almost drunk, even though the bottle of Dom Pérignon she'd just bought remained unopened in the fridge. A tremendous weight had just lifted from her heart, and she floated like a butterfly on a summer breeze.

Mike would arrive any minute and the celebration would begin. She gave up on her lipstick—it really didn't matter much, since she planned to mess it up the moment he walked in. She went to watch for his car from her office. Soft jazz wafted in from the therapy room and she hummed along.

His car turned into the parking garage. She took the champagne out and popped the cork. She had just finished pouring two glasses when she heard him at the door. She put the glasses on the lobby counter and opened the door.

He stepped in, and before he could say a word, she hugged him and kissed him with calculated passion. He froze in surprise for a second. Then he gently disengaged and looked down at her in silence for a heartbeat.

His face held a mix of emotions that she couldn't quite read, but he was clearly exhausted. It had been a rough couple of weeks for him—the shooting in the garage, losing Val, the trial, dealing with Horizon Finance. Well, she was about to see to it that his life got better.

She reached back and picked up the champagne. She handed him a glass and raised hers. "To the best lawyer in the world."

He paused, then gave a half smile and looked over his shoulder. "Where?"

"No false modesty today," Jo said. "You won, and not just in the courtroom. You also took down some very bad guys, solved a murder, and saved my career in the process. To victory!" She tapped her glass against his, drawing a melodious chime from the crystal.

They each sipped their champagne. "Thanks," Mike said, looking into his glass. "There's, um, one loose end we need to wrap up."

A cold wind knifed through her soul. Goff—what had he found? "What is it?" she asked, keeping her voice as casual as possible.

He looked up, but didn't meet her eyes. "Val found Seth Bell's old criminal records, from when he was a juvenile."

Fear gripped her throat and she could hardly breathe. "What . . . what did they show?"

"That Seth violated and killed your sister, Madeline."

So he knew about Maddie. She looked down and took a deep breath to give herself time to think. Then she nodded heavily. "I wanted to heal him. I knew what he was capable of, the threat he posed to women. I thought that with Mind's Eye, I could get inside his head, find what was really wrong, and fix it." She sighed. "It was stupid. I see that now. The chances that something would go wrong were just too high. I knew Seth was depressed, paranoid, and schizophrenic. The odds that he would hurt himself or someone else were always high. Then the truth would come out and people would assume the worst." She took a deep breath and shook her head. "Imagine what Tim Cromwell would have done with this if he knew."

He looked at her skeptically. "Why didn't you tell me?"

"Because if I did, you would have had to tell the other side, right?"

"If they asked about it in discovery, yes," he admitted, but his voice and face remained cold and accusatory.

"I'm sorry," she said. She bit her lip for an instant. "I shouldn't have lied to you, and I feel terrible about it. I just . . . I just couldn't let one bad decision destroy all of this or put Mind's Eye in the wrong hands."

He nodded. "I understand. It would have looked terrible at trial. What Seth did to your sister, the way you tracked him down, the fact that there weren't any witnesses when you treated him, the missing data and video. It would have looked like you used Mind's Eye to plant suicidal impulses in his mind—or at least strengthen the impulses that were there." His eyes were full of judgment. "It would have looked like you murdered him."

Her heart hammered in her chest. "But that's impossible! Mind's Eye is just a collection of sensors and some software—you know that. It has no effect whatsoever on a patient's mind."

"No, but you do. You give your patients a sedative and hypnotize them. That makes them highly susceptible to suggestion, doesn't it? And I know from personal experience that it interferes with their memory of what happens during Mind's Eye sessions. With Mind's Eye guiding you, I'll bet you could plant suggestions very effectively."

She put down her glass and folded her arms. Her panic was turning to anger. "No. First, that would be highly unethical. Second, you shouldn't believe everything you read on the Internet. That's not how hypnosis works. I know. I've studied it at length. You haven't."

"Dr. Goff has."

So that's why Goff hadn't testified. "Really. What did he have to say?"

"He said that you could have used Mind's Eye and hypnosis to steer Seth toward suicide. You could also have given Seth posthypnotic amnesia so that he wouldn't remember much when the session was over."

"That's interesting speculation, but I can assure you that I did no such thing," she said icily. "And in my professional opinion, it would not be nearly as easy as Dr. Goff seems to think. Did he have any actual evidence to back up this fantasy?"

"Not for Seth," Mike acknowledged. He paused and looked her in the eye. "But he thinks you might have done something similar to me. So does Dr. Lay."

She stared at him wide eyed. "That's just insane. I would *never* try to hurt you, Mike. I hope you know that." She paused. "Have you been having suicidal thoughts?"

"No, but I have been getting splitting headaches whenever I think about you in a negative way. I have one now. That could be intentional—you've conditioned me to have a headache whenever I think the 'wrong' thoughts. Or it could be unintentional. You could have predisposed me to trust you—maybe even love you—and the headaches could be caused by the stress of not being able to do that."

"Mike, I care about you. Even if something like that were possible, I would never do it."

"Let's watch the video of my Mind's Eye sessions and confirm that."

She shook her head and laughed, but her voice sounded shrill in her ears. "I can't believe we're having this crazy conversation. We should be out celebrating."

"I can't celebrate until I've seen those videos."

"All of them? There must be at least ten hours' worth."

"Then we'd better get started."

She gave an exasperated sigh. "Look at yourself in a mirror, Mike. You're exhausted and not thinking straight. Go home and get some sleep. If you still want to watch all of those videos in the morning, be my guest."

He rubbed his eyes. "That might be best—but I'll need to take the Mind's Eye hard drive with me. I'll also need any storage drives you might have."

She thought furiously. There had to be a way out of this. Had to be. All she needed was an hour alone with the drives and she would be home free. But Mike knew that as well as she did.

Her mind spun wildly. Should she demand that he leave? Confess and try to persuade him not to go to the police? Run? Every idea that popped into her head had obvious flaws.

He sighed and shook his head slowly, looking emotionally and physically drained. "I can recommend a good criminal attorney."

# CHAPTER 83

Val was walking out of a job interview when her phone rang. It was Mike.

A torrent of conflicting emotions rushed through her. She wanted to give him a piece of her mind for defending Jo in his closing argument. She wanted to thank him with all her heart for helping catch Angy's killer. She wanted to share her dream of being a lawyer. She wanted to make things the way they had been, even though she knew that was impossible.

She stepped out onto the sidewalk and answered her phone. "Mike, how are you doing?" she said, keeping her voice neutral.

"I'm beat, and I've got a headache. How about you?"

"I'm fine. So, what's up?"

"I just spent two hours talking to the police." He sighed. "You were right about Jo. I'm sorry."

She had daydreamed about this moment a dozen times, but she had never quite decided what she would say after Mike's mea culpa—and now she couldn't think of anything. After an awkward pause, she forced out, "Wow, I'm sorry. Um, what happened?"

"You remember how I was seeing that neurologist, Dr. Lay, right? She couldn't find a physical cause for my headaches, and she thought there might be something psychological going on. So she called Dr. Goff and asked him what he thought. He asked me if there was any recurring situation or thought pattern that triggered my headaches. I realized there was: they came whenever I thought something negative about Jo. Then he asked whether anything unusual happened during my Mind's Eye sessions. I said that I didn't really remember much about what happened during them. That was a big red flag for him. He said what I was describing sounded like it might be posthypnotic amnesia. That almost never happens by accident—the hypnotherapist has to specifically block memories of what happens during therapy."

A chill ran through Val as she realized what must have been happening over the past months. "So she was brainwashing you?"

"Sort of. Dr. Goff says there's no such thing as brainwashing someone with hypnosis. But a good hypnotherapist can plant suggestions in your mind and then keep you from remembering what happened. It doesn't work with everyone, but it helps if you're relaxed and you trust the hypnotherapist—like I did. And Mind's Eye would probably let Jo know whether her suggestions and the memory block were working." His tone was matter-of-fact, but she could hear an edge of bitterness in his voice. "Dr. Goff wasn't sure. He said he'd need to see the video from my sessions and talk to Jo to be positive, but he thought it was a real possibility. I didn't want to believe him, of course."

"Of course," Val repeated. "Are they going to arrest her?"

"They already did, about three hours ago."

"That's . . . I guess that's great. Will you be able to testify against her?"

"Yes. The attorney-client privilege only covers conversations related to my representation of her. It doesn't cover everything she says to me. And it sure doesn't cover everything she did to me."

She felt a wave of compassion, tinged with regret. "Hey, I'm sorry for some of the things I said and, well, all of the things I yelled. It wasn't your fault."

"No worries," he said. "You'd been warning me off of Jo from the start. You waved those ethics rules in my face and told me it was a bad idea for me to be seeing her. And you were right."

"I wish I wasn't." Which wasn't quite true, though she did feel sorry for him and a little guilty. "I shouldn't have quit on you."

"You didn't quit on me. You kept digging and finally found out the truth about Jo and Seth. I didn't want to believe it, but after I got off the phone with you, I thought it through and realized you were right."

That didn't make sense. "So why did you give that closing if you knew she was a murderer?"

"A couple of reasons. I wanted to talk to her first, hear what she had to say. I also didn't want the Bells or Horizon Finance to get Mind's Eye. Horizon is probably gone now, of course, but—"

"Wait, what? Why is Horizon Finance probably gone? And what exactly happened with that David Klein slimeball?"

He told her.

When he finished, she said, "That's awesome. I wish I could have seen the look on Klein's face when he saw those cops."

"I would've taken a picture, but my phone was down with their security guys."

She laughed. "And I would've gotten it framed. This all happened over a week ago, right? How come you didn't tell me until now?"

"Because you didn't pick up when I called or reply when I texted."

*Oh, yeah.* "Sorry about that. I'd just gotten Angy's care package and I didn't want to talk to you until I knew how legit it was." That excuse didn't sound particularly good in her ears. "I guess I should have called, huh?"

"Yeah, but we're talking now." He yawned. "So, what's up with you?"

"Well, I just walked out of a job interview. I think they're going to make me an offer."

"That's great! Who is it?"

"Doyle & McCutchen."

"They're a good firm. I know some people there. Feel free to put me down as a reference, of course."

"Thanks." She paused and swallowed a hard lump of pride. "Um, if you haven't filled my position, I'd love to come back."

"I'd love to have you back," he said, his voice soft and tired. "But there may not be anything for you to come back to."

# Chapter 84

*February*

Over the years, Mike had wondered what it felt like to be the client in a high-stakes case. Now he knew. And he would have a lot more sympathy the next time one of his clients called him three times in one day to ask questions or make suggestions, then e-mailed with more.

If he ever had another client.

He sat in a conference room at the San Francisco office of the state bar. His lawyer, Henry Lopez, sat next to him. Mike had initially wanted to represent himself, but quickly realized that he needed someone who specialized in dealing with the bar. Plus, he knew that he would have difficulty being objective about his own case. As the old saying goes, a lawyer who represents himself has a fool for a client.

Henry came highly recommended and had a reputation as one of the best ethics lawyers in the Bay Area, but Mike still had to consciously refrain from second-guessing everything his attorney did. Henry had a dozen other cases, so was he really devoting as much time to Mike's as he should? Even if he were, Mike could still help. He could do research, interview witnesses, write briefs. After a couple of weeks of that, Henry diplomatically told Mike that the best thing he could do was stay out of his lawyer's hair. Mike knew Henry was right. He had even had similar conversations with his own clients from time to time. But it was hard.

It was mostly hard because so much was at stake. Henry had warned him repeatedly that the most likely result was disbarment. Mike had viewed his actions as a little rule-bending in the pursuit of justice; the bar viewed them as a years-long pattern of serious ethical violations. So serious that several of his cases might even need to be retried. The bar would probably throw the book at him.

They were about to find out whether Henry was right. The Office of the Chief Trial Counsel for the bar had finished its investigation and brought Mike and Henry in for a meeting at eleven that morning. They had arrived ten minutes early, and the OCTC staff had parked them in this conference room until the prosecution team was ready for them.

At eleven sharp, the door opened and two lawyers walked in. One was a sixtyish African American woman with a stern face and hair cropped so short that it was little more than a dusting of gray on her skull. The other was a young white man carrying a fat accordion file, which he plopped on the table.

Henry knew them both and introduced the woman as Selma Blades and the man as James Whittaker. Mike recognized both names from the letters Henry had forwarded to him.

They all sat down and Blades put her hand on the bulging file. "Mr. Webster, you have committed nearly a dozen violations of the ethical rules you swore to follow. All of those violations were intentional and involved moral turpitude, and six were serious enough to warrant disbarment." She paused and pulled a document out of the file. "However, in mitigation, the San Francisco District Attorney's Office and the United States Attorney's Office both sent letters informing us that, at considerable risk to yourself, you provided valuable assistance in solving two homicides, including the murder of a San Francisco police officer. They further state that the original complainant in this case,

Horizon Finance, LLC, is under indictment, in part as a result of your efforts. Also, a Horizon Finance employee offered to keep your ethical infractions secret if you agreed to lose your most recent case—an offer you refused."

She put down the paper. "In light of these factors, the OCTC is willing to recommend that your license be suspended for a minimum of two years. Further, you will only be allowed to resume the practice of law if you are able to prove rehabilitation and fitness to practice."

Mike opened his mouth to respond, but Henry laid a hand on his arm.

"Two more things," Blades said. "First, this is a take-it-or-leave-it offer. There will be no negotiation. Second, if you reject this offer, we will seek disbarment."

"Thank you, Selma," Henry said. "Could I have a few minutes to talk with my client?"

"Of course. Just let the secretary outside the door know when you're done."

Once the two OCTC lawyers were gone, Henry turned to Mike. "That's a very good offer. I advise you to take it."

"What are our odds if we go to court? We'll have a decent story to tell, as she basically admitted just now."

"But we won't be telling it to a jury," Henry responded. "We won't even be telling it to a regular superior-court judge. We'll be telling it to a state-bar judge who does nothing but try ethics cases. They won't care how good your story is. They'll care what the rules say and what the OCTC recommends. And even if we somehow win at trial, there's a good chance the Review Department of the bar court will kick us in the teeth. If you ever want to practice again, accept their offer."

Mike nodded and sighed. He knew Henry was right, but he still felt hopeless and numb. "Okay, I'll accept it."

# CHAPTER 85

*March*

It was unnaturally silent in Mike's office, even though the door was open. No indistinct voices coming from other cubicles. No whir of printers or copiers. No ringing phones, hurrying footsteps, or rustling paper. None of the background noise of a busy law office—unnoticeable until it was gone.

Mike had been busy for a while, wrapping up loose ends. First, he had to wind down his practice. Fortunately, Tim Cromwell stepped in to help. Masters & Cromwell bought Mike's practice for six million dollars, which was more than it was really worth. Tim had also agreed to hire everyone and take over all of Mike's cases, even the ones that were likely to lose money.

Then Mike's time was consumed by the two criminal cases he'd helped create. Klein's case had wrapped up two weeks ago. Klein had a lot of information that would be useful to the feds in prosecuting the rest of Horizon Finance, which Mike pointed out to both the US Attorney's Office and Klein's lawyer. After that, it was easy for Mike to broker a deal in which Klein pled guilty to thirty-two counts of money laundering and over two thousand counts of wire fraud—one for each time he moved money anywhere. That would keep Klein in federal prison for the rest of his life, which was fine with him. The alternative was state prison, where he would be unlikely to survive long.

The DA's Office wasn't happy about Klein's deal with the feds, but they would still get to put him on trial for Angy's murder and Klein's other crimes, even if they'd have to hand him back to the feds when they were done. Besides, Mike had helped them catch Klein in the first place, so they couldn't complain too much.

Mike's role in Jo's case had been smaller, but more painful. He had to repeatedly describe the whole humiliating experience and watch video of her manipulating him while he was in Mind's Eye. He did it for the police, for the DA, for the psychology board, and finally for Jo's lawyer, who was considering whether to recommend a plea deal to his client. It had been excruciating. But now it was over. Yesterday she had pled guilty to manslaughter and would spend the next ten years in prison.

Now his to-do list was empty. His e-mail inbox was also empty. So was his office. And his calendar. Empty years stretched out in front of him. But they were nothing compared to the emptiness inside him. Everything was gone. The nightmare he feared for years had finally come true.

All because he wanted justice. Someone once said that laws are like spiderwebs that catch little flies but let hornets and wasps break through. So sometimes Mike had broken through too, to help the little flies and go after the hornets and wasps. And now he had been caught.

At first, he had been shocked and numb. He couldn't quite believe what the bar had done to him. Then he flamed with outrage, furious that he was being punished for pursuing justice too zealously. But the fires of righteous anger burned themselves out after a few weeks, leaving only dead ashes and a sour miasma in his soul.

Last night he had decided to watch *A Man for All Seasons*. He had seen it with his father when he was in high school and had a vague recollection that it was an uplifting movie about a lawyer who was martyred for following God's laws rather than man's. Mike had expected to see himself in the hero, Thomas More. But as he watched the movie, he became uncomfortably aware that he was a lot more like More's hotheaded son-in-law, Will Roper.

One scene in particular made him squirm. A scheming villain had just left More's home. More, who was then Lord Chancellor of England, refused to have the man arrested because he hadn't broken any laws. Roper grew frustrated and said More would give the devil himself the benefit of law. More replied that of course he would. Roper retorted that he'd cut down every law in England to go after the devil. More replied by asking, "And when the last law was down, and the devil turned round on you, where would you hide, the laws all being flat?"

Well, Mike had cut a nice wide road through the law. He had chopped plenty of holes in the legal spiderweb—and handed the devil those silken threads to weave into a rope to hang him with. All he could do now was twist in the wind.

The more he thought about it, the less he blamed the bar. Would the system work if they gave a pass to every lawyer who could argue that he broke a rule because he was pursuing justice? If everyone could cheat if they thought the situation called for it, how long would it be until the only law left was the law of the jungle?

A sudden desire to travel came over him. He needed to get out of there, away from the office, the city, everything. He used to daydream about taking a long semiplanned road trip, but he never had the time. Until now.

Where to go? Yosemite for some hiking and rock climbing? Too close, and he'd done it before a dozen times. Tahoe? Same thing.

San Diego? Maybe. He hadn't been there in ten years, and he'd never driven. Long beaches to the west, camping and hiking to the east, Mexico to the south. Lots to do and see. And Dad was there.

He took his phone out of his pocket and brought up Dad's number. He hesitated for a moment, then pressed the "Call" button.

# Chapter 86

*April*

Jo looked out the window of the bus that was taking her to prison. A parade of identical hills rolled by, covered by dying grass and the occasional shrub hardy enough to survive the arid summer heat. It was only the beginning of April, but already the bus was uncomfortably warm despite the rattling air conditioner blasting away in the front.

A dozen other women rode the bus with Jo. Two of them, prison veterans who had made this trip several times, talked and laughed loudly. One woman cried in the back—until one of the veterans told her to shut up or she'd get her head beaten in. She subsided to quiet sniffling. The rest of the women on the bus rode in silence, avoiding eye contact.

The heat outside did nothing to dispel the cold inside Jo. She felt like an iceberg floating in a dark sea, drifting, aimless and alone.

Everything was gone. The decade of effort she put into her now-worthless degrees. The future she had planned with Mike, which would never happen. Mind's Eye, her great contribution to psychology, was now in Adrian Goff's lab at Stanford. At least it hadn't gone to the Bells or Horizon Finance—Mike had seen to that. But if it ever came out of the lab, Goff would get the glory and Stanford would get the money. Jo would be forgotten at best, and a cautionary tale for future psychology students at worst.

Why had all of that happened? Because she wanted justice for Maddie. Because the system was broken and she took matters into her own hands.

Old anger welled up in her as she remembered what happened. There had been the shock of the initial call at college. Only rich people had cell phones back then and the Nordahls weren't rich, so her parents had called her dorm room. Jo's roommate had friends over, and they were talking so loudly that Jo could barely hear what her mother was saying. She had asked her mother to repeat herself several times. Mother finally shouted, "Maddie is dead!" at the top of her lungs.

The next several months had been a swirling horror. Not only did Jo and her grieving parents have to cope with Maddie's death, they had to see her reputation dragged through the sewer of Seth Bell's imagination. He claimed that he and Maddie went to Shadow Cliffs to drink, do some drugs, and have sex. Jo knew that was a lie, of course. But it was impossible to get the truth out. Seth's parents hired a pack of politically connected lawyers who were only too eager to represent Senator Bell's son for a fraction of their regular rates.

Finally, it was over. Seth went to a California Youth Authority facility and the Nordahls slowly rebuilt their lives. They moved past the whole awful chapter, but they never really got over it. It was always an open wound, ready to start bleeding again if touched.

Jo got her degree, opened her practice, and developed Mind's Eye. She set up her program with the California Department of Corrections and Rehabilitation. And then she ran across Seth's name in another patient's medical records. She should have just ignored it, gone on with developing Mind's Eye. But she couldn't. The old wound had reopened.

She needed to hear Seth admit the truth, to say he was sorry. Or at least that's what she told herself.

He didn't recognize her, and she wouldn't have recognized him on the street. The years had been hard on him, and his mental and physical health had decayed sharply. Was that at least partly the result of guilt over Maddie?

No, she had realized by the end of Seth's second session. He eventually admitted the truth about Maddie, but he didn't feel remorse—or not enough, anyway. So Jo suggested that he feel more guilt. He did. And it turned out that he had cared about Maddie, in his own way. He had wanted to be with her again. The last happy time in his life ended with her death. He had wanted to go back to that time, to her.

From there, it took only a little push. Seth's guilt and his longing both nudged him in the same direction. All Jo did was guide and encourage him. It wasn't vengeance; it was justice for Maddie and protection for the other women Seth might hurt in the future.

Then there was Mike. He had just needed a little encouragement in a very different direction. Healing his anxiety and encouraging him to trust her were really two sides of the same coin. And if the end result was that he fell in love with her, well, that could work out for both of them. They had been good together. If only it could have lasted. They might—

She cut off that train of thought. That wasn't going to happen now, of course. It had all spun out of control. The gleaming future she had built was now a smashed wreck.

The first time she got Mind's Eye working, she had felt like a teenager who just got the keys to a Porsche. The precision and power in her hands were seductive. There had been so much she could do with it. Too much, it turned out.

She sighed and watched the unchanging landscape slide by. Maybe it was best that Stanford had Mind's Eye. They would never use its full potential, but that might not be a bad thing.

Her full potential would also never be used. Even after she got out of prison, she would never be able to practice again. No one would trust themselves to a therapist who had pled guilty to manslaughter. Even if they did, she doubted the board would ever give her a license again.

In a sudden rush, she realized how much she missed it. Missed it so much it was a physical ache in her chest. She had wanted to be a psychologist ever since she was in high school. She had loved the thought of helping people with their problems. She had spent her whole adult life learning to do that and then doing it. And she had been good at it.

Then she invented Mind's Eye and everything changed. She woke up one day and discovered that she was swimming in venture-capital money, in demand for interviews, and able to achieve results that other psychologists could only dream of.

Now it was all gone—except the old desire to heal broken people. Everything else had been stripped away, but that desire was still there, like the stump of a tree blown over in a storm. Could it ever put out new shoots?

If so, how? She was a felon. A convict. Those words would follow her for the rest of her life. And who would trust a felon to help them with their problems? Who would open up to a convict?

Maybe another convict? She certainly had plenty of experience with them.

She realized that the woman in the back of the bus was crying again. She went back to talk to her.

# CHAPTER 87

Ten years ago, Val helped Mike open the Law Offices of Michael Webster. Now she was helping him close it.

Professional movers would come in the morning to take everything that Masters & Cromwell had bought. Tim had told Mike to keep whatever he wanted, which was turning out to be a lot more than Val expected.

"Garbage, right?" Val said, holding up a stack of decade-old court filings from one of Mike's drawers.

He took a quick look at them. "No, no. Those are the summary-judgment papers from the *Nimmagadda* case."

"So? That case ended nine years ago."

"Yeah, but these have a lot of good research on international choice of law."

"Which is now ten years old. You'd need to do it all over again anyway."

"These would be a good start, and I only have them in hard copy."

"So scan them."

"That'll take half an hour."

"Are you ever going to need to brief international choice of law again?"

"You never know. Just pack them, okay?"

She sighed and dropped them in a box. His desk had already produced six bankers boxes of junk, which was about twice what she would have guessed it could hold. There must have been a sort of evil magic to his drawers: each of them held about three times as much stuff as was physically possible. And of course he wouldn't let her throw any of it away.

She reached into the current drawer and pulled out the next pile of random paper. Her hand came out holding a fat stack of greeting cards. They were all from her. Birthday cards, Christmas cards, work-anniversary cards. It looked like he had saved them all.

Her vision went blurry and she sniffed.

He glanced over. "What is it?" His gaze dropped to the cards in her hand. He smiled and reddened slightly. "Good memories. I can take over the desk if you'd rather do the kitchen. You can throw away anything in there that you want."

"I'm going to miss working together."

"Me too. We had a great run."

There was a moment of awkward silence.

"So how's the new job treating you?" he asked.

She shrugged. "It's a job. Boring, but it pays the bills."

"Tim would pay you a lot more than that. He agreed to take on everyone who worked in my office at their old salaries. I'll bet I could get him to include you in that package."

She grinned. "He called me yesterday and offered a raise over what you were paying me."

"Did you take it?"

She shook her head. "I need something that lets me work nine to five with lunches off. I'm taking a full course load, and I can't have a job that eats up sixty hours or more each week."

"A full course load? Wow. How long will it take you to get your BA?"

"I've picked up half the credits I need over the years, so I'm hoping to be done in two years. I might even be able to squeeze it down to a year and a half. And after that, law school."

He shook his head and smiled. "I'm impressed."

She felt a warm glow and smiled back. "You inspired me."

He picked up a stack of law books and dumped them into a box. "Can't say I feel particularly inspirational right now."

"You did a lot of good. And retiring at thirty-nine doesn't sound so bad. What are you going to do now?"

"Well, for starters I'm taking a sort of open-ended trip to see my dad in San Diego. I'm going to throw a couple of duffel bags of clothes in the backseat of my car and make it a road trip. I'll take Highway 1 and enjoy the views. I'll drive when I want to, stop when I want to, and get there when I get there. It'll be fun."

She shook her head in disbelief. "This is not the Mike Webster I knew. Was your brain just taken over by hippies or something?"

He laughed. "The Mike Webster you knew never had a free minute in his calendar and loved it that way. Now he's got at least two free years, maybe a lot more."

"What are you going to do with them?"

He shrugged. "Figure stuff out, I guess."

"Like what?"

"Everything." He sighed and leaned against the bookshelf. "Six months ago, I could see my future. It was like I was standing at the top of a hill with the road all spread out in front of me. I was going to win the Bell case and then the case after that and the case after that. We would keep building the firm, year by year. I'd settle down, probably with Jo. In ten years, I'd basically be Tim Cromwell.

"But then I found out that the whole settling-down thing was just Jo messing with my mind. And after that, the bar took my license and I had to sell the firm. It's like . . . like I'm still standing on that hill, but

the fog blew in and now I can't see the road at all. I can't see anything."
He looked tired and vulnerable and a little lost.

"Well, wherever the road leads, I'll be there for you," she said.

He looked at her with an expression that she couldn't quite read.
His eyes held affection, gratitude, and something else. He crossed the
short distance between them and enveloped her in a hug. She hugged
him back and held him tight.

# CHAPTER 88

It takes about eight hours to drive from San Francisco to San Diego, but Mike stretched it into a three-day trip. He drove along the two-lane coastal highways doing fifty or sixty, rather than eighty, through the desert on I-5. His lunches came from farmers' markets and delis in little coastal towns, and he always stopped at a beach or oceanside bluff to eat them. He stayed in bed-and-breakfasts and took his time over warm artichoke bread and scrambled eggs and coffee in the mornings. After breakfast, he spent an hour or two walking around whatever town he was in—and was regularly amazed at how many antique shops and art galleries a little seaside town could support. Then he'd hit the road around ten.

It was a relaxing trip, but it didn't relax him. His insomnia had come back, and it got worse as he got closer to San Diego. He didn't sleep at all the last night on the road. He also had a vague but unshakable sense that he was driving to his doom.

He finally reached San Diego, checked into his hotel, and headed out to meet Dad for dinner at Eddie V's. Mike was staying at the Marriott on K Street and the weather was nice—as it almost always is in San Diego—so he left early and walked instead of catching a cab.

He meandered through the Gaslamp Quarter rather than take the most direct route. The Gaslamp was the city's historic district, and like most such places it was a little touristy—but not bad. The century-plus-old buildings, brick streets, and a few actual gas lamps gave the place a pleasantly nostalgic air. A good place for a long evening stroll. Which would have to wait for another day. Mike braced himself and turned his steps toward Eddie V's.

Dad waited for him outside the door. He looked great—tan, relaxed, fit. And exactly how Mike would probably look in thirty years if he were lucky. They had always resembled each other, and they looked more alike as the years passed. Seeing his father was like looking into a mirror that showed him the future.

Mike realized that was what had been gnawing at him during the whole trip: the fear of seeing what he might be like in three decades. A man whose life's work had been destroyed, who had been betrayed by a woman he trusted. A man whose life used to mean something, a long time ago.

He thrust that thought down, planted a smile on his face, and strode forward to greet his father. Dad gave him a firm handshake and smiled. "It's wonderful to see you, Mike. I'm really looking forward to dinner."

"It'll be great," Mike said as he opened the door for his father, wondering whether that was true.

"I've heard good things about this place." Dad glanced around the lobby. "Never been here, though. It's a little outside my price range."

"Consider it a down payment on all those Father's Days that I missed." Mike turned to the hostess. "Reservation for two under Webster."

She nodded and picked up two menus. "This way, gentlemen," she said and escorted them through the restaurant.

"You were busy," Dad said as they followed her.

"Not anymore," Mike replied. "Now we're just a couple of semiretired guys with plenty of time on their hands."

"Speak for yourself, son. I work sixty hours a week, sometimes more."

They arrived at their table and Mike waited while the hostess seated them. Mike had requested a patio table when he made the reservation, partially for privacy and partially for the view of San Diego Bay in the setting sun.

When the hostess was gone, Mike said, "I didn't realize you were so busy. What have you been up to?"

"Matthew Twenty-Five, mostly."

That sounded vaguely familiar, but Mike couldn't quite place it. "What's Matthew Twenty-Five?"

"Thought I'd mentioned it to you before: the Matthew Twenty-Five Foundation. It's a ministry that takes the twenty-fifth chapter of Matthew as its mission statement, particularly the last part. Jesus tells the disciples about his second coming. He says he'll invite his followers into heaven, saying, 'I was hungry, and you gave me food. I was thirsty, and you gave me drink. I was a stranger, and you took me in; naked, and you clothed me. I was sick, and you visited me. I was in prison, and you came to me.' He says they'll be confused and ask when they did all of that. And he'll reply, 'When you did it to one of the least of these my brothers, you did it to me.' So that's what we do at Matthew Twenty-Five—we go to prisons, hospitals, and homeless camps. We bring them food, water, clothing, and, most of all, the love of Christ."

Their waiter came and took their orders. Mike had the swordfish. Dad tried to order a salad that happened to be the cheapest thing on the menu, but Mike said they were at a seafood restaurant and he specifically remembered Dad liking crab. Dad objected that the crab was too expensive. They compromised on the ahi tuna for him.

Mike pondered what had become of his father. When Dad left Oakland, he was a sad, broken, and lonely man. A failed pastor and a beaten-down postal worker on the verge of a threadbare retirement. What happened?

"Was Matthew Twenty-Five what got you over it?" he asked at last.

Dad gave him a quizzical look and swallowed. "Got me over what?"

"Losing the church and Mom. I mean, your whole life—everything you'd built—was destroyed. How did you get over it? Was it Matthew Twenty-Five?"

"Sort of." He paused for a moment. "Things were tough in the beginning. I prayed a lot. I kept looking for a new church, but I never found one. Then one day I came across a statue of Jesus as a homeless man sleeping on a park bench, with only the crucifixion wounds on his feet giving him away. God spoke to me deeply through that. It helped me realize just how closely God identifies with 'the least of these'—so closely that on Judgment Day we will be judged by how we treated them. That's what Matthew Twenty-Five is all about—to see Jesus in the homeless, the refugee, the prisoner. The apostle Paul says that the one thing that counts is faith working through love. If we don't have God's love, that's evidence we don't have faith.

"So when a friend called me and told me about the ministry down here and asked if I could help, I knew that's what God was calling me to do." Dad smiled. "There's nothing glamorous about my work, and I don't get the recognition I had as a pastor, but I've never been more fulfilled."

Their food arrived and Dad said grace. It had been a long time since Mike had sat like that, head bowed and listening to his father's voice praying over the food. It brought memories flooding back. Memories of family dinners, with Mom sitting between them at the little kitchen table.

They ate in silence for a few minutes. The swordfish was superb: fresh, flaky, and beautifully presented. And the pinot grigio the waiter had recommended was an excellent complement to the fish. Mike enjoyed his dinner, but couldn't help wondering how many of 'the least of these' could have been fed for the price he paid for it.

"What about Mom?" Mike asked. "How did you get over her?"

Dad put down his fork and looked out over the water. "I didn't. I still love her, and I pray for her every day. She . . ." He sighed and shook his head. He sat in silence, squinting into the sunset. For a moment, Mike saw the sad old man he had been afraid to find.

But the moment passed. Dad turned back to Mike and smiled. "We stay in touch, and she seems to be doing well. I've invited her to come down here and she says she'd like to visit, but she can never find the time."

Mike gave a rueful smile. "I guess I am my mother's son."

Dad nodded. "We used to say that you were like me on the outside and her on the inside."

Mike chuckled. "I suppose." He took a sip of his wine and poked at the remains of his meal in silence for a few seconds. "You know, I'm not particularly busy at the moment."

Dad's smile broadened. "I was hoping you'd say that. A lot of the people we see need legal help of one sort or another. Some of them are quite desperate. We've been thinking of starting a legal clinic. I know you can't actually practice law, but maybe you could help." He took his last bite and chewed while he waited for Mike's answer.

Mike turned the idea over in his head. He didn't want to get too excited, but it might work. It just might. "What's your budget like?" he asked.

"There isn't one," Dad admitted, "but we might be able to interest a donor if we have a good plan."

Mike had expected that. He pulled out his wallet and dropped three fifties on the bill, which covered their meal and a generous tip. He and Dad stood and headed out to the walkway that edged the Bay.

Mike talked as he walked. "Okay, you can keep costs down by using law students rather than hiring lawyers. No promises, but the bar might let me supervise them if I'm under appropriate moral guidance—that would be you." He grew more and more excited as the idea took shape in his head. "Oh, or better yet, I'll see if I can talk them into making this a bar-affiliated program. They love this sort of thing. I can chip in some starter money until donors get on board. And I know some guys down here with some extra office space . . ."

By the time they passed the *Midway*, Mike had the clinic mostly planned. When they stopped for coffee in the Gaslamp an hour later, he wrote a thirty-item to-do list on his phone while Dad sipped a decaf latte and smiled. And when Mike's head finally hit the pillow at eleven thirty, he knew what he would be doing for the next two years. Maybe longer. The fog shrouding his path had cleared and he could see the road ahead of him again.

He slept like a baby.

# AFTERWORD

A few comments on the facts behind the fiction in this book:

*Mind's Eye.* The technology in the story is mostly real. Functional MRI, or fMRI, machines can provide all of the data Jo Anderson got from hers and more. Researchers using fMRI technology can generally identify subjects' emotional states, whether they're lying, whether they've seen a particular image or object before, and other information. As the Science Directorate of the American Psychological Association noted, an fMRI machine "isn't quite a mind reader, but it comes close."

Researchers are also experimenting with ways to use fMRI machines with other elements of Mind's Eye, including EEG machines. Automated microexpression capture hasn't yet been tested with fMRI technology to my knowledge, but intriguing research by teams in Finland and America indicate that this could happen soon—though their accuracy rate is (currently) only about half that achieved by Mind's Eye.

*Hypnosis.* As Dr. Goff notes, the American Psychological Association believes that hypnosis is a valid therapeutic tool, though some psychologists view it with suspicion or prefer to use different terms like "guided meditation." A skilled hypnotherapist can indeed plant powerful suggestions in a patient's mind, which will influence the patient's behavior after the hypnosis ends. Hypnotherapists can also induce posthypnotic amnesia, which causes patients to forget some or all of what happened while they were under hypnosis. Thus, an unethical hypnotherapist like Jo could plant a suggestion in a patient's mind and then hide it from the patient by giving the patient posthypnotic amnesia.

*Medical-Malpractice Law.* I did a fair amount of medical-malpractice defense work early in my career and did my best to recreate the feel and dynamics of those cases in this book. However, I did take some minor liberties with California law—particularly on the procedural front—in order to make the plot flow better.

*San Francisco.* All San Francisco locations are as described in the book, with one minor exception: I took the liberty of setting the first scene at Brenda's before the restaurant's recent expansion. It is now about double the size it was when Mike arranged to be overheard by the jurors in the Lee case, and there are multiple tables that could seat large groups. It's still tough to get a seat there during lunch, but the crawfish beignets are totally worth the wait.

# Acknowledgments

My name is the only one on the book cover, but I am hardly the only one who contributed to this book. I owe a great debt of gratitude to many people, particularly the following:

Anette Acker (wife)—for loving support, honest and insightful criticism, and hundreds of hours spent plotting and editing.

Sue Brower (agent)—for finding the perfect publisher for this book.

Peggy Hageman and Meredith Jacobson (editors)—for making this book better than I ever could have on my own.

Amy Hosford and the rest of the Waterfall Press team—for giving this book a wonderful home and really getting behind it.

Randy Ingermanson (author, beta reader, and programmer)—for being an early sounding board, particularly for the parts involving biotechnology and programming, and for numerous insightful editorial comments.

Per Kjeldaas (beta reader and professor of computer science)—for feedback on an early draft of the book, particularly the parts dealing with computers.

David Lim (Deputy District Attorney)—for answering questions about Bay Area law enforcement agencies I don't deal with regularly.

Cindy Acker, Fred Acker, Chris Ames, Kathy Engel, Emily Kalanithi, Bubba Pettit, Gail Pettit, Donna Tritschler, and Jody Wallem (beta readers)—for taking time to read a rough draft and let me know what worked and what didn't.

The FBI, San Francisco Division (especially Alicia Sensibaugh)—for running an excellent Citizens Academy and answering lots of hard-to-research questions.

# ABOUT THE AUTHOR

 Bestselling author Rick Acker is supervising deputy attorney general in the California Department of Justice. Most recently, he and his team won a string of unprecedented recoveries against the Wall Street players who triggered the Great Recession. Acker has authored several legal thrillers, including *When the Devil Whistles*, which award-winning author Colleen Coble described as "a legal thriller you won't want to miss." He spends most of his free time with his wife and children. You can learn more about Acker and his books at www.rickacker.com.